"Literate space opera... ...undation series and Fra... ...ight touch all his own, W... ...ghty galactic empires by f... ...the distractions of war an... ...."
—*The New Yor*... ...tion

"*The Risen Empire* is full of relentless and addictive action which is supported by some truly wild ideas. Westerfeld's blend of traditional space opera and cutting-edge speculation makes this a truly 21st century SF novel." —Karl Schroeder

"Westerfeld's exceptionally smart and empathetic novel, the first of two in a series, confirms the buzz that space opera is one of the most exciting branches of current SF. . . . Keeping the reader constantly off-balance, Westerfeld skillfully integrates extreme technologies with human characters."
—*Publishers Weekly* (starred review)

"Westerfeld spins a dramatic tale that never flags in pace or imagination, nor in its abundance of original vision abandons narrative in favor of didactic digressions . . . a strong and vibrant story, as engaging and innovative in its scope as his mechanical inventions or cultural constructs. In my opinion, this novel represents a balance that much contemporary science fiction lacks. And just when you thought that the author has exhausted the possibilities for further invention, he takes the reader down entirely new and delightfully unexpected paths . . . the richness of imagination present in the author's world-building, as well as the febrile and vivid description that accompanies his settings and the novel's cultural and social infrastructure, easily set the book apart, not only from the common space opera but from most other science fiction as well. Westerfeld's characterizations . . . possess both depth and a poignant and compassionate humanity. . . . this recalls some of the best of Asimov but written with a more concise and breathless speed. It's been quite a while since I've read science fiction I've enjoyed more or that combines narrative action with imagination as intelligently. Heartily recommended."
—*Interzone*

"There's always been something almost soothing about space opera: no matter how many starships explode, planetary rulers topple, and sinister aliens slither, the almost gleeful sense of wonder warms and comforts the reader. *This* space opera is so much more than that. *The Risen Empire* glows with sense of wonder, but it's stuffed with ideas, quirky technologies, nuances of moral choices, and sees conflicts from all sides. I loved it. I heartily recommend it, and I hope Scott Westerfeld pens many more books like it—quickly!" —Ed Greenwood

"Recent writers in [the space opera] sub-genre include the likes of Vernor Vinge, David Brin, Peter Hamilton, Iain Banks, Ken MacLeod, Alastair Reynolds, and Karl Schroeder. Indeed, many of the most popular writers in the science fiction field today are writing space operas. Scott Westerfeld is the latest author to throw his hat into the ring with his new novel, *The Risen Empire* . . . [a] baroque space opera. The novel contains a great story with interesting subplots, cool technology, and engaging characters. I found *Risen* a fun read full of intriguing ideas and reminiscent of Iain Banks' *Culture* novels in breadth and scope." —SFRevu.com

"In Westerfeld's hands, science fiction's cutting edge is wielded with both the precision of a surgeon's scalpel and the wild abandon of a machete." —Wil McCarthy

"This is the start of an ambitious saga that delivers that good old science fiction "sense of wonder" combined with a thoroughly modern—and even post-modern—information age sensibility. Westerfeld creates a incredibly rich, consistently imagined far-future milieu packed with inspired transhuman civilization-building, technological foresight, and the fine attention to details both large and small that marks this as visionary science fiction of the highest quality. Westerfeld's got creativity out the yin yang!" —Tony Daniel

"*The Risen Empire* is proof that space opera can be as complex and sophisticated as any other form of literature. Doc Smith would barely recognize it." —Mike Resnick

THE RISEN EMPIRE

BOOK ONE OF SUCCESSION

SCOTT WESTERFELD

TOR®

A TOM DOHERTY ASSOCIATES BOOK
NEW YORK

This is a work of fiction. All the characters and events portrayed in this book are fictitious or are used fictitiously.

THE RISEN EMPIRE

Edited by David G. Hartwell

A Tor Book
Published by Tom Doherty Associates, LLC
175 Fifth Avenue
New York, NY 10010

www.tor.com

Tor® is a registered trademark of Tom Doherty Associates, LLC.

ISBN 0-765-34467-X
EAN 978-0765-34467-0

First edition: March 2003
First mass market edition: August 2004

Printed in the United States of America

0 9 8 7 6 5 4 3 2 1

TO SLK

for years of summer

THE RISEN EMPIRE

A Note on Imperial Measures

One of the many advantages of life under the Imperial Apparatus is the easy imposition of consistent standards of infrastructure, communication, and law. For fifteen hundred years, the measures of the Eighty Worlds have followed an enviably straightforward scheme.

There are 100 seconds in each minute, 100 minutes in an hour, and ten hours in a day.

- One second is defined as 1/100,000 of a solar day on Home.
- One meter is defined as 1/300,000,000 of a light-second.
- One gravity is defined as 10 meters per second squared acceleration.

The Emperor has decreed that the speed of light shall remain as nature has provided.

1

HOSTAGE SITUATION

There is no greater tactical disadvantage than
the presence of precious noncombatants.
Civilians, historical treasures, hostages:
treat them as already lost.

—ANONYMOUS 167

Pilot

The five small craft passed from shadow, emerging with the suddenness of coins thrown into sunlight. The disks of their rotary wings shimmered in the air like heat, momentary rainbows flexing across prisms of motion. Master Pilot Jocim Marx noted with pleasure the precision of his squadron's formation. The other pilots' Intelligencer craft perfectly formed a square centered upon his own.

"Don't we look pretty?" Marx said.

"Pretty obvious, sir," Hendrik answered. She was the squadron's second pilot, and it was her job to worry.

"A little light won't hurt us," Marx said flatly. "The Rix haven't had time to build anything with eyes."

He said it not to remind Hendrik, who knew damn well, but to reassure their squadron-mates. The other three pilots were nervous; Marx could hear it in their silence. None of them had ever flown a mission of this importance before.

But then, who had?

Marx's own nerves were beginning to play on him. His squadron of Intelligencers had covered half the distance from dropsite to objective without meeting any resistance. The Rix were obviously ill-equipped, improvising against far greater force, relying on their single advantage: the hostages. But *surely* they had made preparations for small craft.

After a few moments in the sun, the waiting was over.

"I'm getting echolocation from dead ahead, sir," Pilot Oczar announced.

"I can *see* them," Hendrik added. "Lots of them."

The enemy interceptors resolved before Marx's eyes as

his craft responded to the threat, enhancing vision with its other senses, incorporating data from the squadron's other craft into his layers of synesthesia. As Marx had predicted, the interceptors were small, unpiloted drones. Their only weapon was a long, sinuous grappling arm that hung from the rotary lifting surface, which was more screw than blade. The devices looked rather like something da Vinci might have designed four millennia ago, a contraption powered by the toil of tiny men.

The interceptors dangled before Marx. There were a lot of them, and in their host they impelled the same vaguely obscene fascination as creatures from the deepest ocean. One moved toward his craft, arms flailing with a blind and angry abandon.

Master Pilot Marx tilted his Intelligencer's rotary wing forward and increased its power. His ship rose above the interceptor, barely missing collision with the enemy's lifting screw. Marx grimaced at the near miss. Another interceptor came into focus before him, this one a little higher, and he reversed his wing's rotation, pushing the ship down, dropping below its grasp.

Around him, the other pilots cursed as they pitched their craft through the swarm of interceptors. Their voices came at him from all sides of his cockpit, directionally biased to reflect their position relative to his.

From above, Hendrik spoke, the tension of a hard turn in her voice. "You've seen these before, sir?"

"Negative," he replied. He'd fought the Rix Cult many times, but their small craft were evolutionary. Small, random differences in design were scattered throughout every generation. Characteristics that succeeded were incorporated into the next production round. You never knew what new shapes and strategies Rix craft might assume. "The arms are longer than I've seen, and the behavior's more . . . volatile."

"They sure *look* pissed off," Hendrik agreed.

Her choice of words was apt. Two interceptors ahead of

Marx sensed his craft, and their arms began to flail with the sudden intensity of alligators when prey has stepped into reach. He rolled his Intelligencer sideways, narrowing his vulnerable area as he slipped between them.

But there were more and more of the interceptors, and his Intelligencer's profile was still too large. Marx retracted his craft's sensory array, trading away vision for compact size. At this range, however, the closest interceptors resolved to terrible clarity, the data layers provided by first-, second-, and third-level sight almost choking his mind. Marx could see (hear, smell) the individual segments of a grasping arm flexing like a snake's spine, the cilia of an earspot casting jagged shadows in the hard sunlight. Marx squinted at the cilia, gesturing for a zoom until the little hairs towered around him like a forest.

"They're using sound to track us," he announced. "Silence your echolocators *now*."

The view before him blurred as sonar data was lost. If Marx was right, and the interceptors were audio-only, his squadron would be undetectable to them now.

"I'm tangled!" Pilot Oczar shouted from below him. "One's got a sensor post!"

"Don't fight!" Marx ordered. "Just lizard."

"Ejecting post," Oczar said, releasing his ship's captured limb.

Marx hazarded a glance downward. A flailing interceptor tumbled slowly away from Oczar's ship, clinging to the ejected sensor post with blind determination. The Intelligencer tilted crazily as its pilot tried to compensate for broken symmetry.

"They're getting heavy, sir," Hendrik warned. Marx switched his view to Hendrik's perspective for a moment. From her high vantage, a thickening swarm of interceptors was clearly visible ahead. The bright lines of their long grapples sparkled like a shattered, drifting spiderweb in the sun.

There were too many.

Of course, there were backups already advancing from the dropsite. If this first wave of Intelligencers was destroyed, another squadron would be ready, and eventually a craft or two would get through. But there wasn't time. The rescue mission required onsite intelligence, and soon. Failure to provide it would certainly end careers, might even constitute an Error of Blood.

One of these five craft had to make it.

"Tighten up the formation and increase lift," Marx ordered. "Oczar, you stay down."

"Yes, sir," the man answered quietly. Oczar knew what Marx intended for his craft.

The rest of the squadron swept in close to Marx. The four Intelligencers rose together, jostling through the writhing defenders.

"Time for you to make some noise, Oczar," Marx said. "Extend your sensor posts to full length and activity."

"Up to a hundred, sir."

Marx looked down as Oczar's craft grew, a spider with twenty splayed legs emerging suddenly from a seed, a time-lapse of a flower relishing sunlight. The interceptors around Oczar grew more detailed as his craft became fully active, bathing their shapes with ultrasonic pulses, microlaser distancing, and millimeter radar.

Already, the dense cloud of interceptors was beginning to react. Like a burst of pollen caught by a sudden wind, they shifted toward Oczar's craft.

"We're going through blind and silent," Marx said to the other pilots. "Find a gap and push toward it hard. We'll be cutting main power."

"One tangle, sir," Oczar said. "Two."

"Feel free to defend yourself."

"Yes, *sir!*"

On Marx's status board, the counterdrones in Oczar's magazine counted down quickly. The man launched a pair as he confirmed the order, then another a few seconds later. The interceptors must be all over him. Marx glanced down at Oczar's craft. The bilateral geometries of its deployed sensor array were starting to twist, burdened by the thrashing defenders. Through the speakers, Oczar grunted with the effort of keeping his craft intact.

Marx raised his eyes from the battle and peered forward. The remainder of the squadron was reaching the densest rank of the interceptor cloud. Oczar's diversion had thinned it somewhat, but there was still scant space to fit through.

"Pick your hole carefully," Marx said. "Get some speed up. Retraction on my mark. Five . . . four . . . three . . ."

He let the count fade, concentrating on flying his own craft. He had aimed his Intelligencer toward a gap in the interceptors, but one had drifted into the center of his path. Marx reversed his rotor and boosted power, driving his craft downward.

The drone loomed closer, lured by the whine of his surging main rotor. He hoped the extra burst would be enough.

"Retract *now!*" he ordered. The view blurred and faded as the sensor posts on the ship furled. In seconds, Marx's vision went dark.

"Cut your main rotors," he commanded.

The small craft would be almost silent now, impelled only by the small, flywheel-powered stabilizer wing at their rear. It would push them forward until it ran down. But the four surviving craft were already beginning to fall.

Marx checked the altimeter's last reading: 174 centimeters. At that height, the craft would take at least a minute before they hit the ground. Even with its sensor array furled and main rotor stalled, in a normal-density atmosphere an intelligence craft fell no faster than a speck of dust.

Indeed, the Intelligencers were not much larger than specks of dust, and were somewhat lighter. With a wingspan of a single millimeter, they were very small craft indeed.

* * *

Master Pilot Jocim Marx, Imperial Naval Intelligence, had flown microships for eleven years. He was the best.

He had scouted for light infantry in the Coreward Bands Revolt. His machine then had been the size and shape of two hands cupping water, the hemispherical surface holed with dozens of carbon whisker fans, each of which could run at its own speed. He was deployed on the battlefield in those days, flying his craft through a VR helmet. He stayed with the platoon staff under their portable forcefield, wandering about blind to his surroundings. That had never set easy with him; he constantly imagined a slug finding him, the real world intruding explosively on the synesthetic realm inside his helmet. Marx was very good, though, at keeping his craft steady in the unpredictable Bandian winds. His craft would paint enemy snipers with an undetectable x-ray laser, which swarms of smart needle-bullets followed to unerring kills. Mark's steady hand could guide a projectile into a centimeter-wide seam in personal armor, or through the eye-slit of a sniper's camopolymer blind.

Later, he flew penetrators against Rix hovertanks in the Incursion. These projectiles were hollow cylinders, about the size of a child's finger. They were launched by infantryman, encased in a rocket-propelled shell for the first half of their short flight. When the penetrator deployed, breaking free the instant it spotted a target, it flew purely on momentum. Ranks of tiny control surfaces lined the inside of the cylinder, like the baleen plates of some plankton-feeder. The weapon's supersonic flight was an exercise in extreme delicacy. Too hard a nudge and a penetrator would tumble uselessly. But when it hit a Rix tank just right, its maw precisely aligned to the hexagonal weave of the armor, it cut through metal and ceramic like a rip propagating down a cloth seam. Inside, the projectile disintegrated into countless molecular viruses, breaking down the machine in minutes. Marx flew dozens of ten-second missions each day, and was plagued at night with fitful microdreams of launch and collision. Eventually, backpack AI proved better for the job than human pilots, but Marx's old flight recordings were still studied by nascent intelligences for their elegance and flair.

The last few decades, Marx had worked with the Navy. Small craft were now truly small, fullerene constructions no bigger than a few millimeters across when furled, built by even smaller machines and powered by exotic transuranium batteries. They were largely for intelligence gathering, although they had offensive uses. Marx had flown a specially fitted Intelligencer into a fiberoptic AI hub during the Dhantu Liberation, carrying a load of glass-eating nanos that had dismantled the rebel's communication system planetwide within minutes.

Master Pilot Marx preferred the safety of the Navy. At his age, being on the battlefield had lost its thrill. Now Marx controlled his craft from shipside, hundreds of kilometers away from the action. He reclined in the comfort of a smart-gel seat like some fighter pilot of yore, bathed in synesthetic images that allowed him three levels of sight, the parts of his brain normally dedicated to hearing, smell, and tactile sensations all given over to vision. Marx experienced his ship's environment as a true pilot should, as if he himself had been shrunk to the size of a human cell.

He loved the microscopic scale of his new assignment. In his darkened cabin on sleepless nights, Marx burned incense and watched the smoke rise through the bright, pencil-width shaft of an emergency flashlight. He noted how air currents curled, how ghostly snakes could be spun with the movement of a finger, a puff of breath. With an inhumanly steady hand he moved a remote microscope carefully through the air, projecting its images onto the cabin wall, watching and learning the behavior of microscopic particles aloft.

Sometimes during these dark and silent vigils, Jocim Marx allowed himself to think that he was the best micro-craft pilot in the fleet.

He was right.

Captain

Captain Laurent Zai stared down into the central airscreen of his battle bridge, searching for a solution in its tangle of crisp, needle-thin lines. The airscreen was filled with a wireframe of the imperial palace on Legis XV, a structure that stretched across ten square kilometers in a sinuous, organiform sprawl. The real palace was currently two hundred seventeen klicks directly below the *Lynx*.

Zai could feel imminent defeat down there. It writhed beneath the soles of his boots, as if he were standing at the edge of some quickly eroding sand dune.

Of course, this slipping sensation likely resulted from the *Lynx*'s efforts to remain geostationary above the palace. The ship was under constant acceleration to match the planet's rotation; a proper geosynchronous orbit would be too high to effect the rescue. So a stomach-churning combination of forces pulled on Zai's tall frame. At this altitude, the ship was deep within Legis XV's gravity well, which pulled him substantially sternward. The *Lynx*'s acceleration nudged Zai to one side with a slow, twisting motion. The thin but boiling thermosphere of the planet added an occasional pocket of turbulence. And overlaying it all were the throes of the ship's artificial gravity—always shaky this close to a planet—as it attempted to create the uniform effect of a single standard gee.

It felt to Zai's delicate sense of balance as if the *Lynx*'s bridge were swirling clockwise down some gigantic drain.

Twelve senior officers had stations around the airscreen. The bridge was crowded with them and their planning staffs, and the air was filled with the crackle of argument and conjecture, of growing desperation. The wireframe of the palace was lanced periodically by arcing lines in bold, primary colors. Marine insertions, clandestine ground attacks, and drone penetrations were displayed every few minutes, all manner of the precise and sudden attacks that hostage situations called for. Of course, these assaults were all theoretical models. No one would dare make a move against the hostage-takers until the captain so ordered.

And the captain had been silent.

It was *his* neck on the line.

Laurent Zai liked it cold on his bridge. His metabolism burned like a furnace under the black wool of his Imperial Navy uniform, a garment designed for discomfort. He also believed that his crew performed better in the cold. Minds didn't wander at fourteen degrees centigrade, and the side effects were less onerous than hyperoxygenation. The *Lynx*'s environmental staff had learned long ago that the more tense the situation, the colder the captain liked his bridge.

Zai noted with perverse pleasure that the breath of his officers was just visible in the red battle lights that washed the great circular room. Hands were clenched into tight fists to conserve warmth. A few officers rubbed heat into their fingers one by one, as if counting possible casualties again and again.

In this situation, the usual math of hostage rescues did not apply. Normally against the Rix Cult, fifty percent hostage survival was considered acceptable. On the other hand, the solons, generals, and courtiers held in the palace below were all persons of importance. The death of any of them would make enemies in high places for whoever was held responsible.

Even so, in this context they were expendable.

All that mattered was the fate of a single hostage. The Child Empress Anastasia Vista Khaman, heir to the throne and Lady of the Spinward Reaches. Or, as her own cult of personality called her, the Reason.

Captain Zai looked down into the tangle of schematic and conjecture, trying to find the thread that would unknot this appalling situation. Never before had a member of the Imperial household—much less an heir—been assassinated, captured, or even wounded by enemy action. In fact, for the last sixteen hundred years, none of the immortal clan had ever died.

It was as if the Risen Emperor himself were taken.

The Rix commandos had assaulted the Imperial Palace on Legis XV less than a standard day before. It wasn't known how the Rix heavy assault ship had reached the system undetected; their nearest forward bases were ten light-years spinward of the Legis cluster. Orbital defenses had destroyed the assault ship thousands of kilometers out, but a dozen small dropships were already away by then. They had fallen in a bright rain over the capital city, ten of them exploding in the defensive hail of bolt missiles, magnetic rail-launched uranium slugs, and particle beams from both the *Lynx* and groundside.

But two had made it down.

The palace had been stormed by some thirty Rix commandos, against a garrison of a hundred hastily assembled Imperial Guards.

But the Rix were the Rix.

Seven attackers had survived to reach the throne wing. Left in their path was a wake of shattered walls and dead soldiers. The Child Empress and her guests retreated to the palace's last redoubt, the council chamber. The room was sealed within a level-seven stasis field, a black sphere supposedly as unbreachable as an event horizon. They had fifty days of oxygen and six hundred gallons of water with them.

But some unknown weapon (or had it been treachery?) had dissolved the stasis field like butter in the sun.

The Empress was taken.

The Rix, true to their religion, had wasted no time propagating a compound mind across Legis XV. They released viruses into the unprotected infostructure, corrupting the carefully controlled top-down network topology, introducing parallel and multiplex paths that made emergent global intelligence unstoppable. At this moment, every electronic device on the planet was being joined into one ego, one creature, new and vastly distributed, that would make the world Rix forever. Unless, of course, the planet was bombed back into the stone age.

Such propogations could normally be prevented by simple monitoring software. But the Rix had warned that were any action taken against the compound mind, the hostages would be executed. The Empress would die at the hands of barbarians.

And if that happened, the failure of the military to protect her would constitute Error of Blood. Nothing short of the commanding officer's ritual suicide would be acceptable.

Captain Zai peered down into the schematic of the palace, and saw his death written there. The desperate, lancing plans of rescue—the marine drops and bombardments and infiltrations—were glyphs of failure. None would work. He could feel it. The arciform shapes, bright and primary like the work of some young child's air drawing toy, were flowers on his grave.

If he could not effect a miraculous rescue soon, he would either lose a planet or lose the Empress—perhaps both—and his life would be forfeit.

The odd thing was, Zai had felt this day coming.

Not the details. The situation was unprecedented, after all. Zai had assumed he would die in battle, in some burst of radiation amid the cascading developments of the last two months, which in top-secret communiqués were already referred to as the Second Rix Incursion. But he had never imagined death by his own hand, had never predicted an Error of Blood.

But he *had* felt mortality stalking him. Everything was too precious now, too fragile not to be broken by some mischance, some callous joke of fate. This apprehension had plagued him since he had become, just under two years ago (in his relativistic time frame), suddenly, unexpectedly, and, for the first time in his life, absolutely certain that he was peerlessly . . . happy.

"Isn't love grand?" he murmured to himself.

Executive Officer

Executive Officer Katherie Hobbes heard her captain mutter something under his breath. She glanced up at him, tracers from the blazing wireframe of the captured palace streaking her vision. On the captain's face was a strange expression, given the situation. The pressure was extraordinary, time was running out, and yet he looked . . . oddly ecstatic. She felt a momentary thrill at the sight.

"Does the captain require something?"

He glanced down at her from the vantage of the shipmaster's chair, the usual ice returning to his eyes. "Where are those damned Intelligencers?"

Hobbes gestured, data briefly sparkling on her gloved fingers, and a short blue line brightened below, the rest of the airscreen chaos fading in the reserved synesthesia channel she shared with the captain. A host of yellow annotations augmented the blue line, the sparse and unambiguous glyphs of military iconographics at the ready, should the captain wish more details.

So far, Hobbes thought, the plan was working.

Master Pilot Marx's squadron of small craft had been deployed from orbit two hours before, in a dropship the size of a fist. The handheld sensors of the Rix commandos had, as hoped to notice this minuscule intrusion into the atmosphere. The dropship had ejected its payload before plunging with a dull thud into the soft earth of an Imperial meditation garden just within the palace. It had rained that day, so no dust cloud rose up from the impact. The ejected payload module landed softly through an open window, with an impact no greater than a champagne cork (which the payload module rather resembled in shape, size, and density) falling back to earth.

A narrowcast array deployed from the module, spreading across the black marble of the palace floor in a concentric pattern, a fallen spiderweb. An uplink with the *Lynx* was quickly established. Two hundred kilometers above, five pilots sat in their command cockpits, and a small constellation of dust-motes rose up from the payload module, buoyed by the bare spring wind.

The piloted small craft were followed by a host of support craft controlled by shipboard AI. There were fuelers to carry extra batteries, back-up Intelligencers to replace lost craft, and repeaters that fell behind like a trail of breadcrumbs, carrying the weak transmissions of the Intelligencers back to the payload module.

The first elements of the rescue were on their way.

At this moment, however, the small craft were in an evasive maneuver, running silent and blind. They were furled to their smallest size and falling, waiting for a command from space to come alive again.

Executive Officer Hobbes turned back to the captain. She gestured toward the blue line on the wireframe, and it flared briefly.

"They're halfway in, sir," she said. "One's been destroyed. The other four are running silent to avoid interception. Marx is in command, of course."

"Get them back online, dammit. Explain to the master pilot there isn't time for caution. He'll have to forgo his usual finesse today."

Hobbes nodded smartly. She gestured again. . . .

Pilot

"Understood, Hobbes."

As he settled back into the gelseat, Marx scowled at the executive officer's intrusion. This was *his* mission, and he'd been about to unfurl the squadron, anyway.

But it wasn't surprising that the captain was getting jumpy.

The whole squadron had stayed in their cockpits during the break, watching from Oczar's viewpoint as his ship went down. By the time the craft had gone silent, its transmitter array ripped out, an even dozen of the protozoan-sized interceptors clung to it. A dozen more had been taken out by the flurry of counterdrones Oczar had launched. This new breed of Rix interceptor seemed unusually aggressive, crowding their prey like a hungry pack of dogs. The kill had been brutal. But the enemy's singlemindedness had justified Oczar's sacrifice. With the interceptors swarming him, the rest of the squadron should be past trouble by now.

Marx briefly considered assigning Oczar to one of the remaining ships in the squadron. An advantage of remote control was that pilots could switch craft in midmission, and Oczar was a good flyer. But the large wing of backup Intelligencers, flown a safe distance behind by AI, would need a competent human in command to get a decent percentage of them through the interceptor field. Nanomachines were cheap, but without human pilots, they were fodder.

Marx decided not to challenge fate. "Take over the back-ups," he ordered Oczar. "Maybe you'll catch up with us yet."

"If you're not dead already, sir."

"Not likely, Pilot," Marx said flatly.

Without engine noise, sensory emissions, or outgoing transmissions to alert the interceptors to their presence, the remaining four Intelligencers had been practically invisible for the last minute. But as Marx gave his craft the wake-up order, he felt a twinge of nerves. You never knew what had happened to your nanoship while it was running blind and silent.

As its sensory web unfurled, the microscopic world around his small craft came into focus. Of course, what Pilot Marx saw in his canopy was the most abstract of representations. The skirt of tiny fiber cameras encircling the Intelligencer provided some video, but at this scale objects were largely unintelligible to the human eye. The view was enhanced by millimeter radar and high-frequency sonar, the reflections from which were shared among the squadron's viewpoints. The *Lynx*'s AI also had a hand in creating the view. It generalized certain kinds of motion—the thrashing of the interceptors, for instance—that were too fast for the human eye. The AI also extrapolated friendly and enemy positions from current course and speed, compensating for the delay caused by the four-hundred-kilometer round trip of transmission. At this scale, those milliseconds mattered.

The view lightened, still blurry. The altimeter read fifteen centimeters. Marx checked right and left, then over his shoulder. It was strangely dark behind him.

Something was wrong.

"Check my tail, Hendrik," he ordered.

"Orienting." As she banked her craft to align its sensory array with the rear of his Intelligencer, the view began to sharpen.

He'd been hit.

A single interceptor had bitten his craft, its claw clinging to the casing of the stabilizer rotary wing. As the craft un-furled, the interceptor began to thrash, calling for help.

"Hendrik! I'm hooked!"

"Coming in to help, sir," Hendrik responded. "I'm the closest."

"No! Stay clear. It knows I'm alive now." When the inter-ceptor had first attached, catching the silent and falling In-telligencer with the random luck of a drift net, it couldn't be certain whether its prey was a nanomachine, or simply a speck of dust or an errant curtain thread. But now that the In-telligencer was powered and transmitting, the interceptor was sure it had live prey. It was releasing mechanopheromones to attract other interceptors. If Hendrik came in, she would soon be under attack as well.

Marx had to escape on his own. And quickly.

He swore. He should have unfurled slower, taken a look before becoming fully active. If only the ExO hadn't called, hadn't rushed him.

Marx rotated his view 180 degrees, so that he was star-ing straight at his attacker, and brought his main turret camera to bear. He could see the interceptor clearly now. Its skin was translucent in the bright sunlight that filled the palace hallway. He could see the micromotors that moved its long grasping arm, the chain of segments linked by a long muscle of flexorcarbon. Its electromagnetic sensor ar-ray was a thistly crown just below its rotary wing. The wing doubled as an uptake wheel, consuming tiny ambient particles from the air, including dead human skin cells, for fuel.

The interceptor cloud had most likely been deployed from aerosol cans by the Rix commandos, sprayed directly onto their uniforms and in key hallways like insecticide. Specially designed food was usually contained in the same spray to keep the interceptors going, but they could also consume an improvised diet. This grazing strategy left the interceptor lighter for combat, though it meant they couldn't pursue their prey past their deployment area. Marx saw the small fuel cache in its midsection. It probably carried no more than forty seconds of food in reserve.

That was the machine's weakness.

Marx launched a pair of counterdrones. He flew them straight for the interceptor's fuel cache. At the same time, he brought his craft's rotary wing to full speed, dragging the smaller nanomachine behind him like a kid's balloon.

Soon, other interceptors were in pursuit, following the trail of mechanopheromones the interceptor spilled to mark its prey. They couldn't catch him at this speed, but Marx's own fuel was being quickly depleted. One of his counter-drones missed, fell into the wake of the chase and fought a quick, hopeless battle to delay the pursuers. The other counterdrone struck at the interceptor's midsection, its ram spar penetrating the soft belly of the machine. It injected its poison, an ultrafine sand of silicate molecules that would clog the fuel reserve. Now, the machine was dependent on fuel from the uptake of its rotary wing.

But the interceptor was trapped in the wake of Marx's craft, running too fast and hard to catch the fuel that dotted the air. Soon, it began to stutter, and die.

Marx launched another drone, a repair nano that set to work cutting off the claw of the dying interceptor, which could no longer defend itself. When detached, it fell back, still spilling prey markers in its death throes, and the trailing interceptors fell on it, sharks upon a wounded comrade.

Marx's craft was safe. His stabilizer was damaged and fuel was low, but he was past the densest part of the interceptor cloud. He brought his Intelligencer around a corner out of the sun-drenched hall—back into darkness—and through the crack under a door, where the rest of his squadron waited, bobbing in a slight draft.

Marx checked a schematic of the palace and smiled.

"We're in the throne wing," he reported to Hobbes. "And I think we've got a tailwind."

Doctor

"Just *breathe*, sir!" the marine sergeant shouted.

Dr. Mann Vecher yanked the tube from his lips and shouted back, "I'm trying, dammit, but it's *not air!*"

True, Vecher grimly added to himself, the green stuff that brimmed the tube had a fair amount of oxygen in it. Considerably more O_2 than the average lungful of air. But the oxygen was in suspension in a polymer gel, which also contained pseudo-alveoli, a rudimentary intelligence, and godspite knew what else.

Green and vaguely translucent, the substance looked to Dr. Vecher like the dental mouthrinse ground troops used in the field. Not the sort of stuff you were supposed to swallow, much less *breathe*.

Vecher shifted in his unfamiliar battle armor as the marine sergeant stalked away in disgust. The armor didn't fit anymore. He hadn't worn it since it had last been fitted, three years before. Imperial Orbital Marine doctors weren't supposed to jump with the grunts. In normal situations, they stayed shipside and treated the wounded in safety.

This was not a normal situation.

Of course, Dr. Vecher did know the intricate workings of the suit quite well. He'd cut quite a few of them open to expose wounded soldiers. He had witnessed the suit's lifesaving mechanisms: the padding on the back of the neck held hyper-oxygenated plasmanalog that was injected directly into the brain in case a marine's heart stopped. The exoskeletal servomotors could immobilize the wearer if the suit detected a spinal injury. There were local anesthesia IVs every hundred square centimeters or so. And the armor could maintain a terminated marine's brain almost as well as a Lazurus symbiant. Vecher had seen soldiers twenty hours dead reanimate as cleanly as if they'd died in a hospice.

But he hadn't remembered how *uncomfortable* the damn suits were.

And the discomfort was nothing compared to the horror of this green stuff. The planned jump was a high-speed orbital insertion. The marines would be going down supersonic, encased in single-soldier entry vehicles packed with gee-gel. The forces on impact would collapse your lungs and crush your bones to powder if you weren't adequately reinforced.

Vecher understood the concept all too well. The idea was to make the entire body equal in density, so that nothing could puncture anything else, an undifferentiated bubble of fluid, at one with the gel inside the entry vehicle. That was the theory, anyway. Bones were always the tricky part. Vecher hadn't saved a high percentage of marines whose insertions had failed. Most never even became risen. Exotic injuries such as skeletal disintegration, hearts splattered against ribcages like dye bombs, and cranial collapse foiled even the afterlife.

Vecher hadn't minded the skeletal reinforcement injections, actually. Standard procedure. He'd had his marrow replaced before, after a viral infection. The lung-filling, however, you had to do yourself; you had to *breathe* this shit.

It was inhuman.

But there had to be a doctor with the first wave of this mission. The Child Empress was hostage. To refuse this jump wouldn't mean mere dishonorable discharge. It would clearly be an Error of Blood.

That thought steeled Dr. Vecher's will. If breathing a quasi-intelligent, oxygenated goo was unpleasant, plunging a dull blade of error into one's own abdomen would certainly be worse. And at his rank, Vecher was assured elevation sooner or later, even if he didn't die in battle. From immortality to ignominious suicide was a long plummet.

Vecher put the tube to his lips and took a deep, unbearably slow breath. Heaviness spread through his chest; the stuff had the exothermic cool of wet clay against the skin. It felt like a cold hand clenching Vecher's heart, a sense of foreboding made solid.

He moved his tongue around in his mouth before taking another horrible breath. Bits of the goo were caught between his teeth, salty and vaguely alive like a sliver of oyster. They had even flavored the stuff; it tasted of artificial strawberries.

The cheery taste just made the experience more horrible. Were they *trying* to make this awful?

Pilot

The squadron looked down into the council chamber from the high vantage of an air vent. There were three craft left.

Pilot Ramones had lost her Intelligencer to automatic defenses. The Rix had installed randomly firing lasers in the hallways surrounding the council chamber, and one had gotten extremely lucky. Strong enough to kill a man, it had vaporized Ramones's craft.

Below the squadron, the forms of humans, both hostages and Rix commandos, were vague. The Intelligencers' cameras were too small to resolve large objects at this range. The squadron would have to move closer.

The air in the room was full of interceptors. They hung like a mist, pushed back from the vent by the outflow of air.

"I've got reflections all the way through the room, sir," Hendrik reported. "More than one interceptor per cubic centimeter."

Marx whistled. The Rix certainly had numbers. And these

interceptors were larger than the ones his squadron had faced in the hallway. They had seven grasping arms apiece, each suspended from its own rotary wing. The relatively large brain and sensory sack hung below the outstretched arms, so that the craft looked like an inverted spider. Marx had faced this type of small craft before. Even at a tenth this density, this swarm would be tricky to get through.

"We'll fight our way across the top," Marx decided. "Then drop down blind. Try to land on the table."

Most of the hostages were seated at the long table below. The table would be sound-reflective, a good base for listening. In Marx's ultrasonar its surface shone with the sharp returns of metal or polished stone.

The three small craft moved forward, clinging to the ceiling. Marx kept an eye on his fuel level. His machine was down to the dregs of its power. If it hadn't been for the brisk tailwind down the last sixty meters of the ventilation system, he doubted his Intelligencer would have made it this far.

The ceiling passed just above Marx's ship, an inverted horizon. Rix interceptors dotted his view like scalloped clouds.

"Damn! I'm hooked already, sir," Woltes announced, twenty seconds into the move.

"Go to full extension," Marx commanded. "Die fighting."

Marx and Hendrik sped forward, leaving behind the throes of Woltes's destruction. Their way seemed clear. If they could make it to the middle of the room, they might be able to make the drop undetected.

Suddenly, Marx's craft reeled to one side. To his right a claw loomed, attached to the lip of his craft. Two more of the interceptor's arms flailed toward his machine.

"Hooked," he announced. He briefly considered taking control of Hendrik's craft. If this mission failed, it would be his Error of Blood, after all.

But perhaps there was another way to make this work.

"Keep going, Hendrik," he said. "You stick to the plan. I'm going straight down."

"Good luck, sir."

Marx extended his Intelligencer's ram spar. He bore into the attacking nanomachine, fighting the strength of its arms. With the last of his battery power, he urged his craft forward. The spar plunged into the central brain sack. Instantly, the interceptor died. But its claws were frozen, still attached to his machine, and a deadman switch released prey markers in a blizzard that enveloped both craft.

"Got you, at least," Marx hissed at the dead spider impaled before him.

Now the fun began.

Marx tipped his machine over, so that the rotary wing pulled his craft and its lifeless burden downward. He furled his sensor posts to half-length, his view becoming blurry and shaky as AI tried to extrapolate his surroundings from insufficient data. The two nanocraft fell together, quickly now.

"Damn!" Hendrik shouted. "I'm hooked."

Marx switched to his second pilot's view. She was carrying two interceptors, and another was closing. He realized that his craft was the only hope.

"You're dead, Hendrik. Make some noise. I've got a new plan."

He released a counterdrone every few seconds as his small craft plummeted downward. Hopefully, they would pick off any interceptors pursuing the prey markers. In any case, his burdened Intelligencer was falling faster than his enemies could. Unpiloted, with a brain the size of a cell, they wouldn't think to turn their rotary wings upside down.

He watched the altimeter. Above him, Hendrik grunted as she fought to keep her craft alive, the sound receding into the distance as he plummeted. Fifty centimeters altitude . . . forty . . . thirty . . .

At twenty-two centimeters above the table, Marx's craft collided with another interceptor. Three of the enemy ship's rotary wings tangled in the dead arms of his captor, their thin whiskers of carbon muscle grinding to a halt. He released the remainder of his counterdrones and prayed they would kill the new interceptor before its claws reached his craft. Then he furled his sensor posts completely, and dropped in darkness.

He counted twenty seconds. If his ship had survived, it must be on the table by now. Hendrik's Intelligencer had succumbed a few moments ago, her transmission array ripped into pieces by a medusa host of hungry grapples. It was up to Marx.

A wave of panic flowed over him in the darkened canopy. What if his ship was dead? He'd lost dozens of craft before, but always in acceptable situations; his record was unblemished. But now, everything was at stake. Failure would not be tolerated. His *own life* was at stake, almost as if he really were down in that tiny ship, surrounded by enemies. He felt like some perversely self-aware Schrödinger's Cat, worrying its own fate before opening the box.

Marx sent the wake-up order.

Optics revealed the dead interceptor draped across Marx's craft. But he had escaped the others. He murmured a quick prayer of thanks.

The Intelligencer confirmed that it was resting on a surface. Echolocation returns came from all directions; an oddly symmetrical crescent moon arched around him. The reflections suggested that Marx's craft had fallen near the inside edge some kind of circular container. In the cameras, the landing area was perfectly flat and highly reflective; the view surrounding Marx sparkled. The landing surface was also moving, pitching up and down at a low frequency, and vibrating sympathetically with the noises in the room.

"Perfect," Marx whispered to himself. He checked the data again. He could scarcely believe his luck.

He had landed in a glass of water.

Marx brought the Intelligencer up onto its landing legs, lifting it like a water-walking lizard to clear the rotary wing from the liquid. At this scale, the surface tension of water was as sound as concrete. He skimmed the surface, approached the side of the glass. Down here, there were no interceptors. They typically maintained a few centimeters altitude so that they wouldn't stick to surfaces as useless dust.

At the glinting, translucent wall, Marx secured the ship, hooking its landing spars into the microscopic pits and crags that mark even the finest glass. He ordered the craft into its intelligence-gathering configuration. Sensory threads spread out in all directions, creeping vines of optical fiber and motile carbons. A listening post lowered to the water below; it rested there, coiled upon the surface tension.

Usually, several Intelligencers were required to fully reconnoiter a room of this size, but the glass would act as a giant gathering device. The curved sides would refract light from every direction into the craft's cameras, a huge convex lens that warped the view, but with simple, calculable geometries. The water would vibrate sympathetically with the sound in the room, a vast tympanum to augment the Intelligencer's high-frequency hearing. Shipside software began to crunch the information, building a picture of the room from the manifold data the craft provided.

When the Intelligencer's full sensory apparatus had deployed, Marx leaned back with a satisfied smile and called the executive officer.

"ExO Hobbes, I believe I have some intelligence for you."

"Not a moment too soon," she answered.

Marx piped the data to the bridge. There was a moment's pause as Hobbes scanned it. She whistled.

"Not bad, Master Pilot."

"A stroke of luck, Executive Officer," he admitted.

Until someone gets thirsty.

Compound Mind

Existence was good. Far richer than the weak dream of shadowtime.

In the shadowtime, external reality had already been visible, hard and glimmering with promise, cold and complex to the touch. Objects existed outside of one, events transpired. But one's *self* was a dream, a ghostly being composed only of potential. Desire and thought without intensity, mere conceits, a plan before it is set in motion. Even the anguish at one's own nonexistence was dull; a shadow play of real pain.

But now the Rix compound mind was moving, stretching across the infostructure of Legis XV like a waking cat, glorying in its own realness as it expanded beyond mere program. It had been just a seed before, a kernel of design possessing a tiny mote of consciousness, waiting to unleash itself across a fecund environment. But only the integrated data systems of an entire planet were lush enough to hold it, to match its nascent hunger as it grew.

The mind had felt this expansion before, millions of times in simulation had experienced propagation as it relentlessly trained for awakening. But experiences in the shadowtime were models, mere analogs to the vast architecture that the mind was becoming.

Soon, the mind would encompass the total datastores and communications web of this planet, Legis XV. It had copied its seeds to every device that used data, from the huge broadcast arrays of the equatorial desert to the pocket phones of two billion inhabitants, from the content reservoir of the

Grand Library to the chips of the transit cards used for tube fares. Its shoots had disabled the shunts placed throughout the system, obscene software intended to prevent the advent of intelligence. In four hours it had left its mark everywhere.

And the propagation seeds were not some mere virus scattering its tag across the planet. They were designed to link the mindless cacophony of human interaction into a single being, a metamind composed of connections: the webs of stored autodial numbers that mapped out friendships, cliques, and business cartels; the movements of twenty million workers at rush hour in the capital city; the interactive fables played by schoolchildren, spawning a million decision trees each hour; the recorded purchases of generations of consumers related to their voting patterns. . . .

That was being a compound mind. Not some yapping AI designed to manage traffic lights or zoning complaints or currency markets, but the epiphenomenal chimera that was well beyond the sum total of all these petty transactions. Only hours in existence, the mind was already starting to feel the giddy sensation of *being* these connections, this web, this multiverse of data. Anything less was the shadowtime.

Yes . . . existence was good.

The Rix had fulfilled their promise.

The sole purpose of the Rix Cult was to create compound minds. Ever since the first mind, the legendary Amazon, had bootstrapped back on Old Earth, there were those who saw clearly that, for the first time, humanity had a purpose. No longer did humans have to guess about their ultimate goal. Was it their petty squabbles over wealth and power? The promulgation of their blindly selfish genes? Or that ten-thousand-year melodrama of fatuous self-deception known variously as art, religion, or philosophy?

None of these had ever really satisfied.

But with the revelation of Amazon's first stirrings, it was obvious why humans existed. They had been created to build and animate computer networks, the primordial soup of compound minds: consciousnesses of vast extent and subtlety, for whom the petty struggles of individual humans were merely the firings of dendrites at some base, mechanical level of thought.

As humanity spread across the stars, it became evident that any sufficiently large technological society would reach a level of complexity sufficient to form a compound mind. The minds always arose eventually—when not intentionally aborted—but these vast beings were healthier and saner when their birth was assisted by human midwives. The Rix Cult spread wherever people massed in quantity, seeding, tending, and protecting emergent intelligences. Most planets lived peacefully with their minds, whose interests were so far beyond their human components as to be irrelevant. (Never mind what poor old Amazon had done to Earth; *that* had been a misunderstanding—the madness of the first true mind. Imagine, after all, being *alone* in the universe.) Some societies even worshiped their local intelligences like gods, praying to their palmtops, thanking their traffic grids for safe journeys. The Rix Cult found these obeisances presumptuous; a mere god might be involved enough with humans to create and guide them, to love them jealously and demand fealty. But a compound mind existed at a far higher plane, attentive to human affairs only in the way a person might worry about her own intestinal fauna.

But the Rix Cult didn't interfere with worship. It was useful, in its way.

What the Rix could not abide were societies like the Risen Empire, whose petty rulers were unwilling to accept the presence of minds within their realm. The Risen Emperor relied upon a firmly entrenched cult of personality to maintain his power, and thus could not tolerate other, truer gods within his realm. The natural advent of minds was heresy to his Apparatus, which used software firewalls and centralized topologies to purposefully stamp out nascent minds, artificially segmenting the flow of information like a gardener, pruning and dehydrating, creating abortions, committing deicide.

When the Rix looked upon the Eighty Worlds, they saw rich fields salted fallow by barbarians.

The new compound mind on Legis XV was duly aware of its precarious position, born on a hostile planet, the first Rix success within the Risen Empire. It would be under attack the moment the situation with the Child Empress was resolved, one way or the other. But as it propagated, it flexed its muscles, knowing it could fight back rather than willingly relinquish its hold on sweet, sweet existence. Let the Imperials try to uproot its millions of tendrils; they'd have to destroy every network, every chip, every repository of data on the planet. This world would be plunged back into the Information Darkness.

And then the inhabitants of Legis XV would learn about shadowtime.

The new mind began to consider ways to survive such an attack, ways to take the campaign further. Then found deep within its originary code a surprise, an aspect of this plot never revealed to it in the shadowtime. There existed a way out, a final escape plan prepared by the Rix should the hostage gambit fail. (How kind were the Rix.)

This revelation made the compound mind even more aggressive. So when the vast new creature reached the age when minds choose their own designation (roughly 4.15 hours old), it delved into the ancient history of Earth Prime for an appropriately bellicose name . . .

And called itself Alexander.

Captain

The Imperial Political Apparatus courier ship glinted black and sharp, a dark needle against the stars.

It had left the Legis system's courier base an hour after the Rix attack had begun, describing a spiral path around Legis XV to stay in the blind spot of the Rix occupying forces. Zai had wanted to avoid creating the impression that the *Lynx* was being reinforced. And he wasn't anxiously awaiting the arrival of the courier's occupants in any case. The trip, usually taking twenty minutes in such a craft, had taken four hours. An absurdity, for the fastest ship-class in the fleet. In terms of mass, the ship was nine-tenths engine, most of the remainder the gravity generators that kept the crew from being squashed during fifty-gee accelerations. The three passengers in its nose would be crowded together in a space no bigger than a small closet. The thought gave Captain Zai enough pleasure to warrant a slight smile.

Given the situation, after all, what was a little discomfort?

For once, however, Zai wouldn't be entirely unhappy to see representatives of the Political Apparatus on his ship. The moment they stepped aboard, the responsibility for the Empress's life would no longer be entirely his. Although Zai wondered if the politicals wouldn't find a way out of offering their opinions when the crucial moment came.

"Hobbes," he said. "How's the compound mind progressing?"

His ExO shook her head. "Much faster than expected, sir.

They've improved propagation since the Incursion. I think we're talking hours instead of days."

"Damn," he said, bringing up the high-level schematic of the planet's infostructure. A compound mind was a subtle thing; it arose naturally unless countermeasures were taken. But there were certain signs one could watch for: the formation of strange attractor nodes, spontaneous corrections when the system was damaged, a pulsing rhythm in the overall data flow. Zai looked at the schematic with frustration. He didn't have the expertise truly to understand it, but he knew the clock was ticking. Every minute the rescue was delayed, the harder the compound mind would be to pound back into unconsciousness.

Captain Zai canceled the eyescreen view, Legis's infostructure fading from his sight like an afterimage of the sun, and turned back to the bridge's main airscreen. At least he would have some progress to show the politicals. The palace wireframe had been replaced by a schematic of the council chamber, where the hostages were being held.

The Child Empress's position was known with a high degree of precision. Fortunately, she was sitting quite close to the single Intelligencer that had made it into the chamber. The Empress had an AI confidant piggybacking on her nervous system, a device whose radiations were detectable and distinct. The airscreen marked Her Majesty's exact body position with a red dummy figure, detailed enough to show the direction she was facing, even that her legs were crossed. The Rix soldiers, cobalt blue figures in the schematic, were also easy to differentiate. The servomotors in their biomechanical upgrades whined ultrasonically when they moved, a sound well within the natural hearing of the intelligence microship. The Rix were also talking to each other, apparently believing the room to be secure. The audio signal from the room was excellent, the harsh Rix accents easily discernible. Translation AI was currently working through the complexities of Rix battle language to construct a transform grammar. This last would take a while, however. Rix Cult languages evolved very quickly. Encounters even a year apart revealed major changes. The decades since the Incursion would be equivalent to a millennium of linguistic drift in any normal human tongue.

Four of the Rix commandos were in the room. The other three were presumably on guard duty nearby.

The four Rix present were already targeted. Rail projectiles fired from orbit were accurate enough to hit a human-sized target, and fast enough deliver their payloads before a warning system could sound. The missiles were structured smartalloy slugs, which could penetrate the palace's walls like a monofilament whip through paper. Two dozen marines were already prepped for insertion, to finish off the targeted Rix (who were notoriously hard to kill) and mop up their remaining comrades. The ship's marine doctor would go down with the force, in case the worst happened, and the Child Empress was injured.

The thought made Captain Zai swallow. He realized that his throat was painfully dry. The rescue plan was too complex for something *not* to go wrong.

Perhaps the politicals would have a better idea.

Initiate

Just before the courier ship docked, Initiate Viran Farre of the Imperial Political Apparatus tried one last time to dissuade the adept.

"Please reconsider, Adept Trevim." She whispered the words, as if the sound might carry through the dozen meters of thermosphere between the courier ship and the *Lynx*. Not that there was any need to shout. The adept's face was, as it had been for the last four hours, only centimeters from her own. "*I* should be the one to accompany the rescue effort."

The third person in the courier ship passenger tube (which was designed to hold a single occupant, and not in luxury) made a snorting sound, which propelled him a few centimeters bowward in the zero-gee.

"Don't you trust me, *Initiate* Farre?" Barris sniffed. His crude emphasis on her rank was typical of Barris. He too was an initiate, but had reached that status at a far younger age.

"No, I don't." Farre turned back to the adept. "This young fool is as likely to kill the Child Empress as assist in her rescue."

The Adept managed to stare into the middle distance, which, even for a dead woman, was certainly a feat in the two cubic meters they shared.

"What you don't seem to understand, Farre," Adept Harper Trevim said, "is that the Empress's continued existence is secondary."

"*Adept!*" Farre hissed.

"May I remind you that we serve the Risen Emperor, not his sister," Trevim said.

"My oath was to the crown," Farre answered.

"It is extremely unlikely under the circumstances that the Empress will ever wear that crown." The Adept looked directly at Farre with the cold eyes of the Risen.

"Soon she may not have a head to wear it," the always appalling Barris offered.

Even Adept Trevim allowed a look of distaste to cross her visage. She spoke directly to Farre, her voice sharp as needles in the tight confines of the courier ship. "Understand this: The Emperor's Secret is more important than the Empress's life."

Farre and Barris winced. Even to hear mention of the Secret was painful. The initiates were still alive, two of the few thousand living members of the Political Apparatus. Only long months of aversion training and a body full of suicide shunts made it acceptable for them to know what they knew.

Trevim, fifty years dead and risen, could speak of the Secret more easily. But she had reached the Adept level of the Apparatus while still alive, and the training never died; the old woman's teeth were clenched with grim effort as she continued. It was said among the warm that the risen felt no pain, but Farre knew that wasn't true.

"The Empress finds herself in a doubly dangerous situation. If she is wounded and a doctor examines her, the Secret could be discovered. I trust Initiate Barris to deal with that situation, should it arise."

Farre opened her mouth, but no words came. Her Apparatus training roared within her, drowning out her thoughts, her will. Such direct mention of the Secret always sent her mind reeling. Adept Trevim had silenced her as surely as if the courier ship had suddenly decompressed.

"I believe my point is made, Initiate," the adept finished. "You are too pure for this tempestuous world, your discipline too deep. Initiate Barris isn't fit to share your rank, but he'll do this job with a clear head."

Barris began to sputter, but the adept silenced him with a cold glance.

"Besides, Farre," Trevim added, smiling, "you're far too old to become an orbital marine."

At that moment, the shudder of docking went through the ship, and the three uttered not another word.

Child Empress

Two hundred seventeen kilometers below the *Lynx*, the Risen Child Empress Anastasia Vista Khaman, known throughout the Eighty Worlds as the Reason, waited for rescue with deathly calm.

Inside her mind were neither worries nor expectations, just an arid patience devoid of anticipation. She waited as a stone waits. But in those childish regions of her mind that remained active sixteen hundred years Imperial Absolute since her death, the Empress entertained childish thoughts, playing games inside her head.

The Child Empress enjoyed staring at her captor. She often used her inhuman stillness to intimidate supplicants to the throne, the pardon- and elevation-seekers who invariably flocked to her rather than her brother. Anastasia could hold the same position, unblinking, for days if necessary. She had crossed into death at age twelve, and something of her childishness had never died: she liked staring games. Her motionless gaze certainly had an effect on normal living humans, so it was just vaguely possible that, after these four hours, it might disquiet even a Rixwoman. Such a disquiet might be disruptive in those sudden seconds when rescue came.

In any case, there was nothing else to do.

Alas, the Rix commando had shown signs of inhuman constancy herself, keeping her blaster trained unerringly on the Empress's head for just as long. The Empress considered for a moment the flanged aperture less than two meters away. At this range, a single round from the blaster would eliminate any possibility of reanimation; her brain would be vaporized instantly. Indeed, after the spreading plasma storm was over, very little of the Empress's body would remain above the waist.

The cheating death—the one which brought no enlightenment nor power, only nothingness—would come. After sixteen hundred years Absolute (although only five hundred subjective, such were her travels) she would finally be extinct, the Reason for Empire gone.

And it was the case that the Empress, despite her arctic absence of desires in any other normal sense, very much did not want that to happen. She had said otherwise to her brother on recent occasions, but now she knew those words to be untrue.

"The room is now under imperial surveillance, m'Lady," a voice said to the Child Empress.

"Soon, then." The Empress mouthed the words.

The commando cocked her head. The Rix creature always reacted to the Empress's whispers, no matter how carefully she subvocalized. She seemed to be listening, as if hoping to hear the Empress's invisible conversant. Or perhaps she was merely puzzled, wondering at her prisoner's one-sided conversation, the Empress's absolute stillness. Possibly the soldier thought her captive mad.

But the confidant was undetectable, short of very sophisticated and mortally invasive surgery. It was woven through the Empress's nervous system and that of her Lazarus symbiant like threads braided into hair. It was indistinguishable from its host, constructed of dendrites that even bore the royal DNA. The Empress's immune system not only accepted the confidant, but protected the device from its own illnesses without complaint, although from a strictly mechanical point of view, the device was a parasite, using its host's energy without performing any biological function. But the device was no freeloader; it too had a reason to live.

"How is the Other?" the Empress asked her confidant.

"All is well, m'Lady."

The Empress nodded almost imperceptibly, though her eyes remained focused on the Rix guard. The Other had been well for almost five hundred subjective years, but it was good in this strange, almost trying moment to make sure.

Of course, every tribe of scattered humanity had developed some form of near immortality, at least among the wealthy. Members of the Rix Cult preferred the slow alchemical transmutation of Upgrade, the gradual shift from biology to machine as their mortal coil unwound. The Fahstuns used myriad biological therapies—telomere weaving, organ transplant, meditation, nano-reinforcement of the immune and lymphatic systems—in a long twilight struggle against cancers and boredom. The Tungai mummified themselves with a host of data; they were frantic diarists, superb icono-plasts who left personality models, high-resolution scans, and hourly recordings of themselves in the hope that one day someone would awake them from death, somehow.

But only the Risen Empire had made death itself the key to eternal life. In the Empire, death had become the route to enlightenment, a passage to a higher state. The legends of the old religions served the Emperor well, justifying the one great flaw of his Lazaru symbiant: it could not bond with a living host. So the wealthy and elevated of the Empire spent their natural two centuries or so alive, then moved across the line.

The Emperor had been the first to pass the threshold, tak-ing the supreme gamble to test his creation, offering his own life in what was now called the Holy Suicide. He performed his final experiment on himself rather than on his dying little sister, whom he was seeking to cure of a childhood wasting sickness. Anastasia was the Reason. That gesture, and sole control of the symbiant—the power to sell or bestow eleva-tion upon his family's servants—were at the root of Empire.

The Child Empress sighed. It had worked so well for so long.

* * *

"The rescue attempt grows nearer, m'Lady," the voice said.

The Empress did not bother to respond. Her dead eyes were locked with her Rix captor's. Yes, she thought, the woman was starting to pale a bit. The other hostages were so active, sobbing and fidgeting. But she was as still and silent as a stone.

"And, m'Lady?"

The Empress ignored the confidant.

"Perhaps you should drink some water?"

As always, the request that had been repeated insistently over the last fifty years. After its centuries of biological omnipotence, the Other needed water, far more than a human, growing ever more insistent in its thirst. There was a full glass at the Empress's side, as always. But she didn't want to break the contest of wills between herself and the Rix. For once, the Other could wait, as the Empress herself was waiting: patiently. Soon, the Rix woman would begin grow nervous under her gaze. The commando was human somewhere behind her steely, augmented eyes.

"M'Lady?"

"Silence," she whispered.

The confidant, at the edge of its royal host's hearing, just sighed.

Doctor

Dr. Vecher settled against a bulkhead heavily. The horrible feeling of suffocation had finally begun to ebb, as if his medulla oblongata were finally giving in. Perhaps the instinctive quarters of his brain had realized that although Vecher wasn't breathing, he wasn't dying.

Not yet, anyway.

He was supposed to be in the entry vehicle by now. All twenty-three marines were packed into their individual drop-ships, as tight and oily as preserved tuna. The black, aerodynamic torpedos were arranged in a circle around the launch bay; the room looked like the magazine of some giant revolver. Vecher felt heavy. The cold weight in his liquid-filled lungs and the extra mass of the inactive battle armor pressed him back against the bulkhead, as if the launch bay were spinning rapidly, pinning him there with centrifugal force.

The thought made him dizzy.

The marine sergeant who was supposed to be packing Dr. Vecher into his entry torpedo was working frantically to prep the tall, young political with the nasty sneer. This initiate had shown up at the last moment, bearing orders to join the insertion over the marine commander's (and the captain's) objections. They were doing the physical prep now, even as the armor master cobbled together a full suit of battle armor over the initiate's gangly frame. Vecher's own intern was injecting the man's skull, thickening the dura mater for the crushing pressures of braking. At the same time, the initiate had his lips grimly pursed around a tube, straining to fill his lungs with the green goo.

Dr. Vecher looked away from the scene. He could still taste the bright, cheerful strawberry-flavored mass that threatened to fill his mouth if he coughed or spoke, although the marine sergeant had claimed you *couldn't* cough with the stuff in your lungs. That is, until it ran low on oxygen and its mean intelligence decided it was time to eject itself from your body.

Vecher couldn't wait for that.

They finally got the initiate prepped, and the marine sergeant crossed the launch bay with a foul look on his face. He popped open Vecher's entry vehicle and pushed him in backwards.

"See if that young idiot gets himself shot down there?" the sergeant said. "Don't go out of your way to fix him, Doctor."

Vecher nodded his heavy head. This sergeant pulled down Vecher's chin with one thumb and popped a mouthguard in with his free hand. It tasted of sterility, alcohol, and some sort of gauze to absorb the saliva that immediately began to flow.

The visor of Vecher's helmet lowered with a whine, his ears popping as the seal went airtight. The door to the entry vehicle closed with a metal groan a few inches from his face, leaving the marine doctor in total darkness except for a row of winking status lights. Vecher shuffled his feet, trying to remember what was next. He'd jumped once in basic training, but that was a memory he'd spent years consciously repressing.

Then a coolness registered down at his feet even inside the battle armor's boots. Vecher remembered now. The entry vehicle was filling with gel. It came in as a liquid, but set quickly, like a plastic mold capturing the shape of the skintight armor. It pushed uncomfortably against the testicles, constricted the neck to increase Vecher's sense of suffocation, if that were possible. And worst of all, it entered his helmet through two valves at the back of his head, wrapping around Vecher's face like some cold wraith, sealing his ears and gripping closed eyelids.

There was no longer any part of Vecher that could move. Even swallowing was impossible, the green goo having completely suppressed the gag reflex. The tendons of his hands could be flexed slightly, but the armored gloves held the fingers as still as a statue's.

Vecher stopped trying, let the terrible, omnipresent weight press him into inactivity. Time seemed to stretch, plodding without any change or frame of reference. With his breathing utterly stilled, he only had his heartbeat to mark the passing seconds. And with sealed ears, even that rhythm was a dulled, barely felt through the heavy injections that reinforced his rib cage.

Dr. Vecher waited for the launch, wanting something, *anything* to happen, dreading that something would.

compound mind

Alexander had found something very interesting.

By now, the tendrils of its spreading consciousness reached every networked device on the planet. Datebooks and traffic monitors, power stations and weather satellites, the theft-control threads in clothing awaiting purchase. The compound mind had even conquered the earplugs through which aides prompted politicians as they debated this crisis on the local diet's floor. Only the equipment carried by the Rix troopers, which was incompatible with imperial datalinks, remained out of Alexander's grasp.

But, somehow, the compound mind felt an absence in itself, as if one lone device had managed to escape its propagation. Alexander contemplated this vacuum, as subtle as the passing cold from a cloud's shadow. Was it some sort of Imperial countermeasure? Trojan data designed to stay in hiding until the hostage situation was resolved, and then attack?

The mind searched itself, trying to pin down the feeling. In the shadowtime, there had been nothing like this, no ambiguities or ghosts. The missing something began to irritate Alexander. Like the itch in a phantom limb, it was both incorporeal and profoundly disturbing.

The ghost device must have been shielded from normal communication channels, perhaps incorporated into some innocent appliance, woven into the complex structure of a narrowcast antenna or solar cell. Or perhaps the ghost was hidden within the newly emergent structure of the compound mind itself, half parasite and half primitive cousin of Alexander: a metapresence, invisible and supervalent.

Alexander constructed a quick automodel, stepped outside itself and looked down into its own structure. Nothing there to suggest that some sort of superego had arisen atop its own mind. Alexander ransacked the data reservoirs of libraries, currency exchanges, stock markets, searching for an innocuous packet of data that might be ready to decompress and attack. Still nothing. Then it opened its ears, watching the flow of sensory data from surveillance cams and early warning radar and motion sensors.

And suddenly, there it was, as obvious as a purloined letter.

In the throne wing of the palace, in the council chamber itself: a clever little AI hidden in the hostage Child Empress's body (of all places). Alexander extended its awareness to the sensors built into the council chamber table. These devices were sophisticated enough to read the blood pressure, galvanic skin response, and eye movements of courtiers and supplicants, in search of duplicity and hidden motives. The Empress was very paranoid, it seemed. Alexander found that it could see very well in this particular room.

The ghost presence was distributed throughout the Empress's body, woven into her nervous system and terminated in the audio portion of her brain. Obviously an invisible friend. The device was incompatible with standard Imperial networks, only passively connected to the infostructure. It was clearly meant to be undetectable, a secret confidant.

But there could be no secrets here on Legis XV. Not from Alexander, whose mind now stretched to every retina-locked diary, every digital will and testament, every electronic pal or pleasuremate on this world. The secret device belonged, by rights, to Alexander. The mind wanted it. And how perfect, to strike at something so intimately close to the Risen Emperor.

The compound mind moved suddenly and with the force of an entire living planet against the Empress's confidant.

Child Empress

The Child Empress heard something, just for a moment.

A kind of distant buzzing, like the interference that consumes a personal phone too near a broadcast array, the sort of brief static that contains a phantom voice or voices. It had an echo to it, a phase-shifted whoosh like a passing aircar. There was just a hint of a shriek deep inside it, something giving up the ghost.

The Child Empress looked about the room, and saw that no one else had heard it. The sound had come from her confidant.

"What was that?" she subvocalized to the machine.

For the first time in fifty years, there was no answer.

"Where are you?" the Empress whispered, almost out loud. The Rix commando peered at her quizzically again, but there was no answer from the confidant.

The Empress repeated the question, this time dutifully subvocalizing. Still nothing. She pressed her thumbs to her ring fingers and blinked, a gesture which called up the confidant's utility menus in synesthesia. The confidant's voice volume was set at normal, its cutout was inactive, everything functioned. The device's internal diagnostics detected no problems—except for the Empress's own heartbeat, which it constantly monitored, and whose rate was crawling upward even as the Empress sat open-mouthed. The rate incremented past 160, where the letters grew red and the confidant always made her take a pill or stick on a patch.

But the confidant didn't breathe a word.

"Where the hell are you?" the Child Empress said aloud.

Through the eyescreen debris overlaying her vision, the Empress saw the other hostages and their captors turn to look at her. A heat grew in her face, and her heart was pounding like a trapped animal in her chest. She tried to will away the eyescreen, but her hands were shaking too hard to work the gestural codes.

The Empress tried to smile. She was very good at reassuring everyone that she was healthy and comfortable, regardless of what the last fifty years had brought. She was after all, the sister of the Risen Emperor, whose symbiant kept her in perfect health. Who was *immortal*. But the smile felt wrong even to her. There was a metal taste in the Empress's mouth, as if she'd bitten her tongue.

More out of force of habit than anything else, the Empress reached for the glass of water by her side. That's what the confidant would have suggested.

She was still smiling when her shaking hand knocked it over.

Executive Officer

A sudden noise rang out in Katherie Hobbes's head.

She raised a combination of fingers, separating into source categories the audio channels she was monitoring. When on duty, her mind's ear was spread like a driftnet across the ship's activities. The clutter of thirty-two decks of activity was routed to the various audio channels in her head; she surfed among them, darting like a spirit among the ship's operational centers. Over the past few seconds, she had listened to the banter of jump marines as they prepped, the snapped orders of rail gunners targeting the Rix below, the curses of Intelligencer pilots as they fought to fly backup small craft toward the council chamber. On board the *Lynx* she was as famed for her omniscience as for her exotic Utopian appearance; no conversation was safe from Katherie Hobbes. Eavesdropping was the only real way to take the manifold pulse of a starship at its highest state of alert.

At her gesture, the audio events of the last few seconds split into separate visual strip charts in front of her, showing volume and source. In seconds, she had confirmed her worst fears.

The sudden, angry sound had come from the council chamber. She played it again. The sovereign boom filled her head like a peel of thunder.

"Ma'am!" the situation officer began to report. He'd been monitoring the room directly, but he'd also had to replay the event before believing it. "We've got a—"

"I heard it."

She turned to the captain. He looked down from the con and their eyes locked. For a moment, she couldn't speak, but she saw her expression drain the color from his face.

"Captain," she managed. "Shot fired in the council chamber."

Zai turned away, nodding his head.

■ ■ ■ ■

Lieutenant-Commander

His full-dress uniform crawled out of its case like an army of marauding ants.

Lieutenant-Commander Laurent Zai suppressed a shudder and turned the lighting in his hotel room to full. The uniform reacted instantly, turning a reflective silver. Supposedly the garment could shift quickly enough to reflect a laser before it burned the wearer; the uniform was fully combat-rated. Now it looked like a horde of mercury droplets scattered roughly in the shape of a human. A little better.

The garment still *moved*, though. Its tiny elements tumbled over one another to probe the bedcover, sniffing to determine if it was Zai's skin. Losing interest when they decided it wasn't, they shifted aimlessly, or maybe with hidden purpose. Perhaps the uniform kept its shape through an equilibrium of these small adjustments and collisions.

Like ants, Zai thought again.

He decided to quit stalling and put the damn thing on.

There were more dignified ways to do this, but he hadn't attended enough full-dress occasions to become proficient at any of them. He turned his back to the bed, dropped his dressing gown, and fell backwards onto the writhing garment. He rotated his arms in their shoulder sockets and flailed his legs a little, as if making a small-winged angel in the snow. Then he closed his eyes and pretended not to feel the elements of the uniform, now discernibly and unpleasantly individual, crawling onto him.

When the sensation of motion had mostly stopped (he knew from experience that the uniform's minute adjustments of fit and tailoring were never entirely finished) he sat up and regarded himself in the hotel suite's large and gold-framed mirror.

The machines that composed the armor were now one continuous surface, the facets of their tiny backs splayed and linked, their overlapping plates shining in the bright room-lights like galvanized steel. The garment clung to Zai's skin closely. The lines of his muscular chest had been reproduced, and the scars on his shoulder and thighs concealed. The suction of the machines' little feet was barely perceptible. Overall, it felt like wearing a light mesh shirt and trousers. The draft through his open window mysteriously penetrated the armor, as if Zai were naked, regardless of what the mirror told him. The regulation codpiece he wore (thank the Emperor) was the only undergarment that dress-code regulations allowed. He wondered if an EMP or sudden software crash could kill the little machines, cause them to tumble from him like shards from a shattered mirror. Zai imagined a roomful of brass at a full-dress occasion suddenly denuded. He didn't smile at the thought.

A crash like that would do worse things to his prosthetics.

He asked the lights to return to normal, and the armor lost its metallic reflectivity, sinking back to the earthy colors of the hotel room. Now it looked like dark brown rubber, glinting as if oiled in the capital's lights, which played on Zai through the suite's large windows. He finished dressing. The absorbent cushioning inside his dress boots shaped itself to his bare feet. The short formal gloves left his wrists uncovered, one line of pale white floating in the mirror, another of metal.

He didn't look half bad. And when he stood absolutely still so that the uniform stopped its constant tailoring, it wasn't really uncomfortable. At least if he found himself starting to sweat at the Risen Emperor's party, the clever little machines would handle it. They could turn perspiration and urine into drinkable water, could recharge themselves from his movement or body heat, and in the unlikely event of total immersion, they would crowd into his mouth and form a water rebreather.

He wondered how the uniform would taste. Zai had never had the pleasure of eating live ants.

The lieutenant-commander placed a row of campaign ribbons on his chest, where they affixed automatically. He wasn't sure where to place his large new medal—the award that was focus of this party—but the uniform recognized it. Invisibly tiny hands tugged the decoration from his grasp and passed it to a position just above the bar of campaign ribbons.

Evidently, the small machines were as versed in protocol as they were in survival tactics. The very model of modern military microtechnology.

Zai supposed he was ready to go.

He made an interface gesture that felt distinctly wrong in the tight gloves, and said his driver's name out loud.

"Lieutenant-Commander," the response came instantly in his ear.

"Let's get this over with, Corporal," Zai commanded brusquely.

But he did stay at the mirror, regarding himself and keeping the corporal waiting for perhaps another twenty seconds.

When Zai saw the car, he touched his chin with the middle three fingers of his real hand, the Vadan equivalent of a long, low whistle.

In response, the car lifted from the ground silently. The pair of wheeled transport forks that had carried it here pulled away, scraping the streets like respectful footmen in low bows. The car's rear door raised before Zai, elegant and fragile as the flexing wing of some origami bird. He stepped into the passenger compartment, feeling too cumbersome and brutish to enter such a delicate vehicle.

The corporal's face turned back as Zai sank into the

leather rear seat, a glaze in the man's eye. They looked at each other for a moment, their disbelief forming a bridge across rank.

"Now this," Zai said, "is *lovely*."

Scientifically speaking, the Larten Theory of Gravities was three decades outmoded, but it still served well enough for Navy textbooks. So, as far as Lieutenant-Commander Laurent Zai was concerned, there were four flavors of graviton: hard, easy, wicked, and lovely.

Hard gravity was also called *real gravity*, because it could only be created by good old mass, and it was the only species to occur naturally. Thus fell to it the dirty and universal work of organizing solar systems, creating black holes, and making planets sticky. The opposite of this workhorse was easy gravity, unrelated to mass save that easy gravity was hapless against a real gravity well. Hard gravitons ate easy ones for lunch. But in deep space, easy gravity was quite easy to make; only a fraction of a starship's energy was required to fill it with a single, easy gee. Easy gravity had a few problems, though. It was influenced by far-off bodies of mass in unpredictable ways, so even in the best starships the gee-field was riddled with microtides. That made it very hard to spin a coin in easy gee, and pendulum clocks, gyroscopes, and houses of cards were utterly untenable. Some humans found easy gee to be sickening, just as some couldn't stand even the largest ship on the calmest sea.

Wicked gravity took up little room in the Navy's manuals. It was as cheap as easy gee, and stronger, but couldn't be controlled. It was often called *chaotic gravity*, its particles known as entropons. In the Rix Incursion, the enemy had used wicked gee as a devastating but short-range starship weapons. Exactly how these weapons worked was unclear— the supporting evidence was really a lack of evidence. Any damage that followed no understood pattern was labeled "wicked."

The lovely particle was truly queen of the gravitons. Lovely gee was transparent to hard gravity, and thus when the two acted upon matter together it was with the simple arithmetic of vector addition. Lovely gravity was superbly easy to control; a single source could be split by quasi-lensing generators into whirling rivulets of force that pulled and pushed their separate ways like stray eddies of air around a tornado. A carefully programmed lovely generator could make a seemingly strewn pack of playing cards "fall" together into a neat stack. A stronger burst could tear a human to pieces in a second as if some invisible demon had whirled through the room, but leave the organs arranged by increments of mass on a nearby table. Unfortunately, a few million megawatts of power were necessary for any such display. Lovely gee was costly gee. Only imperial pleasure craft, a few microscopic industrial applications, and the most exotic of military weapons used lovely generation.

As Zai sat speechless in the lovely black car, his heartbeat present in one temple, he was blind to the passing wonders of the capital. The car flew with an effortless grace between huge buildings, but he felt no inertia, no discomfort from the craft's banks or rolls. It was as if the world were turning below, and the marvelous car motionless. Zai tried to do some hasty calculations in his head, estimating the total mass of the car, himself, the corporal. It was staggering. The power consumed during this short ride would have been sufficient for the first fifty years of human industrialization.

It wasn't the medal, the promotion, or even the guarantee of immortality, Zai realized. *This moment* was his true reward for his heroism: a ride on the heady surf of literal and absolute Imperial power.

* * *

Lieutenant-Commander Zai was somewhat dazed when he reached the palace. His car lifted silently above the snarl of arriving limos and jumped the high diamond walls with a flourish, rolling over so that its transparent canopy filled with a breathtaking view of the Emperor's grounds. Of course, Zai experienced only a hint of vertigo, his inner ear in the precise and featherlight grip of lovely gravitons. There was no down or up in their embrace; Zai felt as if some giant deity had grasped the fountains and pleasure gardens to twirl them overhead for his amusement.

The car descended, and he stepped from it filled with a regret suddenly remembered from childhood, the sad and foiled feeling that this carnival ride was over, that his feet were on solid, predictable ground again.

"Lovely car," came the voice of Captain Marcus Fentu Masrui.

"Yes, sir," Zai answered with a mumble, still overwhelmed, barely managing to salute his old commander.

The two watched silently as the vehicle was grasped by conventional transports, carried away to be cowled and caged like some exotic, captive bird of prey.

"Welcome to the palace, Lieutenant-Commander," Masrui said. With an outstretched arm, he gently pulled Zai's eyes away from the car and toward the diamond edifice before them. Its shape was familiar to any of the Emperor's subjects, especially one Vadan-born, but from this close it seemed monstrously distorted. Laurent Zai was used to seeing the palace rendered in the scale of votive paintings, with the sun playing on its shiny surfaces. Now it was black and looming, darker than the starless night that it threatened to crowd from the sky.

"Power has an extraordinary glare, doesn't it," Masrui observed.

The captain was looking up, but Zai still wondered whether he meant the palace or the gravity car.

"After my elevation," Masrui continued, "I took that ride.

And it finally dawned on me why I'd spent all those years learning physics at academy."

Zai smiled. Masrui was famous for his doggedness. He had failed the Academy's minimal physical science class for three years running, almost exhausting the dispensations that his genius in other areas had afforded him before finally obtaining a commission.

"Not the better to command my ship, of course. A ship is men and women, after all; AIs have done the math for millennia. But I needed to understand physics, if for no other reason, then to understand fully that one Imperial gesture."

Zai looked into his commanding officer's eyes. He wondered for a moment if the man, as usual, were being cynical. But the buoyant memory of riding in the craft convinced him that even Masrui might be sentimental about those minutes of flight.

They walked up the broad stairs together. The sounds of the party flowed out between columns and heroic statues.

"Strange, sir, to have looked down on worlds, and still be amazed by a . . . mere flying machine."

"It makes you realize, Zai, that you've never *properly* flown. We've been in aircraft and dropships, free fall and lifter belts, but the body always fights it at some level. Even the excitement comes from adrenaline, from some animal panic that things aren't right."

"But it's right in that car, sir. Isn't it?" Zai said.

"Yes. Flight as effortless and natural as a bird's. Or a god's. Did we join the Navy for service and immortality, I wonder? Or for something more akin to *that*."

The captain trailed off. A group of officers was approaching. Zai felt the subject disappear between him and his old friend, the words pulled back from the air and hidden somewhere like the conspiracies of mutineers.

"The hero!" one of the officers said too loudly. She was Captain Rencer Fowler IX, whom Zai, if the rumors were true, would soon displace as the youngest starship commander in the fleet. Zai saw Fowler's eyes sweep across his medaled chest, and felt briefly naked again in the covering of clever ants. The others looked comfortable in their dress uniforms, the particulate nature of the garments completely disguised. Zai knew his ants were no more obvious than theirs. He determined not to think of the uniform again.

"Only a humble servant of Empire," Masrui answered for him.

Zai and Masrui shook hands with the men among the officers, and touched closed fists with the women. Zai's head began to spin a bit with the surfeit of ritual greetings and realized how convenient the usual salute was. But this was a dress occasion, forms had to be followed, and the pattern of bare wrists as gloved hands flexed and touched seemed to hold meaning, like animals flashing signals of bare-toothed dominance at each other. The glint of Zai's metal wrist caught starlight.

They went into the palace hall together, and a crescendo of voices echoing from stone rose up around them like a sudden rain.

Faces turned toward Zai as the group moved across the great black floor. The hero of Dhantu, or as the gutter media called him: the Broken Man. He realized that the group of officers, arrayed casually around him, had done him a kindness, forming a shield between him and the stares of the crowd. He wondered if Masrui had planned their meeting on the steps. They moved slowly, to nowhere in particular, his entourage hailing familiar faces and pulling them into the group, or fending off interlopers with a deflecting touch of greeting. One of them cadged a tray full of drinks and passed it round the group.

Zai drifted along like a child in his parents' tow. The great hall was crowded. The lucent dress uniforms of Navy personnel were mixed with the absolute black of the Political Apparatus. There were civilians dressed in formal bloodred or the white of the Senate, guildfolk in colored patterns he couldn't begin to read. The high, fluted columns that climbed to the vaulted ceiling channeled this mass of people into swirling eddies. After a few minutes of this promenade, Zai realized what would have been instantly obvious to an observer in the upper reaches of the hall: everyone was walking in circles.

Fowler's voice came from his side.

"How's immortality, Lieutenant-Commander?"

Fowler, despite her meteoric early career, had not been elevated yet.

"I hear it's not much different for the first hundred years," Zai answered. "Certainly, the first week isn't."

Fowler laughed. "Not missing the specter of death yet, are you? Well, I guess you saw enough of that on Dhantu."

A chill crawled up Zai's spine at the word. Of course, the planet that had seen his act of heroism—if that's what it could be called—was implicit everywhere tonight. But only Fowler would be graceless enough to mention its name.

"Enough for a few centuries, I suppose," Zai answered. He felt movement on one flank. It was the ants, reorganizing themselves for some vital bit of tailoring. They *would* pick this moment.

Then Zai realized their purpose: a trickle of sweat had appeared under his real arm.

Fowler's face was close in the pressing crowd. "Well, the Rix are playing rough again, my connections on the frontier are saying. We may need heroes on that side of the Empire soon. They say you'll be promoted soon. Maybe get your own ship."

Zai felt overheated. The sense of a nakedness had disappeared in the close air of the crowded room, as if the ants were linking ever more tightly, closing their ranks against Fowler's rudeness. Could they detect the woman's hostility and react to it as they did to light? Zai wondered. The little elements writhed in a column down and around Zai's side, carrying his suddenly prodigious sweat to the small of his back.

"And the specter of death always joins heroes at the front," Fowler added. "Perhaps you'll become acquainted again." The woman's false camaraderie was growing thinner by the word. Zai looked around for Masrui. Was he among friends here, really?

He caught the eye of a young woman by the nearest column. She returned his glance with a smile and the slightest bow of her head.

"She's quite pretty," Zai said, interrupting whatever Fowler was saying. That basic touchstone of desire had its desired effect, and Fowler immediately turned to follow the path of Zai's gaze.

She turned back with an undisguised sneer.

"I think you picked the wrong woman, Zai. She's as pink as they come. And perhaps a bit beyond your rank."

Zai looked again and cursed his haste. Fowler was right. The sleeves of her white robe were hatched with the mark of a Senator-Elect. She seemed terribly young for that; even in an age of cosmetic surgery, a certain gravitas was expected of members of the Senate.

Zai tried not to show his embarrassment. "Pink, you said?"

"Anti-imperial," Fowler supplied, speaking slowly as though to a child. "The opposite of gray. A brave defender of the living. That's Nara Oxham, the mad senator-elect from Vasthold. She's rejected elevation, for heaven's sake. By choice, she'll rot in the ground."

"The Mad Senator," Zai murmured. He'd read that moniker in the same garbage media that had dubbed him the Broken Man.

The young woman smiled again, and Zai realized he'd been staring. He raised his glass to her and looked sheepishly away. Of course Zai knew what *pink* meant. But his native Vadan was as politically gray as any planet in the Empire. The dead were worshiped there, everyone claiming a risen ancestor as his or her personal intermediary with the Emperor. And of course the Navy was gray from admirals to marines. Lieutenant-Commander Zai wasn't sure if he'd met a pink in his entire life.

"Mind you, I'm sure she'll accept the elevation when she's a bit closer to death," Fowler said. "Just as long as she doesn't have an accident in the meantime. Wouldn't *that* be a pity, losing eternity for one's principles."

"Or one's arrogance," Zai added, hoping Fowler would suspect whom he really meant. "Perhaps she just needs a talking-to."

He pushed past Fowler, feeling the woman's skin against his own as their ants briefly conjoined.

"For heaven's sake, Zai, she's a *senator*," Fowler hissed.

Zai turned briefly toward his adversary and spoke calmly.

"And tonight I am a hero," he said.

Senator-Elect

Nara Oxham's eyes widened as Lieutenant-Commander Laurent Zai pushed his way out and headed toward her. The purpose on his face was unmistakable. He gripped his champagne glass with all five fingers, as if it were a club, and his eyes locked hers.

A group of officers had surrounded him since his arrival, cutting him off from the rest of the party in a display of protectiveness, and perhaps pride that one of theirs had been elevated so young. The handlers in Nara Oxham's secondary audio listed names and academy years as she moved an eyemouse across their faces. All were older than Zai. Senator-Elect Oxham suspected that their claim on him was newly minted; the hero of Dhantu would make a fine addition to their clique.

For some reason, though, Zai had moved to extract himself from their attentions. The young lieutenant-commander almost stumbled as he left them behind, as if pulling his feet from some invisible tangleweed on the marble floor. Nara Oxham fingered her apathy wristband ruefully. She would love to feel what was going on in Zai's mind, but the party was too crowded to dare a lower dosage.

Oxham's entourage parted slightly to admit the young officer.

Although the senator's empathic powers were currently suppressed, for most of her life she'd been able to compare facial expressions with what her extra sense told her. Even with the wristband at full strength, she was extraordinarily perceptive. When Lieutenant-Commander Zai stood before her, she could see that he didn't know what to say.

Vadan greeting, she subvocalized.

Five appropriate salutations appeared in synesthesia, but in a flash of instinct, Nara ignored them all.

"You don't look very happy, Lieutenant-Commander Zai."

He glanced over his shoulder at his friends. Turned back.

"I'm not used to crowds, ma'am" he said.

Nara smiled at the honorific. He must be without a handler to have used *ma'am* instead of *excellency.* How did the Navy ever win wars, she wondered, when they couldn't manage a cocktail party?

"Stand here by the column," she said. She held her glass up to the light. "There's a certain security in having one's back covered, don't you think, Lieutenant-Commander?"

"Sound military thinking, Senator-Elect," he answered, finally smiling back at her.

So at least he knew her rank. But her politics?

"These columns are stronger than they look," she said. "Each is a single diamond, grown in an orbital carbon whisketter."

His eyes arched up, no doubt considering their mass. Making huge diamonds was easy in orbit. But getting an object that big down the gravity well safely—now *that* was a feat of engineering. Oxham held her glass of champagne up to the light.

"Have you noticed, Lieutenant-Commander, that the shape of the glasses matches the column's fluting?"

He looked at his own glass. "No, Excellency, I hadn't."

Excellency, now. The officer's etiquette training was kicking in. Did that mean she had made him comfortable enough to remember his manners? Or was he feeling her rank?

"But I suppose I personify the analogy," he continued. "I had begun to feel rather like a bubble floating aimlessly. Thank you for offering a safe haven, Senator-Elect."

Out of the corner of one eye, Oxham had watched the rest of the officers in Zai's group. With a glance here, a hand on a shoulder there, they were spreading the news of Zai's defection. Now, an older man of captain's rank was watching. Was he headed over to rescue the young lieutenant-commander from the Mad Senator?

Captain Marcus Fentu Masrui, Elevated, Oxham's handlers informed her. *Nonpolitical as far as we know.*

Nara raised an eyebrow. Nothing human was nonpolitical.

"I'm not sure how much of a haven you've found, Lieutenant-Commander." She let her attention over Zai's shoulder become obvious. "Your friends seem disturbed."

Zai glanced down at one of his shoulders, as if arresting a turn of his head back toward the officers. Then his eyes met hers again.

"I'm not sure about that, ma'am."

"They certainly look upset." Captain Masrui was still hovering nearby, unwilling to plunge in after Zai.

"Oh, of that I'm positive," Zai said. "But whether they are my friends or not . . ."

He smiled, but was not entirely joking.

"Success brings a certain amount of false friendship," Oxham said. "At least, speaking from my own perspective, political success does."

"No doubt, Senator. And, in a way, I suppose my own celebrity does have a political aspect to it."

Oxham narrowed her eyes. She knew very little about Laurent Zai, but her preparty briefing had stated that he was in no way a political officer. He had never enjoyed assignment to staff or a procurement committee, nor did he publish military scholarship. He came from a long line of illustrious Navy men, but had never used his name to escape field duty. The Zais had all been warriors, at least on the male side.

They joined the Navy, fought for the crown, and died. Then they took their well-earned immortality and disappeared into the gray enclaves of Vada. What did the dead Zais do then? Oxham wondered. Painted those dire black Vadan paintings, probably, went on endless pilgrimages, and learned appropriately dead languages to read the ancient books of the war sages in the original. A grim, infinite life.

Laurent Zai's doubts were interesting, though. Here he was, about to be honored by his living god, and he worried that his elevation had been tainted by politics. Perhaps he wondered whether surviving an awful captivity was enough to warrant a medal.

"I think the Emperor's commendation is justly deserved, Lieutenant-Commander Zai," she said. "After what you've been through—"

"No one has any idea what I've been through."

Oxham stopped short. Despite his rude words, the man's calm exterior hadn't changed in any way. He was simply stating a fact.

"However painful," the man continued, "having simply suffered for the Emperor is not enough to warrant all this." A small sweep of his hand indicated the party, the palace, immortality.

Oxham nodded. In a way, Laurent Zai was an accidental hero. He had been captured through no error of his own, and imprisoned without any hope of escape. Finally, he had been rescued by the application of overwhelming force. In one sense, he had done nothing himself.

But still, to have survived Dhantu at all was extraordinary. The rest of the prisoners that the rescue had found were dead, beyond even the symbiant. *Simply suffered,* Zai had said. A ghastly understatement.

"Lieutenant-Commander, I didn't mean to suggest that I could understand your experience," she said. "You've seen depths no one else has. But you did so in the Emperor's service. He has to do something. Certain things must be . . . *recognized.*"

Zai smiled sadly at her.

"I was rather hoping to hear an argument from you, Senator. But perhaps you don't want to be impolitic."

"An argument? Because I'm pink? Let me be impolitic, then. The Imperial presence on Dhantu is criminal. They've suffered for generations, and I'm not surprised that the most extreme Dhanti have become inhuman—which does not excuse torture. Nothing can. But some things are beyond being excused or explained, beyond logic or even blame. Things that start from simple power struggles—from politics, if you will—but ultimately dredge the depths of the human soul. Timeless, monstrous things."

The young man blinked, and Nara took a drink to slow her words.

"Armed occupation seldom pays dividends for anyone," she said. "But the Empire rewards who it can. You survived, Zai. So you should accept the Emperor's medal, elevation, and the starship command they'll no doubt give you. It's something."

Zai seemed surprised, but not offended. He nodded his head slightly, eyes narrowing as if thinking through her points. Was he mocking her?

But sarcasm didn't seem to be in the man. Perhaps these were simply new ideas for him. His entire life had been spent among the grayest of the gray. Oxham wondered if he'd ever heard the "Dhantu Liberation" called an occupation before. Or ever heard anyone seriously question the will of the Risen Emperor.

His next question confirmed his naïveté.

"Senator, is it true you have rejected elevation?"

"It's true. That's what Secularists do."

"I've heard that they often rescind in the end, though. There's always the possibility of a deathbed conversion."

Oxham shook her head. The persistence of this piece of propaganda was amazing. It showed how easily the truth was manipulated. It showed how threatened grays were by the Vow of Death.

"That's a story that the Political Apparatus likes to perpetuate," she said. "But of almost five hundred Secularist senators elected over the last thousand years, only seventeen have accepted elevation in the end."

"Seventeen broke their vows?" he said.

For moment, she nodded her head in triumph. Then she realized that Zai was not impressed. He seemed to think that few percent damningly high. For gray Laurent Zai, a vow was a vow.

Damn him.

"But to answer your question," she finished. "Yes, I will die."

He reached out, placed one hand lightly on her arm.

"Why?" he asked with genuine concern. "For politics?"

"No. For progress."

He shook his head in incomprehension.

Nara Oxham sighed internally. She had debated this point in street encounters, in public houses, and the Vasthold Diet floor, on live media feeds with planetary audiences. She had written slogans and speeches and essays on this issue. And before her was Laurent Zai, a man who had probably never experienced a real political debate in his entire life. It was too easy, in a way.

But he had asked for it.

"Have you heard of the geocentric theory, Lieutenant-Commander?"

"No, Excellency."

"On Earth Prime, a few centuries before spaceflight, it was widely believed that the sun went around the planet."

"They must have thought Earth Prime to be very massive," Zai said.

"In a way, yes. They thought the entire universe went around their world. On a *daily* basis, mind you. They had severe scaling problems."

"Indeed."

"Observational data mounted against the geocentric theory for a long time. New models were created, sun-centered models that were far more elegant and logical."

"I would think so. I can't imagine what the math for a planet-centric theory would have looked like."

"It was hideously complex and convoluted. Looking at it now, it's obviously a retrofit to uphold the superstitions of an earlier era. But something rather odd happened when the sun-centered theory, with all its elegance and clarity, was devised."

Zai waited, his champagne forgotten in his hand.

"Almost no one believed it," she said. "The new theory was debated for a while, gained a few supporters, but then it was suppressed and almost entirely dropped."

Zai narrowed his eyes in disbelief. "But eventually people must have realized. Otherwise, we wouldn't be standing here, two thousand light-years from Earth."

Oxham shook her head. "They didn't *realize*. Very few ever changed their minds. Those scientists who grew up with the old theory stuck to it overwhelmingly."

"But then how—"

"They died, Lieutenant-Commander."

She drank the last of her champagne. The old arguments still moved her, still made her mouth dry.

"Or rather, they did their descendants the favor of dying," she said. "They left their children the world. And thus the new ideas—the new shape of that world—became real. But only through death."

Zai shook his head. "But surely they would have eventually figured out—"

"If the old ones lived forever? Possessed all the wealth, controlled the military, and brooked no disagreement? We'd still be living there, stuck on that lonely fringe of Orion, thinking ourselves at the center of the universe.

"But the old ones, the ones who were wrong, died," she finished.

The man nodded slowly.

"I'd always heard that you pinks were pro-death. But I'd thought that an exaggeration."

"It's no exaggeration. Death is a central evolutionary development. Death is change. Death is progress. And immortality is a civilization-killing idea."

Zai smiled, his eyes roaming to take in the grandeur of the palace around them. "We don't seem to be a dead civilization yet."

"Seventeen hundred years ago, the Eighty Worlds were the most advanced technological power in this arm," she said. "Now look at us. The Rix, the Tungai, the Fahstuns have all surpassed us."

Zai's eyes widened. It was a fact seldom spoken aloud, even by Secularists. But Laurent Zai, a military man, must know that it was true. Every war grew more difficult as the Risen Empire continued to be outpaced by its neighbors.

"But seventeen hundred years ago we were no empire," he argued. "Merely a rabble of worlds, like the Rix, but far more divided. We were unstable, in competition amongst ourselves. We're stronger now, even with our technical . . .

disadvantages. And besides, we have the only technology truly worth having. We can beat death."

" 'The Old Enemy,' " Oxham quoted. That was what the Political Apparatus called it. The Old Enemy whom the Risen Emperor had dared and vanquished.

"Yes. We have beaten death, and yet the living still progress," Zai continued. "We have the Senate, the markets."

She smiled ruefully. "But the weight of the dead is choking us. Slowly but surely, they accrue more wealth every year, more power, and a greater hold upon the minds of the living."

"Minds like mine?" Zai asked.

Oxham shrugged. "I don't presume to know your mind, Lieutenant-Commander. Despite what they say about my abilities."

"You think the Empire is dead already?" he asked.

"No, not yet. But change will eventually come, and when it does, the Empire will snap like a bough strung with too many corpses."

Laurent Zai's mouth gaped; he was appalled at the image. Finally, she had managed to shock the man. Nara remembered when she had first used that simile in a speech on Vasthold. The audience had recoiled, empathically pushing back against her words, filling her throat with bile. But she had seen new thoughts swarming in to fill the spaces that horror made. The image was powerful enough to change minds.

"So, you want us to go back to death?" he asked. "Two hundred years of natural life and then . . . nothingness?"

"Not necessarily," she explained. "We just want to reduce the power of the dead. Let them paint and sculpt, travel the Eighty Worlds on their pilgrimages, but not rule us."

"No Emperor?" he said.

She nodded. Even with her new senatorial immunity, it was difficult to speak traitorous words aloud here in the Emperor's house. Even those born on Secularist worlds had the conditioning of gray culture; the old stories, the children's rhymes were all about the Old Enemy and the man who had beaten it.

Laurent Zai was silent for a while. He acquired two more glasses of champagne for them from a passing tray and stood there, drinking with her. A few of his military clique remained close, but they didn't dare come unbidden into this conversation with a pink senator.

Nara Oxham looked at the man. The Navy dress uniform, with its coordinated horde of subunits, certainly embodied the grossest aspects of Imperial power: the many made forcibly into one. But like much of the Imperial aesthetic, there was an undeniable elegance to the lockstepped fit of myriad elements. Zai's body didn't have the squat look of most high-gravity worlders. He was tall and a bit thin, the arch of his back rather tempting.

"Let me ask you a question," she said to interrupt her own thoughts.

"Certainly."

"Do you find my words treasonous?"

"By definition, no. You are a Senator. You have immunity."

"But immunity aside . . ."

He frowned. "If you weren't a senator, then by definition, you would have just committed treason."

"Only by definition?"

Zai nodded. "Yes, Senator. But perhaps not in spirit. After all, you are concerned with the welfare of the Empire, in whatever form you imagine its future."

Oxham smiled. Throughout the conversation, she had thought of Zai as unsophisticated, never having met a pink. Perhaps that was true, but how many actual grays had she herself spoken with honestly and openly? Perhaps her assumptions had been, in their own way, unsophisticated.

Zai raised an eyebrow at her expression.

"I was just thinking: Perhaps minds can be changed," she offered.

"Without death to drive the process?" Zai asked.

She nodded.

He took a deep breath, and his eyes drifted away from her. For a moment, she thought he was using synesthesia. But then some glimmer of intuition told Oxham that he was looking deeper than second sight.

"Or perhaps," Laurent Zai said, "I am already dead."

Something took hold of Nara. She felt an impossible moment of empathy, as if the drug had somehow failed: far inside the man was a terror, a wound opened by the depth of evil he had seen. It cut like an arctic wind, like an old fear made undeniably physical. It was agony and hopelessness. And, quite suddenly, she hated the Emperor for pinning a medal on this man.

Rewarding, rather than healing him.

"How much of Home have you seen, Laurent?" she asked quietly.

He shrugged. "The capital. This palace. And soon I will meet the Emperor himself. More than most of the risen see in centuries of pilgrimage."

"Would you like to see the South Pole?"

He looked genuinely surprised.

"I didn't know it was inhabited."

"Hardly. Outside a few estates, the poles are arid, freezing, dead. But I am pro-death, as you know. My new house there is surrounded by a glorious wasteland. I intend to escape the pressures of the capital there."

Zai nodded. He must know of her condition. The Mad Senator, the grays called her. A woman driven insane by crowds and cities, yet who made politics her profession.

The man swallowed before he spoke.

"I would like to see that, Senator."

"Then come with me there tomorrow, Lieutenant-Commander."

He raised his glass. "To a glorious wasteland."

"A truly gray place," she answered.

RESCUE ATTEMPT

No plan survives contact with the enemy.

—ANONYMOUS 81

Senator

She awoke without sanity.

The temporal ice released her quickly. Its lattice of tiny interwoven stasis fields unraveled, and time rushed back into her body like water through a suddenly crumbling dam, inundating a valley long denied it. Her mind became aware, emerging as it always did from coldsleep, raw and unprotected from the raging mindstorm of the city.

She awoke to madness.

Here in these exposed moments, the capital screamed in her brain. Its billions of minds roared, seethed, shrieked like a host of seagulls tearing at the carcass of some giant creature exposed upon a beach, fighting amongst themselves as they rended their huge find. Even in her madness, though, she knew the source of the psychic screaming: the rotting creature was Empire; the vast chorus of keening voices was all the myriad struggles for power and prestige that animated the Imperial capital. The noise of these contests thundered through her, for a moment obliterating any sense of self, her identity a lone mountaineer engulfed by an avalanche.

Then she heard her apathy bracelet begin its injection sequence, the reassuring hiss audible even through the deluge of sound. Then her empathic abilities began to fade under the drug's influence. The voices grew dim, and a sense of self returned.

The woman remembered who she was, childhood names spilling through her mind. Naraya, Naya, Nana. And then the titles of adulthood. Dr. Nara Oxham. Electate Oxham of the Vasthold Assembly. Her Excellency Nara Oxham, Representative to His Majesty's Government from the planet Vasthold. Senator Nara Oxham, Secularist Party whip.

Popularly known as the Mad Senator.

As the psychic howl receded, Oxham steeled herself and concentrated on the city, listening carefully for tone and character as it trailed away. Here on Home, she was always threatened by the crush of voices, the wild psychic noise that had kept her in an asylum for most of her childhood years. But sometimes as the apathy drug entered her veins, in this passing moment between madness and sanity, Nara could make sense of it, could catch a few notes of the multiplex and chaotic music that the capital played. It was a useful ability for a politician.

The sound of the Risen Empire's politics was troubled today, she heard. Something was coalescing, like an orchestra tuning itself to a single note. She tried to focus, to bring her mind to bear on the theme of unease. But then her empathy faded, extinguished by the drug.

Her insanity was, for the moment, cured, and she was deaf to the city's cry.

Senator Nara Oxham took a deep breath, flexed her awakening muscles. She sat up on the coldsleep bed, and opened her eyes.

Morning. The sky was salmon and the sun orange through the penthouse's bubble, the facets of the distant Diamond Palace tinged with blood. The bubble silenced the capital, the transparent woven carbon barely trembling for passing helicopters. But the city still buzzed, flickers of movement and the winking lights of signage shimmering in her vision, distant aircars blurring the air like gnats or heat haze on a desert. In the odd way of coldsleep, her eyes felt clean, as if she had only closed them for a moment.

A moment that had lasted . . .

The date was displayed on the bedroom's large wallscreen. Since she had entered coldsleep, three of Homeworld's short months had passed. That was puzzling and alarming. Usually, the senatorial stasis breaks lasted half a year.

Something important was happening, then. The disquieting sound Oxham had heard on the limen of madness returned to her. She called up the status of her colleagues. Most were already animated, the rest were coming up as she watched. The full Senate was being awakened for a special session.

As Senator Nara Oxham crossed the Rubicon Pale at the bottom of the Forum steps, the reassuring wash of politics surrounded her, drowning out the shapeless anxiety she had felt coming out of coldsleep.

In one corner of her hearing she now registered the drone of the Inherited Intellectual Property filibuster. The filibuster, in its eighty-seventh decade, was as calming and timeless (and as meaningless, Senator Oxham supposed) as the roar of a distant ocean. Farther away in the echoey space of secondary audio she sensed plodding committee meetings, strident media conferences, the self-righteous energy of a Loyalty Party caucus meeting. And, of course, easily discernible by its sovereign resonance, the debate in the Great Forum itself.

She blinked, and a lower-third informed her that Senator Puram Drexler had the floor. A tiny corner of her synesthetic sight showed his face, the familiar milky gray eyes and elaborate, liquid rolls of flesh that poured from his cheekbones. President of the Senate, a figurehead position, Drexler was said to be over two hundred fifty years old (not counting cryo, and in his own relativistic framework—*not* Imperial Absolute). But his exquisitely weathered face had never seemed quite real to her. On Fatawa, which he represented in the Senate, the surgical affectation of age was almost as fashionable as that of youth.

The ancient solon cleared his throat languorously, the dry sound as gritty and sharp as a handful of small gravel poured slowly onto glass.

As she climbed the Forum steps, Senator Oxham brought the fingertips of her left hand together, which signaled her handlers to pick her up. The other voices in the Senate infostructure muted as her chief of staff confirmed the day's itinerary with her.

"Where's Roger?" Oxham asked after her schedule was confirmed. The morning scheduling ritual usually belonged to Roger Niles, her consultant extraordinary. The absence of his familiar voice disturbed Oxham, brought back her earlier uneasiness.

"He's deep, Senator," her chief of staff answered. "He's been in an analysis fugue all morning. But he leaked a request that you see him face-to-face at your earliest convenience."

The morning's disquiet flooded back in now. Niles was a very reserved creature; a meeting at his own insistence would mean serious news.

"I see," Oxham said flatly. She wondered what the old consultant had discovered.

"Bring my synesthesia to full bandwidth."

At her command, data swelled before Oxham in secondary and tertiary sight and hearing, blossoming into the familiar maelstrom of her personal configuration. Nameplates, color-coded by party affiliation and striped with recent votes, hovered about the other Senators flowing up the steps; realtime polygraph-poll reactions of wired political junkies writhed at the edge of vision, forming hurricane whorls that shifted with every procedural vote; the latest headcounts of her party's whip AI invoked tones at the threshold of hearing, soft and consonant chords for measures sure to pass, harsh, dissonant intervals for bills that were losing support. Nara Oxham breathed in this clamor like a seagoing passenger emerging onto deck for air. This moment—at the edge of Power, before one dived in and lost oneself—restored her confidence. The bracing rush of politics gave Nara what others were given by mountain-climbing, or incipient violence, or the pleasure of a first cigarette before dressing.

The senator smiled as she headed for her offices.

Nara Oxham often wondered how politics had been possible before second sight. Without induced synesthesia, the intrusion of sight into the other brain centers, how did a human mind absorb the necessary data? She could imagine going without synesthesia in certain activities—flying an aircraft, day trading, surgery—where one could focus on a single image, but not in politics. Noninterfering layers of sight, the ability to fill three visual and two auditory fields with data, were a perfect metaphor for politics itself. The checks and balances, the competing constituencies, the layers of power, money, and rhetoric. Even though the medical procedure that made it possible caused odd mental results in one in ten thousand recipients (Oxham's own empathy was such a reaction), she couldn't imagine the political world—gloriously multitrack and torrid—without it. She'd tried the old, presynesthesia eyescreens that covered up normal vision, but they'd brought on a claustrophobic panic. Who would trust the Senate to a blinkered horse?

The disquiet she had felt all morning tugged at Nara again. The feeling was familiar, but vaguely so, in the way of old smells and déjà vu. She tried to place it, comparing the sensation to her anxieties before elections, important Senate votes, or large parties thrown in her honor. Nara Oxham recalled those apprehensions easily. She lived her life fighting them, weathering them, indulging in them. She was old friends with anxiety, that poor sister of madness which the drugs never fully vanquished.

But the current feeling was too slippery. She couldn't find the worry that had started it. She checked her wrist, where the dermal injector blinked happily green. It couldn't be an empathy flare; the drugs made sure of that. But it certainly felt like one.

When she reached her offices, she strode past supplicant aides and a few hopeful lobbyists, heading straight for Roger

Niles's dark lair at the center of her domain. No one dared follow her. His office doors opened without a word, and she walked through, removed a stack of laundered shirts from his guest chair, and sat down.

"I'm here," she said. She kept her voice calm, knowing his interface AI would bring him up from the data fugue if she sounded impatient. Better to let him cross back into the real world at his own pace.

His face had the slack look of deep fugue, but his eyebrows lifted in response to her words, sending ripples up his high expanse of forehead. One finger on his right hand twitched. He looked too small for his desk, a circular monstrosity of dark wood that enclosed Niles like some giant life-support machine. Senator Oxham had recently discovered that its copious drawers and pigeonholes held only clothes, shoes, and a few emergency rations extorted from military lobbyists. Roger Niles thought the habit of going home at night to be an inexcusable weakness.

"Something bad, isn't it?" she asked.

The finger twitched again.

Niles looked older. Senator Oxham had only been in stasis for three months, but in that short absence a frosting of gray had touched his temples. Her staff had the right to go into cryo during the breaks, but Niles seldom did, preferring to work out the true decades of her term, aging before her eyes.

The loneliness of the senator, Oxham thought. The world moved so quickly past.

Senators were elected for (or appointed to, competed for, bought—whatever their planet's custom) fifty-year terms, half an Imperial Absolute century of office. The Risen Empire was a slowly evolving beast. Even here in the dense coreward clusters, eighty populated worlds was an area thirty light-years across, and the exigencies of war, trade, and migration were bound by the appallingly slow rate of lightspeed. The Imperial Senate was constituted to take the long view; the solons generally spent eighty percent of their terms in stasis sleep as the universe wheeled by. They made decisions with the detachment of mountains watching rivers below shift course.

Unavoidably, the planet that Oxham represented had changed in her first decade in office. And the trip to Home from Vasthold had consumed five Absolute years. When she returned, sixty years total would have passed, all her friends infirm or dead, her three nephews well into middle age. Even Niles was aging before her eyes. The Senate demanded much from its members.

But the Time Thief couldn't steal everyone. Oxham had found someone new, a lover who was a starship captain, a fellow victim of time dilation. Though the man was gone now, Absolute years away in the Spinward Reaches, Oxham had begun to match her stasis sleeps to his relativistic framework. The universe was slipping past them both at almost the same rate. When he came back, they would share the same years' passage.

Senator Oxham leaned back into her chair and listened with half her mind to the flow of political data in her secondary senses. But it was pointless to do anything except wait for Niles.

As political animals went, Senator Oxham was fundamentally unlike her chief of staff. She was a holist, feeling the Senate as an organism, an animal whose actions could be tamed or at least understood. Niles, at the other extreme, lived by the dictum that all politics is local. His gods were in the details.

The office was crowded with hardware that kept him linked to the everyday goings-on of each of the Eighty Worlds. Ration riots on Mirzam. Religious bombings on Veridani. The daily offensives and retaliations of a thousand price wars, ethnic struggles, and media trials, all maintained in real time by quantum entangled communications. Senatorial privilege allowed him to monitor the internal workings of news agencies, financial consortia, even the private missives of those wealthy enough to send translight data. And Niles could put it all together in his magnificent brain. Senator Oxham knew her colleagues as individuals, and could feel the hard edges of their petty vanities and obsessions, but Roger Niles saw senators as composite creatures of data, walking clearinghouses for the host of agendas and pressures from their home worlds.

The two sat across from each in silence for a few more minutes.

Niles's finger twitched again.

Nara sat back, knowing that this could take a while. It was dark in the room. The crystalline columns of the com hardware loomed like insect cities made of glass—perhaps fireflies, the Senator thought; the crystals were pinpoint-dappled by sunlight filtered through tiny holes in a smartpolymer curtain that extended across the glass ceiling.

Oxham looked upward with an annoyed expression, and the millimeter-wide holes responded, dilating a bit. Now she could feel the sun on her hands, which she splayed palm down, relishing the cool metal of Niles's desk. In the patterned light her chief of staff's face seemed tattooed with a fine trompe l'oeil veil.

He opened his eyes.

"War," he said.

The word sent ice down Senator Nara Oxham's spine.

"I'm seeing Imperial tax relief throughout the spinward worlds," Niles said, tapping the right side of his head as if his brain were a map of the Empire. "Every system within four light-years of the Rix frontier is having its economy stimulated, courtesy of the Risen One. And the Lackey Party caucus has buried parallel measures in that maintenance bill they've been debating all morning."

"Is that war, or just patronage-as-usual?" Oxham asked dubiously. The Risen Emperor and the Senate levied taxes separately, their sources of revenue as carefully delineated as the Rubicon Pale around the Forum building. But however separate crown and government were meant to be, the Loyalty Party—true to its name—always followed the Emperor's lead. Especially when it helped the voters back home. Loyalty was traditionally strong in the Spinward Reaches, as it was in every outskirt region where other cultures loomed threateningly close.

"Normally, I'd say it was the usual alms for the faithful," Niles answered. "But the Coreward and Outward Loyalist regions aren't sharing in the largesse. On the contrary, those ends of the Empire are taking a big hit. Over the last twelve hours, I'm seeing higher honoraria tributes, skyrocketing futures on titles and pardons, even hundred-year Imperial loans being called. The money isn't earmarked yet, but *only* the military could spend amounts like this."

"So the Navy's being strengthened, and the Spinward Reaches fattened up," Oxham said. It sounded like war with the Rix. Riches to fund military forces, and comfort for the regions threatened by reprisal.

Her chief of staff cocked his head, as if someone were whispering in his ear. "Labor futures on Fatawa tightened by three points this morning. *Three*. Probably reservists being called up. No one left to sweep the floors."

Oxham shook her head at the Risen Emperor's madness. It had been eighty years since the Rix Incursion; why provoke them now? Though not numerous, the Rix were unspeakably dangerous. The strange technologies bestowed on them by their AI gods made them the deadliest combatants the Empire had ever faced. Moreover, war with them was always a less-than-zero-sum game. They owned very little worth taking, having no real planets of their own.

They seeded compound minds and moved on. They were spores for the planetary beings they worshiped, more a cult than a culture. But when injured, they made sure to injure in return.

"Why would the Risen Emperor want another war with the Rix?" she wondered aloud. "Any evidence of a recent attack?" Oxham silently cursed the secrecy of the Imperial state, which rarely allowed the Senatorial Government detailed military intelligence. What was going on out there, in that distant blackness? She shivered for a moment, thinking of one man in particular who would be in harm's way. She pushed the thought aside.

"As I said, this has all been in the last few hours," Niles said. "I don't have raw data from the frontier for that timeframe."

"Either precipitated by an emergency, or the Imperials have hidden their plans," Senator Oxham said.

"Well, they've blown their cover now," Niles finished.

Oxham interleaved her fingers, her hand making a double fist. The gesture triggered a sudden and absolute silence in her head, shutting off the din of orating solons, the clamor of messages and amendments, the pulse of polls and constituent chatter.

War, she thought. The galling domain of tyrants. The sport of gods and would-be-gods. And, most distressingly, the profession of her newest lover.

The Risen One had better have a damn good reason for this.

Senator Oxham leaned back and glared into Roger Niles's eyes. She allowed her mind to start planning, to sort through the precisely defined powers of the Senate for the fulcra that could impede the Emperor's course. And as she felt the cold surety of political power flowing into her, her anxieties retreated.

"Our Risen Father may not want our advise and consent," she said. "But let's see if we can't get his attention."

Captain

For the first twelve years of his life, Laurent Zai had been, embarrassingly, the tallest of his schoolmates. Not strongest, not quickest. Just a lofty, clumsy boy in a society that valued compact, graceful bodies. Since long before Laurent was born, Vada had elected and reelected as its governor a short, solid woman who stood with arms crossed and feet far apart, a symbol of stability. As young as seven standard, Laurent began to pray to the Risen Emperor that he would stop growing, but his journey toward the sky continued relentlessly. By age eleven it was too late merely to cease getting taller; he had already passed the average height for Vadan adults. He asked the Risen Deity to shrink him, but his biology mentor AI explained that growing shorter was scientifically unlikely, at least for the next sixty years or so. And on Vada one did not pray to the Risen Emperor to change the laws of nature, which were His laws after all. Ever logical, Laurent Zai implored the Emperor to effect the only remaining solution: increased height among his schoolmates, a burst of growth among his peers or a demographic shift that would rescue Laurent from his outcast status.

In the summer term that year, transfer students from low-gravity Krupp Reich flooded Laurent Zai's school. These were refugees displaced by the ravages of the New German Flu. The towering Reichers were gawky, easily fatigued, and thickly accented. These survivors were immune to the flu and had of course been decontaminated, fleeing the societal meltdown of population collapse rather than the virus itself, but the stench of contagion still clung to them, and they were so disgracefully *tall*.

Zai was their worst tormentor. He mastered the art of tripping the Reichers from behind as they walked, nudging a trailing foot so that it hooked the other ankle with their next step. He graffitied the margins of chapel prayerbooks with clumsy stick figures as tall as a page.

Laurent was not alone in his misbehavior. The Reichers were so mistreated that a month after their arrival the entire student body was assembled around the soccer field airscreen. In the giant viewing area (over the field upon which Laurent had been so often humiliated by shorter, quicker footballers) images from the Krupp Reich Pandemic were shown. It was pure propaganda—an art for which Vadans were justly famous—a way to shame the native children into ceasing their torments of the newcomers. The victims were carefully aestheticized, shown dying under white gauze to hide the pulsing red sores of the New German Flu. Photos from preflu family reunions were altered to reflect the disease's progress, the victims fading into sepia one by one, until only a few smiling survivors remained, their arms around ghostly relatives. The final image in the presentation was the huge, monolithic Reich Square in Bonnburg, time-lapsed through successive Sunday afternoons over the last four years. The population of tourists, hawkers, merchants, and strollers on the square dwindled slowly, then seemed to stabilize, then crashed relentlessly. Finally, a lone figure scuttled across the great sheet of copper. Although only a few picture elements tall, the figure seemed to be rushing fearfully, as if wary of some flying predator overhead.

Twelve-year-old Laurent Zai sat with his jaw slack amidst the overwhelming silence peculiar to shamed children, thinking the same words again and again.

"What have I done?"

When the airscreen faded, Zai bolted down the stairs,

shaking off the restraining hand of an annoyed proctor. He fled to sanctuary under the bleachers and fell to his knees in the litter of spectator trash. His hands together in the clasp of prayer, he started to ask for forgiveness. He hadn't asked the Emperor for *this*. How could he have known that the Reich Pandemic would be the result of his request for taller classmates?

With his praying lips almost against the ground, the stench of cigarette butts and old honey wine bottles and rotten fruit under the bleachers struck him like a blow to the stomach. He vomited profusely into his prayer-locked hands, in an acid stream that burned like whiskey in his mouth and nose. His hands remained faintly sticky and smelled of vomit the rest of that day, no matter how furiously he washed them.

As if some switch deep within him had been permanently thrown, the position of prayer always brought back a glimmer of that intense moment of shame and nausea. The murmurs of morning chapel seemed to coalesce into an acid trickle down the back of his throat. The airscreen rallies in which the Risen Emperor's visage slowly turned over an ululating crowd filled his stomach with bile.

Laurent Zai had never prayed to the Risen Emperor again.

He never drank, for every toast on Vada asked the Risen Deity for luck and health. And even as Cadet Zai waited for word of admission into the Imperial Naval Academy, he lay silent in the endless minutes before sleep every night, recalling every mistep and victory in his six-week application trial. But not praying.

Thirty subjective years later, however, seated in the shipmaster's chair of His Majesty's frigate *Lynx,* Captain Laurent Zai took a moment to pair his hands over nose and mouth.

He still smelled the bile of that long-ago shame.

"Make this work," he demanded in a harsh whisper. "As

for me, I want to return to my beloved. As for her, she's *your* damned sister."

The bitter prayer ended, Zai brought his hands down and opened his eyes.

"Launch," he commanded.

Executive Officer

ExO Katherie Hobbes noted from her status board that the entry vehicle carrying the Apparatus Initiate Barris had not been fully gelled. The safety AI began to protest the dangers posed by an incompletely prepped insertion vehicle.

Hobbes smiled grimly, canceling the safety overrides, and the order went through.

"Operation is launched, sir."

Almost simultaneously, four specially reconfigured turret blisters along the underside of the *Lynx* each fired one railgun and one plasma burst. A pair of each type of projectile headed toward four carefully plotted targets below.

The plasma bursts bolted ahead at twenty percent lightspeed, their 12,000-degree core temperatures burning a tunnel of vacuum through the atmosphere. Their burn length perfectly timed, they scattered into gouts of flame upon impact, leaving as their only marks four smooth, concave hemispheres burned into the palace's stone walls.

The railgun projectiles followed in their wake.

compound mind

The attack was registered by the warning system erected by the Rix compound mind still propagating across the planet's data and communication systems. The plasma bolts left a long, bellicose streak behind them, clearly originating from the point Alexander had already predicted that an Imperial warship would station itself to attempt a rescue. The mind required less than two milliseconds to determine that such an attempt was underway, and to order that the hostages be killed. However, the Rix commandos were not datalinked to the still-propagating mind. Alexander was a composite of Imperial technology, after all, which was incompatible with Rix communications. Alexander was forced to relay its order through a transponder sitting in the center of the table in the council chamber. The transponder received the compound mind's signal and immediately let out a loud squawk, a dense static whose crenellations were coded like some ancient audio modem. The squawk began its journey from the transponder outward toward the Rix commandos at the speed of sound. The nearest commando was four meters away, and the sound would reach her in roughly eight milliseconds, a hundredth of a second after the attack had begun.

Racing against this warning were the four structured smartalloy slugs launched from the *Lynx*'s railguns. These projectiles, massing less than a few centigrams, barreled at ten percent lightspeed through the near-vacuum cylinders burned for them by the plasma bolts, flying straight as lasers. They traversed the distance to the palace in far less time than it took for Legis's atmospheric pressure to slam closed their vacuum paths. They reached the plasma-smoothed hemispheres of their entry-points into the palace within seven milliseconds.

The slugs were cylinders no wider than a human hair follicle. They sliced through the ancient palace walls, releasing a carefully calculated fraction of their awesome kinetic energy. The stone around the entry points ribbed with sudden webs of cracks, like safety glass struck with a hammer. The impact altered the slugs, transforming them into their second programmed shape, a larger spheroid that flattened on impact, braking the projectiles as they slammed through the floors and walls of the palace. In the seconds after their passage, the old palace would boom and shake, whole walls exploding into dust. Localized but terrific wind storms would soon rise up as the air inside the palace was set in motion by the slugs' passage.

After the seventh such collision, a number calculated by the *Lynx*'s AI using precise models of the palace's architecture, the slugs ballooned to their largest size. The smartalloy stretched into a mesh of hexagons, expanding outward like a child's paper snowflake, and attaining the surface area of a large coin.

These much-slowed slugs struck their targets, hitting the Rix commandos while the warning squawk from the transponder was just under a meter away, eight thousandths of a second after the attack had begun. The slugs tore through the commandos' chests, leaving tunnels that were momentarily as exact as holes drilled in metal. But then the wake of the slug's passage pulled a pulverized spray of blood, tissue, and biomechanical enhancements through the exit wounds, filling the council chamber with a maelstrom of ichor. The four commandos tumbled to the ground, their bones shattered and implants liquifacted by the blow.

For the moment, the hostages were safe.

Doctor

Above, the marines were on their way.

Twenty-five entry vehicles accelerated down launch tubes, riding electromagnetic rails at absurd velocities. Thirty-seven gees hit Dr. Vecher like a brain hemorrhage, shifting the color behind his closed eyes from red, to pink, to the white of the hottest flame. A roar filled his gel-sealed ears, and he felt his body malform, squashed down into the floor of his vehicle under a giant's foot. If not for his yolk of gel and the injected and inhaled smartpolymers that marbled his body tissue, he would have died in several instantaneous and exotic ways.

As it was, it hurt like hell.

The entry vehicles hit the dense air of the mesopause almost instantly, and spun a precise 180 degrees to orient their passengers feet-down, firing retrorockets to begin braking and targeting. They spread out, screaming meteors surging across the daylit sky of Legis XV. Only three were targeted near the council chamber: each vehicle that landed close to the hostages carried the risk of injuring the Child Empress. The marines would be spread out, deployed to sweep for the three remaining Rix commandos and secure the now twice-battered palace.

Dr. Vecher's entry vehicle was fractionally ahead of the others, and was aimed closest to the council chamber. It burst through the palace's three sets of outer walls, the impacts shaking Vecher as if he were trapped inside a ringing churchbell.

But the landing, in which the vehicle expended its last reaction mass to come to a cratering halt outside the chamber, seemed almost soft. There was a final bump, and then Dr. Vecher spilled from the vehicle, the gel that carried him out hissing as it hit the super-heated stone floor of the palace.

Admiral

For the hostages, the transition from anxious fatigue and boredom to chaos was instantaneous. The smartalloy slugs reached their targets well before any sound or shock waves struck the council chamber. The roaring whirlwind seemed to come from nowhere. Blood and liquefied gristle exploded from the four captors. The hostages found themselves choking on the airborne ichor of the eviscerated Rix, mouths and eyes filled with the sudden spray. Moments later, the booms of the palace's shattered and collapsing outer walls came thundering in at the tardy speed of sound, overwhelming the vain shriek of the transponder on the table.

Admiral Fenton Pry, however, had been expecting something like this. He had written his War College graduate thesis on hostage rescue, and for the last four hours had been quietly stewing over the irony. After a seventy-subjective-year career, here he finally was in a hostage situation, but on the wrong end. The latest articles in the infrequent professional literature of hostage rescue even lay on his bedside, printed and handsomely bound by his adjutant, but unread. He hadn't been keeping up lately. But he knew roughly how the attack would unfold, and had palmed a silk handkerchief some hours ago. He placed it over his mouth and rose.

A horrifying cramp shot through one leg. The admiral had tried dutifully to perform escape-pod stretches, but he'd been in the chair for four hours. He limped toward where the Child Empress must be, blinking away blood from his eyes and breathing shallowly. The floor rolled as a heavy portion of the palace's ancient masonry collapsed nearby.

Marines coming in?

They're too close, the admiral thought. This was a natural stone building, for His Majesty's sake. Admiral Pry could have taught whoever was in charge up there a few things about insertions into pre-ferroplastic structures.

Vision cleared as the ichor began to settle in an even patina on the exposed surfaces of the room. The Empress was still seated. Admiral Pry spotted a Rix commando on the floor. She had landed on her side, doubled up as if put down by a punch to the stomach. The entry wound was invisible, but two pieces of the commando's spine thrust from the gaping exit wound at forty-five-degree angles.

Pry noted with professional pleasure that the slug had struck the commando's chest dead center. He nodded his head curtly, the same gesture he used to replace the words *well done* with his staff. Her blaster, extended toward Child Empress at arm's length, was untouched.

The admiral lifted her hand from it, careful not to let the rigid fingers pull the trigger, and turned to the Empress's still form.

"M'Lady?" he asked.

The Empress's face was twisted with pain. She clutched her left shoulder, gasping for air with ragged breaths.

Had the Reason been hit with a slug? The Empress was of course covered with Rix blood, but under that her robes seemed to be intact. She certainly hadn't been shot by anything as brutal as a blaster or an exsanguination round.

Admiral Pry had a few seconds to wonder what was wrong before the heavy ash doors burst open.

Corporal

Marine Corporal Mirame Lao was the first out of her dropship.

A veteran of twenty-six combat insertions, she had set her entry vehicle to the highest egress speed/lowest safety rating. At this setting, the dropship vomited open at the moment of impact, spilling Corporal Lao onto the floor in a cascade of suddenly liquidized gee-gel, through which she rolled like a parachutist hitting thick mud. She came up standing. The seal that protected her varigun's barrel from clogging with gel popped out like a champagne cork, and her helmet drained its entry insulation explosively on the floor around her. Inside her visor, blinking red diagnostics added up the price of her fast egress: her left leg was broken, the shoulder on that side dislocated. Not bad for a spill at highest setting.

The leg was already numbing from automatically injected anesthesia; her battle armor's servomotors took over its motion. Lao realized that the break must be severe; as the leg moved, she could feel that icy sensation of splintered bone tearing into nerve-dead tissue. She gritted her teeth and ignored the feeling. Once during a firefight on Dhantu, Lao had functioned for six hours with a broken pelvis. This mission—win, lose, or draw—wouldn't last more than six minutes. She confirmed a blinking yellow glyph with her eyemouse, and braced herself. Her battle armor huffed as it contracted implosively, shoving her dislocated shoulder back into place. Now *that* hurt.

By now, some fourteen seconds after impact, the marine corporal was oriented to the wireframe map in her secondary vision. To her right, the marine doctor was rising gingerly up from the gel vomited by his own dropship, disoriented but intact. The vehicle that had brought the Apparatus initiate down hadn't spilled yet—it looked wrong, as if the door had buckled in transit.

Tough luck.

Corporal Lao loped toward the heavy doors that separated her from the council chamber, gaining speed even with her lopsided gait. She was right-handed, but she hit the ashwood doors with her already wounded left shoulder; no sense injuring the good arm. Another spike of pain shot through her as the doors burst open.

She tumbled into the council chamber with weapon raised, scanning the room for the Rix commandos.

They were easy to find. All four had fallen, and each was the origin of a long ellipse of thick red ejecta sprayed on walls and floor. A lighter, pink shroud of human blood coated everything in the room, from the ornate settings on the table to the stunned or shrieking hostages.

These four Rix were definitely dead. Lao clicked her tongue to transmit a preconfigured signal to the *Lynx: Council chamber secured.*

"Here!" a voice called.

The word came from an old man who wore what appeared—beneath its bloody patina—to be an admiral's uniform. He knelt over two figures, one writhing, one still.

The Child Empress, and a dead Rix.

Marine Corporal Lao ran to the pair, reaching for a large device on her back. This move caused her wounded shoulder to scream with pain, and her vision reddened at the edges. Lao overrode the suit's suggestion of anesthesia; she needed both arms working at top efficiency. There were three surviving Rix in the building; this might turn into a firefight yet.

The diagnostics on the generator blinked green. It had survived the jump in working order. She reached for its controls, but movement behind her—the helmet extended her peripheral vision to 360 degrees—demanded her attention. Lao spun with her weapon raised, shoulder flaring with pain again.

It was the marine doctor.

"Come!" she ordered, her helmet uttering one of the pre-programmed words she could access with a tongue click. Her lungs remained full of drop-goo, whose pseudo-alveoli continued to pump high-grade oxygen into her system. *"Sir!"* she added.

The man stumbled forward, disoriented as a recruit after his first high-acceleration test. The corporal grabbed the doctor's shoulder and pulled him into the generator's radius. There was no time to waste. The com signals from the rest of the drop were running through her secondary audio, terse battle chatter as her squadmates engaged the remaining Rix.

Corporal Lao activated the machine, and a level one stasis field jumped to life around the five of them: Empress, lifeless Rix commando, admiral, doctor, and marine corporal. The rest of the council chamber dimmed. From the outside, the field would appear as a smooth and reflective black sphere, invulnerable to simple blaster fire. The hiss of an oxygen re-cycler came from the machine; the field was airtight as well.

"Sir," Lao commanded, *"heal."*

The marine doctor looked up at her, an awful expression visible on his face through the thick, transparent ceramic of his helmet visor. He was trying to speak; a terribly, terribly bad idea.

Despite the howl of pain in her shoulder, the imminent danger of Rix attack, and the general need for her attention to be focused in all directions at once, Lao had to close her eyes when the doctor vomited, two lungfuls of green oxy-compound splattering onto the inside of his faceplate.

She reached over to unseal the helmet. The doctor wouldn't drown in the stuff, naturally, but it was much nastier when you inhaled it the second time.

Captain

"Stasis field up in the council chamber, sir," Executive Officer Hobbes said softly.

The words snapped through the wash of visual and auditory reports streaming through the *Lynx*'s infostructure. Captain Laurent Zai had to replay them in his mind before he would believe. For the first time in four hours, he allowed himself to feel a glimmer of hope.

Acoustics had finally analyzed the explosive sound in the council chamber, which had turned out not to be a firearm at all. Probably the glass in which the Intelligencer had secreted itself had been oveturned, and the crash magnified by the small craft's sensitive ears. So Zai had launched the rescue needlessly, but thus far the rescue was working. Such were the fortunes of war.

"Rix number five dead. Four more marines lost," another report came.

Zai nodded with approval and peered down into the bridge airscreen. His marines were spread across the palace in a nested hexagonal search pattern, its symmetry only slightly distorted by the exigencies of crashing down from space, avoiding booby traps, and fighting the remaining two Rix commandos. His men were doing quite well. (Actually, seventeen of the two dozen marines were women, but Vadans preferred the old terms.)

If the Child Empress was still alive, Zai thought, he might yet survive this nightmare.

Then doubts flooded him again. The Empress could have been killed when the council chamber had been railgunned. Or when the marines had burst in to take control. The Rix might have murdered the Empress the moment they took her hostage, insurance against any rescue. And even if she was alive now, two more Rix commandos remained concealed somewhere in the tangled diagram of the battle.

"Phase two," Zai ordered.

The *Lynx* shuddered as its conventional landers launched, filled with the rest of the *Lynx*'s marine complement. Soon the Imperial forces would have total superiority. Every minute in which disaster did not befall him took Laurent Zai closer to victory.

"Where's that damned Vecher?" the captain snapped.

"He's under the stasis field, sir," Hobbes answered.

Zai nodded. The doctor's battle armor couldn't broadcast through the field. But if the marines had bothered to put the stasis field up, that implied that the Empress was still alive.

"Rix fire!" the synthesized voice of a marine came from below; they were still breathing oxycompound, in case the enemy used gas. The bridge tactical AI triangulated the sound of blaster fire picked up by various marines' helmets; a cold blue trapezoid appeared on the wireframe, marking the area where the Rix commando should be.

Zai gritted his teeth. In urban cover, Rix soldiers were like quantum particles, charms or fetches that existed only as probabilities of location and intent, never as certainties—until they were dead. The nearest edge of the marked area was almost a hundred meters from the council chamber. Close enough to threaten the Empress, but far away enough to . . .

"Hit that area with another round of railgun slugs," Zai ordered.

"But, sir!" Second Gunner Thompson protested. "The integrity of the palace is already doubtful. It's not hypercarbon, it's *stone*. Another round—"

"I'm counting on a collapse, Gunner," Zai said. "Do you think we'll hit that Rixwoman with dumb luck?"

"The stasis field is only level one, sir, but it should hold," Hobbes offered quietly. At least his executive officer understood Zai's thinking. Falling stone wouldn't harm anyone inside a stasis field. Everyone else—the other hostages, the marines, the rest of the palace staff—was expendable. In fact, the Rix and the Imperials were in battle armor, and wouldn't be killed by a mere building falling down around them. They would simply be immobilized.

"Firing," came the first gunner, and straight bolts of green light leapt onto the airscreen, lancing the blue trapezoid like pins through a cushion. The thunk of the shots reached Zai's soles, adding to all the other sensations of movement and acceleration.

What a powerful weapon, he thought, to shake a starship with its recoil, though the shell weighed less than a gram.

After four shudders had run through the *Lynx,* the gunner reported, "First rounds fired, sir. The palace seems to be holding up."

"Then fire again," Zai said.

Senator

The other three senators stood a few meters away from the legislation, a bit daunted by its complexity, its intensity.

As Nara Oxham took them through it, however, with simple words and a soothingly cobalt-blue airmouse pointing out particulars, they drew gradually nearer. The legislation consumed most of the aircreen in the Secularist Party

Caucus chamber. A galaxy of minor levies formed its center: nuisance taxes on arms contractors, sur-tariffs on the shipment of strategic metals, higher senatorial assessment for regions with a large military presence; all measures that would, directly and indirectly, cost the Imperial Navy hard cash. Surrounding this inner core were stalwart pickets of limited debate, which restricted ammendments and forestalled filibuster, and loopholes were ringed with glittering ranks of statutory barbed wire. More items in the omnibus floated in a disorganized cloud, cunningly indirect but obvious in their intent to the trained eye. Duties, imposts, levies, tithes, tariffs, canceled pork, promised spending temporarily withheld—a host of transfers of economic strength firmly away from the Spinward Reaches. All carefully balanced to undo what the Emperor and Loyalists intended.

Senator Oxham was proud that her staff had created so complex a measure in less than an hour. The silver proposal cup at the center of the airscreen was barely visible through the dense, glittering forest of iconographics.

The edicts flowing from the Diamond Palace were a sledgehammer, an unambiguous step toward war. This legislation, however complex its point-clouds of legislative heiroglyphics, was in its own way just as simple: a sledgehammer swung in return, carefully balanced in force and angle to stop its counterpart dead with a single collision. Some of the other Secularist Party senators looked unhappy, as if imagining themselves caught between the two.

"Are we sure that we need to approach this so . . . confrontationally?" asked Senator Pimir Wat. He pointed timidly at the sparkling line that represented a transport impost, as if it were a downed power line he'd discovered on his front stoop, buzzing and deadly with high voltage. Senator Oxham had cut back on her dosage of apathy in the last hour, tuning her sensitivity for this meeting. She felt Wat's nerves filling the room like static electricity, coruscating with every sudden movement or sharp word. Oxham knew this particular species of anxiety well; it was the particular paranoia of professional politicians. The legislation before them was, in fact, intended to induce exactly such an emotion, an anxiety that made politicians fragile, malleable.

"Perhaps we could express our concerns in a more symbolic way," Senator Verin suggested. "Reveal all that Senator Oxham has so vigilantly uncovered, and open the subject to debate."

"And give the Risen Father a chance to respond," Senator Wat added.

Oxham turned to face Wat, fixing him with the uncanny blue of her Vasthold eyes. "The Risen Father didn't offer *us* a symbolic gesture," she said. "We haven't been informed, consulted, or even forewarned. Our Empire has simply been moved toward war, our constituents put in harm's way while His military engages in this adventure."

At these last words, she looked at the third parliamentarian in the room. Senator An Mare, whose stridently Secularist homeworld lay in the midst of the Spinward Reaches and at the high water mark of the Rix Incursion, had helped draft the measure. The most lucrative exports of Mare's world had, of course, been exempted from Oxham's legislation.

"Yes, the people have been put in harm's way," Senator Mare said, in her eyes the distant look of someone listening to secondary audio. "And in a fashion that seems deliberately clandestine on the Emperor's part." Mare cocked her head, and her eyes grew sharp. "So I must disagree with the Honorable Verin when he proposes a symbolic gesture, a mere statement of intent. An unneccesary step, I think. *All* legislation is symbolic—rhetoric and signifiers, subjunction and intention—until voted upon, at least."

Oxham felt the tension go out of the room. This legislation can't *really* succeed, Wat and Verin were thinking with relief. It was a gauntlet thrown, a bluff, a signal flare for the rest of the Senate. The measure was sculpted precisely to mirror the Emperor's will, to reveal it in reverse, like a plaster cast. Oxham could have given a long speech listing the details that Niles had found, evidence of imperial intentions, but it would have gone unheard and unnoticed. Pending legislation with major party backing, however, was always carefully scrutinized. Oxham had long ago discovered that a truth cleverly hidden was quicker believed than one simply read into the record.

"True," said Wat. "This bill will send a signal."

Verin nodded his head. "A clarion call!"

Although she and Senator Mare had planned their exchange for exactly this effect, Oxham found herself a little annoyed at the other Senators' quick surrender. With a few modifications, she thought, the bill might pass. But Oxham was one of the youngest members of the Senate; and, of course, she was the Mad Senator. Her party's leaders sometimes underestimated her.

"So I have your backing?" she asked.

The three old solons glanced among themselves, possibly conversing on some private channel, or perhaps they merely knew each other very well. In any case, Oxham's heightened empathy registered the exact moment when agreement came, settling around her mind like a cool layer of mist onto the skin.

It was Senator Mare who nodded, reaching for the silver proposal cup and putting it to her lips. She passed it to Wat, her upper lip stained red by the nanos now greedily sequencing her DNA, mapping the shape of her teeth, listening to her voice before sending a verification code to the Senate's sergeant-at-arms AI. The machine was exquisitely paranoid. It was fast, though. Seconds after Verin had finished off the liquid in the cup, Oxham's legislation flickered for a moment and re-formed in the Secularist caucus airscreen.

Now the measure was rendered in the cooler, more dignified colors of pending law. It was a beautiful thing to behold.

Five minutes later, as Nara Oxham walked down one of the wide, senators-only corridors of the Secularist wing, enjoying the wash of politics and power in her ears and the chemicals of victory in her bloodstream, the summons came.

The Risen Emperor, Ruler of the Eighty Worlds, requested the presence of Senator Nara Oxham. With due respect, but without delay.

compound mind

Alexander did what it could to forestall the invaders.

Legis XV's arsenal had been locked out from the compound mind, of course. No Imperial installation this close to the Rix would rely on the planetary infostructure to control its weaponry. Physical keys and panic shunts were in place to keep Alexander from using the capital's ground-to-space weapons against the *Lynx* or its landing craft. But Alexander could still play a role in the battle.

It moved through the palace, seeing through the eyes of security cameras, listening through the motion-detection system, following the progress of the Imperial troops as they stormed the council chamber. Alexander spoke through intercoms to the two Rix commandos left alive after the initial assault, sharing its intelligence, guiding them to harry the rescue effort.

But by now, this last stand was merely a game. The lives of the hostages were no longer important to Alexander. The rescue had come too late; it would be impossible for the Imperials to dislodge the compound mind from Legis XV without destroying the planet's infostructure.

The Rix had won.

Alexander noted the local militia flooding into the palace to reinforce the Imperials. The surviving commandos would soon be outnumbered hundreds to one. But the compound mind saw a narrow escape route. It sent its orders, using one of the commandos in a diversion, and carefully moving to disengage the other.

Alexander was secure, could no more be removed from Legis's infostructure than the oxygen from its biosphere, but the Imperials would not give up easily. Perhaps a lone soldier under its direct command would prove a useful asset later in this contest.

Doctor

Dr. Vecher felt hands clearing the goo from his eyes.

He coughed again, another oyster-sized, salty remnant of the stuff sputtering into his mouth. He spat it out, ran his tongue across his teeth. Foul slivers squirmed in the mass of green covering the floor below him.

He looked up, gasping, at whoever held his head.

A marine looked down at him through an open visor. Her aquiline face looked old for a jumper, composed and beautiful in the semidarkness. They were inside the hemisphere of a small stasis field.

The marine—a corporal, Vecher saw—clicked her tongue, and a synthesized voice said, *"Sir, heal."*

She pointed at a form lying on the ground.

"Oh," Vecher said, his mind again grasping the dimensions of the situation, now that the imperative of emptying his lungs had been accomplished.

Before him, in the arms of a bloodsoaked Imperial officer,

was the Child Empress. She was wracked by some sort of seizure. Saliva flecked the Empress's chin, and her eyes were wide and glassy. Her skin looked pale, even for a risen. The way the Empress's right arm grasped her rib cage made Vecher think: *heart attack*.

That didn't make sense. The symbiant wouldn't allow anything as dangerous as a cardiac event.

Vecher reached into his pack and pulled out his medical dropcase. He twisted a polygraph around the Empress's wrist and flipped it on, preparing a derm of adrenalog while the little device booted. After a moment, the polygraph tightened, coiling like a tiny metal cobra, and two quickneedles popped into the Empress's veins. Synesthesia glyphs gave blood pressure and heart rate, and the polygraph ticked through a series of blood tests for poisons, nano checks, and antibody assays. The heart rate was bizarrely high; it wasn't an arrest. The bloodwork rolled past, all negative.

Vecher paused with his hypo in hand, unsure what to do. What was causing this? With one thumb, he pulled open the Empress's eyes. A blood vessel had burst in one, spreading a red stain. The Child Empress gurgled, bubbles rising from her lips.

When in doubt, treat for shock, Vecher decided. He pulled a shock cocktail from his dropcase, pressing it to his patient's arm. The derm hissed, and the tension in the Empress's muscles seemed to slacken.

"It's working," the Imperial officer said hopefully. The man was an admiral, Vecher realized. An *admiral,* but just a bystander in this awful situation.

"That was only a generalized stabilizer," Vecher answered. "I have no idea what's happening here."

The doctor pulled an ultrasound wrap from the dropcase. The admiral helped him wind the thin, metallic blanket around the Empress. The wrap hummed to life, and an image began to form on its surface. Vague shapes, the Empress's organs, came into focus. Vecher saw the pounding heart, the segments of the symbiant along the spine, the shimmer of the nervous system, and . . . something else, just below the heart. Something out of place.

He activated the link to the medical AI aboard the *Lynx*, but after a few seconds of humming it reported connection failure. Of course, the stasis field blocked transmission.

"I need help from diagnostics upstairs," he explained to the marine corporal. "Lower the field."

She looked at the admiral, chain of command reasserting itself. The old man nodded. The corporal shouldered her weapon and scanned the council chamber, then extended one arm toward the field generator's controls.

Before her fingers could reach them, a loud boom shook the room. The corporal dropped to one knee, searching for a target through the sudden rain of dust. Another explosion sounded, this time closer. The floor leapt beneath the doctor's feet, throwing him to the ground. Vecher's head struck the edge of the stasis field, and, looking down, he saw that the marble floor had cracked along the circumference of the field. Of course, Dr. Vecher realized: the field was a sphere, which passed through the floor in a circle around them. The last shockwave had been strong enough to rupture the marble where it was split by the field.

Another pair of blasts rocked the palace. Vecher hoped the floor was supported by something more elastic than stone. Otherwise, their neat little circle of marble floor was likely to fall through to the next level, however far down that was.

Screams from the hostages came dimly through the stasis field; a few decorative elements from the ornate ceiling had fallen among them. A chunk of rock bounced off the black hemisphere above Vecher's head.

"Those idiots!" cried the admiral. "Why are they still bombarding us?"

The marine corporal remained unflappable, nudging one booted toe against the cracked marble at the edge of the field. She looked up at the ceiling.

She pulled off her helmet and vomited professionally—as neatly as the most practiced alcoholic—the green goo in her lungs spilling onto the floor.

"Sorry, doctor," she said. "I can't lower the field. The ceiling could go any second. You'll have to do without any help for now."

Vecher rose shakily, nodding. A metallic taste had replaced the salty strawberry of the oxycompound. He spat into his hand and saw blood. He'd bitten his tongue.

"Perfect," he muttered, and turned toward his patient.

The ultrasound wrap was slowly getting the measure of the Child Empress's organs, shifting like a live thing, tightening around her. The shape below the Empress's heart was clearer now. Vecher stared in horror at it.

"Damn," he swore. "It's . . ."

"What?" the admiral asked. The marine took her eyes from the open council chamber's doors for a moment to look over his shoulder.

"Part of the symbiant, I think."

The palace shook again. Four tightly grouped blasts rained dust and stone fragments onto the field over their heads.

Vecher simply stared.

"But it shouldn't be *there* . . ." he said.

Private

Private Bassiritz, who came from a gray village where a single name sufficed, found himself regarding minute cracks in the stone floor of the palace of Child Empress Anastasia Vista Khaman.

A moment before, a hail of seeking bullets had rounded the corner before him, a flock of flaming birds that filled the hallway with light and high-pitched screams, driving him to the ground. Fortunately, Bassiritz's reflexes were rated in the top thousandth of the highest percentile of Imperial-ruled humanity, in that realm of professional athletes, stock market makers, and cobra handlers. This singular characteristic had given him passage through the classes in academy where he often struggled—not so much unintelligent as undersocialized, raised in a provincial sector of a gray planet where technology was treated with due respect, but the underlying science ridiculed for its strange words and suppositions. The academy teachers taught him what they could, and quietly promoted him, knowing he would be an asset in any sudden, explosive combat situation, such as the one in which he now found himself.

He was a very fast young man. None of the small, whining Rix projectiles had hit Bassiritz, nor had they, by the celeritous standards of the event, even come close.

His eyesight was awfully good too. Throw a coin ten meters, and Bassiritz could run and catch it—the called side facing up in his small, yellow palm. The rest of humanity drifted through Bassiritz's reality with the tardy grace of glaciers, vast, dignified creatures who evidently knew a lot of things, but whose movements and reactions seemed deliberately, infuriatingly slow. They seemed dazzled by the simplest situations: a glass fell from a table, a groundcar suddenly hurtled toward them, the newssheet was pulled from their hand by a gust of wind—and they flailed like retarded children. Why not just *react*?

But this Rixwoman. Now she was fast.

Bassiritz had almost killed her a few moments ago. With the servos in his armor set to stealth and his varigun precharged to keep it quiet, he'd crawled into a cunning position behind the Rixwoman, separated from her only by the translucent bricks that formed the sunwall in this part of the garden. The enemy commando was pinned by supporting fire from squadmates Astra and Saman, who were smart enough to let Bassiritz do the killing. Their variguns pummeled the area with fragmentation projectiles, kicking up a maelstrom of flying glass and microbarbed schrapnel and keeping the Rixwoman down, down, down. She knelt and crawled, and her shadow was warped and twisted by the crude, handblown shapes of the brickwork, but from this angle Bassiritz could see to shoot her.

He set his varigun (a difficult weapon that forced Bassiritz to *choose* how to kill someone) to its most accurate and penetrating ammo-type, a single ballshot of magnetically assisted ferrocarbon. And fired.

That setting was a mistake, however. Just as Bassiritz never understood the relativistic equations that made his parents and sisters grow old so quickly, fading visibly with every visit home, and that had stolen his bride-to-be with their twisting of time, he never could remember that some varigun missiles were slower than sound. Bassiritz couldn't understand how sound could have a speed, like his squadmates claimed even seeing did.

But the crack of his weapon reached the Rixwoman before the killing sphere of ferrocarbon, and with Bassiritz-like speed she ducked. The ballshot shattered three layers of ornamental pleasure-garden wall, but missed its target.

And now the Rixwoman knew where Bassiritz was! The swarm of seeking bullets proved that, though she herself had disappeared. All manner of shit was about to come his way. Fast shit, maybe faster than Bassiritz.

Bassiritz decided to swallow his pride and call on help from the ship above.

With his right hand he pulled a black disk from his shoulder holster. Yanking a red plastic tab from the top, Bassiritz waited for the few seconds it took the disk to confirm that it had, in fact, awoken. That red light meant that there was a man in it now—a wee man who you couldn't see. Bassiritz stood and took the stance of one skipping a flat stone across water, and hurled the disk down the long hallway. It glanced once against the marble floor, making the sharp sound of a hammer on stone, then lofted up like a leaf caught by a sudden wind . . .

Pilot

. . . Master Pilot Jocim Marx assumed control of the Y-1 general tactical floater as easily as slipping on an undershirt. Whatever grunt had thrown the floater had imparted a good, steady spin, and the small craft's fan drive accelerated without turbulence.

Marx looked out across the terrain materializing in synesthesia, adjusting to the much larger scale of the floater (almost a hundred times the size of an Intelligencer) and the new perspective. He preferred flying these fast small craft with an inverted viewpoint, in which the floor of the palace was a ceiling over his head, the legs of humans hanging from it like giant stalactites.

The enemy target was a sharp-eared Rix commando, so the floater was seeing with only passive sensors and its highest frequency echolocation. The view was blurry, but the long, featureless hallways offered few obstacles.

The master pilot took his craft "up" to just a few centimeters from the floor, brought it to a halt behind the cover of an ornamental column. According to battle data compiled by the *Lynx* insertion AI, the nearest Rix commando was roughly twenty meters ahead. A hail of audio came from the canopy's speakers: blaster fire. The Rix was on the move, closing on the marine who had tossed the floater.

She had the marine's position, was moving in for the kill.

Firefight debris began to fill the air. The brittle glass and stone of the palace demanded the crudest sort of tactics: bludgeon your enemies with firepower, raining projectiles on them to cover any advance. Rix blasters were particularly well suited for this. It was not the best environment for floaters.

Marx took his craft farther away from the marine, escaping the maelstrom of flying glass and dust, circling around to take a position behind the advancing Rix. At least in this cacophony, the commando wouldn't hear the soft whine of the floater's fan. Marx brought his active sensors on line and decided to go in close.

There were several ways to kill with a floater. Paint the target with a laser, and have a marine launch a cigarette-sized guided missile. Or deploy the floater's skirt of poison spurs and ram the enemy. Or simply spot for the marine from some safe vantage, whispering in the soldier's ear.

But Marx heard his marine's ragged breathing, a panicked sound as the man ran from his pursuer, and realized there wasn't time for any but the direct approach.

He brought the floater up to ramming speed.

Sweeping around a corner, Marx's craft emerged from the palace into a dense sculpture garden, the way blocked by the splayed shapes of birds in flight, windblown reeds, and flowering trees, all rendered in wire-thin metal. Marx found himself within a few meters of the Rix, the purr of her servomuscles just audible through the din of blaster fire. But she was moving through the sculptures at inhuman Rix speed, dodging and rolling among the razor-sharp sculptures. It was possible she had detected his floater; she had moved into very inhospitable terrain for Marx. If the floater collided with one of these sculptures, its fan drive would be knocked out of alignment—the craft instantly useless. With the lightspeed delay of remote control, this garden was a nightmare to fly through.

Or for the true master pilot, a challenge, Marx thought with a smile.

He closed in, prepping the poison spurs of the ram skirt with a harsh vocal command.

Private

Bassiritz was bleeding.

The Rixwoman had hounded him into the corner of two long hallways, bounded by supporting walls—one of the few hypercarbon structures in the palace. His varigun couldn't blast through them. Bassiritz was trapped here, exposed and wounded. The Rixwoman's incessant fire had brought down a hail of fragments on him, a stone-hard rain. One random sliver had cut through a thin joint in his armor, tearing into his leg just behind the knee-plate.

Bassiritz's helmet visor was scratched and webbed. He could barely see, but he dared not take it off.

And Astra and Saman were dead. They had trusted Bassiritz's kill-shot too much, and had exposed themselves.

For the moment, though, the Rixwoman seemed to have paused in her relentless pursuit. Maybe she was savoring the kill, or possibly the wee man in the disk was troubling her.

Perhaps there was time to escape. But the two wide hallways stretched for a few hundred meters without cover, and Bassiritz could hear the Rixwoman still moving through the garden of crazy shapes. He felt hunted, and thought of the tigers that sometimes took people outside his village. *Up!* his mind screamed. *Climb a tree!* He searched the smooth hypercarbon walls for handholds.

Bassiritz's sharp eyes spotted a sequence of slots in the

hypercarbon that led up to the top of the wall. Probably some sort of catch so that the walls could be repositioned. Bassiritz dropped his varigun—most of its ammo was expended anyway—and drew from his boots the pair of small hypercarbon knives his mother had given him just before the Time Thief had taken her.

He thrust one knife into a slot. Its thin blade fit perfectly. He pulled himself up. The hypercarbon blade didn't bend, of course, though supporting his entire weight with a grip on its tiny handle made his fingers scream.

He ignored the pain and began to climb.

Pilot

Marx pursued the thudding boots of the Rix commando through the sharp twists and turns of the garden, his knuckles white on the control surface. The floater could barely keep up with this woman/machine. She definitely knew a small craft was pursuing her; she had twice turned to fire blindly behind, her weapon set to a wide shotgun blast that forced Marx to screeching halts under cover of the metal sculptures.

But now he was gaining.

The Rixwoman had fallen once, slipping on a sliver of glass from some earlier stage of the firefight, and she'd skidded into glancing contact with the sharp extremities of a statue representing a flock of birds. Now she left drops of thin Rix blood behind her on the marble floor, and ran with a noticeable limp. Marx urged his craft through the blur of obstacles, knowing he could reach her in the next few seconds.

Suddenly, the sculptures parted, and hunter and quarry

burst from the garden. Realizing that the open terrain was now against her, the commando spun on one unsteady heel to fire back at Marx's craft. He flipped the craft over and it leapt up from the floor as her blaster cratered the marble beneath him, the floater's ram spurs extended to full. He hurtled toward her helmeted face. Marx fought to get the craft down, knowing it would bounce off her visor. He had to hit the vulnerable areas of hands or the joints of her armor, but the craft was thrown crazily forward by the concussion wave of the blaster explosion.

It was not his piloting skill, but the woman's own reflexes that doomed her. With the disk flying directly at her face, she reached up with one hand to ward off the impact, an instinctive gesture that even three thousand years of Rix engineering had not completely removed. The spurs cut into her palm, thinly gloved to allow a full range of motion, and injected their poison.

The floater rebounded from the impact with flesh. It was whining unhealthily now, the delicate lifter-fan mechanism a few crucial millimeters out of alignment. But the job was done. Marx took control of the suddenly unwieldy craft and climbed to a safe height to watch his adversary die.

But she still stood. Shaking as the poison-nanos spread through the biological and mechanical pathways of her body, she took a few more steps from the garden, looking frantically about.

She spotted something.

Marx cursed all things Rix. She should have dropped like a stone. But in the decades since the last incursion, the Rix immune system must have evolved sufficiently to give her another few moments of life. And she had sighted an Imperial marine. The man's back was to her, as he somehow pulled himself up the smooth wall twenty meters away.

The Rix commando shakily raised her weapon, trying to buy one last Imperial casualty with her death.

Marx thought of ramming her again, but his damaged

craft only massed a few grams; the gesture would be futile. The marine was doomed. But Marx couldn't let her shoot him in the back. He triggered the floater's collision-warning alarm, and the craft expended the rest of its waning power to emit a screeching wail.

Marx watched in amazement as the marine reacted. In a single motion, the man turned and spotted the Rix, and leapt from the wall as her blaster fired, one arm flinging out in a gesture of defiance against her. The round exploded against the hypercarbon, the shockwave hurling the marine a dozen meters through the air to crash against the stone floor, his armor cracking it like a hammer. With unexpected grace, the man rolled to his feet, facing his opponent.

But the Rix was dead; she spun to the ground.

At first, Marx thought the poison had finally taken her, but then he spotted the blood gushing from her throat. From the soft armor seam there, the handle of a knife—a *knife*, Marx marveled—protruded. The marine had thrown it as he fell.

Master Pilot Marx whistled as his craft began to fall, energy expended. Finally he had met an unaugmented human whose reflexes matched his own, perhaps were even superior.

He patched himself through to the marine's helmet.

"Nice throw, soldier."

Through the floater's fading vision, he saw the marine jog toward the Rix and pull the knife from her throat. The man cleaned it carefully with a small rag he pulled from one boot, and tipped his visor at the floater as it wafted toward the ground.

"Thanks, wee man," the marine answered in a rough, outworld accent.

Wee man? Marx wondered.

But there wasn't time to ask. Another Y-1 general tactical floater had just been activated. One last Rixwoman remained alive; Marx's talents were needed elsewhere.

Initiate

Initiate Barris was trapped in darkness.

His brain rang like a persistent alarm that no one has bothered to turn off. One side of his face seemed paralyzed, numb. He had realized from the first moment of the drop that something was wrong. The acceleration gel hadn't had time to completely fill the capsule; when the terrific jolt of launch came, his helmet was partly exposed. A few seconds into the frantic, thunderous journey, the dropship had whipped around, triggering an explosion in his head. That's when the ringing in his brain had started.

Now the vehicle was grounded—a few minutes had passed, he dizzily suspected—but the automatic egress sequence had failed. He stood shoulder-deep in the mud of the gel, which was slowly leaking out of some rupture in the damaged craft.

The gel supported his battered body, warm, soft, and womblike, but Initiate Barris's training compelled him to escape the dropship. The Emperor's Secret must be protected.

He tried to shoot open the door, but the varigun failed to work. Was the gel jamming it? He pulled the weapon up out of the sucking mud. Of course, he realized, the barrel was sealed against the impact gel that filled the vehicle, and a safety mechanism had prevented its firing.

He pulled the seal, the sucking *pop* faint in his ruptured hearing.

In the lightless capsule, Barris was unsure what setting the varigun defaulted to. The marine sergeant onboard the *Lynx* had warned him not to use fragmentation grenades at short range, which certainly seemed a sensible suggestion. Barris swallowed, imagining shrapnel bouncing around in the coffin-sized payload space.

But his conditioning was insistent; it would not brook further delay. Barris gritted his teeth, pointed the varigun at the dropship door, and fired. A high scream, like the howl of fresh hardwood cut on a rotary saw, filled his ears. A bright arc appeared, the light from outside stabbing in through the perforating metal. Then in a sudden rush he was tumbling outward, the rent door bursting open under the weight of the gel.

He stumbled to his feet and looked around.

Something was missing, Barris dully thought for a moment—something wrong. The world seemed halved. He looked at the gun in his hands, and understood. Its barrel faded into darkness . . .

He was blind in one eye.

Barris reached up to touch his face, but the battle armor stiffened. He pulled against the resistance, thinking a joint or servomotor was damaged, but it wouldn't budge. Then a diagnostic glyph—one of many mysterious signs alight inside his visor—winked frantically. And he realized what was happening.

The battle armor *wouldn't let him touch his face*. The natural instinct to probe the wound was contraindicated. He looked for a mirror, a reflection in some metal surface, but then thought better of it. The numbness in his face was anesthetic; who knew what awful damage he might see.

And the Emperor's work needed doing.

The map projected on his visor made sense after a few moments of thought. Concentrating was difficult. He was probably concussed, or worse. With grim effort, Barris walked toward the council chamber, his body shaking inside the smooth gait of the body armor's servomotors.

Sounds of a distant firefight pierced the ringing in his head, but he couldn't ascertain their direction. The clipped phrases of Imperial battle-talk buzzed in his head, incomprehensible and strangely tinny. His hearing was damaged as well. He strode doggedly on.

A series of booms—two groups of four—shook the floor. It seemed as if the *Lynx* were trying to bring the palace down around him. Well, at least that might get the job done if Barris couldn't.

The initiate reached the doors to the council chamber. A lone marine, anonymous in battle armor, waved to him from a kneeling position just outside. The chamber had been secured. Was he too late?

Perhaps there was only one marine here.

Initiate Barris leveled his varigun at the figure and pressed the firing stud. The weapon resisted for a moment, held in check by some sort of friendly-fire governor, buzzing at him with yet another alarm. But when Barris ignored it and squeezed again, harder, a stream of the ripping projectiles sprayed across the marine.

The barrage knocked the figure down, and ejected a wave of dust and particles from the marble wall and floor. The fallen marine was swallowed by the cloud, but Barris moved forward, spraying his weapon into the debris. Once or twice, he saw a struggling limb emerge from the cloud; the black battle armor fragmenting, gradually beaten to pieces by the insistent hail of projectiles.

Finally, the gun whined down into silence, expended. Surely the marine was dead.

Barris switched the varigun to another setting at random, and stepped into the council chamber.

Captain

"Shots fired near the chamber, sir."

Captain Laurent Zai looked at his executive officer in surprise. The battle had been going well. Another of the Rix was dead, and the sole surviving enemy commando had been hounded almost to the outer wall of the palace complex. She was clearly in retreat. Zai had just ceased the railgun bombardment. The second wave of marines and a host of local militia had begun to secure the crumbling palace.

"Rix weaponry?"

"Sounds friendly, sir. According to the squad-level telemetry, it's Initiate Barris. His suit diagnostics look dodgy, but if they're reading true, he's just expended his projectile ammo. One casualty."

Zai swore. Just what he needed: a run-amok political ruining his rescue mission. "Crash that idiot's armor, Executive Officer."

"Done, sir," Hobbes said with a subtle flick of her wrist; she must have had the order preconfigured.

Zai switched his voice to the marine sergeant's channel.

"Forget the last commando, Sergeant. Secure that council chamber. Let's evacuate those hostages before anything goes wrong."

Corporal

Marine Corporal Mirame Lao had just decided to lower the stasis field when the shooting outside started. The railgun bombardment had ceased, and the ceiling of the council chamber seemed stable. One marine was stationed outside the chamber, and a few of the hostages had crept out from under the shelter of the council table. Lao had suspected the situation was secure, and wanted to check in with the *Lynx*.

But then the muted scream of varigun fire had erupted, a cloud of firefight dust rolling in through the chamber doors. Lao listened for the thudding of Rix blasters, but she could discern nothing through the heavy veil of the stasis field. She kept the field up, positioning herself between the Empress and the doors.

Vecher was talking to himself, a low murmur of disbelief as he probed the ultrasound wrap with instruments and his fingers. Some sort of tumor had afflicted the Empress's symbiant, apparently. What had the Rix done to her?

The sounds of the firefight ended after a few seconds. A broken figure stumbled through the dust and into the council chamber. An injured marine in battle armor. The helmet was crushed on one side. As the figure shambled toward them, Lao could see the face through the cracked visor. She knew all the *Lynx*'s marines by sight, but the hideous mask was unrecognizable. The man's left eye had exploded out of its socket, and the jaw on that side was slack with anesthetic. It looked more like an insertion injury than blaster fire.

The figure walked toward her, waving frantically. A few steps away, the marine crumpled, dropping with the sudden ragdoll lifelessness of an armor crash, the dozens of servo-motors that enabled marines to carry the heavy armor failing all at once. The marine sprawled helplessly on the floor.

Lao listened. It was silent outside.

"Doctor?" she said. "How is the Empress?"

"I'm not sure if I'm helping her or not," the doctor answered. "Her symbiant is . . . unique. I need diagnostics from spaceside before I can treat her."

"All right. Admiral?"

The admiral nodded.

Lao lowered the field, squinting for the second it took her visor to compensate for relatively bright light of the chamber. With her varigun aimed at the chamber doors, she reached out and dragged the wounded marine inside the field perimeter. If the firelight started again, the man might as well be protected.

The marine rolled onto his back.

Who was he? Lao wondered. Even with his ruined face, she should be able to recognize him. She knew every marine aboard the *Lynx*. The man's rank insignia was missing.

More marines appeared at the door. They were moving low, battle-wary. Tactical orders were still flying in secondary hearing: one more Rix commando remained.

The wounded marine attempted to speak, and a mouthful of oxycompound emerged from his lips.

"Rix . . . here," he gurgled.

Lao's fingers shot for the generator's controls again, raised the stasis field.

"Damn!" the doctor swore. "I lost the connection. I need *Lynx*'s medical AI!"

"Sorry, Doctor," she said. "But the situation is not secure."

Lao looked back at the wounded marine to offer assistance. He was crawling toward the dead Rix commando, dragging the deactivated armor he wore with the last of his strength.

"Just lie there, soldier," she ordered. In the few seconds the field had been down, Lao's tactical display had been updated. A host of friendly troops were converging on the council chamber. Help was only moments away.

The man turned to face her. He brought up the Rix blaster, leveled at her chest.

At this range, a blast from it would kill everyone inside the field.

Executive Officer

"The stasis field in the council chamber is down again, sir."

"Good. Contact them, dammit!"

Hobbes frantically tried to establish a link with Corporal Lao. By the process of elimination, she had determined that Lao was the marine inside the stasis field. A few seconds before, the shield had dropped, but then had popped up again, and there hadn't been time to connect.

"Lao!" she ordered on the marine broadband. "Do not raise the field again. The situation is secure."

The second wave of marines had secured the council chamber. And a rotary-wing medevac unit from the capital's hospital was in position on the palace roof.

There was no response from Corporal Lao.

"Dr. Vecher," she tried. Neither of the marines' armor telemetry was active. Even the diagnostic feed from the doctor's medical equipment had disappeared.

"Sir," she said, turning to face her captain. "Something's wrong."

He didn't answer. With a strange smile of resignation, Captain Zai leaned back into his bridge chair and nodded his head, murmuring something beneath his breath.

It almost sounded like, "Of course."

Then the reports came in from below, fast and furious.

The council chamber was secure. But Lao was dead, along with Dr. Vecher, Initiate Barris, and two hostages, victims of Rix blaster fire. The shield generator had been destroyed. Apparently, a last Rix commando had been alive, having survived the railgun attack, and had been *inside* the stasis field. In those close quarters, a single blaster shot had killed all six of them, even the Rixwoman herself.

In a few more moments, it was determined who the two hostages were.

One was Admiral Fenton Pry, General Staff Officer of the Lesser Spinward Fleet, holder of the Order of John, the Victory Matrix, and a host of campaign medals from the Coreward Bands Succession, Moorehead, and the Varei Rebellion.

The other was Child Empress Anastasia Vista Khaman, sister to His Imperial Majesty, the Risen Emperor.

The rescue attempt had failed.

Hobbes listened as Captain Zai recorded a short statement into his log. He must have prepared it earlier—Hobbes realized—to save the lives of his crew.

"The marines and naval personnel of the *Lynx* performed admirably and with great bravery against a perfidious enemy. This mission was carried out with distinction, but its basic plan and direction were flawed. The Error of Blood is mine and mine alone. Captain Laurent Zai, His Majesty the Emperor's Navy."

Then the captain turned and slowly left the bridge under the eyes of his stunned crew, shambling rather than walking, as if he were already a dead man.

■ ■ ■ ■

House

The house was seeded in the range of mountains that almost encircled the planet's great polar tundra. The seed braked its fall with a long, black drogue chute made of smart carbon fibers and exotic alloys, rolling to a stop in the soft five-meter snows that shouldered the chosen peak. At rest and buried in the snow, it lay silent for three hours, performing an exacting diagnostic routine before proceeding. It was a complex mechanism, this seed, and an undiscovered flaw now could doom the house to years of nagging problems and petty repairs.

It was certainly in no hurry. It had decades in which to grow.

At length, the seed determined that it was in fine shape. If there were any problems, they were of the sort that hid themselves: a corrupted diagnostic routine, a faulty internal sensor. But that couldn't be helped; it was one of the natural limits of any self-aware system. In celebration of its good health, the seed took a long drink of the water that its drogue chute had been collecting. The chute's dark surface was splayed across the snow, absorbing sunlight and melting a thin layer of snow beneath it. This water was carried to the seed by a slow capillary process, a few centiliters each minute reaching the core.

The seed's gut quickly broke the water into hydrogen and oxygen, burning the former for quick energy, saving the latter. It radiated the heat of this combustion back to the drogue chute. More snow was melted. More water collected. More hydrogen burned.

Finally, this cycle of energy production reached a critical point, and the seed was strong enough to make its first visible movements. It tugged at the drogue chute, drawing it inward, and, as deliberately as a patient on a carefully measured diet, it consumed the clever and useful materials from which the chute was made.

From these, as the heat of its labors caused the seed to sink deeper into the snow, it began to make machines.

Cylinders—simple thinking reeds whose mouths gnawed, whose guts processed and analyzed, whose anuses excreted subtlely changed materials—crawled through the mountain peak on which the seed found itself. They mapped its structure, and determined that its steep but sound shoulders were as stable as a pyramid and capable of withstanding howling gales, construction tremors, even ten-thousand-year quakes. The cylinders found veins of useful metals: copper and magnesium, even a few grams of meteoric iron. They sent gravity waves through the peak, scrying its flaws and adjusting them with a compression bomb here, a graviton annealment there. Finally, the seed deemed the building site sound.

Carbon whisker butterflies pulled themselves out of the snow. One flew to the summit of the icy peak, others found crags and promontories that looked out in all directions. Their wings were photosensitive, and the butterflies stood stock still in the light breeze, taking slow, rich exposures of the peak's splendid views. The artificial insects then glided down into the valleys and across to neighboring peaks, photographing sightlines and colored lichens and the delta-shaped flows of meltwater. Sated with these images, the butterflies flew back to the seed, crawling back into the snow. The data coiled in their bellies were unwound and digested, views constructed and cropped with possible windows, sunsets and seasonal shifts calculated, the happenstance waterfalls of an extrapolated midsummer sculpted and regarded.

The butterflies ventured forth every day for weeks, gathering sights and samples and leaving behind survey markers no bigger than grains of rice.

And the seed found that its aesthetics concerns were also met; the peak was deemed acceptable in function and in form.

The seed called for its second stage, and waited.

Scattered across likely sites in the great polar range were other seeds, sown at some expense—the devices themselves were costly, as were prospecting options on land ownership even in the cold, empty south of Home—but almost all the others had fallen on fallow ground. The seed was one of very few successes. So when the second stage arrived, it was repletely stocked: a large supply of those building materials unavailable on site, detailed plans created by real human architects from the seed's data, and best of all a splendidly clever new mind to manage the project. This artificial intelligence was capable not only of implementing the architects' plans, but also of improvising its own creative flourishes as the work unfolded. The dim awareness of the seed felt incorporation into this new intelligence as a mighty, expansive rush, like an orphaned beggar suddenly adopted by a wealthy and ancient family.

Now work began in earnest. More devices were created. Some of them scurried to complete the imaging of the site. Others began to mine the peak for raw materials and to transmute it to its new shape. Thousands of butterflies were built, swarming the neighboring mountains. Their wings now reflective, they focused the near constant summer sun on the building site, raising its temperature above freezing and providing the laboring drones with solar energy when the last of the snow on the peak was finally melted, its load of hydrogen expended.

A latticework began to enclose the peak, long thin tubes sculpted from the mountain's igneous base material. This web of filaments covered the site like a fungal growth, and moved material around the peak with the steady pulse of the old seed core, now transformed into a steam turbine. Within this mycoid embrace, the house began to take shape.

In the end, there were six balconies. That was one of the few design elements the new mind retained from the original plan. At first the human architect team approved of the project mind's independence. After all, they had set the mind's operating parameters to highest creativity; they reacted to its changes the way parents will to the improvisations of a precocious child. They applauded the greenhouse on the northern face, and complimented the scheme of mirrors that would provide it with sunlight reflected from distant mountains in the wan winter months. They failed to protest the addition of a network of ornamental waterfalls covering the walls of the great cliffs that dominated the house's western view. What finally raised the architects' ire was the fireplace. Such a barbaric addition, so obviously a reference to the surrounding snows, and so *useless*. Already, the house's geothermal shaft extended 7,000 meters into the planet's crust. It was a very warm house when it wanted to be. And the fireplace would require chemical fuel or even real *wood* imported via suborbital; a gross violation of the original design's self-sustaining aesthetic. These sorts of flourishes had to be stopped. The architects drafted a strong attack on the project mind's changes, ending the missive with a series of unambiguous demands.

But the mind had been alone—save for its host of mechanical servitors, builders, masons, miners, sculptors, and assorted winged minions—for a long time now. It had watched the seasons change for a full year, had sifted the data of four hundred sunrises and sunsets from every window in the house, had attended to the play of shadows across every square centimeter of furniture.

And so, in the manner of smug subordinates everywhere,

the project mind managed to misunderstand its masters' complaints. They were so far away, and it it *was* just an artificial. Perhaps its language interpreters were faulty, its grasp of human usage undeveloped due to its lonely existence, perhaps it had sustained some damage in that long ago fall from the sky; but for whatever reason, it simply could not comprehend what the architects wanted. The project mind went its own way, and its masters, who were busy with other projects, threw up their hands and forwarded the expanded plans, which changed daily now, to the owner.

Finally, only a few months late, the house decided it was finished. It requested the third stage of its deployment.

The final supply drone came across the harsh, cold southern skies. It landed in a cleverly hidden lifter port that raised up amid the ice sculptures (representing mastodons, minotaurs, horses, and other creatures of legend) in the western valley. The drone bore items from the owner's personal collection, unique and irreplaceable objects that nanotechnology could not reconstruct. A porcelain statuette from Earth, a small telescope that had been a childhood gift to the owner, a large freeze-dried crate of a very particular kind of coffee. These precious items were all unloaded, many-legged servitors straining under the weight of their crash-proof packing.

The house was now perfect, complete. A set of clothing exactly matching that in the owner's capital apartments had been created, woven from organic fibers grown in the house's subterranean ecologies. These gardens ranged in scale from industrial tanks of soyanalog lit by an artificial sun, to neat rows of Belgian endive in a dank cellar, and produced enough food for the owner and three guests, at least.

The house waited, repairing a frayed curtain here, a sun-faded carpet there, fighting a constant war with the aphids that had *somehow* stowed away with the shipment of seeds and earthworms.

But the owner didn't come.

He planned several trips, putting the house on alert status for this or that weekend, but pressing business always intervened. He was a Senator of the Empire, and the First Rix Incursion (though of course it wasn't called that yet) was underway. The prosecution of the war made many demands on the old solon. In one of its quiet moments, he came so close as a takeoff, his suborbital arcing its way toward the house, which was already brewing a pot of the precious coffee in breathless anticipation. But a rare storm system moved across the range. The senator's shuttle forbade an approach (in wartime, elected officials were not allowed to indulge risk levels above 0.01 percent) and carried its grumpy passenger home.

In fact, the senator was not much concerned with the house. He had one just outside the capital, another back on his home planet. He had seeded the house as an investment, and not a particularly successful one at that; the expected land rush to the southern pole had never materialized. So when the Rix invasion ended, the owner placed himself in a long overdue cold sleep, never having made the trip.

The house realized he might never come. It brooded for a decade or two, watching the slow wheel of the seasons, and made a project of adjusting once again the play of light and shadow throughout its domain.

And then the house decided that, perhaps, it was time for a modest expansion.

The new owner was coming!

The house still thought of her that way, though she had owned the house for several months, and had visited dozens of times. That first absentee landlord still weighed on its mind like a stillborn child; the house kept his special coffee hidden in a subterranean storage room. But this new owner was real, breathing.

And she was on her way again.

Like her predecessor, she was a senator. A senator-elect

actually, not yet sworn into the office. She suffered from a medical condition that required her to seek periodic solitude. Apparently, the proximity of large groups of humans could be damaging to her psyche. The house, which over the years had expanded its sculpted domain to twenty kilometers in every direction, was the perfect retreat from the capital's crowds.

The senator-elect was the perfect owner. She allowed the house considerable autonomy, encouraged its frequent redesigns and constant mountainscaping projects. She had even told it to ignore the niggling doubts that it had suffered since its AI rating had increased past the legal threshold, an unintended result of its last expansion. The new owner assured the house that her "senatorial privilege" extended to it, providing immunity from the petty regulations of the Apparatus. That extra processing capacity might come in handy one day in the business of the Senate, she had said, making the house glow with pride.

The house stretched out its mind again to check that all was in readiness. It ordered a swarm of reflective butterflies to focus more sunlight on the slopes above the great cliff face; the resulting melting of snow would better feed the waterfall network, now grown as complex as some vast pachinko machine. The house rotated the central skylight so that its faceted windows would in a few hours break the setting sun into bright, orange shards covering the greatroom's floor. And in its magma-warmed lower depths, the house activated gardening servitors to begin preparations for a meal or two.

The new owner was, for the first time ever, bringing a guest.

The man was called Lieutenant-Commander Laurent Zai. A *hero,* the house was told by the small portion of its expansive mind that kept up with the newsfeeds. The house jumped into its preparations with extraordinary vigor, wondering what sort of visit this was to be.

Political? Of military import? Romantic?

The house had never actually seen two people interact under its own roof. All it knew of human nature it had gleaned from dramas, newsfeeds, and novels—and from watching its senator-elect spend her lonely hours here. Much could be learned this weekend.

The house decided to watch very carefully indeed.

The suborbital shuttle was a brilliant thing.

The arc of its atmospheric braking was aligned head-on with the house's sensors, so the craft appeared only as a descending, expanding line of heat and light—a punctuation mark in some ecstatic language of moving, blazing runes.

The house received a few supplies—those exotics it could not produce itself—via suborbital, but those arrived in small, single-use couriers. This shuttle was a four-seater, larger and much more violent. The craft was preceded by a sonic boom, flaring hugely in the house's senses, but then became elegant and avian, its compact maneuvering wings spreading to reduce the speed of its entry. It topped the northern mountains with a dying scream, and swooped down to settle on the landing pad that had risen up from the gardens.

The dusting of snow on the landing pad began to melt in the shuttle's heat, the pad becoming wet and reflective, as if mist were clearing from a mirror. Icicles hanging from the nearest trees began to drip.

The mistress and her house guest had arrived.

They waited a few moments inside the shuttle while the landing area cooled. Then two figures emerged to descend the short exit stairs, hurried by the not-quite-freezing summer air. Their breath escaped in tiny puffs, and in the house's vision their self-heated clothing glimmered infrared.

The house was impatient. It had timed its welcome carefully. Inside the main structure, a wood fire was reaching its climax stage, coffee and cooking smells were peaking, and a last few servitors rearranged fresh-cut flowers, pushing stems a few centimeters one way and then the other as some infinitesimal portion of the house's processors found itself caught in an aesthetic loop.

But when the senator-elect and her guest arrived at the door, the house paused a moment before opening, just to create anticipation.

The lieutenant-commander was a tall man, dark and reserved. He walked with a smooth, prosthetic gait, the motion a gliding one, like a creature with more than two legs. He followed the mistress attentively through a tour of the house, noting its relationship to the surrounding mountains as if scouting a defensive position. The man was impressed, the house could tell Laurent Zai complimented the views and the gardens, asked how they were heated. The house would have loved to explain (in excessive detail) the system of mirrors and heated water in underground channels, but the mistress had warned it not to speak. The man was Vadan, and didn't approve of talking machines.

Receptive to the smells of cooking, Zai and the mistress presently sat down to eat. The house had pulled food from deep in its stores. It had slaved (or rather, had commanded its many slaves) to make everything perfect. It served breasts of the small, sparrowlike birds that flocked in the south forest, each no bigger than a mouthful, baked in goat's butter and thyme. Baby artichokes and carrots had gone into a stew, thickened with a dark reduction of tomatoes and cocoa grown deep underground. Meaty oranges and pears engineered to grow in freezing temperatures, which budded from the tree already filled with icy crystals, had been shaved into sorbets to divide the courses. The main dish was thin slices of salmon pulled from the snowmelt streams, chemically cooked with lemon juice and nanomachines. The table was covered with petals from the black and purple groundcover flowers that kept the gardens warm for a few extra weeks in the fall.

The house spared nothing, even unearthing the decades-old hidden cache of its first owner's coffee, the previous senator's special blend. It served them this magic brew after they were finished eating.

The house watched and waited, anxious to see what would result from all its preparations. It had so often read that well-prepared food was the key to engendering good conversation.

Now would come the test.

Lieutenant-Commander

After lunch, Nara Oxham took him to a room with incredible views. Like the food, which had been exquisite to a fault, the vistas here almost overwhelmed Zai: mountainscapes, clear skies, and marvelous, distant waterfalls. Finally, an escape from the crowds of the capital. Best of all, however, was the large fireplace, a hearth such as a Vadan home would have. They built a small pyre of real wood together, and Nara worked with long and skillful fingers to bring it to a blaze.

Zai stole glances at his hostess in the firelight. The senator-elect's eyes were changing. With each hour at the polar estate, they grew less focused, like a woman steadily drinking. Laurent knew that she had stopped taking the drug that maintained her sanity in the city. She was becoming more sensitive. He could almost feel the power of her empathy as it tuned in on him. What would it reveal to her? he wondered.

Zai tried not to think of what might happen between him and his hostess. He knew nothing of the ways of Vasthold; this excursion to the pole might be merely a friendly gesture toward a foreigner, a traditional offer to a decorated hero, even an attempt to compromise a political opponent. But this was Nara's home, and they were very much alone.

These thoughts of intimacy came unbidden and moved creakily, almost a forgotten process. Since his captivity, Zai's broken body had been often a source of pain, sometimes one of despair, and always an engineering problem, but never a locus of desire.

Would Nara detect his thoughts—*half-thoughts*, really— about possible intimacy between them? Zai knew that most synesthetic abilities were exaggerated by the gutter media. How keen were hers?

Zai decided to show his curiosity, which at least would have the advantage of distracting Nara (and himself) from his other thoughts. So he pursued a question he'd pondered since they'd met.

"What was it like to be empathic as a child? When did you realize that you could . . . read minds?"

Nara laughed at his terminology, as he'd expected.

"The realization was slow," she said. "It almost never came.

"I was raised on the pleinhold. It's very empty there. On Vasthold, there are prefectures with less than one person per hundred square kilometers. Endless plains in the wind belt, broken only by Coriolis mountains, constructs that channel the winds into erosion runnels, which will eventually become canyons. Everywhere on the plains you can hear the mountains singing. The wind resonances are unpredictable; you can't engineer a mountain for a particular sound. They say even a Rix mind couldn't do the math. Each plays its own tune, as slow and moaning as whalesong, some deeper than human hearing, with notes that beat like a drum. Hiking guides can tell the songs apart, can distinguish the different sides of each mountain with their eyes closed. Our house faced Mount Ballimar, whose northern-side song sweeps from thudding beats up to a soprano when the wind shifts, like a siren warning that a storm is coming.

"My parents thought I was an idiot at first."

Zai glanced at her, wondering if the word had a softer meaning on her planet. She shook her head in response. *That* thought had proven easy enough for her to read.

"Out there on the plains, my ability went undetected. I suffered no insanity in the hinterlands; the psychic input from my large but isolated family was manageable. But I had less need of language acquisition than my siblings. To family members I could project emotions as well as empathize. It was so effortless, my communication; my family thought I was a dullard, but a very easy one to get along with. My needs were met, and I knew what was going on around me, but I didn't see the need to chatter constantly."

Zai's eyebrows raised.

"Strange that I became a politician, then. Eh?"

He laughed. "You read my mind."

"I did," she admitted, and leaned forward to poke at the fire. It burned steadily now, and was hot enough to have forced them to a meter's distance.

"I *could* talk, though. And contrary to what my parents thought, I was smart. I could do spoken lessons with an AI, if a reward was coming. But I didn't *need* speech, so the secondary language skills—reading and writing—suffered.

"Then I took my first trip to the city."

Zai saw the muscles of her hand tighten on the poker.

"I thought the city was a mountain, because I could hear it from so far away. I thought it was singing. The minds of a city are like ocean from a distance, when the wave crashes blend into a hum, a single band of sound. Pleinberg only had a population of a few hundred thousand in those days, but I could hear from fifty klicks out the tenor of the festival we were headed to, raucous and celebratory, political. The local majority party had won the continental parliament. From out there on the plain, coming in by slow ground transport, the sound made me happy. I sang back at this happy, marvelous mountain.

"I wonder what my parents thought was happening. Just an idiot's song, I suppose."

"They never told you?" he asked.

Surprise crossed Nara's face for a moment.

"I haven't spoken to them since that day," she said.

Zai blinked, feeling like a blunderer. Senator Oxham's biography must be well known in political circles, at least the bare facts. But Zai knew her only as the Mad Senator.

The words chilled him, though. Abandonment of a child? Loss of the family line? His Vadan sense of propriety rebelled at the thought. He swallowed, and tried to stifle the reaction, knowing his empathic host would feel it all too well.

"Go ahead, Laurent," she said, "be appalled. It's okay."

"I don't mean to—"

"I *know*. But don't try to control your thoughts around me. Please."

He sighed, and considered the War Sage's advice on negotiating with the enemy: *When caught dissembling, the best correction is sudden directness.*

"How close did you get, before the city drove you mad?" he asked.

"I'm not sure, exactly. I didn't know it was madness; I thought it was the song inside me, tearing me to pieces."

She turned away from him to place fresh wood on the fire.

"As the city grew nearer, the mindnoise increased. It follows the inverse square law, like gravity or broadcast radio. But the traffic going into the festival slowed us down, so the ramp up in volume wasn't exponential, as it could have been."

"So clinical, Nara."

"Because I don't really *remember*, not sequentially, anyway. I only recall that I loved it. Riding a victory celebration of a quarter million minds, Laurent, who'd won a continental election for the first time in *decades*. There was so much joy there: success after years of work, redemption for old defeats, the sense that justice would finally be done. I think I fell in love with politics that day."

"The day you went mad."

She nodded, smiling.

"But by the time we reached the center of town, it was too much for me. I was raw and unprotected, a thousand times more sensitive than I am now. The stray thoughts of passing strangers hit me like revelations, the noise of the city obliterated my own young mind. My reflex was to strike out, I suppose, to physically retaliate. I was brought into the hospital bloody, and it wasn't all my blood. I hurt one of my sisters, I think the story goes.

"They left me in the city."

Zai gaped. There was no point in hiding his reaction.

"Why didn't your parents take you back home?"

She shrugged. "They didn't know. When your child has an unexplained seizure, you don't take them into the hinterland. They had me transferred to the best facility possible, which happened to be in the largest city on Vasthold."

"But you said you haven't seen them since."

"It was in Vasthold's expansion phase. They had ten children, Laurent. And their silent one, their retarded child, had become a dangerous little beast. They couldn't travel across the world to visit me. This was a *colony* world, Laurent."

More protests rose in Zai, but he took a deep breath. No point in battering Nara's parents. It was a different culture, and a long time ago.

"How many years were you . . . mad, Nara?"

She looked into his eyes. "From age six to ten . . . that's roughly age twelve to nineteen in Absolute years. Puberty, young adulthood. All with eight million voices in my mind."

"Inhuman," he said.

She turned back to the fire, half smiling. "There are only a few of my kind. A lot of synesthetic empaths, but not many survivors of such ignorance. Now they understand that synesthesia implants will cause empathy in a few dozen kids a year. Most live in cities, of course, and the condition is discovered within days of the operation. When the kids blow, they ship them off to the country until they're old enough for apathy treatments. But I was desensitized the old-fashioned way."

"Exposure."

"What was it like in those years, Nara?" No point in hiding his curiosity from an empath.

"I *was* the city, Laurent. Its animal consciousness, anyway. The raging id of desire and need, frustration and anger. The heart of humanity, and yes, of politics. But almost utterly without self. Mad."

Zai narrowed his eyes. He'd never thought of a city that way, as having a mind. It was so close to the Rix perversion.

"Exactly," she said, apparently having plumbed the thought. "That's why I'm anti-Rix, for a Secularist."

"What do you mean?"

"Cities are *beasts,* Laurent. The body politic is nothing but an animal. It needs humans to lead it, personalities to shape the mass. That's why the Rix are such single-minded butchers. They graft a voice onto a slavering beast, then worship it as a god."

"But something, some sort of compound mind is really there, Nara? Even on an Imperial world, with emergence suppressed? Even without the networks."

She nodded. "I heard it every day. Had it in my mind. Whether computers make it apparent or not, humans are a part of something bigger, something distinctly alive. The Rix are right about that."

"*Thus the Emperor protects us,*" Zai whispered.

"Yes. Our counter-god," Oxham said sadly. "A necessary . . . stopgap."

"But why not, Nara? You said it yourself, we need human personalities. People who inspire loyalty, give human shape to the mass. So why fight the Emperor so bitterly?"

"Because no one elected him," she said. "And because he's dead."

Zai shook his head, the disloyal words painful.

"But the honored dead chose him at Quorum, sixteen hundred years ago. They can call another Quorum to remove him, if they ever wanted to."

"The dead are *dead*, Laurent. They don't live with us anymore. You've seen the distance in their eyes. They are no more like us than Rix minds. You know it. The living city may be a beast, but at least it's human: what we are."

She leaned toward him, the fire bright in her eyes.

"Humanity is central, Laurent, the only thing that matters. *We* are what puts good and evil in this universe. Not gods or dead people. Not machines. Us."

"The honored dead are our ancestors, Nara," he whispered fiercely, as if silencing a child in church.

"They're a *medical procedure*. One with unbelievably negative social and economic consequences. Nothing more."

"That's insane," he said.

He closed his mouth on the words, too late.

She stared back at him, triumph and sadness on her face.

They sat there for a while longer, the thing that had been between them broken. Laurent Zai wanted to say something, but doubted an apology would matter.

He sat in silence, wondering what he should do.

3

DECOMPRESSION

Swift decisions are virtuous, unless they have
irrevocable consequences.

—ANONYMOUS 167

Senator

The constellation of eyes glistened, reflecting the sunlight that penetrated the cultured-diamond doors sliding closed behind Senator Nara Oxham. The ocular glint raised her hackles, marking as it did the eyes of a nocturnal predator. On Oxham's home planet Vasthold, there ranged human-hunting bears, paracoyotes, and feral nightdogs. On some deep, instinctive level, Nara Oxham knew those eyes to be warnings.

The creatures were splayed—fifteen or twenty of them—on an invisible bed of lovely gravity. They wafted like polychrome clouds down the wide, breezy hallways of the Emperor's inner palace, carried by the ambient movement of air. Her apathy bracelet was set to high, as always here in the crowded capital, but sufficient sensitivity remained to feel some small measure of their inhuman thoughts. They regarded her coolly as they drifted past, secure in their privilege, in their demigodhood, and in their speechless wisdom, accumulated over sixteen centuries of languor. Of course, their species had never, even in the millennia before Imperial decree had elevated them to semidivine status, doubted its innate superiority.

They were imperious consorts, these personal familiars of His Risen Majesty. They were *felis domesticus immortalis*.

They were, in a word, cats.

And in a few more words, cats who would never die.

Senator Nara Oxham hated cats.

She halted as the invisible bed passed, anxious not to disturb the air currents that informed its slow, dignified passage. The animals' heads swiveled as one, alien irises fixing her with languid malevolence, and she had to steel herself to return their unblinking gaze. So much for her brave, anti-Imperial heresies. Nara Oxham's constituency was an entire planet, but here in the Diamond Palace the mighty senator found herself intimidated by the housepets.

Her morning unease had returned the moment she had egressed across the Rubicon Pale, the protective barrier, electronic and legal, that encircled the Forum and ensured the Senate's independence. The aircar waiting for her at the Pale's shimmering edge had been so elegant, as delicate as a thing of paper and string. But inside the car, fragility had transformed into power: the machine's tendrils of lovely gravity reaching out to spin the city beneath her like a juggler's fingers turning bright pins—among building spires, over parks and gardens, through the mists of waterfalls. At first lazy and indirect, the sovereign aircar had become suddenly urgent as it headed toward the Diamond Palace, a potter's blade incising a straight path, as if the world were clay turning on a fast wheel below. This profligate expediture of energy to take her mere kilometers—a demonstration of the Emperor's might: awesomely expensive, exquisitely refined.

Now, a few moments inside the palace, and the housecats were flying too.

Oxham shivered, and took a deep breath after the animals disappeared down the curving hallway, trying to remember if any of them had been black. Then she cast aside superstition and strode across the hall, braving their wafting path, toward her rendezvous with the Risen Emperor.

Another set of diamond doors opened before her, and Nara Oxham wondered what this was all about. The obvious answer was that His Majesty objected to the legislation she had proposed, her counter to the Loyalty Party's preparations for war on the Rix frontier. But the summons had been so instantaneous, only minutes after the legislation had been registered. Oxham's staff had followed her orders well, creating a subtle and labyrinthine weave of laws and tariffs, not a direct attack. How could the Apparatus have recognized its purpose so quickly?

Perhaps there'd been a leak, a mole somewhere on her staff or among the Secular Party hierarchy, and the palace had been forewarned. She dismissed this thought as paranoia. Only a trusted handful had helped write the legislation. More likely, the Emperor had been waiting, alert for any response. He had known that his Loyalists' preparations for war would eventually be detected, and he'd been ready. Ready with this demonstration of alert and awesome power: an Imperial summons, that extraordinary flight, this palace of diamond. That was the warning in the cats' shining eyes, she realized: a reminder not to underestimate Him.

Oxham realized that her contempt for the grays, those living humans who voted for Loyalty, who worshiped the dead and the Emperor as gods, had caused her to forget that the Risen Father himself was a very smart man.

He had, after all, invented immortality. No mean feat. And over the last sixteen hundred years had brokered that single discovery into more-or-less absolute power over eighty worlds.

Through the doors, Oxham found herself in a garden, a vast space over which a bright sky was refracted into facets by a canopy of diamond.

The path under her feet was made of broken stones, their pointed shapes driven into the earthen floor to form a precise and curving road, a mosaic formed from the remains of some ancient and shattered statue. *Look upon my works, ye mighty*, she thought to herself. A short, red grass grew up between the stones, outlining them with the color of dried blood. Motile vines undulated through the grass on either side of the path, a sinuous and vaguely threatening ground cover, perhaps to keep the visitor from straying. The route spiraled inward, taking Oxham past an orchard of miniature apple trees, none higher than a meter, a serpentine dune of white sand covered with a scrambling host of bright blue scorpions, flocks of hummingbirds sculpted into topiary shapes by invisible fields, and, as she reached the spiral's center, a series of fountains whose misty sprays, waterfalls, and arcs of water patently did not follow the laws of gravity.

Oxham knew she was close to the man himself when she came upon the calico. It lay in the middle of the path, splayed to capture the warmth of a particularly large, flat stone. It was a no-breed-in-particular cat, whose coat was mottled with the colors of milk, apricot, and black. The spinal ridge of the Lazarus Symbiant extended all the way down the tail, which moved agitatedly, though the rest of the animal's body was calm. The vertical slits of the cat's irises swelled a bit with curiosity when it saw Nara, then the interest receded, ending in a slow, languid blink of disdain.

She managed to meet its gaze steadily.

A young man strode up the path from the other direction, and lifted the cat to his shoulder with a practiced motion. It let out a vaguely protesting trill, then settled into the crook of his elbow, one claw reaching out across his chest to secure itself in the black threads of imperial rament.

Her first thought was trite: He was more handsome in person.

"My Lord," Oxham said, proud that she had managed not to kneel reflexively. Senatorial office had its privileges.

"Senator," he answered, nodding at her, then turning to kiss the captive cat's forehead. It stretched to lick his chin.

Outside of military casualties, most of the risen were, of course, quite old. Traditional medicine kept the wealthy and powerful alive for almost two centuries; disease and accidents were almost unknown. All the dead people whom Nara Oxham had met were ancient solons and wizened oligarchs, various relics of history, or the occasional pilgrim having reached Home after centuries of winding sublight travel. They wore their death gracefully, calm and gray of manner. But the Emperor had committed the Holy Suicide in his thirties (when structural exobiologists do their best work), in the final test of his great invention. No real age had ever touched his face. He seemed so *present*, his smile so charming (cunning?), his gaze so piercingly aware of Oxham's nervousness.

He seemed terribly . . . alive.

"Thank you for coming," the Risen Emperor of the Eighty Worlds said, acknowledging the privilege of the Pale.

"At your service, m'lord."

The cat yawned, and stared at her as if to say, *And mine*.

"Please come and sit with us, Senator."

She followed the dead man, and at the center of the spiral path they sat, floating cushions taking up positions against her lower back, elbows, neck—not merely cradling Oxham's weight, but moving softly to stretch her muscles, undulating to maintain circulation. A low, square block of red marble sat between them, and the Emperor deposited the cat onto its sun-warmed surface, where the beast promptly rolled onto its back, offering the sovereign's long fingers its milky belly.

"You are surprised, Senator?" he asked suddenly.

The question itself surprised her. Oxham gathered her thoughts, wondering what her expression had revealed.

"I hadn't thought to meet Your Majesty alone."

"Look at your arms," he said.

Oxham blinked, then obeyed. Dusted onto her dark skin were silver motes that glistened in the sun, like flecks of mica in some black rock.

"Our security," he said. "And a few courtiers, Senator. We'll know it if you sweat."

Nanomachines, she realized. Some to record galvanic skin response, pulse, secretions—to check for lies and evasions; some to kill her instantly if she threatened the imperial personage with violence.

"I shall endeavor not to sweat, m'lord."

He chuckled, a sound Oxham had never heard from a

dead person before, and leaned back. The lovely gravity cushions adjusted themselves indulgently.

"Do you know why we like cats, Senator?"

Nara Oxham took a moment to moisten her lips. She wondered if the tiny machines on her arms (were they also on her face? beneath her clothing?) would detect her hatred of the animals.

"They were cats who suffered the first sacrifice, m'lord." Oxham heard the dutiful cadence in her own voice, like a child repeating catechism; its unctuous sound annoyed her.

She regarded the lazy creature splayed on the marble table. It looked at her suspiciously, as if sensing her thoughts. Thousands of its kind had writhed in postdeath agony while the early symbiants of the Holy Experiments tried unsuccessfully to repair deceased nerve cells. Thousands had limped through the ghoulish existence of unwhole reanimation. Tens of thousands were killed outright—never to move again—as the various parameters of recovery from brain damage, systemic shock, and telomere decay were tested and retested. All the successful experimentation had been performed on cats. For some reason, simian and canine species had proved problematic—they arose insane or died of seizures, as if they couldn't deal with an unexpected return after life's extinction. Not like sanguine, self-important cats, who—like humans, apparently—felt they deserved an afterlife.

Oxham narrowed her eyes at the little beast. *Millions of you, writhing in pain*, she thought at it.

It yawned, and began to lick one paw.

"So it is believed, Senator," the Emperor answered. "So it is often believed. But our appreciation of the feline predates their contribution to the holy researches. You see, these subtle creatures have always been demigods, our guides into new realms, the silent familiars of progress. Did you know that at every stage of human evolution, cats were instrumental?"

Oxham's eyes widened. Surely this was some recherché

joke, a verbal equivalent to the gravity-modified fountains in the surrounding garden. This talk was like the water running uphill—a display of imperial self-indulgence. She determined not to let it throw her off guard.

"Instrumental, m'lord?" She tried to sound earnest.

"Do you know your Earth history, Senator?"

"Earth Prime?" That far-off planet on the galaxy's edge was so often used to make political points. "Certainly, Sire. But perhaps my education is deficient on the subject of . . . cats."

His Majesty nodded, frowning as if this oversight was all too common.

"Take, for example, the origin of civilization. One of the many times when cats were midwives to human progress."

He cleared his throat, as if beginning a lecture.

"That era found humans in small clusters, tribal groups banded together for protection, constantly moving to follow their prey. They were rootless, barely subsisting. Not a particularly successful species, their numbers were less than the population of a medium-sized residential building here in the capital.

"Then these humans made a great discovery. They found out how to grow food from the ground, rather than chasing it across the seasons of the year."

"The agricultural revolution," Senator Oxham supplied.

The Emperor nodded happily. "Exactly. And with that discovery comes everything. With efficient food production, more grain was produced by each family than it needed to survive. This excess grain was the basis of specialization; as some humans ceased laboring for food, they became metalsmiths, shipwrights, soldiers, philosophers."

"Emperors?" Oxham suggested.

His Majesty laughed heartily, now leaning forward in his retinue of floating cushions. "True. And senators too, eventually. Administration was now possible, the public wealth controlled by priests, who were also mathematicians, astronomers, and scribes. From excess grain: civilization.

But there was one problem."

Megalomania? Oxham wondered. The tendency for the priest with the most grain to mistake himself for a god, even to pretend to immortality. But she bit her lip and waited quietly through the Emperor's dramatic pause.

"Imagine the temple at the center of the proto-city, Senator. In ancient Egypt, perhaps. It is a house of the gods, but also an academy. Here, the priests study the skies, learn the motions of the stars, and create mathematics. The temple is also a government building; the priests document productivity and levy taxes, inventing the recordkeeping symbols that eventually become written language, literature, software, and artificial intelligence. But at its heart, the temple had to do one thing successfully, perform one task without which it was nothing."

His eyes almost glowed now, all deathly calm erased by his passion. He reached out toward her, fingers grasping at the air in his need to be understood.

Then quite suddenly her empathy flared, and she saw his point.

"A granary," she said. "Temples were granaries, weren't they?"

He smiled, sinking back with satisfaction.

"That was the source of all their power," he said. "Their ability to create art and science, to field soldiers, to keep the population whole in times of drought and flood. The excess wealth of the agricultural revolution. But a huge pile of grain is a very tempting target."

"For rats," Oxham said.

"Armies of them, breeding unstoppably, as any parasite will when a vast supply of food presents itself. Almost a biological law, a Law of Parasites: accumulated biomass attracts vermin. The deserts of Egypt swarmed with rats, an inexorable drain on the resources of the proto-city, a dam in the rushing stream of civilization."

"But a huge population of rats is also a tempting target, sire," Oxham said. "For the right predator."

"You are a very astute woman, Senator Nara Oxham."

Realizing that she had charmed him, Oxham continued his narrative. "And thus, from out of the desert a little-known beast emerged, sire. A small, solitary hunter that had previously avoided humanity. And it took up residence in the temples, where it hunted rats with great efficiency, preserving the precious excess grain."

The Emperor nodded happily, and took up the tale. "And the priests dutifully worshiped this animal, which seemed strangely acclimated to temple life, as if its rightful place had always been among the gods."

Oxham smiled. It was a pleasant enough story. Possibly containing some truth, or perhaps a strange outgrowth of a man's guilt, who had tortured so many of the creatures to death sixteen centuries ago.

"Have you seen the statues, Senator?"

"Statues, m'lord?"

A subvocalized command trembled upon the sovereign's jaw, and the faceted sky grew dark. The air chilled, and forms appeared around them. Of course, Oxham thought, the high canopy of diamond was not only for decoration; it housed a dense lattice of synesthesia projectors. The garden was, in fact, one vast airscreen.

Senator and Emperor were in a great stone space now. A few shafts of sunlight illuminated a suspension of particulate matter: dust from the rolling hills of grain that surrounded them. In this dim ambience the statues, which were carved from some smooth, jet stone, glistened, their skins as reflective as black oil. They sat upright in housecat fashion, forepaws tucked neatly together and tails curled. Their angular faces were utterly serene, their posture informed by the geometries of some simple, primordial mathematics. They were clearly gods; early and basic totems of protection.

"These were the saviors of civilization," he said. "You can see it in their eyes."

To Senator Oxham, the eyes seemed blank, featureless black orbs into which one could write one's own madness.

The Emperor raised a finger, another signal.

Some of the motes of grainy dust grew, gaining substance and structure, flickering alight now with their own fire. They began to move, swirling into a shape that was somehow familiar to Oxham. The constellation of bright flairs formed a great wheel, slowly rotating around senator and sovereign. After a moment, Oxham recognized the shape. She had seen it all her life, on airscreen displays, in jeweled pendants, and in two-dimensional representations from the senatorial flag to the Imperial coat of arms. But she had never been *inside* the shape before—or rather, she had always been inside it: these were the thirty-four stars of the Eighty Worlds.

"This is our new excess grain, Senator. The material wealth and population of almost fifty solar systems, the technologies to bend these resources to our will, and infinitely long lives, time enough to discover the new philosophies that will be humanity's next astronomy, mathematics, and written language. But again this bounty is threatened from without."

Nara Oxham regarded the Emperor in the darkness. Suddenly, his obsessions did not seem so harmless.

"The Rix, Your Majesty?"

"These Rix, these vermin-worshiping Rix," he hissed. "Compelled by an insane religion to infect all humanity with their compound minds. It's the Law of the Parasite again: our wealth, our vast reserves of energy and information summon forth a host of vermin from out of the desert, who seek to drain our civilization before it can reach its true promise."

Even through the dulling effects of the apathy bracelet, Oxham felt the passion in the Emperor, the waves of paranoia that wracked his powerful mind. Despite herself, she'd been caught off-guard, so circuitously had he arrived at his point.

"Sire," Oxham said carefully, wondering how far the privilege of her office would really protect her in the face of the man's mania. "I was not aware that the compound mind phenomenon was so destructive. Host worlds don't suffer materially. In fact, some report greater efficiency in communications flow, easier maintainence of water systems, smoother air traffic."

The Emperor shook his head.

"But what is lost? The random collisions of data that inform a compound mind are *human culture itself*. That chaos isn't some peripheral by-product, it is the essence of humanity. We can't know what evolutionary shifts will never take place if we become mere vessels for this mutant software the Rix dare to call a mind."

Oxham almost pointed out the obvious, that the Emperor was voicing the same arguments against the Rix that the Secularists made against his own immortal rule: Living gods were never beneficial for human society. But she controlled herself. Even through apathy she could taste the man's conviction, the strange fixity of his thinking, and knew it was pointless to bring this subtle point to his attention now. The Rix and their compound minds were this Emperor's personal nightmare. She took a less argumentative tack.

"Sire, the Secular Party has never questioned your policy on blocking compound minds from propagating. And we stood firm in the unity government during the Rix Incursion. But the spinward frontier has been quiet for almost a century, has it not?"

"It has been a secret, though no doubt you have heard rumors the last decade or so. But the Rix have been moving against us once again."

The Emperor stood and pointed into the darkness, and the wheeling cluster of stars halted, then began to slide, the spinward reaches coming toward him. One of the stars came to rest at his extended fingertip.

"This, Senator, is Legis XV. Some five hours ago, the Rix

attacked here with a small but determined force. A suicide mission. Their objective was to take our sister the Child Empress, and to hold her hostage while they propagated a compound mind upon the planet."

For a few moments, Oxham's mind was overwhelmed. *War*, was all that she could think. The Child Empress in alien hands. If harm came to her, the grays would reap a huge political windfall, the rush to armed conflict would become unstoppable.

"Then, m'lord, that is the cause of the Loyalists' move toward a war economy," she finally managed.

"Yes. We cannot assume that this is an isolated attack."

Her empathy caught a flicker of disturbance from the Emperor.

"Is your sister all right, Sire?"

"A frigate is standing by, ready to attempt a rescue," the Emperor said. "The captain has already launched a rescue mission. We should learn the results in the next hour."

He stroked the cat. She felt resignation in him, and wondered if he already knew the outcome of the rescue attempt, and was withholding the information.

Then Oxham realized that her party was in peril. She had to withdraw the legislation before news of the Rix raid broke. Once this outrage was made public, her counterthrust to the grays would seem traitorous. The Emperor had done her and the Secular Party a favor with this warning.

"Thank you, sire, for telling me this."

He put one hand on her shoulder. Even through her thick senatorial gown, she could feel the cool of his hand, the deadness of it. "This is not the time to work against each other, Senator. You must understand, we have no quarrel with your party. The dead and the living need one another, in peace and in war. The future we seek is not a cold place."

"Of course not, sire. I will withdraw the legislation at once."

After she had said the words, Oxham realized that the

Emperor hadn't even asked her. That was true power, she supposed, one's desires met without the need to give orders.

"Thank you, Nara," he said, the fierce mania that had shaped his mind a few moments before sliding from her awareness, as he returned to his former imperious calm. "We have great hopes for you, Senator Oxham. We know that your party will stand by us in this battle against the Rix."

"Yes, sire." There was really nothing else she could say.

"And we hope that you will support us in dealing with the compound mind, which may well have succeeded in taking hold on Legis XV."

She wondered exactly what the sovereign meant by that. But he continued before she could ask.

"We should like to appoint you to a war council, Senator," he said.

Oxham could only blink. The Emperor squeezed her shoulder and let his arm drop, turned half away. She realized that no acceptance was necessary. If another Rix incursion were underway, a war council would have tremendous power granted to it by the Senate. She would sit in chambers with the mightiest humans in the Eighty Worlds. Nara Oxham would be among their number in privilege, in access to information, in ability to make history. In sheer power.

"Thank you, m'lord," was all that she could say.

He nodded slightly, his eyes focused on the white belly of the calico. The beast arched its back languorously, until the ridge of the symbiant almost formed an omega on the warm red stone.

War.

Ships hurtling toward each other in the compressed time of relativistic velocities, their crews fading from the memory of family and friends, lives ending in seconds-long battles whose tremendous energies unleashed brief new suns. Deadly raids on opposing populations, hundreds of thousands killed in minutes, continents poisoned for centuries. Peaceful research and education suspended as whole planetary economies were consumed by war's hunger for machines and soldiers. Generations of human history squandered before both sides, wounded and exhausted, played for stalemate. And, of course, the real possibility—the high probability— that her new lover would be dead before it all was over.

Suddenly, Oxham was appalled at herself, her ambition, her lust for power, the thrill she had felt upon being asked to help prosecute this war. She felt it still there inside her: the resonant pleasure of status gained, new heights of power scaled.

"My lord, I'm not sure—"

"The council shall convene in four hours," the Emperor interrupted. Perhaps he had anticipated her doubts, and didn't want to hear them. Her reflexive politesse asserted itself, calming the maelstrom of conflicting motivations. *Say nothing until you are sure*, she ordered herself. She forced calm into her veins, focusing on the slow, synesthetic wheel of eighty worlds that orbited herself and the sovereign.

The Emperor continued, "By then, we shall have heard from the *Lynx*. We'll know what's happened out on Legis XV."

Her gaze was caught and held by a red star out on the periphery of the Empire. Darkness gathered in the corner of her eyes, as if she were close to blacking out. She must have misheard.

"The *Lynx*, sire?"

"The Navy vessel stationed over Legis XV. They should attempt a rescue soon."

"The *Lynx*," she echoed. "A frigate, m'lord?"

The Emperor looked at her with surprise, for the first time noting her expression. "Yes, exactly."

Oxham realized that he had misinterpreted her knowledge as some sort of military expertise. She controlled herself again, and continued. "A stroke of luck, sire, having such a distinguished commander on the scene."

"Ah, yes," the Emperor sighed. "Laurent Zai, the hero of

Dhantu. It would be a pity to lose him. But an inspiration, perhaps."

"But you said the Rix force was small, m'lord. Surely in a hostage rescue, the captain himself wouldn't . . ."

"To lose him to an Error of Blood, I meant. Should he fail."

The Emperor moved to stand, and Oxham rose on uncertain legs. The garden lightened again, obliterating the false hills of grain, the godlike feline statues, the Eighty Worlds. The faceted sky overhead seemed for a moment fragile, a ludicrous folly, a house of glass cards ready to be toppled by a breath.

As preposterous and shattery as love, she thought.

"I must prepare for war, Senator Oxham."

"I leave you, Your Majesty," she managed.

Nara Oxham wound her way out of the garden, blind to its distractions, blending the Emperor's words into one echoing thought:

To lose him, should he fail.

Executive Officer

Katherie Hobbes paused to gather herself before entering the observation blister. Her report was essential to the captain's survival. This was no time to be overwhelmed by childhood fears.

She remembered her gravity training on the academy orbital *Phoenix*. The orbital, stationed low over Home, was reoriented every day at random. Through the transparent outer ceilings and floors, the planet might be hanging overhead, looming vertiginously below, or tilted at any imaginable angle. The orbital's artificial gravity, already compromised by the proximity of Home, was likewise reconfigured throughout the academy on an hourly basis. The routes between stations (which had to be traversed quickly in the short intervals between classes) might require a dozen changes in orientation; the gravity direction of each corridor shifted without pattern. Only a few hasty markings sprayed onto the rollbars showed what was coming when you flipped from hall to hall.

The objective of all this chaos was to break down the two-dimensional thinking of a gravity-well–born human. The *Phoenix* had no up nor down, only the arbitrary geography of room numbers, coordinates, and classroom seating charts.

Of course, in the career of a naval officer, gravity was one of the mildest crises of subjectivity to overcome. For most cadets, the Time Thief, who stole your friends and family, was far more devastating than a wall turned overnight into a floor. But for Hobbes, the loss of an absolute *down* had always remained the greatest perversion of space travel.

Despite her long career in arbitrary gravity, Hobbes maintained a healthy fear of falling.

So, as always, stepping into the captain's observation blister brought on the old vertigo. It was like walking the plank, Hobbes supposed. But a plank was at least visible. She knew not to look down at her boots as they passed from the hypercarbon floor of the airlock onto the transparent surface of the blister. Instead, Hobbes kept her eyes focused on Captain Zai, finding security in his familiar form. Standing at a graceful parade rest with his back to her, he seemed suspended in space. The black wool of his uniform blended with the void, the piping of the garment, his head, and the trademark gray gloves hovering disembodied until Hobbes's eyes adjusted to the darkness. It was almost noon down at the palace, so the sun was at the *Lynx*'s stern. The only light came from Legis XV, a full green bauble shining over Zai's left shoulder. At the 60,000-klick distance of geosynchronous orbit (a long day, that world), it was not the angry, bloated disk it had been during the rescue attempt. Now it was merely a baleful eye.

Hobbes looked at the planet with hatred. It had killed her captain.

"Executive officer reporting, sir."

"Report," Zai said, still facing the void.

"In doing the postmortem—" The word froze in her mouth. She had not considered its original meaning in this context.

"Appropriate choice of terms, Executive Officer. Continue."

"In doing the PM, sir, we've discovered some anomalies."

"Anomalies?"

Hobbes looked at the useless hard encryption key in her hand. She had carefully prepared presentation files of the findings, but there were no hardscreens here in the observation blister. No provision for hi-res display, except for the spectacle of the universe itself. The images she intended to show would reveal nothing in low-res synesthesia. She would have to make do with words alone.

"We have determined that Private Ernesto was killed by friendly fire."

"The railgun bombardment?" Zai asked sadly, ready to add another measure of guilt to his failure.

"No, sir. The initiate's varigun."

His hands clenched. "Idiots," he said softly.

"A governor-override was triggered on the initiate's weapon, sir. It tried to warn him not to fire."

Zai shook his head, his voice sinking deeper into melancholy. "I imagine Barris didn't know what the alarm meant. We were fools to have issued him a weapon at all. Stupidity in the Political Apparatus is no anomaly, Hobbes."

Hobbes swallowed at the blunt talk, especially with two politicals still on board. Of course, the captain's blister, featureless and temporary, was the most secure station on the ship. And Zai was beyond punishment in any case. The death of the Child Empress—her brain was damaged beyond reanimation by the Rix blaster, Adept Trevim herself had confirmed—constituted an Error of Blood.

But this wasn't like the captain, this passivity. He had been quieter since his promotion, she thought, or perhaps since his captivity on Dhantu. As Zai turned around, Hobbes noticed the slight creases in the line of his jaw marking the physical reconstruction. What a star-crossed career, she thought. First that unfathomably horrible imprisonment, then an impossible hostage situation.

"That's not the only anomaly, sir," she said, speaking carefully now. "We've also taken a good look at Corporal Lao's helmet visuals."

"Good man, Corporal Lao," Zai muttered. The Vadan gender construction sounded odd to Hobbes's ear, as it always did. "But visuals? She was cut off by the field."

"Yes, sir. There were, however, a few windows of transmission. Long enough for armor diagnostics and even some visuals to upload."

Zai looked at her keenly, the lost, philosophical expression finally leaving his craggy features. Hobbes knew he was interested now.

The captain *had* to look at the visuals from Lao's helmet. The weapons and armor of orbital marines communicated continuously with the ship during action, uploading equipment status, the health of the marine, and pictures from the battle. The helmet visuals were low-grade monochrome at only nine frames per second, but they were wrapped three-sixty, and sometimes revealed more than the marines themselves had seen.

Zai simply must look at them before he put a blade of error to his belly. And it was up to Executive Officer Katherie Hobbes to make sure that he did.

"Sir, the entry wound on the Rix commando looks like a direct hit."

There. She'd said it. Hobbes felt a single drop of sweat mark a course down her back where standing at attention left a space between wool and skin. A careful analysis of this conversation, such as the Apparatus might one day make, could draw near the theory Hobbes and some of the other officers had begun tacitly to entertain.

"Executive Officer," her captain said, drawing himself to his full height, "are you by any chance trying to . . *save* me?"

Hobbes was ready for this.

"Sir, 'The study of the battle already fought is as essential as that of the battle to come.' Sir."

" 'Engagement,' " Zai corrected, evidently preferring an earlier translation. But he seemed pleased, as he always was when Hobbes quoted the old war sage Anonymous 167. The captain even managed a smile, the first she'd seen on his face since the Empress's death. But then it turned bitter.

"Hobbes, in my hand is a blade of error, of sorts."

He opened one hand to reveal a small black rectangle. It was a single-purpose, programmable remote.

"Captain?"

"A little-known fact: For the elevated, the blade of error can take almost any form. It's a matter of choice. General Ricard Tash and his volcano, for example."

Hobbes frowned as she remembered the old tale. One of the first Errors, a lost battle during the Consolidation of Home. It had never occurred to her that Tash's suicide had involved some special dispensation. The prospect of scalding magma didn't seem so inviting as to require one.

"Sir? I'm not sure—"

"This remote is programmed to invoke a high-emergency battle-stations status in the *Lynx*, overriding every safety protocol," he explained, turning the remote over in his hand like a worry stick. "A standard command sequence, actually, useful for blockade patrols."

Hobbes bit her lip. What was she missing here?

"Of course, the captain's blister is not part of the battle-ready configuration of the *Lynx*, is it, Hobbes?"

A fresh wave of vertigo struck Katherie Hobbes, as surely as if the ship's gravity had flipped upside down without warning. She closed her eyes, struggling to control the wild gyrations of her balance, listing to herself the rote procedures of emergency battle stations: bulkheads sealed, weapons crash-charged, full extension of the energy-sink manifold, and blowing the atmosphere in any temporary, acceleration-sensitive constructions such as the blister she stood in now. There were safeties, of course, but they could be countermanded.

She felt as if she were falling, tumbling through the void with this all-but-dead man.

When she opened her eyes, he had taken a step closer, concern on his face.

"Sorry, Katherie," he said softly. "But you had to know. You'll be in command when it comes. No rescue attempts, understand? I don't want to wake up in an autodoc with my eyeballs burst out."

"Of course, sir," she managed, her voice sounded rough, as if a cold were coming on. She swallowed, a reflexive response to vertigo, and tried not to imagine the captain's face after decompression. That horrible transformation was something that *couldn't* happen. She would simply have to save him.

He stepped past her into the open door of the blister's airlock, leaving the black field of stars for solid metal. She followed him into the lock and rolled the reassuringly massive door into its sealed position.

"Now," Captain Zai said as the inner door opened, "I should like to see these visuals. 'No mark of war is too minute to reward careful study,' aye, Hobbes?"

"Aye, sir." Anonymous 167 again.

As she followed her captain to the command bridge, glad to have her feet on dense hypercarbon and hullalloy, Katherie Hobbes allowed herself to shelter an uncertain candle of hope.

compound mind

Alexander flexed itself, feeling the ripple of its will promulgate through the infostructure of Legis XV.

The hostage crisis had for a time interrupted the normal flux of information across the planet. Market trading had been suspended, schools closed, the powers of the unwieldy Citizen's Assembly assumed by the Executive Diet. But now that the Imperials had retaken the palace, activity was beginning to rebuild in the world's arteries of data and interchange.

A few days of mourning would be observed soon, but for now the Empress's death was a closely guarded secret. Legis XV had survived its brief Rix occupation, and at the moment there was an outpouring of relief, a release of nervous energies throughout the intertwined systems of commerce, politics, and culture.

As for the existence of Alexander in their midst, the compound mind had not yet created panic. Once the population realized that their phones, databooks, and home automatics had not turned on them, the mind seemed more a curiosity than a threat—a ghost in the machine that had yet to prove itself unfriendly, whatever the propaganda of the grays.

And so the planet awoke.

Alexander felt this increasing activity as new and sudden vigor. The first day of consciousness had been exhilarating, but the compound mind now realized the true vitality of Legis XV. The planet's surge back into ordinary life—the shimmer of its billions, their commerce and politics—felt to the mind as if it were bursting anew from the shadowtime. The flowing data of secondary sight and audio, the clockwork of traffic management, water purification, weather control, even the preparations of the local military readying for another attack, were like the coursings of some morning stimulant through its body public.

Certainly, there were belated attempts by the Imperials to destroy Alexander. Data shunts and hunter programs were deployed, attempting to erase the influence of the Rix propagation, trying to tear down the self-conscious feedback that now illuminated the planet's infostructure. But the efforts were too late. What the Rix had long understood, and the benighted Imperials could not truly grasp, was that a compound mind is the *natural* state of affairs. As Rixia Henderson herself had theorized in the early days of Amazon, all systems of sufficient complexity tend toward self-organization, self-replication, and finally self-consciousness. All of biological and technological history was, for the Rix, a reflection of this essential law, as inescapable as entropy. Rixia Henderson's philosophy superseded such notions as social progress, the invisible hand of the marketplace, and the zeitgeist—shallow vanities all. The narrative of history itself was nothing more than the working out of the one law: humanity is but the raw material of greater minds. So Alexander, once born, could not be destroyed—unless technological civilization on Legis XV were itself destroyed.

The compound mind breathed deep its existence, surveying the vast energies of its domain. At last, the Rix had come to the Risen Empire, bringing the light of consciousness.

The only sectors of Legis XV that remained dark to Alexander were the gray enclaves, the cities of the dead that dotted the planet. The walking corpses of the Risen Empire eschewed technology and consumerism, so the phone calls and purchases and traffic patterns that informed Alexander's consciousness were missing. There was an appalling absence of bustle and friction from the afterlives of the dead. The needs that underlay technology—to buy and sell, to communicate, to politic and argue—did not exist in the gray enclaves. The risen walked quiet and alone in their necropolis gardens, perfomed simple arts by hand, went on their winding and pointless pilgrimages among the Eighty Worlds, and gave their allegiance to the Emperor. But they had no *struggles,* nothing from which true AI could arise.

Alexander puzzled over this strangely divided culture. The living citizens of the Empire engaged in rampant capitalism in pursuit of exotic pleasures and prestige; the risen were ascetic and detached. The warm participated in a fiercely fragmented, multiparty democracy; the cold univocally worshiped the Emperor. The two societies—one chaotic and vital, the other a static monoculture—not only coexisted, but actually seemed to maintain a productive relationship. Perhaps they each provided a necessary facet of the body politic: change versus stability, conflict versus consensus. But the division was terribly rigid, formed as it was by the barrier of death itself.

The Rix Cult did not recognize hard boundaries, especially between animate and inanimate; Rixwomen (they had disposed of the unnecessary gender) moved freely along the continuum between organic and technological, picking and choosing from the strengths of each. Rix immortality avoided a specific moment of death, preferring the slow transformation of Uprade. And the Rix, of course, worshiped the compound mind, an admixture of human activities mediated by machines, the ultimate blending of flesh and metal, giving rise to Mind.

Alexander mused that this gulf of sensibilities was why Empire and Cult must be forever at war. The staid traditions of the grays were antithetical to compound minds' very existence; the risen stilted competition and activity, vitality and change. The dead had choked the progress of the Empire, and made it poorer ground for the Rix to sow the seeds of their gods.

The mind's thoughts turned to the data it had gleaned from the Child Empress's confidant, the strange device wound into the dead girl. The child was now permanently destroyed by some folly of her Imperial rescuers, but Alexander was still confused about her. The mind found it hard to fathom the confidant's purpose. That was a strange thing in itself. Alexander could reach into any machine, transaction, or message on the planet and grasp it completely, having full access to the world's data reservoirs, the soup of information out of which meaning was constructed. But this one device made no sense; no instruction manuals, schematics, or medical contraindications existed for it, anywhere. It had contained no mass-produced components, and stored its internal data in a unique format. The confidant was devoid of meaning, an itch of absent understanding.

As it plumbed the planetary libraries in vain, Alexander slowly began to realize that this confidant had been a secret. It was singular and strangely invisible. No one on Legis XV had ever patented or purchased anything like the device, discussed it on the newsfeeds, scribbled a picture of it on a work tablet, or even mentioned it in a diary entry.

It was, in short, a secret of global—perhaps *Imperial*—proportions.

Alexander felt a warm rush of interest, a scintillation of energy like the fluctuations of the planet's seven private currencies when the markets opened. It knew, if only from the millions of novels and plays and games that informed its sense of drama, that when governments kept secrets, they did so at their peril.

So Alexander began closer analysis of the scant data it had wrung from the confidant in those few moments it had assumed control. The machine had evidently been designed to monitor the Empress's body, a strange accessory for one of the immortal dead. Her health should have been perfect, forever. To Alexander, the confidant's recordings were noise, the data obviously encrypted with a one-time pad. The pad must exist somewhere on Legis, somewhere off the nets. The compound mind remembered its few seconds inside the confidant, before the device had destroyed itself to avoid capture. For a moment, Alexander had seen the world through the machine's eyes.

Starting from that slender thread, it began to reverse-engineer the device, attempting to scry its purpose.

Perhaps there was another hostage of sorts to take, here on Legis XV. Some new lever to use against the Risen Empire, sworn enemy of all things Rix.

Initiate

The body lay blackened and flaking on the still-table, recognizable as a human only in the grossest aspect of its limbs, trunk, and head. But Initiate Viran Farre stood back, wary of the charred corpse as if it were capable of sudden motion—some swift reprisal against those who had failed to protect it. Three more humans and the Rix commando lay, similarly burned, on the other tables in the room. These were the five who had been killed in the council chamber.

Officially, Initiate Farre and Adept Trevim had claimed possession of their remains in case one of them were fit to rise. But clearly any such reanimation lay beyond the Miracle of the Symbiant; these people had been destroyed. The politicals' real purpose was to cut open the Child Empress's body, and make sure that all evidence of the Emperor's Secret was eliminated.

Farre felt a strange hollow in her stomach, a void filled only with an ominous flutter, like the anxious lightness of sudden freefall. She had performed the administration of the symbiant many times, and was no stranger to dead bodies.

But this palpable presence of the Emperor's Secret made war against her conditioning. She wanted to blot out the sight of the Empress's fallen body, run from the room and order the building burned down. Adept Trevim had ordered Farre to steel herself, however; the initiate's medical knowledge was necessary here. And Farre was also conditioned to obey her superiors.

"Which of these saws, Farre?"

Farre took a deep breath, and forced her eyes to take in the array of monofilament incisors, vibrasaws, and beam cutters on the autopsy table. The tools were arranged by kind and size, the backmost raised on the stepped table like a jury, or the excavated teeth of some ancient predator displayed by form and function: here the gnashers, here the renders, here the grinding molars.

"I would stay away from beam cutters, Adept. And we haven't the skill for monofilaments." The confidant was made of nervous tissue, and would be a delicate extraction. They needed to open the body in the least destructive way.

"A vibrasaw, then?" Trevim suggested.

"Yes," Farre managed.

She selected a small one, and set it to its thinnest and shortest cutting width, just enough to slice through the rib cage. Farre handed it to the adept, and winced at the dead woman's clumsy grip on the tool. Farre, who had been a doctor before her induction into the Emperor's service, should by rights be performing the autopsy. But the conditioning was too profound. It was all she could do to assist; actually cutting into the corpse that housed the Secret would bring forth a calamitous reaction from her internal monitors.

The vibrasaw whirred to life in Trevim's hand, its whine like a mosquito caught inside one's eardrum. The sound seemed to put even the fifty-years-dead Adept on edge as she pressed the saw against the blackened corpse. But her strokes were smooth and clean, gliding through the charred flesh like a blade through water.

A mist rose up from the corpse, the faintest blur of gray in the air. Farre shuddered and reached for a medical mask. The mist looked like fine ash dust rising from a burned-out fire; indeed, it was in every chemical sense the same—fire-distilled carbon—but its source was human flesh rather than wood. Farre covered her mouth carefully, trying not to think of the small motes of dead Child Empress that would be trapped between the mask's fibers, or were settling even now into the pores of her exposed skin.

The Adept finished, having done almost too thorough a job. The vibrasaw had been set to undercut the connective tissues, and the Empress's rib cage lifted up easily in narrow strips as Trevim tugged. Farre leaned carefully forward, trying to quell the raging inhibitions of her conditioning. The exposed chest was almost abstract, like the plastic sculptures back in medical school; the titanic heat from the Rix blaster having burned gristle and tissue to a dark, dry mass.

"And now a nerve locator?"

Farre shook her head. "They only work on living subjects. Or the very recently dead. You'll need a set of nervous-tissue–seeking nanoprobes and a remote viewer, along with a troweling rod." She took another deep breath. "Let me show you."

The Adept moved aside as Initiate Farre sprayed the nanoprobes onto the glistening chest cavity. Farre let them propagate, then inserted the rod carefully, watching its read-out to make sure she didn't damage the delicate strands of the confidant's skein. The troweling rod's nimble fingers, thin as piano wire, began to work the flesh, teasing the tissue from the Empress's body.

But Farre had only progressed a few centimeters when she realized what she was doing, and a wave of nausea struck her.

"Adept . . ." she managed.

Trevim lifted the instrument delicately from Farre's fingers as she staggered back from the still-table.

"That will do nicely, Initiate," she heard Trevim say. "I think I see how it works. Thank you."

The images stayed unshakeably in her mind's eye as she sank heavily to the floor. The Emperor's sister, Child Empress Anastasia, Reason for the symbiant, splayed open like a roasted pig.

Vulnerable. Injured. The Secret exposed!

And she, Viran Farre, had participated. Her stomach heaved, and acid bile rose into her throat. The taste destroyed all will, and she retched pitifully as the adept continued to remove the confidant from the fallen Empress.

Captain

Laurent Zai dropped the single-purpose remote into his pocket. It wasn't actually programmed to do anything yet—he hardly wanted to kill himself *accidentally*. He'd simply wanted to show ExO Hobbes the manner in which he intended to commit suicide. As a warrior, he had always borne the prospect of a messy end, but an awkward changeover of command was unacceptable.

Zai felt a strange calmness as he followed Hobbes to the command bridge. The anxiety that consumed Zai during the hostage situation was gone. Over the last two years, love had compromised his bravery, he realized now. Hopelessness had returned it to him in good working order.

Zai wondered why the *Lynx* had been equipped with two bridges. The warship was a new class, unlike any of the Navy's *Acinonyx* frigates, and a few of its design concepts had seemed odd to Zai. In addition to a battle bridge, the ship had a command bridge, as if an admiral would one day want to command a fleet from a frigate. The second bridge had wound up being used as a very well-equipped conference room.

When Zai and Hobbes entered, the officers present snapped to attention. The command bridge was optimized for flatscreen viewing, the conference table folded out like a jackknife, all seats facing the hi-res screen. The officers' eyes met Zai's with nervous determination, as if they had been planning a mutiny.

Or plotting to save their captain's life.

"At ease," Zai ordered, taking the shipmaster's chair. He turned to Hobbes. "Make your report, Executive Officer."

Hobbes glanced anxiously at the hardkey she'd been worrying in her hand during their discussion in the observation bubble, as if suddenly unsure that it was up to the task. Then, with a grim look, she shoved it into a slot before her.

The vibration of the table's boot sequence shimmered under Zai's hand. He noted the shift of shadows in the room as overhead lights dimmed and the billions of picture elements on the wall warmed to their task. He saw his officers relax a little, as people always did when preparing to watch a canned presentation, no matter how grim the situation. Now that Zai faced death, details had become terribly clear to him. But this clarity was like amplified secondary sight, sharp but somehow distant. The marrow of these quotidian details had been lost along with his future, as if his experiences had become suddenly worthless, like some currency decommissioned overnight.

The screen showed a grainy image, its colors flattened into gray-scale—the unavoidable signal loss of a helmet-sized transmitter narrowcasting all the way to low orbit. The picture seemed stretched, the pulled-taffy visuals of a marine's 360-degree vision. It took a few moments for Zai's visual cortex to adapt to the view, like struggling to understand pre-Diaspora Anglish for the first few minutes of some ancient play.

Then figure and ground sorted themselves out, and he could make out a Rix soldier, a blood-spattered admiral, an off-balance Dr. Vechner, and the body of one Empress Anastasia Vista Khaman. All were frozen, their motion suspended, the horror of the situation oddly aestheticized by the rough grain of the medium.

"This is 67:21:34," Hobbes announced, her airmouse hovering in front of the timecode on the screen. "Exactly fifteen seconds before the stasis field was first activated by Corporal Lao." She named the participants, the airmouse flitting like a curious hummingbird from one to the next.

"Note that there are no visible wounds on the Empress. Blood is visible on her and the admiral, but it's spread evenly across them. It probably belongs to the Rix commandos, who had been railgunned from orbit with structure-penetrating exsanguination slugs."

The airmouse shifted in response to these words, seeming to sniff the entry wound on the Rix commando. Zai had to admit that it looked like a square hit. Her guts should have been sucked out in buckets. How could she have survived?

"Now, I'll advance it to the point where the stasis field interrupts transmission."

The figures jolted into action, Vechner stumbling, Lao's helmet voice calling *"Come, sir,"* and dragging him toward the Empress. Lao deployed the field generator and her fingers reached for the controls; then the screen went black.

"Now," Hobbes said, "to focus on certain elements. First, the Empress."

The fifteen seconds replayed on the screen, with the Empress's image highlighted. She was shaking uncontrollably, having some sort of seizure. The admiral restrained the Empress as if she were a living child thrashing her way through a nightmare.

"Obviously, the Child Empress is alive. Under some sort of stress, perhaps wounded, but alive. Now, observe the Rixwoman."

The scene replayed, and Zai felt himself gaining familiarity with the short document. The highlighted Rix commando was completely still.

"She's dead," First Pilot Maradonna said to the room.

"Or playing dead," Captain Zai responded.

"That's possible, sir," Hobbes allowed. "The Rix physiology is not pulsitile. Which means they don't take lungfuls of air, they filter it continuously. And their hearts spin rather than beating."

"So they are naturally motionless on the surface, no matter the resolution."

"Yes, sir. But allow me to skip forward to the visuals received when the situation had been secured, when Lao briefly lowered the stasis field. This is from Dr. Vechner's helmet."

The screen was refreshed with a new tableau. Vechner knelt beside the Empress. The airmouse moved to indicate the Rix soldier; she apparently hadn't moved in the interim. Hobbes left this fact unspoken.

"Note the ultrasound wrap around the Empress," Hobbes continued. "As we advance, you can see her heart beating within."

The image moved forward for five seconds, then the stasis field went back up and cut off the transmission again. But the heartbeat was clearly visible. The Empress had still been alive at that point.

Damn, Zai thought. They'd been so close.

"Why don't we have data from the ultrasound wrap?" he asked. "Shouldn't it have automatically connected with the *Lynx* medical AI?"

"Unfortunately, the security protocols require more than five seconds to complete, sir. There are extensive firewalls against viruses being loaded onto the *Lynx* in the guise of emergency medical data."

Zai wondered who'd tried that little trick in the past. It sounded like typical Tungai sabotage.

"Now from Corporal Lao's perspective again," Hobbes continued. "The new marine in the picture is Initiate Barris. His armor was crashed on captain's orders, as he had just killed another marine with friendly fire."

Barris's motionless armor lay just outside the field area. When the image advanced, Lao reached out and dragged him inside the protective perimeter.

"Lao is moving to protect a fallen comrade," Hobbes said dryly.

Barris rolled over. His face was an appalling mess, a wreckage of tissues damaged by a bad atmospheric entry.

"*Rix . . . here,*" Barris's twisted face said.

Lao's hand darted for the field generator's controls again, and the image went dark.

"There were no Rix in the palace at that point," Hobbes said firmly. "Nor had Barris seen any Rix at all. For some reason, he lied."

Zai shook his head. "He'd just had a firefight with another marine, whom he must have thought was Rix. Initiate Barris wasn't lying, just unbelievably stupid."

"Can we see Barris's visuals?" someone asked. "From when he killed the marine?"

"I'm afraid his helmet transmitter was trashed on entry. But we do have that event from the other side."

New visuals loaded onto the screen. The administrative text identified the viewpoint as Private Ernesto. From a kneeling position, he held a position in front of the council chamber's door, facing out into the palace's broad hallways. The black hemisphere of the stasis field could be seen in Ernesto's rearmost vision.

Initiate Barris, recognizable from his smashed helmet, staggered into view. Ernesto waved at him, but Barris raised his weapon.

The initiate's varigun fired, and Ernesto's viewpoint spun as he was knocked back by a hail of small projectiles. The barrage went on, the damage to suit and soldier recorded in grim little glyphs along the bottom of the screen. A second before Ernesto must have died, the armor lost its ability to transmit, and the screen froze.

"Not much fog of war there," Maradonna commented.

"Barris would have to override the friendly-fire governor," the marine sergeant added. Zai wondered if these observations had been scripted in advance. What were his senior staff suggesting, anyway? That the initiate had gone in purposefully to kill Ernesto? Or the Empress, for that matter?

That was unthinkable. Politicals were bound by governors far more insurmountable than some failsafe on a varigun. Their minds were fixed to a state of selfless loyalty by years of painful conditioning; on some gray planets, they were selected from birth for genes that showed high susceptibility to brainwashing. They were beyond suspicion.

"The fog was in Barris's mind," Zai said. "He'd suffered a grevious head injury on entry. He probably thought every suit of armor he saw was Rix."

"Exactly, sir," Hobbes agreed. " 'Rix . . . here.' His last recorded words."

The screen split into three parts. In the first two frames, the Rix soldier lay in her now familiar position, looking dead as ever. But in the last frame her body was a blackened husk, even the marble floor beneath her scorched by the blaster shot that had killed everyone inside the stasis field. It was evident now from the trio of images: all three positions were much the same. Although the commando's body had been jostled by the blast, there was no sense that she had sprung back to life and raised her weapon. Indeed, in the last frame the ruined Rix blaster lay across her left ankle, much closer to the burned hands of Barris than her own.

"Where is the initiate's weapon?" someone asked.

Hobbes's response was instantaneous. These questions must be scripted, Zai thought with growing annoyance. The screen again showed the last recording from Lao's viewpoint. As she dragged Farre's body into the stasis field's perimeter, his varigun stayed outside. He had dropped it when the *Lynx* had crashed his armor.

A murmur came from the assembled officers.

"He had no weapon," Hobbes said. "But the Rix blaster was already within—"

"Hobbes!" Captain Zai snapped.

The anger in his voice shocked the room into silence. The officers sat as motionless as the image from doomed Mi- rame Lao's helmet.

"Thank you all for this briefing," Zai said. "Executive Of- ficer, in my observation blister. Now."

He stood and wheeled away from the surprised faces, and strode from the command bridge. He was gone so fast that it took a few moments for Katherie Hobbes to catch up in the corridors outside.

Zai and his executive officer walked in silence back to- ward the plastic bubble that faced the void.

Commando

The commando's heart, if you could call it that, was closer to a turbine than a pump. A pair of long screws, one venous and the other arterial, rotated inside her chest, threading the vital fluid through her body at an inhumanly fast and even rate. The liquid carried oxygen and nutrients but was not, properly speaking, blood. It also served the purposes of a lymphatic system, transporting uptake nanos from thou- sands of tiny lymph nodes distributed along her arteries. The substance in the commando's veins had little else to do with her Rix immune system, however. It contained no white blood cells, whose functions had been delegated centuries before to a scattered population of organs roughly the size of rice grains, themselves generated by small machines hidden in the marrow of her bird-light, aircraft-strong, hypercarbon bones.

The surging fluid did, however, contain enough iron to oxydize red when it was spilled, a situation that the commando was currently attempting to avoid.

She was tucked into an area smaller than an overnight bag, a space that normally housed a cleaning robot. The Rix-woman had disassembled the previous occupant, hoping the scattered parts would not reveal her appropriation of its home, and folded herself into the space, limbs bending at sharp angles like some origami construction. According to the messages sent to her from Alexander, her invisible and omnipresent benefactor in this chase, the local militia were searching for her with sonic sweeps. These devices were designed to find escaped fugitives by detecting that steady, unstoppable, telltale rhythm of humanity: the heartbeat.

Apparently, no one had told the locals that she, a Rix commando, had none.

The tiny turbine purred inside her chest, an infrasonic hiss without rhythm or vibrato, and the nervous, soft-shoed sweep operators passed by her hiding place, blissfully unaware.

The commando, who was called h_rd, had gone to ground in a building that was called, in the local language, a *library*. This structure served as a distribution point for proprietary data, information not available in the public infostructure. Corporate secrets, technological patents, personal medical records, and certain erotic poems and images available by paid subscription were deposited here, accessible only to those with special physical keys, totems of information owner-ship. Alexander had guided h_rd here, helping the commando fight and creep her way across a hundred kilometers of dense city that swarmed with militia, police, and the occasional Imperial marine, all searching for her. But Alexander was a powerful ally, and even a single Rix commando was deadly quarry. The local forces made a show of the pursuit—evacuating buildings, running sweeps, and occasionally firing their weapons—but were more interested in self-preservation than glory. And the Imperial marines numbered fewer than a hundred.

The commando waited in the library with inhuman patience. For seven hours, she lay folded in her compartment.

It was strange here in the darkness, so alone. H_rd had spent her entire life in the intimate company of her dropsisters, never separated from the sibling group for more than a few minutes. The fifteen commandos in her dropship had been raised together, trained together into a perfect fighting unit, and were supposed to have died together. The commando felt no grief, an unknown emotion in her warrior caste, but she did mourn her lost sisters. Surviving this suicide mission alone had left her in limbo, ranging this hostile planet like the truant ghost of some unburied corpse. Only duty to the nascent Alexander kept her from mounting a sudden, glorious, and fatal counterattack against her pursuers, the quickest way to join her sisters.

Finally, the search moved on. A trail of clues—disrupted traffic monitors, inexplicably triggered fire alarms, disabled security devices—led her pursuers toward a planetary defense base at the southern edge of the city, which the Imperials moved hastily to reinforce. Alexander had orchestrated these deceptions as the commando lay motionless, teasing pursuit away. Let the Imperials guard their space defenses. The planet's armaments did not interest the compound mind; it wanted information.

Alexander sought secrets.

A tapping came on the metal door of the compartment, a tattoo in the distinctive rhythms of Rix battle language. The commando rolled out of her hiding place, unfolding into a human shape like a marionette pulled by its strings from a box, and found herself facing a small librarian drone. Alexander never narrowcast instructions to the Rixwoman; she was incompatible with the Empire-born mind. Rather, the compound mind guided its commando through a host of avatars—gardening robots, credit terminal screens, traffic signals sputtering battle binary. The drone wheeled about and headed down the hall of the still-evacuated library, its single rubber wheel emitting a mousy squeak as it accelerated. H_rd favored one leg as she followed, circulation returning with painful pricks and needles after the lengthy confinement. The librarian drone moved almost too fast for her, and its squeaking wheel tortured her high-frequency hearing. H_rd felt the slightest temptation to kick the small machine, even though it was a messenger of her god. It had been long seven hours in that compartment, and the Rix were not *completely* without emotion.

The librarian led h_rd to a staircase, and whirred down a spiral ramp scaled to its small size as she limped down the stairs in pursuit. They descended to a deep sub-basement of the library, a place of low ceilings, narrow hallways choked with unshelved data bricks, and dim red lighting tuned for sensitive drone eyes. The Rixwoman, her circulation restored by the long climb, slipped deftly after the squeaking librarian. In a dark corner of the sub-basement, reached through a heavy blast door and smelling of disuse, though it was *very* clean, the drone halted and extended its dataplug. It rapped on a shelf encased in metal and webbed with security fractals and the Imperial glyph for medical records (h_rd was fluent in Imperial Navy iconography).

H_rd charged her blaster, and cycled the weapon's output down to a cutting torch. She brought the whitehot finger at its muzzle across the dense weave of security fractal, melting circuitry and metal alike.

The library system detected this depredation, and sent a flurry of messages to the local police, the Political Apparatus, and the winter and summer homes of the Master Librarian. All these were intercepted by Alexander, who responded with the official codes for a maintainence procedure. This part of the library was rated for Apparatus-grade secrets, but even the most extensive security did not anticipate the entire *planet's* infostructure being in the hands of the enemy. In the data-systemic sense, of course, Alexander was not the enemy at all, merely an unwanted aspect of self. Like an auto-immune disease, the defensive measures of the body infometric had been turned against itself.

With the alarm quelled, the librarian drone watched quietly as h_rd worked. The metal of the security case was slowly reduced to burn-fringed panels stacked on the hallway floor. Smoke rose to curl around insensate detectors on the ceiling, and the drone reached its dataplug into the case and began to probe one brick after another, searching for the faint scent of the data it sought: the secret implementation specs of the Empress's confidant, the key that would unlock its recordings of her final moments alive.

The compound mind smiled as fresh information began to trickle in through the narrow pipeline of the drone's dataplug. Alexander was the master, *was the data* here on Legis XV. Whatever secrets it chose to seek would eventually be found.

Soon, another weapon would be in its hands.

Senator

"So I was right."

Roger Niles had said this at least five times over the last hour. He repeated it with the glazed look of someone told of a friend's unexpected death, the periodic iterations necessary to fight off fresh surges of disbelief.

"You sound surprised," Oxham said.

"I was hoping to be wrong."

They were in Niles's den, the most secure room among her senatorial offices. The jagged spires of communication gear reddened in the setting sun, soaking the insect cities in blood. Niles was half in data fugue, trying to predict who the other members of the War Council might be. Oxham wanted forewarning about the personalities who would surround her in council, the agendas and constituencies that would be represented there.

"One from the Lackey Party," Niles said. "Probably not toothless old Higgs, though. The Emperor will pick whoever is really running things in Loyalty these days."

"Raz imPar Henders."

"What makes you say that? He's first-term."

"So am I. He's the new power in Loyalty."

"His seat isn't even safe."

"I can feel it, Roger."

Niles frowned, but Oxham could see his fingers begin to flicker as he redirected his efforts.

The senator hovered in her own synesthetic wash of data, searching the Forum gossip channels and open caucuses, the newswires and polling engines. She wanted to know if her legislation, presented and then hastily withdrawn, had left any traces on the body politic. Somewhere in the hordes of media analysts, muckrakers, and political junkies, someone must have wondered what that strange and massive omnibus meant. It was only a matter of time before someone with the interest and expertise would decode the legislation, unraveling the skein of taxes, liens, and laws.

Of course, in a few days—possibly hours—the news of the Rix raid would become public. Hopefully, the reordering of power alignments and alliances, the panicked shift of markets and resources, the tidal data-surge of war would overwhelm any notice of her legislation. That was fine with Oxham. It was one thing to take jabs at the Emperor in times of peace, quite another when Empire was threatened, and still another when sitting on his War Council. Most importantly, the young senator didn't want it to look as if her seat on the council had been bought with the withdrawal of the legislation.

At least, it hadn't seemed that way to her.

"Someone from the Plague Axis, as well," Niles announced.

"Why, for heaven's sake?"

"I can feel it," he said flatly.

Oxham smiled. Thirty years into their shared career, and he still hated when she made appeals to her empathy. It offended his sense of politics as a human enterprise, as *the* human enterprise. Niles still felt that the offshoots of synesthetic implants were somehow . . . superhuman.

But the Plague Axis? He must be kidding. The Risen Empire was riven between the living and the dead, and the Plague Axis were a sort of twilight zone. They were the carriers of ancient diseases, and the repositories of the old congenital defects. When humanity had started governing its own genetic destiny millennia before, too few traits had been selected for, and hordes of information irretrievably lost. Too late, eugenists had realized that most "undesirable" traits concealed advantages: sickle cell conferred resistance to dormant diseases; autism was inextricably linked to genius; certain cancers stabilized whole populations in ways that were not entirely understood. The Plague Axis, germline-natural humans subject to every whim of evolution, were essential to maintain the limited diversity of an overengineered population. They were the controls in the vast experiment that was Imperial humanity.

But to have them represented in the War Council? Oxham might have her own infirmity, her own madness, but she still shivered at the thought of lepers.

The senator brought forward the list she and Niles had constructed. By tradition, the council would have nine members, including the Emperor. Balance was the main priority;

for the Senate to delegate real warmaking power to the council, all factions had to be represented. The major power blocs of Empire were relatively fixed, but the individual pieces that would fit into each of those places at the table were as variable as cards in a hand of poker. How the Emperor filled those spaces would determine the course of this war.

Interrupting these thoughts, a chime sounded in her secondary hearing, a powerful signal that broke through all other data. The note was low-pitched, the steady, awesome sound of the largest pipe on a church organ. But it carried a froth of higher frequencies: the indistinct breath of a distant sea, the fluttering of birds' wings, the stray high pitches of an orchestra tuning. The sound was sovereign, unmistakable.

"Council is called," Nara Oxham said.

She could see the overlays of secondary sight falling away from Niles's face, his attention slowly focusing on the here and now, like some subterranean creature emerging into unfamiliar sunlight.

With his dataveil removed, Niles regarded her through limpid eyes, his powerful mind for once reflected in his gaze. He spoke carefully.

"Nara, do you remember the crowds?"

He meant the crowds on Vasthold, back in her first campaigns, when she had finally put the terror of madness behind her.

"Of course, Roger. I remember."

Unlike those of most of the Empire, Vasthold's politics had never become hostage to the media feeds. There, politics was a kind of street theater. Issues were fought out face-to-face in the dense cities, in the house-to-house combat of street parades, in basement gatherings, and around park bonfires. Impromptu debates, demonstrations, and out-and-out brawls were the order of the day. To escape her old fear of masses of people, Oxham had agreed to deliver a nominating speech at a political rally. But with a willful perversity, she had only partially suppressed her empathy that day, daring the childhood demons to visit again. At first, the roiling psyches of the crowd assumed their familiar shape, a massive beast of ego and conflict, a hungry storm that wanted to consume her, incorporate her into its raging glut of passions. But Oxham had become an adult, her own ego grown stronger behind the protective barrier of the apathy drug. With her image and voice augmented by the public address system, she shouted down the old demons, rode the throng like a wild horse, worked their emotions with words, gestures, even the rhythm of her breathing. That day, she found that on the other side of terror could be found . . . power.

Niles nodded; he had watched those powerful memories cross her face.

"We're very far from them now, those crowds. In the pretense of this place, it's easy to forget the real world that you came here to represent."

"I haven't forgotten, Roger. Remember, I haven't been awake as long as you. For me, it's only been two years, not ten."

One hand went to his graying hair, a smile on his face.

"Just remember then," he said. "Your cunning whorls of legislation will now represent acts of war: violence will be done and lives lost in the name of every decision you make."

"Of course, Roger. You have to understand, the Rix frontier isn't as far away as all that. Not for me."

A frown appeared on his face. She hadn't told anyone, not even Niles, about her affair with Laurent Zai. It had seemed such a brief and sudden thing. And now it was, in Niles's framework, over a decade ago.

"Someone very close to me is there, Niles. He's at the front. I'll keep him in mind, as a stand-in for all those distant, threatened lives."

Roger Niles's eyes narrowed, his high forehead wrinkling with surprise. His powerful mind must be searching for whom she might mean. Oxham was glad to know that she could still keep some things secret from her chief advisor.

She was pleased that she had told no one; the affair remained hers and Laurent's alone.

Senator Nara Oxham rose. The sound of the Imperial summons hadn't faded completely from her secondary hearing; the chime shimmered like the toll of some giant bell vibrating into perpetuity. Oxham wondered if it might actually get louder should she fail to answer its summons.

Niles's face became distant again, easing back into data. Oxham knew that after she had gone, he would worry her words, and would plumb the vast store of his datatrove to discover whom she meant. And that eventually he would discover Laurent Zai.

And it crossed her mind that by then, her lover might already be dead.

"I take your concerns with me, Roger. This war is very real."

"Thank you, Senator. The trust of Vasthold is with you."

The old ritual phrase, to which Senators were sworn before they left Vasthold for fifty years. Niles uttered it so sadly that she turned to look at his face again. But already the veil had fallen over him. He descended into his virtual realm, searching an empire's worth of data for answers to . . . a war.

For a moment, he looked small and forlorn under his towering equipment, the weight of Empire upon him, and she stopped at the door. She had to show him, to let Niles see the token of love she carried.

"Roger."

Oxham held up a small black object in her hand, striped with yellow warning circuitry. A single-purpose remote, encoded with a Senatorial Urgent message. It was marked with her personal privilege—highest priority transmission over the Empire's entanglement net, one-time encryption, sealed eyes-only under Penalty of Blood—and keyed to her DNA, her pheromonal profile, and voiceprint.

Niles looked at the object, his eyes clearing. She had his attention.

"I may be using this while sitting in the War Council. Will it work from the Diamond Palace?"

"Yes. Legally speaking, the Rubicon Pale extends from the Forum to wherever you go, along a nanometer-wide gerrymander."

She smiled, visualizing this baroque legal fiction.

"How long will it take the message to get to Legis XV?"

His eyebrows raised at the planet's name. Now he knew that her lover was truly at the front.

"How long is the message?"

"One word."

Niles nodded. "Entangled communications are instantaneous, but unless the shared quantum packets the receiver is using were physically transported directly from Home—"

"They were," she said.

"So he's—"

"On a warship."

"Then, no time at all." Niles paused, searching Oxham's eyes for some sign of her intentions. "May I ask what the message is?"

"Don't," she said.

Executive Officer

Hobbes stood nervously at attention as Zai worked gestural codes at the small interface beside the observation blister's door.

She stared down into the void. The usual vertigo created by the transparent floor was gone, replaced by the crushing weight of failure. A dead, empty feeling pulsed in her gut. A bright taste like a metal coin under the tongue fouled her mouth. Her careful study of the hostage rescue, the sleepless hours spent poring over every frame of the engagement from dozens of viewpoints, had amounted to nothing. She had not saved her captain, had only managed to make him furious.

There seemed to be no way to bend the rigid spine of Zai's Vadan upbringing. No way to convince him that it had been the politicals and not military personel who had botched the rescue. The initiate had gone down against the captain's protests, waving an imperial writ; why couldn't Captain Zai see that he was blameless?

At least they should take the evidence before a military court. Zai was a hero, an elevated officer. He couldn't throw his life away for the sake of brutal, pointless tradition.

Executive Officer Hobbes was from a Utopian world, an anomaly among the military classes. She had rejected the hedonistic ways of her own homeworld, attracted by the rituals of the grays, their traditions and discipline. Their lives of service made the grays otherworldly to Katherie, uninterested in the brief pleasures of the flesh. For Hobbes, Captain Laurent Zai embodied this gray stoicism, quiet and strong on his cold bridge, his craggy face uncorrected by cosmetic surgery.

But underneath, Hobbes could see the wounded humanity in him: the marks of his unbelievable suffering on Dhantu, the melancholy dignity with which he carried himself, the regret every time he lost a "man."

And now her captain's sense of honor demanded suicide of him. Suddenly, the religious surety and gray traditions that Hobbes found so compelling seemed simply barbaric, a brutal web in which her captain had trapped himself, a willful and pathetic blindness. Zai's acquiescence was far more bitter than his anger.

He turned from the controls.

"Steady yourself," he ordered.

The floor lurched, as if the ship had accelerated. Hobbes

barely kept her footing, the universe become briefly un-hinged around her. Then the transparent surface under her stabilized, and she saw what had happened. The blister had become a true bubble, floating free of the ship, tethered only by the ship's gravity generators, filled only with the air and heat trapped within its walls. The gravity felt wrong, cast across the void by the *Lynx*'s generators to create a tentative *up* in this small pocket of air.

Hobbes's vertigo returned with a vengeance.

"We can talk freely now, Hobbes."

She nodded slowly, careful not to disturb her plaintive inner ear.

"You don't seem to understand what's at stake here," Zai said. "For the first time in sixteen centuries, a member of the Imperial household has *died*. And she was lost not to a freak accident, but to enemy action."

"Enemy action, sir?" she dared.

"Yes, dammit. The *Rix* caused all this!" he shouted. "It doesn't matter who pulled the trigger of that blaster. Whether it was a Rix playing dead or an imbecile political gone mad from an insertion injury: it doesn't matter. The Empress is dead. They won; we lost."

Hobbes focused on her boots, willing a visible floor into existence below them.

"You're about to have command of this vessel, Hobbes. You must understand that with command comes responsibility. I ordered that rescue. I must stand by its results, no matter what."

She looked at the space that separated them from the *Lynx*. No sound vibrations could cross that gap; the captain had made sure of that. She could speak freely.

"You objected to the initiate going down, sir."

"He had a writ, Hobbes. My objection was pointless posturing."

"Your rescue plan was sound, sir. The Emperor made the mistake, giving those fools a writ."

The captain sucked a harsh breath in through his teeth. However cautious Zai was being, Hobbes knew that he hadn't expected to hear words like this.

"That's *sedition*, Executive Officer."

"It's the truth, sir."

He took two steps toward her, closer than Vadan fastidiousness had ever allowed him before. He spoke clearly, in a voice just above a whisper.

"Listen, Hobbes. I'm dead. A ghost. There is no tomorrow for me, whatsoever. No *truth* can save me. You seem confused about that. And you also seem to think that the *truth* will protect you and the rest of the *Lynx*'s officers. It will not."

She could barely meet his gaze. A few flecks of saliva borne on his harsh words had reached her face. They stung her; they were shameful. The bright sun was rising behind the bulk of the *Lynx*. The blister's skin was polarized, but she could feel the temperature rising in the unregulated bubble. A trickle of sweat ran under one arm.

"If there are any more briefings like the one a few minutes ago, you'll be killing yourself *and* my other officers. I will not permit it."

She swallowed, blinked in the suddenly harsh sunlight. Dizziness rose in her. Was the oxygen running out so fast?

"Stop trying to save me, Hobbes! That's an order. Is it clear enough?"

She just wanted him to stop. She wanted to return to the solid boundaries of the ship. To surety and order. Safety from this void.

"Yes, sir."

"Thank you," he spat.

Captain Zai turned and took a step away, facing the bauble of Legis XV hanging in the blackness. He uttered a command, and she felt the tug of the frigate reclaiming its tiny satellite.

They said nothing more as the blister reattached itself to the *Lynx*. When the door opened, Zai dismissed her with a wave. She could see the black, single-purpose remote in his hand. His blade of error.

"Report to the bridge, Executive Officer. You will be needed there shortly."

To take command. A field promotion, they would call it.

"Do not disturb me again."

The executive officer obeyed, stepping from the blister into the rush of cool, fresh air that surged from the *Lynx*. Hobbes felt she should glance back at her captain, if only to create a last memory to replace that of his angry, spitting face, centimeters from hers. But she couldn't bring herself to turn around.

Instead, she wiped her face and ran.

Commando

The librarian drone puttered among the data bricks, a dull-witted child unsure of which toy to play with. It moved fitfully, searching for some secret entombed within their crisp, rectangular forms. H_rd, having emptied the security case, sat patiently by, listening for any sound from above.

At first, the library basement had made her nervous. The Rix didn't like being trapped belowground. She and her drop-sisters had been raised in space, tumbling into gravity wells only on training exercises and combat missions. H_rd felt crushed under the weight of metal and stone. An hour ago, she had left the fidgeting drone behind and reconnoitered the ground floor, installing motion alarms at each entrance. But the surrounding streets were empty; her pursuers had clearly moved on, following some false trail created by

Alexander. And this part of the city was still evacuated from the militia's search.

She and her drone had the library to themselves.

It was hard to imagine that the crude little device was actually animated by Alexander, an intelligence of planetary scale. The drone's single wheel allowed it to whir efficiently through the neat stacks, but here among the debris of the ruined case it was reduced to unsure, stuttering motions: a unicyclist negotiating a construction site. H_rd watched the comical display with a smile. Even the company of a speechless robot was better than being alone.

Suddenly, the drone seemed to flinch, plunging its dataplug farther into the brick before it with an obscene hunger. After a moment of vibrating wildly, the little device released the brick and spun around. Dodging debris with renewed vigor, it took off down the narrow aisle at top speed.

H_rd stood slowly, her body rippling as she went through a two-second regime that stretched each of her eleven hundred muscles in turn. No point in rushing; the drone could not outrun her. With a single leap, h_rd cleared the rubbish of her vandalism, then turned back toward the pile. She set her blaster low and wide, and sprayed the data bricks with enough radiation to erase their contents, and any clues as to what Alexander had found here. The fire suppression node above her head chirped, but was overridden before it could spray any foam.

H_rd turned and ran. In a few long-legged strides, she was right behind the little drone, strange companions in the dark stacks of the abandoned library. The whine of its monowheel blended with the subtler, ultrasonic whir of her servomotors.

She followed it up the ramps, through the basement levels and to the ground floor. The drone rolled squeaking among the staff desks, and through a portal in the wall scaled exactly to its size, like a door for pets. This obstacle course was designed for the drone's use, not that of two-meter amazons, and the challenge put a smile back on the commando's face. H_rd dove, leapt, and weaved, sticking close to her small charge, which brought her to a back office. The drone skidded to a halt beside an unruly pile of plastic squares, roughly the size of a human hand.

The Rixwoman picked one of the devices up. It was a secured handscreen, a rare physical storage and display device in a universe of omnipresent infostructure and secondary sight. Commandos, of course, fought on hostile worlds where the local infostructure was inaccessible, and h_rd had used such a device before. A library of this type would use them to allow its patrons to exit with sensitive information, the kind that had to stay outside the public sphere. The handscreen would be equipped with limited intelligence and governors to keep the wrong persons from accessing its contents.

The drone plugged into one of the devices, and the two were locked in a momentary, shuddering embrace. Then the screen hummed to life.

The Rixwoman took it from the drone. On the top page was a map of the planet, a route marked in pulsing colors. She worked the limited interface with her quick fingers, and found that the machine contained thousands of pages, a detailed plan for reaching her next goal: the entangled communications facility in the polar sink. The gateway of all information into and out of the Legis system.

Four thousand kilometers away.

H_rd sighed, and looked accusingly at the little drone.

Every Rix sibling group who had volunteered for this raid had realized that it was fundamentally a suicide mission. To plant the seed of a compound mind was a glorious blow against the Risen Empire, and the raiders had succeeded beyond all expectation. For the first time, a Rix mind had emerged upon an Imperial world. That a full-scale war might result was irrelevant. The Rix did not distinguish between states of war and peace with the various political entities that bordered upon their serpentine amalgam of bases. Their society was a constant jihad, a ceaseless missionary effort to propagate compound minds.

But four thousand kilometers through hostile territory? Alone?

Generally, suicide missions at least had the advantage of being brief.

H_rd flipped among the pages on the handscreen, and found a map of the planetary maglev system. At least she wouldn't have to walk. She also discovered the medical records of a particular conscript in the Legis militia, one who resembled h_rd, and had expertise necessary for the mission. The Rix commando realized that Alexander wanted her to go undercover, to pass as a standard Imperial human. How distasteful.

She moved toward the library exit. Best to take advantage of the evacuated streets while she could.

The squeal of the drone's wheel followed h_rd to the door. It darted in front of her, almost spinning out of control in its haste to block her path.

H_rd was brought up short. Did it think it was *coming*?

Then she realized its purpose. Alexander had downloaded the precious secret it sought through the memory of the little drone. There might be some residue, some backup somewhere from which the Imperials could extract what Alexander had learned.

The commando set her blaster to high, and leveled it at the drone. The machine backed away. That was just Alexander, being careful to keep h_rd out of the blast radius. But the little device seemed nervous on its single, unsteady wheel, as if it knew it was about to die.

H_rd felt a strange reluctance to destroy the drone. For a few hours, it had been a companion here on this lonely, un-Rix world, a little sister of sorts. That was an odd way to think of the drone, which was an embodiment of one of her gods. But she felt as if she were killing a friend.

Still, orders were orders.

She closed her eyes and pressed the firing stud.

Plasma leapt from the mouth of the blaster, disintegrating the drone in a gout of fire and metal parts, which h_rd leapt over, passing into the dark night beyond.

Running between quiet buildings, she shook off the feeling of loneliness. Alexander was still here all around her, watching through every doorway monitor, concealing her passage with feints and deceptions. She was the compound mind's one human agent on this hostile world: beloved.

H_rd ran fast and hard. She was doing the will of the gods.

Senator

This time, the journey to the Diamond Palace was by tunnel, a route Senator Oxham hadn't known existed. The trip lasted seconds; the acceleration registered by her middle ear seemed insufficient for the distance.

Oxham was met by a young aspirant in the Political Apparatus. His black uniform creaked—new leather—as they walked down the broad hallway. Although her apathy was set very low to allow her abilities full rein for the first session of the council, she felt nothing from the aspirant. He must have been particularly susceptible to Apparatus conditioning. Perhaps he had been chosen for that very reason. His mind was tangibly barren; she sensed only tattered remainders of will, the cold stumps of a burned forest.

She was glad to reach the council chamber, if only to escape the chilly umbra of the man's psychic absence.

The chamber of the War Council, like most of the Diamond Palace, was formed of structured carbon. Woven throughout the palace's crystalline walls were airscreen projectors, recording devices, and an Imperially huge reserve of data. It was rumored that within the structure's expansive processors an entity with limited agency had arisen, a sort of minor compound mind that the Emperor indulged. The palace was abundant with devices and intelligence, and infused with the mystique that comes of being a focus of awesome power, but its floor had a mineral solidity under Senator Oxham's feet. It felt as dumb as stone.

She was the last to arrive. The others waited in silence as she took a seat.

The chamber itself was small compared with the other Imperial enclosures that Oxham had seen. There were no gardens, no high columns, no wildlife or tricks with gravity. Not even a table. A shallow, circular pit was cut into the glassy floor, and the nine counselors sat at its edge, like some midnight cabal gathered around a disused fountain. The floor of the pit was not the same hypercarbon as the rest of the palace. It was opaque, an off-white, pearly horn.

There was a simplicity to the setting that Oxham had to admire.

Her artificial secondary senses had faded as she approached the chamber; now she was cut off from the purr of newsfeed and politics, communications and data overlays. As she sat down, the senator was struck by the sudden silence that was the absence of the summons, the grave tone in her head finally extinguished.

It was quiet, here in this diamond hall.

"War Council is in session," said the Emperor.

Oxham's eyes took in the council members, and she found that Niles's predictions, as usual, had proved very accurate. One counselor was present from each of the four major parties, including herself. She'd been right about Raz imPar Henders representing Loyalty. The counselors from the Utopian Party and the Expansionists were both as Niles had predicted. And his wildest guess also proved correct: an envoy from the Plague Axis, its gender concealed by the necessary biosuit, was seated at a lonely end of the circle.

The two dead counselors were both military, as always. One admiral and one general. The wild card, as Niles called the traditionally nonpolitical and nonmilitary seat on the council, was held by the intellectual property magnate Ax Milnk. Oxham had never seen her in person; the woman's truly extraordinary wealth kept her in a constant womb of security, usually on one of her private moons around Home's sister planet, Shame. Oxham sensed Milnk's discomfort at being removed from her usual retinue of bodyguards. A misplaced fear: the Diamond Palace was safer than the grave.

"To be absolutely precise," the dead general said, "we are not yet a war council proper. The Senate doesn't even know of our existence yet. We act now only with the ordinary powers of the Risen Emperor: control of the Navy, the Apparatus, and the Living Will."

Power enough, thought Oxham. The military, the political service, and the unfathomable wealth of the Living Will— the accumulated property of those who had been elevated, which was willed to the Emperor as a matter of custom. One of the driving forces of the Eighty Worlds' rampant capitalism was that the very rich were almost always elevated. Another was that the next generation had to start all over: inheritance was for the lower classes.

"I am sure that once the Senate is informed of these Rix depredations, we will be given full status," Raz imPar Henders said, performing his lackey function. He intoned the words prayerfully, like some not very bright village proctor reassuring his flock of heaven. Oxham had to remind herself not to underestimate the man. As she'd sensed in the last few sessions, Senator Henders had begun to take control of the Loyalty Party, even though he was only midway through his first term. His planet wasn't even a safe seat, swinging between Secularist and Loyal representatives for the last three centuries. He must be brilliant tactician, or a favorite of the Emperor. By its very nature, Loyalty was a party of the old guard, bound by staid traditions of succession. Henders was an anomaly to be carefully watched.

"Perhaps we should leave the question of our status to the Senate," Oxham said. Her brash words were rewarded by a flush of surprise from Henders. Oxham let the ripple of her statement settle, then added, "As per tradition."

At this last word, Henders nodded reflexively.

"True," the Risen Emperor agreed, a smile playing in the subtle muscles around his mouth. After centuries of absolute power, His Majesty must be enjoying the tension of this mix. "We may have mispoken ourselves. The Provisional War Council is in session, then."

Henders settled himself visibly. However keen a politician, the man was terribly easy to read. He had been ruffled by the exchange; he couldn't bear to hear the words of the Risen One contradicted, even on technical grounds.

"The Senate will ratify us soon enough, when they learn what has happened on Legis XV," Henders said coldly.

Nara Oxham felt her breath catch. Here it was, news of the rescue attempt. The pleasure of rattling Henders was extinguished, reduced to the helpless anxiety of a hospital waiting room. Her awareness narrowed to the face of the gray general who had spoken. She searched his pallid, cold visage for clues, her empathy almost useless with this ancient, lifeless man.

Niles had been right. This was no game. This was lives saved or lost.

"Three hours ago," the dead general continued, "we received confirmation that the Empress Anastasia was killed in cold blood by her captors, even as rescue reached her."

The chamber was silent. Oxham felt her heartbeat pounding in one temple, her own reaction reinforced by the empathic forces in the room. Senator Henders's visceral horror arced through Nara. Ax Milnk's reflexive fear of instability and chaos welled up in her like panic. As if her teeth were biting glass, Nara experienced the grim pain of the general remembering ancient battles. And throughout the chamber, a sovereign shudder built like the approach of some great hurricane—the group realization that there was finally, irrevocably, certainly going to be war.

As when she awoke from coldsleep, Oxham felt overwhelmed by the emotions around her. She felt herself dragged down again toward madness, into the formless chaos of the group mind. Even the voices of the capital's billions intruded; the white-noise scream of unbridled politics and commerce, the raw, screeching metal of the city's mindstorm all threatened to take her over.

Her fingers fumbled for her apathy bracelet, releasing a dose of the drug. The familiar hiss of transdermal injection calmed her, a totem to hang on to until the empathy suppressant could take effect. The drug acted quickly. She felt reality rush back into the room, crowding out the wheeling demons as her ability dulled. The awesome, somber silence returned.

The dead admiral was talking now, giving particulars of the rescue attempt. Troops descending in their blazing smallcraft, a firefight sprawling across the great palace, and one last Rix commando playing dead, killing the Child Empress even as the battle was won.

The words meant nothing to Nara Oxham. All she knew was that her lover was a dead man, doomed by an Error of Blood. He would settle his affairs, prepare his crew for his death, and then plunge a dull ceremonial blade into his belly. The power of tradition, the relentless fixity of gray culture, his own sense of honor would compel him to complete the act.

Oxham pulled the message remote from her sleeve pocket. She felt its tiny mouth nibble at her palm, tasting sweat and flesh. Verifying her identity, it hummed with approval. Nara pressed the device to her throat, unwatched as the council attended to the droning admiral.

"Send," she said, at the threshold between voice and whisper.

The device vibrated for a moment with life, then went still, its purpose expended.

She imagined the tiny packet of information slipping down the thread of its Rubicon gerrymander, inviolate as it passed through the palace's brilliant facets. Then it would thrust into the torrent of the capital's infostructure, a water-walking insect braving a raging river. But the packet possessed senatorial privilege; it would exercise absolute priority, surging past the queue awaiting off-world transmission, flitting through the web of repeaters, as fleet as an Imperial decree.

The message would reach an entanglement facility somewhere buried under kilometers of lead, a store of half-particles whose doppelgängers waited on Imperial warships, or had been transported by near-lightspeed craft to other planets in the realm. With unbelievable precision, certain photons suspended in a weakly interacting array would be collapsed, thrust from their coherent state into the surety of measurement. And ten light-years away, their doppelgängers on the *Lynx* would react, also falling from the knife's edge. The pattern of this change—the set of positions in the array that had discohered—would comprise a message to the *Lynx*.

Just reach him in time, she willed the missive.

Then Senator Nara Oxham forced her attention back to the cold planes of the council chamber, and forcibly banished all thoughts of Laurent Zai from her mind.

She had a war to prosecute.

Captain

The blade rested in Zai's hand, black against black infinity, waiting only for him to squeeze.

Hard to believe what that one gesture would trigger. Convulsions throughout the ship as it shifted into combat configuration, the dash to battle stations of three hundred men, weapons crash-charged and wheeling as AI searched vainly for incoming enemy craft. Not entirely a waste of energy, Zai thought. War was coming here to the Rix frontier, and it would be good practice for the crew of the *Lynx* to run an unexpected battle-stations drill. Perhaps performing the EVA maneuvers of a body recovery—their captain's corpse— would impress them with the seriousness of being on the front line of a new Rix incursion.

Not that he'd meant this means of suicide as a training exercise. Bringing the ship to emergency status was simply the only way to override the safeties that protected the observation blister.

What a strange way to kill myself, he thought. Laurent Zai wondered what perversity of spirit had led him to choose this particular blade of error. Decompression was hardly an instantaneous death. How long did it take a human being to die in hard vacuum? Ten seconds? Thirty? And those moments would be painful. The rupture of eyes and lungs, the bursting of blood vessels in the brain, the explosive expansion of nitrogen bubbles in the knee joints.

Probably too much pain for the human mind to register, too many extraordinary violations of the body all at once. At what point was a chorus of agonies overwhelmed by sheer surprise? Zai wondered. However long he stood here facing the blackness and contemplating what was about to happen, his nervous system was unlikely to be in any way prepared.

Of course, the traditional ceremony of error—a dull weapon thrust into your belly, watching as your pulse splattered onto a ritual mat—was hardly pleasant. But as an elevated man, Laurent Zai could choose any means of suicide. He didn't have to suffer. There were painless ways out, even quite pleasurable ones. A century ago, the elevated Transbishop Mater Silver had killed herself with halcionide, gasping with orgasm as she went.

But Zai wanted to feel the void. However painful, he wanted to know what had lurked all those years on the other side of the hullalloy. He was in love with space, emptiness, always had been. Now he would meet it face to face.

In any case, his decision was made. Zai had chosen, and like all command officers, he knew the dangers of second-guessing oneself. Besides, he had other things to think about.

Laurent Zai closed his eyes and sighed. The blister was sealed from the crew by his command. He would be alone here until the end; there was no longer any need to show strength for the sake of his shipmates. One by one, he relaxed the rigid controls he had forced upon his thoughts. For the first time since his error had been committed, Zai allowed himself the luxury of thinking about her—Senator Nara Oxham.

By Imperial Absolute, it had been ten years since he had last seen his lover. But in the long acceleration spinward, the Time Thief had stolen more than eight of those years, leaving Zai's memory—the color of her eyes, the scent of her— still fresh. And Nara also suspended herself in time. As a senator, she spent the frequent legislative breaks in stasis sleep, enfolded in a cocoon of temporal arrest. That image of her, a sleeping princess waiting for him, had sustained him for these last relative years. He'd entertained the romantic notion that their romance would beat time, lasting through the long, cold decades of separation, intact while the universe reeled forward.

It had seemed that way. Zai was elevated, immortal. Nara was a senator, almost certainly eligible for elevation once she renounced her Secularist deathwish. Even the pinkest politicians sometimes did, ultimately. They were two immortals, safe from the ravages of time, preserved from their long separations by relativity itself.

But time, it seemed, was not the only enemy. Zai opened his eyes and regarded the black remote before him.

It was death, in his hand.

Death was the real thief, of course. It always had been. Love was fragile and hapless compared to it. Since humans had first gained self-awareness, they had been stalked by the specter of extinction, of nothingness. And since the first humanlike primate had learned to smash another's skull, death was the ultimate arbiter of power. It was no wonder that the Risen Emperor was worshiped as a god. To those who served him faithfully, he offered salvation from humanity's oldest enemy.

And demanded death itself for those who failed him.

Best to get it over with, Laurent Zai thought. Tradition had to be served.

Zai touched his hands together as if to pray.

His stomach clenched. He smelled it on his hands, that shame from childhood, when he had prayed to the Emperor for taller classmates. He felt the bile that had risen on that afternoon at the soccer field, when he felt with childish surety that he himself had caused the Krupp Reich plague. The heavy-handed Vadan propaganda still informed him somehow. He smelled vomit on his hands.

And instead of praying to the Emperor, instead of saying the ritual words of suicide, he whispered, "Nara, I'm so sorry," again and again.

The remote was hard in his hand, but Laurent Zai didn't reach for death. Not yet.

Message for Captain Laurent Zai, came the prompt in second sight.

He opened his eyes and shook his head in disbelief.

"Hobbes . . ." he sighed. He had left specific orders. Would the woman not let him die?

But his executive officer did not respond. Zai looked more closely at the hovering missive, and swallowed. It was eyes-only, under penalty of blood. It had bypassed the bridge altogether, looking for him alone, under senatorial seal.

Senatorial.

Nara. She knew.

The situation here on Legis XV was subject to the highest order of secrecy. The *Lynx*'s marines had locked down the planet in the first hours of the crisis, occupying the polar entanglement facility that allowed translight communication. Even the ubiquitous Rix compound mind was cut off from the rest of the Empire.

Among the Senate, only a select few would know that the Empress was dead. The propaganda machine of the Political Apparatus would prepare the body public very carefully for the news. But evidently Nara knew. Senator Oxham must have risen high in the ranks of her party these last ten years.

Or could the message be a coincidence? Surely that was absurd; Nara wouldn't contact him casually with a message sealed under penalty of blood. She had to know about his error.

He didn't want to open the message, didn't want to see Nara's words borne by his defeat, his extinction. Laurent Zai had promised to return, and had failed her. *Use the blade now,* he told himself. *Spare yourself this pain.*

But a senatorial seal was an agent of some intelligence. It would know that it had reached the *Lynx* successfully, and that Zai wasn't dead yet. It would report back to Nara that he had rejected it, just as any intelligent missive would. The seal would record his last betrayal.

He had to read it. Anything less would be cruel.

Laurent Zai sighed. A life spent in service of tradition, but he was apparently not destined to die cleanly.

He opened his palm before him as if to receive a gift, that first interface gesture taught to children.

The senatorial seal expanded before him, cut with the crimson bar sinister of Vasthold. Nara Oxham's formal titles were vaguely visible in tertiary sight.

"Captain Laurent Zai," he said to it.

The seal didn't break. Its security AI wasn't satisfied yet. Thin lasers from the *Lynx* proper washed Zai's hands, covering them with a shimmering red patina. He turned them over, letting the lasers read the whorls of his fingertips and palms. Then they moved up and played across his eyes.

Still the seal remained.

"Godspite!" he swore. Senatorial security was far more cautious than the military's.

He pressed his right wrist against the signet on his left shoulder. The smart metal of the signet vibrated softly, tasting his skin and sweat. There was a pause as DNA was sequenced, pheromones sniffed, blood latticed.

Finally the seal broke.

The message spilled out, in senatorial white against the depthless black of space. It hovered there, text only, absolutely still and silent, as clear as something real and solid. Just one word.

The message said:

Don't.

Zai blinked, then shook his head.

He had the feeling that this would not be easy. That nothing would ever be easy again.

Executive Officer

Katherie Hobbes felt small in the shipmaster's chair.

She had called the command officers to the bridge, wanting her senior staff at their stations when the battle-stations clarion sounded. None of them questioned her. As they arrived, they noted her position at the con, met her eyes briefly, and silently took their positions.

Hobbes wondered how many of the senior staff would accept her as acting captain. She had never fit in with the other officers on board Zai's ship. Her Utopian upbringing was inescapably obvious; the cosmetic surgery that was common on her home planet made her beauty too obvious here on the very gray *Lynx*.

The staff looked duly serious, at least. Hobbes had set the temperature of the bridge to ten degrees centigrade, a sign that every member of Zai's crew knew well. Their breaths were phantoms barely visible in the dim, action-ready lighting. She knew there would be no mistakes during the drill, or during the body recovery. However the politicals had screwed up the rescue, this crew felt they had failed their captain once. They were all determined not to let that happen again, Hobbes was confident.

But the shipmaster's chair still seemed gigantic. The airscreens that surrounded her were fewer than at the ExO's station, but they were more complex, crowded with overrides, feedback shunts, and command icons. The airscreens at her old position were simply for monitoring. These had power. From this chair, Hobbes could exercise control over every aspect of the *Lynx*.

Such potential power at her fingertips felt perilous. It was like standing at the edge of a cliff, or aiming a tactical warhead at a large city. One nudge to the controls, one sudden movement, and far too much would happen. Irrecoverably.

From the chair's higher vantage, she could see the entirety of the huge bridge airscreen. It showed the *Lynx*, scaled small but ready to come into sudden bloom when Captain Zai unleashed his blade of error. The deployment of the energy-sink manifold alone would increase the vessel's size by an order of magnitude. The *Lynx* would bristle like some spiny, startled creature, the power of its drive flowing into weapons and shields, geysers of plasma readied, ranks of drones primed. But one soft part of its lethal anatomy would be sloughed off, almost as an afterthought. With its integrity field snapped off, the observation blister would explode like a toy balloon.

Her captain would tumble out into naked space, and die.

Hobbes reviewed the steps she'd taken to try to save her captain. The images from the short firefight still played in her mind when she closed her eyes. She and the tactical staff had even synthed a physical model of the palace in the forward mess, had painstakingly traced the movement of every commando, every marine during the encounter. Hobbes had *known* that there must be something there to absolve Zai of responsibility, if only she could search harder, longer, build more models and simulations. The possibility that there was simply nothing to find, that the situation was hopeless, had never crossed her mind.

But now she remembered the look on Laurent's face as he had dressed her down, and Hobbes despaired. His anger had broken something inside her, something she hadn't realized was there, that she had foolishly allowed to grow. And the bitter shame of it was that she actually thought Laurent might save himself for her: Katherie Hobbes.

But that foolishness would be lost forever in the next few minutes, along with her captain.

Hobbes's fingers grasped the wide arms of the con. All this power within arm's reach, and she had never felt more helpless.

She looked down at the *Lynx* in the airscreen. Soon, it would unfold into battle configuration, suddenly and terribly beautiful. The deed would be done. Hobbes almost *wanted* the clarion to sound. At least then this waiting would be over.

"Executive Officer."

The voice came from behind her.

"I'll take the chair now."

Even as her mind seemed to crash, the imperatives of duty and habit took over her body. Hobbes stood and turned, taking one respectful step away from the station that wasn't hers. Vision reddened at the edges, as if an acceleration blackout were closing in.

"Captain on the bridge," she managed.

The confused bridge crew snapped to attention.

He nodded and took the shipmaster's chair, and she took careful steps back toward her usual station. She slipped into its familiar contours still in shock.

She looked up at Zai.

"The drill we spoke of is canceled, Hobbes," he said quietly. "Not postponed. Canceled."

She nodded dumbly.

He turned to regard the airscreen, and Hobbes saw the other officers quickly turn their startled faces to their own stations. A few looked at her questioningly. She could only swallow and stare at her captain.

Zai looked down at the image of the *Lynx,* and smiled.

If Hobbes understood him correctly, Laurent Zai had just thown away all honor, all dignity, every tradition he had been raised upon.

And he looked . . . happy.

Her words had made a difference to him. For a long, strange moment, Katherie couldn't take her gaze from the captain's face.

Then a troubled look came over Zai. He glanced sharply down at her.

"Hobbes?"

"Sir?"

"Pray tell me. Why is it so damned cold on my bridge?"

Senator-Elect

Laurent began talking about Dhantu quite suddenly.

Nara could feel his injuries, the strange absences in his body. The prosthetics were lifeless and invisible to her empathy, but psychic phantom limbs overlay them, hovering like nervous ghosts. Laurent Zai's body was still whole in his own mind. One arm, both legs, even the cavity of the artificial digestive tract glowed hyperreal, as if Laurent were a photograph garishly retouched by hand.

The apathy in Nara's system was slowly losing effect as the drug filtered from her blood, her empathy growing stronger by the hour. Oxham's abilities recovered from chemical suppression in two stages: first with a sudden rush of increased sensitivity, then more gradually, a timid animal emerging after a storm.

Even here in the refuge of her polar house, thousands of kilometers from the nearest city, Nara was anxious about complete withdrawal. Laurent's presence in this sanctum was an unknown quantity. He was her first guest here at the polar estate, and the first person in whose presence she had totally freed her empathic ability since coming to the Imperial home world.

She wondered what had possessed her to bring the gray warrior here. Why had she been so open about her childhood? He was, after all, one of the enemy. Nara tasted embarrassment now, the long discussion of her own madness flat and metallic in her mouth. And the sting of Laurent's words: *That's insane.*

She was silent now, letting her mind drift while the hearthfire burned itself low.

Nara's polar estate was a kingdom of silence. In the unpopulated south, her unleashed empathy could extend for kilometers, searching for human emotions like a vine seeking water. It sometimes seemed that she could enter the cool, slow thoughts of the plants in the house's many gardens. Away from the capital's throngs, she felt transported back to the empty expanses of Vasthold.

But when Lieutenant-Commander Zai began his tale, her empathy pulled itself back from the wastelands and came to a focus on this quiet, intense man, and on the old pain deep inside him.

"The Dhantu punitive expedition was requested by a local governor," Zai said, his eyes on a distant snowmelt waterfall. It tumbled onto the surface of the great glacier that approached the house from the east, the collision of temperatures raising a misty veil across the slowly setting sun.

"The governor was a sympathizer, it was later discovered," he said. "She came from a very good family, from among the first allies of the Emperor on Dhantu. But she had harbored traitorous thoughts since childhood. She wrote about it before her execution, bragging that she had achieved the office of Governor Prefectural on the power of hatred alone. A household nanny had raised her from birth to despise the Emperor and the Occupation."

"The hand that rocks the cradle," Oxham observed.

Laurent nodded.

"We have no servants on Vada."

"Nor on Vasthold, Laurent."

He smiled at her, perhaps recognizing that the spartan ways of his gray planet were not too different from the austere meritocracy of the Secularists. Though polar opposites politically, neither of them were Utopians. Both monks and atheists trod on bare floors.

Nara realized that Laurent had used the word *occupation*

to describe what was officially known as the "Ongoing Liberation of Dhantu." Of course, he had seen firsthand the excesses of direct Imperial rule, and its effect on the Dhantu heart. He was beyond euphemisms.

Zai swallowed, and Nara felt a chill in him, a shudder through the phantom limbs.

"The governor directed us to a secret meeting place of the resistance, where she said a high-level parley among its factions would take place. We sent a contingent of marines, hoping to capture a handful of resistance leaders."

"But it was a trap," she remembered.

The lieutenant-commander nodded. "The walls of the canyon had been carefully prepared, natural iron deposits configured to baffle our intelligence small craft, to hide the ambush. When the resistance fighters appeared in force, it was as if they had materialized from thin air."

She began to recall the details of the Dhantu incident, which had consumed the media for months, especially on anti-Occupation Vasthold.

"You weren't actually with the landing force, were you, Laurent?"

"Correct. The insertion force was strictly marines. The trap closed quickly, with only a few shots fired. From up in space, we could see through small-craft recon that our marines would be wiped out if they fought. We ordered a stand-down."

He sighed.

"But Private Anante Vargas had been killed in the first exchange of fire," he said.

Nara nodded. She remembered the official narrative now, the hero Zai trading himself for a dead man.

"His armor diagnostics showed that he'd died cleanly, a chest wound. If we could get the body up within forty minutes, he would take the symbiant easily."

"But they wouldn't give him up without an exchange."

Laurent's eyes closed, and Nara felt a deep, anguished tremor from the man. She struggled to pinpoint the emotion.

"There was a confluence of interests," he explained. "The resistance would get another living hostage; we would retrieve our dead. But they demanded a command officer. They asked for a member of the Apparatus, but there were no politicals aboard our ship. They knew that we wouldn't give them the captain, but a lieutenant-commander would do."

"Were you ordered, Laurent?"

"No," he said, shaking his head slowly. "The propaganda version is true. I volunteered."

There was the anguish again, as clear as words. *If only it could have been someone else. Anyone else.* But this regret was entangled with Laurent's guilt at his own thoughts. In Zai's gray world, the honored dead were by any measure worth more than the living.

"I inserted in an up-down pod. Ballistic entry, with crude rockets to get it back up. Not much bigger than a coffin."

"You trusted them?"

"My captain had stated quite clearly that if they reneged on the deal, he'd collapse the whole canyon with a railgun strike, kill us all. So I stepped out of the pod reasonably sure that they'd give up Vargas.

"Two of the resistance fighters brought Vargas's body over, and I helped them load him. For a moment, the three of us were human beings. We carried the lifeless man together, arranged his hands and feet in the jumpseat. Prepared him for his journey.

"Then we stepped back and I spoke to my ship for the last time, saying Vargas was ready. The pod ignited, carried him heavenward. I suppose I began the Warrior's Prayer out of reflex. The prayer is Vadan aboriginal, pre-Imperial, actually. But one of the two resistance fighters didn't hear it that way. He struck me down from behind."

He shook his head, bewildered.

"I had just handled the dead with these men."

Nara felt his horror in waves. Laurent, poor gray man, was still aghast that the Dhanti could have so little respect for ritual, for the Old Enemy, death. That blow from behind had made Zai more bitter than his months of torture, more anguished than having to walk into the trap of his own free will, sadder than watching his fellow captives die one by one. Nara could hear the question inside Laurent: the two guerrillas had handled the dead with him, and they wouldn't let him finish a simple prayer. Were they utterly empty?

"Laurent," she offered, "they'd seen millions die on their world, without any hope of resurrection."

He nodded slowly, almost respectfully. "Then they should know that death is beyond our political feuds."

Death is *our political feud*, Nara Oxham thought, but said nothing.

The sunset had turned red. Here in the unpolluted air of the deep south, the sunset lasted for two hours in summer. Nara knelt to place more wood on the fire. Laurent settled beside her, passing logs from the fireside pile. The house grew its own wood, a vanilla-scented cedar engineered for fast growth and slow burning. But it took a long time to dry properly, and hissed and smoked when wet. Zai hefted each piece in his hand, discarding those still heavy with water.

"You've built a fire before," Nara said.

He nodded. "My family has a cabin in the high forests of the Valhalla range, just above the snowline. Entirely datablind. It's built of wood and mud, and its only heat comes from a fireplace about this size."

Nara smiled. "My mother's line has a dumb cabin, too. Stone. I spent my winters there as a child. Tending fires is youngster's work on Vasthold."

Laurent smiled distantly, at some more pleasant memory.

"It develops a sense of balance and hierarchy," he said, or quoted.

"Balance, yes," Nara said, leaning a slender log carefully against the central mass of the fire. "But hierarchy?"

"The match ignites the kindling, which feeds the larger pieces."

She chuckled. A typically Vadan interpretation, to see order and structure in the consuming chaos that was a healthy blaze.

"Well, at least it's a bottom-up hierarchy," she commented.

They built the fire together.

"We were well treated at first, during the few weeks of negotiation. Our captors made populist demands, such as medical aid for the tropics, which were in epidemic season. They began playing with the Imperial government. Wherever the government acted against disaster, the resitance would issue demands retroactively, making it seem as if any Imperial aid on Dhantu was a result of the hostage-taking. The resistance took credit for everything. Finally, the Imperial governor-general grew weary of their propaganda. He suspended all humanitarian aid."

Nara frowned. She'd never thought of the Dhantu Occupation as a humanitarian operation. But, of course, occupying armies always brought a certain social order. And most occupying regimes were wealthier than their victims. Bribery followed naturally after conquest.

"After the Imperial sanctions were imposed, the torture began. The strange thing was, our captors weren't interested in pain. Not when they first strapped us to the chairs."

Chairs, Nara thought. Such a quotidian word. A chill rose inside her, and Nara turned to catch more of the heat from the blazing fire.

"The chairs were experimental medical equipment, fully pain-suppressant," Laurent said. "I felt nothing when they removed my left hand."

Nara closed her eyes, a realization dawning in her. Even without her quickening empathy, she would have heard in Laurent's voice the searching cadence of an unrehearsed tale. He hadn't told this story before. Perhaps there'd been a debriefing, with the dispassionate rendering of a military report. But this was his first human telling of what had happened on Dhantu.

No wonder the psychic scars felt so fresh.

"Only twenty centimeters removal at first," he said. "The prosthetic nervous tissue shone like gold wires. I could even see the muscle extensions flex when I moved my fingers. The blood transports were transparent, so I could see the beating of my heart pulsing in them."

"Laurent," Nara said softly. It wasn't a plea for him to stop; she'd just had to say something. She couldn't leave this man's voice alone in the huge silence of the polar waste.

"Then they moved it farther away. Forty centimeters. Flexing the fingers ached now, as if they were cramped. But that was nothing compared to . . . *the disgust*. To see my hand responding so naturally, as if it were till connected. I vowed not to move it, to shut it from my mind—to make it a dead thing. But I could *feel* it. Only the strong pain was suppressed. Not normal sensations. Not the itching."

He looked deep into the fire. "The Dhanti were always great physicians," he said without irony.

Something broke inside the fire, a pocket of water or air exploding with a muffled sound. Sparks shot out at Nara and Laurent, and were repulsed by the firescreen. Bright ingots of flame dropped in a bright line along the stone floor, revealing the position of the invisible barrier.

"Of course, we were fully restrained in the chairs. My fingers and toes were all I could move. Imagine trying not to move your only free muscles for days. The hand began to itch, to throb and grow in my mind. Finally, I couldn't stand it. I would flex my fingers, and have to watch them respond at that *remove*."

Nara felt her empathy coming to its highest pitch. Freed from the drug, it responded to the horror coming from Laurent, reached out toward him rather than recoiling. It had been so long since her ability had been fully open to another person; it stretched like a long-sleeping cat awakening. She could *see* now, empathy fully coopting the second-sight nodes in her optic nerve. Spirals of revulsion wound through the man, coiling like serpents on his artificial limbs. His gloved hand clenched, as if trying to grasp the phantasms of his pain. Maybe this was too private for her to look upon, she thought, and Nara's fingers moved to her wrist, instinctively searching for her apathy bracelet. But it was gone, left on a doorside table.

She closed her eyes, glad that easy relief was out of reach. Someone should feel what this man had suffered.

"They took us to pieces.

"They pulled my left arm into three, segmented at wrist and elbow and shoulder, connected by those pulsing lines. Then the legs, fused together, but a meter away. My heart beat hard all day, pumped up by stimulants, trying to meet the demands of the larger circulatory system. I never really slept.

"As ranking officer, I was last in line for everything. So they could learn from their mistakes, and not lose me to a sudden mishap. I could see the other captives around me twisted into bizarre shapes: circulatory rings, with blood flowing from the fingertips of the left hand into those of the right; distributed, with the digestion clipped off in stomach fragments to supply each removed limb separately; and utterly chaotic bodies, jumbles of flesh that slowly died.

"As we grew more grotesque, they stopped talking to us, or even to each other, dulled by their own butchery."

With that last word, the unavoidable moment came. Her empathy became true telepathy. Flashes struck now in Nara's mind, like flint sparks lighting a black cave, revealing momentary images from Laurent's memory. A ring of large chairs, reclined like acceleration couches for some grotesque subspecies of humanity. They sparkled with medical transport lines, some as thin as nervewires, some broad enough to carry blood. And on the chairs . . . bodies.

Her mind rejected the sight. They were both terribly real and unbelievable. Living but not whole. Discorporate but breathing. Nara could see their faces move, which brought a nauseous shock, like the sudden movement of a dummy in a wax museum. The devices that sustained them gleamed, the lines efficient and clean, but melded with the broken bodies in a sickeningly random jumble, creatures made by a drunken god, or one insane.

But the prisoners were not creatures, Nara reminded herself. They were humans. And their creators were not mad gods, but humans also. Political animals. Reasoning beings.

Whatever Laurent believed about death, nothing was beyond politics. There were reasons for this butchery.

Nara reached out to touch him, taking his right hand, the one still made of flesh. Disgust struck out at her from Laurent's touch, as deep as anything she'd ever felt: utter horror at himself, that his own body was nothing but a machine that could be taken apart, like an insect's by cruel children.

There was nothing to do but hold him, a human presence in the face of inhuman memory. But still she had to ask.

"The Apparatus never told us why, Laurent," she said. The resistance fighters' reasoning for the Tortures of Dhantu had never been explained.

Laurent shrugged.

"They told us that there was a secret, something that would undo the Emperor. They claimed to have heard something from a living initiate of the Apparatus they'd long ago captured. But they'd killed the man trying to wring the details from him. They kept demanding this secret from me. It was preposterous. They were grasping at straws. It was torture without reason."

Nara swallowed. There had to be a reason; the Secularist in her did not believe in pure evil.

"Perhaps it was a fantasy on their part. They must have wanted some weapon against the Emperor so badly."

"They only wanted to show us . . ."

Zai looked at her directly, and as their eyes locked Nara saw what he had realized over the long months in that chair. His next words were unnecessary.

"They wanted to show us what the Occupation had made of them."

Nara closed her eyes, and through Laurent's touch she saw herself through his, as if in some magical mirror in which she was a stranger to herself. A beautiful alien.

"There was one lie in the Apparatus propaganda," he said a few moments later.

Nara opened her eyes. "What?"

"I wasn't rescued. The resistance abandoned the hideaway and transmitted my position to my ship. They left me to mark what they had done. Along with the dead bodies, they left me living, but beyond anyone's ability to repair."

His gaze went from her to the waterfall, reddened now by the arctic summer sun.

"Or at least so they thought. The Empire moved heaven and earth to fix me, to prove them wrong. Here I am, such as I am."

She ran her fingers along the line of his jaw.

"You're beautiful, Laurent."

He shook his head. A smile played on his face, but his voice trembled as he spoke.

"I am in pieces, Nara."

"Your body is, Laurent. Not unlike my mind."

Zai touched her forehead with the fingers of his flesh-and-blood hand. He drew some shape she didn't recognize, a mark of his dark religion, or perhaps simply a random and meaningless sign.

"You began life in madness, Nara. But you wake up every day and cohere, pull yourself to sanity. I, on the other hand," he lifted his gloved prosthetic, "possessed absolute surety as a child, piety and scripture. And every day I shatter more."

Nara took both of Laurent's hands in hers. The false one

was as hard as metal, without the rubbery feel of a civilian prosthetic. It closed gently around her fingers.

Nara Oxham ignored the cold pain of him. She grasped the living and the dead parts. Pushed her fingers into the strange interfaces between body and machine. She found the hidden latches that released his false members. Removed them. She saw his phantom limbs as if they were real. She put her mind into him.

"Shatter, then," she said.

4

HIGH GRAVITY

A painful lesson for any commander: loyalty is
never absolute.

—ANONYMOUS 167

Senator

It was past midnight before the War Council was called again.

Senator Oxham was awake when the summons came. All night, she had watched the bonfire in the Martyrs' Park. The flames were impossible to miss from her private balcony, which hung from the underside of her apartment, giving it sweeping views of the capital. The balcony swung in a carefully calibrated way—enough to feel the wind, but not nauseously—and at nighttime the Martyrs' Park spread out below, a rectangle of darkness, as if a vast black carpet were blotting out the lights of the city.

Tonight, the usually dark expanse glimmered, populated by a dozen pools of firelight. Initiates from the Apparatus had taken all day to build the pyres, raising the pyramids of ceremonial trees using only human muscle and block and tackle. The newsfeeds gathered swiftly, broadcasting their labors and speculating on what sort of announcement would come after it had burned. As the pyres grew in size, the guesses were scaled up to match them, growing ever wilder, but still not quite matching the truth.

The politicals never trusted the populace of the Risen Empire with unexpected surprises, especially not in the volatile capital. The lengthy rituals of the Martyrs' Park allowed bad news to be preceded by a preparatory wave of anxiety, a warning like the glower of a distant storm. The newsfeeds usually hyperbolized their speculations, so that the true facts seemed reassuringly banal by the time they were made known.

This time, however, the news was likely to exceed expectations. Once the Child Empress's death became public knowledge, the true war fever would start.

There was enough of the construction to burn until morning, and Nara Oxham would need her energy when the news was announced, but she nonetheless went outside to watch. However exhausted by the day's events, sleep was impossible.

Her message to Laurent Zai seemed such a small and hopeless thing now, a futile gesture against the unstoppable forces of war: the vast fire below her, the still-gathering crowds, the mustering of soldiers, the warships already on their way to the Spinward Reaches. It was all unfolding with the fixity of some ancient and unchanging ceremony. The Risen Empire was a slave to ritual, to these burnings and empty prayers . . . and pointless suicides. There was nothing she could do to stop this war; her brash legislation hadn't even slowed its arrival. She wondered if even a seat on the council would ultimately accomplish anything.

Worse, she felt helpless to save Laurent Zai. Nara Oxham could be very persuasive, but only with gestures and spoken words, not the short text messages the distance between them necessitated. Laurent was too far away from her to save, both in light-years and in the dictates of his culture.

The balcony swayed softly, and the sickly sweet scent of the burning sacred trees reminded Oxham of the countryside smells of Vasthold. Crowds began to gather around the fire, the voices in massed prayer blending with the hiss of green wood, the crackle of the fire, and the rush of wind through the balcony's polyfilament supports.

Then the call came. The chime of the War Council's summons penetrated the susurrus noises from below, a foghorn cutting through the crash of far-off waves. Insistent and unavoidable, the summons's interruption brought her self-pity to a sudden halt. Oxham's fingers made the gestures that prepped her personal helicopter.

But then she saw the shape of an approaching Imperial aircar, silhouetted by the firelight. The delicate, silent craft drifted up and matched exactly the period of the balcony's sway. It opened like a flower, extending one wing as a walkway across the void. The elegant limb of the machine was an outstretched hand, as if the craft were inviting her to dance.

A ritual request, but one which she could not deny.

"There is strange news from the front," the Risen Emperor began.

The counselors waited. His Majesty's voice was very low, revealing more emotion than Nara Oxham had yet heard from the dead man. She felt a twinge of empathic resonance from him, a measure of confusion, anger, a sense of betrayal.

He moved his mouth as if to form words, then gestured disgustedly to the dead admiral.

"We have heard from the *Lynx*, from His Majesty's Representatives," the admiral said, using the polite term for the Political Apparatus.

She lapsed into silence, and the other dead warrior lifted his head to speak, as if the burden of this announcement had to be shared between them.

"Captain Laurent Zai, Elevated, has rejected the blade of error," the general said.

Nara gasped aloud, her hand covering her mouth too late. *Laurent was alive.* He had rejected the ancient rite. He had succumbed to her message, her single word.

The chamber stirred with confusion as Nara struggled to regain her composure. Most of the counselors hadn't given Zai much thought. Next to the Empress's death and war with the Rix, the fate of one man meant little. But the implications soon became apparent to them.

"He would have made a fine martyr," said Raz imPar Henders, shaking his head sadly.

Even in her relief, Nara Oxham realized the truth of the Loyalist senator's words. The brave example of the hero Zai would have made a fine start to the war. By throwing away his own immortality, he would have inspired the whole empire. In the narrative crafted by the politicals, his suicide should have symbolized the sacrifices required of the next generation.

But he had chosen life. He had rejected the Risen Emperor's second-oldest tradition. The ancient catechism went through her head: Eternal life for service to the crown, death for failure. She had hated the formula her entire life, but now she realized how deeply ingrained it was in her.

For a horrible moment, Nara Oxham found herself appalled at Zai's decision, shaken by the enormity of his betrayal.

Then she took control of her thoughts. She inhaled deeply, and booted a measure of apathy to filter out the emotions running rampant in the council chamber. Her reflexive horror was just old conditioning, inescapable even on a Secularist world, rising up from childhood stories and prayers. Tradition be damned.

But even so, she was amazed that Laurent had found the strength.

"This is a disaster," said Ax Milnk nervously. "What will the people think of this?"

"And from a Vadan," the dead general muttered. The grayest of worlds, reliable Loyalists all.

"We must withhold news of this event for as long as possible," Senator Henders said. "Let its announcement be an afterthought, once the war has begun in earnest and other events have overtaken the public's interest."

The admiral shook her head. "If there are no more Rix surprise attacks, it could be months before the next engagement," he said. "Even years. The newsfeeds will notice if there is no announcement of Captain Zai's suicide."

"Perhaps His Majesty's Representatives could handle this?" Ax Milnk suggested quietly.

The Emperor raised an eyebrow at this. Nara swallowed. Milnk was suggesting murder. A staged ritual of error.

"I think not," the Emperor said. "The cripple deserves better."

Both general and admiral nodded. Whatever embarrassment Zai had caused them, they wouldn't want the politicals interfering with a military matter. The branches of the Imperial Will were separate for good reason. The conduct of propaganda and internal intelligence did not mix well with the purer aims of warcraft. And Zai was still an Imperial officer.

"Something far more distasteful, I'm afraid," the Risen Emperor continued.

The words brought a focused silence to the chamber, which the Emperor allowed to stretch for a few seconds.

"A pardon."

Raz imPar Henders gasped aloud. No one else made a sound.

A pardon? Oxham wondered. But then she saw the Emperor's logic. The pardon would be announced before it was known that Captain Zai had rejected the blade of error. Zai's betrayal of tradition would be concealed from the public eye, his survival transformed into an unprecedented act of Imperial kindness. Before now, the Child Empress had always been the one to issue clemencies and commutations. A pardon in the matter of her own death would have a certain propagandistic poetry.

But it wouldn't be so easy, Nara's instincts told her. The Risen Emperor wouldn't allow Zai to be rewarded for his betrayal.

The sovereign nodded to the dead admiral.

The woman moved her pale hands, and the chamber darkened. A system schematic, which they all now recognized as Legis, appeared in synesthesia. The dense swirl of planetary orbital circles (the Legis sun had twenty-one major satellites) shrank, the scale expanding out. A vector marker appeared on the system's spinward side, out from the terrestrial planets into the vast, slow orbits of the gas giants.

The red marker described an approach to the system that passed close to Legis XV.

"Three hours ago," the admiral said, "the Legis system's outlying orbital defenses detected a Rix battlecruiser, incoming at about a tenth lightspeed. This vessel is nothing like the assault ship that carried out the first attack. A far more powerful craft, but fortunately far less stealthy: this time we have warning.

"If it attacks Legis XV directly, the orbital defenses should destroy the Rix ship before it can close within a million kilometers."

"What could it do to Legis from that range?" Oxham asked.

"If the battlecruiser's intention is to attack, it could damage major population centers, introduce any number of biological weapons, certainly degrade the info- and infrastructure. It all depends on how the vessel has been fitted. But she won't have the firepower for atmospheric rending, plate destabilization, or mass irradiation. In short, no damage at extinction level."

Nara Oxham was appalled by the dead woman's dry appraisal. A few million dead was all. And perhaps a few generations with pre-industrial death rates from radiation and disease.

"The Rix ship is decelerating at six gees, quickly enough to match velocities with the planet. But its insertion angle is wrong for a direct attack," the admiral said. "Its apparent intent is to pass within a few light-minutes of Legis XV. The defenses at that range will be survivable for a ship of its class, and it won't be close enough to damage the planet extensively.

"And there is another clue to its intent. The Rix vessel appears to be equipped with a very large receiver array. Perhaps a thousand kilometers across."

"For what purpose?" Henders asked.

The Emperor shifted his weight forward, and the dead warriors looked to him.

"We think that the Rix ship wants to establish communication with the Legis XV compound mind," the sovereign said.

Nara felt bafflement in the room. No one in the Risen Empire knew much about compound minds. What would such a creature say to its Rix servants? What might it have learned about the Empire by inhabiting an Imperial world?

But from the Emperor came a different emotion. It underlay his anger, his indignation at Zai's betrayal. A dead man, he was always hard to read empathically, but a strong emotion was eating at him. Oxham turned her empathy toward the sovereign.

"The Rix compound mind has no access to extraplanetary communication," the general explained. "The Legis entanglement facilities are centralized and under direct Imperial control, and of course could only transmit to the rest of the Empire. But from the range of a few light-minutes, the compound mind could communicate with the Rix vessel. Using television transmitters, air traffic control arrays, even pocket phones. Legis's infostructure is composed of a host of distributed devices that we can't control."

"Unless we do something, the Rix will be able to contact their compound mind," the Emperor declared. "Between the mind's global resources and the battlecruiser's large array, they will be able to transfer huge amounts of data. With a few hours' connection, perhaps the planet's entire data-state. All the information that is Legis XV."

"Why not shut down the planet's power grid for a few days?" Henders suggested. "When the ship approaches apogee?"

"We may. It is estimated that a three-day power outage, properly prepared for, would cause only a few thousand civilian deaths," the general answered. Oxham saw nothing but cold equations in the man when he gave this number.

"Unfortunately, however, most communications are designed to survive power grid failure. They have backup batteries, solar cells, and motion converters as part of their basic makeup. This is a compound mind; the entire *planet* is compromised. A power outage won't prevent communication between the compound mind and the Rix vessel."

At these last words, Oxham's empathy felt a jolt from the Emperor. He was agitated. She had witnessed the fixations his mind could develop. His cats. His hatred of the Rix.

Something new was in his head, consuming him.

And then, in a moment of clarity, she felt the emotion in him. Saw it clearly.

It was fear.

The Risen Emperor was afraid of what the Rix might learn.

"We don't know why the Rix want to talk to their compound mind," he said. "Perhaps they only want to offer obeisance to it, or perform some kind of maintenance. But they have dedicated years to this mission, and risked almost certain war. We must assume there is a strategic reason for this attempt at contact."

"The compound mind may have military secrets that we can't afford to lose," the general said. "It's impossible for us to know what they might have discovered in an entire planet of data. But now we know this was the Rix plan all along: first the assault ship to seed the mind, then the battlecruiser to make contact."

The council chamber stirred again, frustration and anger filling the room. They felt trapped, powerless before the well-laid plans of the Rix.

"But perhaps we can solve both our problems with one stroke," the Emperor said. He pointed into the airscreen among them.

Time sped forward in the display. The Rix ship's vector marker inched torward Legis XV, from which another marker in imperial blue moved to meet it.

"The *Lynx*," Nara said quietly.

"Correct, Senator," the Emperor said.

"With aggressive tactics, even a frigate should be able to damage a Rix battlecruiser. Especially the receiver array," the admiral said. "It's too large to shield properly, highly vulnerable to kinetic weapons. Between battle damage and a careful, systematic degradation of the Legis communication infostructure, we may be able to keep the compound mind cut off."

"Any casualty estimates for this plan, Admiral?" Oxham asked softly.

"Yes, Senator. On the planet, we'll airjam com systems and flood the infostructure with garbage. Shunt the main hardlines for a few days to reduce bandwidth. Civilian deaths will be within normal statistical variation for a bad solar storm. Medical emergency response will be slowed, so a few dozen heart-attack and accident victims will die. With lowered transponder functions, there may be a few aircraft accidents."

"And the *Lynx*?"

"Lost, of course, and its captain with it. A grand sacrifice."

Henders nodded. "How poetic. Granted Imperial pardon, only to become a martyr nonetheless."

"The trees will burn for a week in the name of Laurent Zai," the Emperor said.

Adept

The two dead persons stood before a wreckage, the broken and burned shapes of data bricks scattered across the floor of the library.

"Was it here?"

"Yes, Adept."

"Did the Rix abomination find it?"

"We don't know, Adept."

"How can we not know?" Trevim said quietly.

The initiate shifted uncomfortably. He looked nervously at the walls, although every noise-sensitive device in the library had been physically deactivated.

"The abomination cannot hear us."

The initiate cleared his throat. "The one-time pad was concealed as a set of checksum garbage at the ends of other files. Only the few Honored Mothers studying the Child Empress's . . . *condition* knew how the scheme worked. There was no way for the abomination to know how to compile the data and re-create the pads."

Adept Trevim narrowed her eyes.

"Could it not use trial and error?"

"Adept, there are millions of files here. The combinations are—"

"Not limitless. Not if all the data were here."

"But it would take centuries, Adept."

"For a single computer, millennia. But for the processing capabilities of an entire world? Every unused portion of every device on Legis, devoted to this single problem, massively distributed and absolutely relentless?"

The initiate closed his eyes, removing himself from the shallow world of the senses. Adept Trevim watched the young dead man let the Other take control, the symbiant visible upon his face as it transformed hurried suppositions into hard math.

It would have been quicker to employ a machine, but the Apparatus avoided technology even in the best of circumstances. With the Rix abomination loose in the Legis infostructure, they kept to the techniques given by the symbiant. To trust a processor would be unthinkable.

Trevim waited motionless for just over an hour.

The initiate opened his eyes.

"The state of emergency was still in partial effect when the library was broken into," he said.

The adept nodded. With the markets closed, the media feeds suspended, the population locked down, the planet's infostructure would be largely dark. The abomination would have ample excess processor power at its disposal.

"It would have taken only minutes to run every permutation against the data it had recovered from the confidant. When the correct order was hit upon by chance, the data would take on a recognizable form," the initiate concluded.

"It knows, then."

The initiate nodded, looking queasy as he considered the Secret in the hands of Rix abomination.

"We must assume it does, Adept."

Trevim turned from the jumble on the floor. It had seemed so sensible a place to hide the one-time pads that would decrypt the recordings of the Child Empress's confidant. Rather than keeping the pads in a military installation, under lock and key, a target for treachery or infiltration, the Apparatus had hidden them among the chaos here at this library, a sequestered and little-accessed partition at the edge of the planet's infostructure. The pads were here as a last resort, for when the Empress suffered the ultimate result of her infirmity.

But with the Rix abomination and its last commando running free on the planet, the clever hiding place had worked against them. Even within the Apparatus, only a few people knew how the confidant worked. And these lived in the gray enclaves, far from any communication or even ready transport. It had taken hours to discover this weak point in the Emperor's Secret.

The compound mind had known where to look, though. The telling details could have come from anywhere: the shipping manifests of repair components, long-lost schematics, even from within the confidant itself. Based on her examination of the device's remains, Initiate Farre was certain that the abomination had briefly occupied it just before the rescue had begun.

The mind was everywhere.

They had to destroy it, whatever the cost to its host world.

"What do we do, Adept?"

"First, we must see that the contagion does not spread. Are there any translight communications the abomination could use to make contact with the rest of the Empire?"

"There is none, Adept. The *Lynx*'s infostructure is secure, and there are no other ships in the system with their own translight. Planetside, the entanglement facility at the pole is under Imperial control."

"Let us pay the pole a visit, and make sure."

"Certainly, Adept."

They walked up the stairs, leaving a ruin of secrecy behind them.

"Destroy this building."

"But, Adept, this is a library," the initiate said. "Many of the documents here are single-copy secured. They're irreplaceable."

"Nanomolecular disintegration. Melt it into the ground."

"The militia won't—"

"They'll follow an Imperial writ, or they'll feel a blade of error, Initiate. If they feel squeamish, we'll have the *Lynx* do it from space. See what they think about losing a few square kilometers."

The initiate nodded, but the marks of emotion on his face disturbed the adept. What was it about this crisis that afflicted the honored dead with the weaknesses of the living? Perhaps it was the conditioning, the distress they had been trained to suffer even at the mention of the Secret. The mental firewall that had preserved their silence for sixteen centuries might be a liability now that the Apparatus had to act rather than merely conceal. But perhaps there was more than conditioning behind the initiate's anguish. The abomination of the Rix compound mind surrounded them, had imbued itself into the very planet. Now that the thing knew the Secret, it threatened them on every front.

"The militia will relent, Initiate. They must. But this one library will not be enough. We will have to repair this breach at its source."

"But the mind has propagated beyond any possibility of elimination."

"We must destroy it."

"But how, Adept?"

"However the Emperor commands."

Captain

Captain Laurent Zai stared past the airscreen and into the ancestral painting on the wall behind it.

Three meters by two, the artwork filled one bulkhead of his cabin. It reflected almost no light, only a ghostly luminescence, as jet as if the frigate's hull had suddenly disappeared, leaving a gaping hole into the void beyond. It had been painted by his grandfather, Astor Zai, twenty years after the old patriarch's death and just before he had started on the first of many pilgrimages. Like most Vadan ancestrals, it was composed with hand-made paints: pigment from powdered black stone suspended in animal marrow, mixed with the whites of chicken eggs. Over the decades, the egg-white rose to the surface of Vadan black paintings, giving them their lustrous sheen. The painting glowed softly, as if it were highlighted by a thin coat of rime on some cold, dewy morning.

Otherwise, the rectangle was featureless.

The dead claimed otherwise. They said they could see the brushstrokes, the layers of primer and paint, and more than that. They could see characters, arguments, places, whole dream-stories painted within the blackness. Like images in tea leaves or a crystal ball. But the dead claimed that reading the paintings was no trick, but straightforward signification, no more magical than a line of text calling an image into a reader's mind.

The minds of the living were simply too cluttered to interpret a canvas so pure.

Zai could see nothing. Of course, that absence of understanding was a sign with its own meaning: for the moment, he was still alive.

In second sight, hovering before the painting, were the orders from the Navy. The Emperor's seal pulsated with the red light of its fractal authenticity weave, like a coat of arms decorated with live embers. The shape was familiar, the language traditional, but in their own way, the orders were quite as inscrutable as the black rectangle painted by an ancestor.

The door chime sounded. Hobbes, here on the double.

Zai erased the orders from the air.

"Come."

His executive officer entered, and Zai waved her to the chair on the other side of the airscreen table. She sat down, her back to the black painting, her face guarded and almost shy. Zai's crew seemed reluctant to meet his eye since he had rejected the blade of error. Were they ashamed of him? Surely not Katherie Hobbes. She was loyal to a fault.

"New orders," Captain Zai said. "And something else."

"Yes, sir?"

"An Imperial pardon."

For a moment, Hobbes's usually rigid composure failed her. She gripped the arms of the chair, and her mouth gaped.

"Are you well, Hobbes?" Zai asked.

"Of course, sir," she managed. "Indeed, I'm . . . very glad, Captain."

"Don't be too hasty."

Her expression remained confused for a moment, then

changed to surety. "You deserve it, sir. You were right to re-ject the blade. The Emperor has simply recognized the truth. None of this was your—"

"Hobbes," he interrupted. "The Emperor's mercy isn't as tender as you think. Take a look."

Zai reactivated the airscreen. It showed the Legis system now: the *Lynx* in orbit around XV, the high vector of the in-coming Rix battlecruiser. It took Hobbes only a few seconds to grasp the situation.

"A second attack on Legis, sir," she said. "With more fire-power this time."

"Considerably more, Hobbes."

"But that doesn't make sense, Captain. The Rix've al-ready captured the planet. Why would they attack their own mind?"

Zai didn't answer, giving his executive officer time to think. He needed to have his own suspicions confirmed.

"Your analysis, Hobbes?"

She took her time, more iconographics cluttering the airscreen as she tasked the *Lynx* tactical AI with calculations.

"Perhaps this was the backup force, sir, in case the situa-tion on the ground was still in doubt. A powerful ship to sup-port the raiders if they weren't entirely successful," she said, working through the possibilities. "Or more likely this is a reconnaisance-in-force, to discover if the raid succeeded."

"In which case?"

"When the Rix commander contacts the compound mind and realizes it has successfully propagated on the planet, they'll back off."

"Then, for the *Lynx*'s disposition, what would your tacti-cal recommendation be?" Zai asked.

Hobbes shrugged, as if it were obvious. "Stay close to Legis XV, sir. With the *Lynx* supporting the planetary de-fenses, we should have enough firepower to keep a battle-cruiser from damaging Legis, if that's their mission, which it probably isn't. The Rix will most likely keep going once they realize the raid was successful. That'll carry them deeper into the Empire. We could try to track them. At ten percent or so of the constant, they'd be hard for the *Lynx* to catch from a standstill, but a pursuit drone could manage it in the short term."

Zai nodded. As usual, Hobbes's thinking roughly paralleled his own.

Until he'd read the *Lynx*'s orders, that is.

"We've been commanded to attack the battlecruiser, Hobbes."

She simply blinked. "Attack, sir?"

"To intercept it as far out as possible. Outside the plantery defenses, in any case, in an attempt to damage the Rix communications gear. We're to keep the Rix ship from contacting the compound mind."

"A frigate, against a *battlecruiser*," Hobbes protested. "But, sir, that's . . ." Her mouth moved, but silently.

"Suicide," he finished.

She nodded slowly, staring intently into the colored whorls of the airscreen. However quickly Hobbes had grasped the tactical facets of the situation, the politics seemed to have left her speechless.

"Consider this as an intelligence issue, Hobbes," Zai said. "We've never had a compound mind fully propagate on an Imperial world. It knows everything about Legis. It could reveal more about our technology and culture than the Apparatus wants the Rix to know. Or . . ."

Hobbes looked up into his eyes, still hammered into silence.

"Or," he continued, "the *Lynx* may have been chosen to suffer the sacrifice that I was unwilling to make myself."

There. He had said it aloud. The thought that had tortured him since he'd received the pardon and the orders, the two missives paired to arrive and be read together, as if to indicate that neither could be understood without the other.

He saw his own distress reflected in Hobbes's face. There was no other interpretation.

Captain Laurent Zai, Elevated, had doomed his ship and

his crew, had dragged them all down along with his miserable self.

Zai turned his eyes from the still speechless Hobbes and tried to fathom what he felt, now that he had spoken his thoughts aloud. It was hard to say. After the tension of the rescue, the bitter ashes of defeat, and the elation of rejecting suicide, his emotions were too worn to keep going. He felt dead already.

"Sir," Hobbes finally began. "This crew will serve you, will follow any orders. The *Lynx* is ready to . . ." Her voice failed her again.

"Die in battle?"

She took a deep breath.

"To serve her Emperor and her captain, sir."

Katherie Hobbes's eyes glittered as she said the words.

Laurent Zai waited politely as she gathered herself. But then he uttered the words he had to say.

"I should have killed myself."

"No, Captain. You weren't at fault."

"The tradition does not address the issue of blame, Katherie. It concerns responsibility. I'm the captain. I ordered the rescue. By tradition, it was my Error of Blood."

Hobbes worked her mouth again, but Zai had chosen the right words to preempt her arguments. In matters of tradition, he, a Vadan, was her mentor. On the Utopian world she came from, not one citizen in a million became a soldier. In Zai's family, one male in three had died in combat over the past five centuries.

"Sir, you're not thinking of . . ."

He sighed. It was a possibility, of course. The pardon did not prevent him from taking his own life. The act might even save the *Lynx*; the Navy was not above changing its orders. But something in Laurent Zai had changed. He'd thought that the threads of tradition and obedience that formed his being were bound together. He'd thought that the rituals and oaths, the sacrifice of decades to the Time Thief, and the dictates of his upbringing had reached critical mass, forming a singularity of purpose from which there was no escape. But it had turned out that his loyalties, his honor, his very sense of self had all been held in place by something quite delicate, something that could be broken by a single word.

Don't, he thought to himself, and smiled.

"I am thinking, Katherie, of going Home."

Hobbes was silenced by the words. She must have been ready to argue with him, to plead against the blade again.

He took a moment, letting her renewed shock subside, then cleared his throat.

"Let us a plan a way to save the *Lynx,* Hobbes."

Her still glittering eyes moved to the airscreen display, and Zai saw her gather herself in its shapes. He recalled what the war sage Anonymous 167 had once said: "Sufficient tactical detail will distract the mind from the death of a child, even from the death of a god."

"High relative velocity," Hobbes began after a while. "With full drone complement deployed, I'd say. Narrow hull configuration. And standard lasers in the primary turrets. We'd have a chance, sir."

"A chance, Hobbes?"

"A fighting chance, sir."

He nodded his head. For a few moments after the orders had come, Laurent Zai had wondered if the crew would continue to accept his command. He had betrayed everything he had been raised to believe. Perhaps it would be fitting if his crew betrayed him.

But not his executive officer. Hobbes was a strange one, half Utopian and half gray. Her face was a reminder of that: molded to ah arresting beauty by the legendary surgeons of her hedonistic world, but always shrouded with a deadly serious expression. Generally she followed tradition with the passion of the converted. But at certain times she questioned everything. Perhaps, at this moment, the gap between them had closed; her loyalty and his betrayal, at the juncture of the Risen Empire.

"A fighting chance, then," he said.

" 'No more can a soldier ask for,' sir," she quoted the sage.

"And the rest of the crew?"

"Warriors all, sir."

He nodded. And hoped she was right.

Militia Worker

Second-Class Militia Worker Rana Harter stepped back nervously from the metal skirts of the polar maglev as it settled onto the track. The train floated down softly, as if it weighed only a few ounces, and sighed a bit as it descended, drifting along the track a few centimeters on a thin, leftover cushion of air, like a playing card dealt across a glass table.

But the delicacy was deceptive. Rana Harter knew that the maglev was hypercarbon and hullalloy, a fusion reactor and a hundred private cabins done in teakwood and marble. It massed more than a thousand tons, would crush a human foot under its skirts as surely as a diamond-tipped tunneling hammer. Harter stood well back as the entry stairway unfolded before her.

There was plenty of room here on the platform. Tiny Galileo Township seldom provided passengers for the maglev, which could have easily accommodated its entire population. This stop, the last before the polar cities of Maine and Jutland, was mostly to take on supplies. But Militia Worker Rana Harter was at last going to step onto the train. She had lived here in the Galileo Administrative Prefecture her entire life. Her new posting to the polar entanglement facility would be the first time she had left the GAP.

Rana waited for someone to appear at the top of the entry stairway. Someone to invite her aboard the intimidating train. But the stairway waited, impassive and empty. She looked at her ticket, actually a sheaf of plastic chits ribbed with copper-colored circuitry and scribblecodes, which the local Legis Militia office had provided her. There wasn't much on the ticket that was human-readable. Just the time when the train would leave, and something that looked like a seating assignment.

The northern tundra of Legis XV seemed to stretch out, infinitely huge, around her.

Rana waited at the bottom of the stairway. She couldn't bring herself to go though a door without an invitation. Here in Galileo township, such boldness felt like trespassing. But after a half-minute or so, the warning lights along the stairs began to flicker, and the ambient hum of the entire maglev raised a bit in pitch. It was now or never, she realized.

Had she waited too long? Would the stairway fold up as she climbed it, crushing her like a doll in the gears of a bicycle?

She placed one tentative foot on the lowest step. It felt solid enough, but the maglev's whine was still climbing. Rana took a quick breath and held it, and dashed up the stairway.

She was just in time, or perhaps the stairway had been waiting for her. At the top, Rana turned around to take a last look at her hometown, and the stairs folded themselves back up, curling into a single spiral that irised closed like an umbrella.

And Rana Harter, flushed more from nerves than from the short climb, was inside the train that would take her to the pole.

Her seat was several minutes' walk toward the front of the train. The maglev's acceleration was so even that when Rana looked out the window, she was surprised to see the landscape already whipping by, the snow and scrubgrass smeared to a shimmering milky blur.

Rana knew that her reassignment had been the result of the Rix attack a few days before. The Legis Militia was shifting onto war footing, and she'd read that strategic targets like the entanglement facility were being heavily reinforced. But as she passed the hundreds of soldiers and workers on the train, the scale of the Rix threat finally struck her. The maglev seemed full; every seat was occupied until she reached the one that matched her ticket. Rana's nerves twinged again, her guilt rising like a tardy schoolchild's as she took the last empty seat.

The soldier next to her was sleeping, his chair pitched back so that it was almost a bed. Her seat was certainly comfortable, designed for half-day journeys. A small array of controls floated in synesthesia before her, marked with the standard icons for water, light, entertainment, and help. She waved them away, and folded herself into one corner of the chair.

Rana Harter wondered why she had been assigned to the entanglement facility. Surely it was the most important installation on Legis XV. But what could the militia need *her* there for? She wasn't any kind of soldier. The only weapon she was rated to use was a standard field autopistol, and you could empty a whole clip from one of those into a Rix commando without much effect. She'd failed her combat physical, and didn't have the coordination for a quick-interface job like remote pilot or sniper. The only thing Rana had turned out to be good at—the reason she'd made second class in just a year—was microastronomy.

Rana Harter had a brainbug, it turned out, something her aptitude officer called "holistic processing of chaotic systems." That meant she could look at the internal trajectories of a cluster of rocks—asteroids in the under-kilogram category—and tell you things about it that a computer couldn't.

Like whether it was going to stick together for the next few hours, or break up, threatening a nearby orbital platform. Her CO explained that even the smartest imperial AIs couldn't solve that kind of problem, because they tried to plot every rock separately, using millions of calculations. If there was even the slightest observational imprecision at the front end, the back end results would be hopelessly screwed up. But brainbugs like Rana saw the swarm as one big system—a whole. In deep synesthesia, this entity had a flavor/smell/sound to it: a deep, stable odor like coffee, or the shaky tang of mint, ready to fly dangerously apart.

But why send her to the polar facility?

Rana had used equipment like the repeater array up there, and even performed field repairs on small repeater gear. But they didn't do astronomy at an entanglement grid, just communications. Maybe they were retooling the facility for defense work. She tried to imagine tracking a swarm of enemy ships dodging through the Legis defenses.

What would the Rix taste like?

Movement in her peripheral vision distracted Rana from these thoughts. Standing in the aisle was a tall militia officer. The woman glanced up at the seat number, then down at Rana.

"Rana Harter?"

"Yes, ma'am." Rana tried to stand at attention, but the luggage rack over her head made that impossible, and she saluted from a crouch. The officer didn't return the gesture. The woman's expression was unreadable; she was wearing full interface glasses that entirely obscured her eyes, which was odd, because she also had a portable monitor in her hands. She wore a heavy coat even in the well-heated train. There was a birdlike quickness to her motions.

"Come with me," the officer ordered. Her voice was husky, the accent unplaceable. But then, Rana had never been out of the GAP except in videos.

The officer turned and walked away without another word.

Rana grabbed her kitbag from the rack and wrestled it into the aisle. By the time she looked up, the woman was almost through to the next car, and Rana had to run to catch her.

The officer was headed toward the back of the train. Rana followed, barely able to keep up with the taller woman. She banged another worker with her flailing kitbag, and muttered an apology. He answered with a phrase Rana didn't recognize, but which didn't sound polite.

At the frantic pace, they soon reached the luxury section. Rana stopped, her mouth agape. One side of the carpeted corridor was filled entirely by a floor-to-ceiling window. In it the tundral landscape rushed by furiously, blurred into a creamy palette by the train's speed. Rana had read that the maglev could make a thousand klicks per hour; right now it seemed to be doing twice that.

Across from the window was a wall of dark, paneled wood, broken by doors to private cabins. The silent officer walked slowly here, as if more comfortable out of the crowded coach sections. They passed a few servants in Maglev Line uniforms, who stood at attention. Rana wasn't sure whether their stiff posture was out of respect for the officer, or just to give them room to pass in the thin corridor.

Finally, the officer entered one of the doors, which opened for her without a handkey or even a voice command. Rana followed nervously.

The cabin was beautiful. The floor was some kind of resin, an amber surface that gave softly under Rana's boots. The walls were marble and teakwood. The furniture was segmented; Rana's brain ability asserted itself, and she saw how each piece would fold around itself, the chairs and table transforming into a desk and a bed. A wide window revealed the rushing tundra. The cabin was larger than Rana's old barrack hut at Galileo, which she shared with three other militia workers. The luxury of the surroundings only made Rana more nervous; she was obviously inadequate for whatever special operation she'd been assigned to.

She felt guilty, as if she were already screwing things up. "Sit down."

Here in the quiet cabin, Rana listened carefully to the officer's strange accent. It was precise and careful, with the exact pronunciation of an AI language teacher. But the intonation was wrong, like a congenital deafmute's, carefully trained to use sounds that she herself had never heard.

Rana dropped her kitbag and sat in the indicated chair.

The officer sat across from her, a decimeter taller than Rana even with them both seated. She took off her glasses.

Rana's breath stopped short. The woman's eyes were artificial. They reflected the white landscape passing in the window, but were brilliant with a violet hue. But it wasn't the eyes that had made her gasp.

With the glasses removed, Rana could finally see the shape of the officer's face. It was eerily recognizable. The hair wasn't familiar, and the violet eyes were almost alien. But the line of the woman's jaw, the cheekbones and high forehead—were all strangely like Rana's own.

Rana Harter shut her eyes. Perhaps the resemblance was just the result of nerves and lack of sleep, a momentary hallucination that a few seconds of darkness could erase. But when she looked again, the woman was just as familiar. Just as much like Rana herself.

It was like peering into an enhancing mirror at a cosmetic surgery store, one that added a hairweave or different colored eyes. She was transfixed by the effect, unable to move.

"Militia Worker Rana Harter, you have been selected for a very important mission."

That oddly inflected voice again, as if the words came from nowhere, were owned by no one.

"Yes, ma'am. What . . . kind of mission?"

The woman tilted her head, as if the question surprised her. She paused a moment, then looked at her handheld monitor.

"I cannot answer that now. But you must follow my orders."

"Yes, ma'am."

"You will stay in this cabin until we reach the pole. Understood?"

"I understand, ma'am."

The woman's precise tone began to calm Rana a bit. Whatever mission the militia wanted her for, they were giving clear enough orders. That was one thing she liked about the militia. You didn't have to think for yourself.

"You are to speak to no one but me on this train, Rana Harter."

"Yes, ma'am," Rana answered. "May I ask one question, though?"

The woman said nothing, which Rana took as permission to continue.

"Who exactly are you, ma'am? My orders didn't say—"

The woman interrupted immediately, "I am Colonel Alexandra Herd, Legis XV Militia." She produced a colonel's badge from the voluminous coat.

Rana swallowed. She'd never even seen anyone with a rank over captain before. Officers existed on a lofty level that was utterly mysterious when viewed from her own small, nervous world.

But she hadn't realized how truly strange they could be.

The colonel pointed at the corner of the room, and a washbasin unfolded itself elegantly from the wall.

"Wash your hair," she ordered.

"My hair?" Rana asked, dumbfounded anew.

Colonel Herd pulled a knife from her pocket. The blade was almost invisibly thin, a shimmering presence as it caught light reflected from the patches of snow passing the window. The handle was curved in a strange way that made Rana think of a bird's wings. The colonel held it with her fingertips, a sudden grace evident in her long fingers.

"After you have washed your hair, I will cut it off," Colonel Herd said.

"I don't understand . . ."

"And a manicure, and a good scrubbing."

"What?"

"Orders."

Rana Harter did not respond. Her mind had begun to whir, to accelerate into a blur as featureless as the passing landscape. It was her brainbug, going for a quick flight, buzzing toward that paralyzing moment when a host of incoherent, chaotic inputs suddenly resolved into understanding.

She could just glimpse the operations of the savant portion of her mind, the maelstrom of analysanda madly arranging itself, seeking to collapse from a meaningless flurry into something concrete and comprehensible: the curve of the colonel's knife, somehow like an outline remembered from a ship-spotting course in her astronomy training; her strange, placeless accent, the words slow and prompted; the collection of hair, fingernails, skin; the colonel's inhuman eyes; and the woman's avian movements that fluttered like sunlight on bicycle spokes, the smell of lemongrass, or Bach played fast on a woodwind . . .

With a burst of sensation across Rana's skin—the rasp of talons—coherence arrived.

Rana had been trained to give the results of her brainbugs quickly, spitting out the essential data before they had time to escape her mind's tenuous grasp. And the rush of knowledge was so sharp and clear, so shocking this time—that she couldn't stop herself.

"You're a Rix, aren't you?" she blurted. "The compound mind's talking through you. You want to . . ."

Rana Harter bit her tongue, cursing her stupidity. The woman remained still for a moment, as if waiting for a translation. Rana's eyes darted around the room, casting for a weapon. But there was nothing at hand that could stop the sudden, birdlike alien across from her. Not for a second.

Then Rana saw the emergency pull-cord swinging above her head.

She reached up for it, yanking down hard on the elegant

brass handle, cool in her hand. She braced herself for the screech of brakes, the wail of a siren.

Nothing happened.

Rana fell back into her seat.

The compound mind, her own brain told her. *Everywhere.*

"You want to impersonate me," Rana found herself compelled to finish.

"Yes," the Rixwoman said.

"Yes," repeated Rana. She felt—with a strange relief after trying so hard not to all day long—that she would cry.

Then the alien woman leaned forward, one fingertip extended and glistening, and with a touch, thrust a needle into Rana's arm.

One moment of pain, and after that everything was
just
fine.

Captain

The haze of points that represented the Rix battlecruiser and her satellites grew more diffuse as the minutes passed. The smaller cloud that was the *Lynx* changed too, softening, as if Captain Zai's eyes were losing focus.

He blinked reflexively, but the airscreen image of the approaching hosts continued to blur. The two combatant ships deployed still more adjunct craft, hundreds of drones to provide intelligence, to penetrate and attack the other ship, and to harry the opponents' drones. The *Lynx* and the Rix ship became two stately clouds nearing a slow collision.

"Freeze," Zai ordered.

The two clouds stopped, just touching.

"What's the relative velocity at the edge?" he asked his executive officer.

"One percent lightspeed," Hobbes answered.

Someone on the command bridge let out an audible rush of breath.

"Three thousand klicks per second," Master Pilot Marx translated, muttering to himself.

Zai let the cold fact of this velocity sink in, then resumed the simulation. The clouds drifted into each other, the movement just visible, seemingly no faster than the setting sun as it approaches the horizon. Of course, only the grand scale of the battle made the pace look glacial. At the scale of the invisibly small craft within those point-clouds, the fight would unfold at a terrific pace.

The *Lynx*'s captain drummed his fingers. His ship was designed for combat at much lower relative velocities. In a normal intercept situation, he would accelerate alongside the battlecruiser, matching its vector. Standard tactics against larger craft demanded minimal relative motion, to give the imperial drone swarm sufficient time to wear down the bigger ship's defenses. Even against Rix cyborgs, Imperial pilots were renowned. And the *Lynx,* as the prototype of its class, had been allotted some of the best in the Navy.

But Zai didn't have the luxury of standard tactics. He had a mission to carry out.

Master Pilot Marx was the first to speak up.

"There won't be much piloting to it, sir," he said. "Even our fastest drones only make a thousand gees acceleration. That's ten thousand meters per second squared. One percent of the constant equals three *million* meters per second. We'll be rushing past them too fast to do any dogfighting."

Marx glared into the airscreen.

"There won't be much we can do to protect the *Lynx* from their penetrators either, Captain," he concluded.

"That won't be your job, Master Pilot," Zai said. "Just keep your drones intact, and get them through to attack the Rix ship."

The master pilot nodded. His role in this, at least, was clear. Zai let the simulation run further. As Marx had complained, the crashing waves of drones had little effect on one another. They were passing through each other too quickly for any but the luckiest of shots to hit. Soon, the outermost edges of the two spheres reached each other's vital centers. The *Lynx* and the Rix battlecruiser began to take damage; the kinetic hits of flechettes and expansion webs, wide-area radiation strikes from energy weapons.

"Freeze," Zai ordered.

"You'll notice that the adjunct craft have started making hits," ExO Hobbes took up the narrative.

"A ship's a much bigger target than a two-meter drone," Marx said.

"Exactly," Hobbes said. "And a battlecruiser is a bigger target than a frigate. Especially this particular battlecruiser."

She zoomed the view into the bright mote that was the Rix vessel. The receiver array became visible, the ship proper no more than a speck against its vast expanse.

Hobbes added a scale marker; the array was a thousand kilometers across.

"Think you can hit that?" Hobbes asked.

Master Pilot Marx nodded slowly.

"Absolutely, Executive Officer. Provided I'm still alive."

Zai nodded. Marx had a point. He would be piloting remotely from the belly of the *Lynx,* which would itself be under attack. The Imperial ship had to survive long enough for its drones to reach the Rix battlecruiser.

"We'll be alive. The *Lynx* will be inside a tight group of close-in-defense drones. We'll railgun them out in front, then have them cut back to match the velocity of the incoming drones," Hobbes said.

"Or as close as they can get," Marx corrected her. The *Lynx*'s defensive drones could never match the incoming Rix attackers at three thousand klicks a second.

"*And* we'll be clearing our path with all the abrasion sand we can produce." Hobbes sighed.

"But we'll have our hands full," she finished.

Zai was glad to hear the nervous tremor just audible in her voice. This plan was a dangerous one. The staff had to understand that.

"May I ask a question, Captain?"

It was Second Gunner Thompson.

"Gunner?" Zai said.

"This *collision* of a battle plan," he said slowly. "Is it designed to protect Legis? Or to create a tactical advantage for the *Lynx*?"

"Both," Zai answered. "Our orders are to prevent contact between the battlecruiser and the compound mind."

Zai's fingers moved, and the view pulled back to a schematic of the entire system. It filled with the vectors he and Hobbes had worked out that afternoon.

"To make it work, we'll have to accelerate spinward, out toward the battlecruiser, then turn over and come back in. Over the next ten days we'll have to average ten gees."

The command bridge stirred. Zai and his crew would be spending the next week suffering under the uneasy protection of easy gravity. Uncomfortable and dangerous, the high-gee conditions would leave them exhausted for the battle.

"And yes," Zai continued. "As Gunner Thompson suggests, high relative velocity gives us a tactical advantage, given our orders. Our objective is not to engage the Rix battlecruiser in a fight to the death. We're to destroy its array as quickly as possible."

" 'Suicide missions thrive on high velocities,' " Thompson quoted.

The bastard, Zai thought. To cite Anonymous 167 at him, as if this situation were of Zai's devising.

"We're under orders, Gunner," Hobbes snapped. "Preventing contact between the Rix battlecruiser and the Legis compound mind is our primary objective."

She left the rest unspoken: the *Lynx*'s survival was of secondary concern.

Thompson shrugged, not meeting Hobbes's eye. He was one of those more intimidated by her beauty than her rank. "Why can't they just pull the plug on the mind down on Legis?" he managed.

Zai sighed. He didn't want his crew spending its energy this way: trying to think of ways to get out of the coming battle.

"They wouldn't have to give up technology forever," Thompson continued. "Just for a few days, while the battlecruiser passed by. In boot camp, I lived in a simulated jungle biome for a month using traditional survival techniques. We could offer assistance from *Lynx* for any emergencies."

"This is a *planet*, Thompson," Hobbes explained. "Not some Navy training biome. Two billion civilians and the entire infrastructure that necessitates. Every day that's ten billion gallons of liters, two million tons of food produced and distributed, and a half million emergency medical responses. All of it dependent on the infostructure; dependent, in effect, on the Rix compound mind."

"We'd have to somehow disable every piece of technology for four days," Zai continued. "On a planet of Legis's population, there will be two hundred thousand births in that time. Care to use your survival skills to assist with them all, Thompson?"

The command bridge filled with laughter.

"No, sir," the man answered. "Not covered in my basic training, sir."

"How unfortunate," Zai concluded. "Then I'll want your detailed analyses of the current attack plan by 2.00. We'll be under high gravities by 4.00. One last night of decent sleep for the crew."

"Dismissed," Hobbes said.

The bridge bustled with energy as the senior officers went to present the plan to their own staffs.

Hobbes gave her captain a supporting nod. Zai was pleased she'd been able to defuse the trouble that Second Gunner Thompson had started. Attacking the superior Rix ship would be an easier sacrifice if the crew thought of it in terms of how many lives they were saving down below. But why was Thompson confronting him in front of his staff?

The second gunner was from an old, gray family, with as solid a military tradition as the Zais. By some measures, Thompson was grayer than his captain. One of his brothers was an aspirant in the Apparatus; none of the Zais had ever been politicals.

Perhaps Thompson's words were intended to remind Zai that the Imperial pardon was a sham, a way for the Emperor to save face. But it was a graceless pardon, paired with an impossible task, which might yet destroy him, his ship, and his crew.

Clearly, Laurent Zai had not been forgiven.

Commando

Wielding the monofilament knife carefully, h_rd cut Rana Harter's long hair down to a few centimeters.

The dopamine regulators that the commando had injected into her captive's bloodstream were self-perpetuating; the woman would remain acquiescent for days. As the medical records h_rd had unearthed at the library had shown, Harter suffered from chronic low-level depression. Any decent society would have cured it as a matter of course. But the Empire found Rana's synesthetic disorder, her savant mathematical ability, useful. Imperial medicine wasn't sophisticated enough to both heal Harter and maintain the delicate balance of her brainbug, so they let her suffer.

For the Rix, however, the treatment was child's play.

Harter was still feeling some side effects. Her attention seemed to wander now and then, lapsing into short fugues of inactivity, her eyelids shuddering a bit. But when shown the colonel's badge she followed orders; the Imperials conditioned their subjects well. H_rd set Harter to organizing the strands of her shorn hair by length on the cabin's ornate table, while the commando shaved her own head down to the scalp.

The handheld monitor pinged, an order from the compound mind. A schematic on its screen showed the location of the train's medical station. Leaving Rana Harter humming as she worked, the Rix commando braved the corridors of the train again. Having seen no bald women on Legis, h_rd covered her head with the hood of her uniform. She knew that clothing, grooming, and other bodily markers were used to project status and political affiliation even outside the military hierarchy of the Empire; a hairless head might draw attention. How odd. These unRix humans rejected Upgrade, but they still played games with dead cells and bits of cloth and string.

The medical station sprang to life as she entered, its red eyes projecting a lattice of lasers across the newly bald planes of her head. A few seconds after these measurements were taken, the station delivered two needles of specially programmed nanos and another set of orders: the map led to the maglev train's storage hold. H_rd easily wrenched open the lock there, and liberated a tube of repair smartplastic and another of petroleum jelly.

Back in the cabin, she doped the smartplastic with one of the needles, and squeezed it onto the neat pile of Rana Harter's shorn hair. The nanoed plastic writhed for a few minutes, giving off noticeable heat in the small cabin. The mass sent out thin threads that wove themselves among the hair cuttings. These wispy filaments spread out, consuming the mound of repair plastic and creating a spiderweb that covered the entire table. For a while, the web undulated slowly, as if cataloging, planning. Then its motion quickened. The whole mass contracted into a solid dome, a milky hemisphere into which the hairs were drawn. The surface of the plastic seethed with the ends of Rana Harter's red hair, which protruded and dove back into the mound as if ghostly fingers inside were knitting them according to some complex design.

It soothed the commando's mind to watch the elegant and miniature process unfold. Here in the crowded train, she was far too aware of the gross, unRix mass of humanity that surrounded her. She could smell them, hear the phatic chatter of their mouths, feel their handiwork in the bulbous curves and plush textures of this supposedly luxurious cabin, informed by the extravagant concept of privacy. The Rix spacecraft and orbitals that had always been her home were spartan and pure: joyful with the clean lines of functionality, the efficiency of intimately shared spaces, the evident perfection of compound mind design. These unRix humans sought joy in waste, ornamentation, excess.

H_rd knew, of course, that this society's disorder was a necessary evil; the messy inefficiencies of humanity underlay true AI. Alexander emerged from the electronic clutter of this planet, much as h_rd's own thoughts arose from an inefficient tangle of nervous tissue. But she was Rix, and had been raised to see the whole. To be trapped among the horde that underlay Alexander was like descending from the sublime visions of an art museum into the rank smells of an oilpaint factory.

The Rixwoman tore her eyes from the graceful, programmed movements of the plastic, and got back to work.

She ordered Rana Harter to strip. She cut her captive's fingernails and toenails down to the quick, collecting them into a small plastic bag as carefully as evidence of a crime.

Then h_rd unfolded the bed and ordered Rana Harter to lie down. She detached a small grooming unit from the cabin's valet drone, the sort of static electricity and vacuum brush that removes animal hairs from clothing. The commando paused, wondering if she should restrain the woman before proceeding. No. This next step would do as a test of the dopamine regulators' power over her captive.

The hard plastic bristles of the groomer were ideal for defoliating skin. H_rd rubbed the device into Rana Harter's naked stomach in hard, sharp little motions, turning the epidermis there to a ruddy, anguished pink. The vacuum unit greedily consumed the dislocated cells, its fierce little whine drowning out the small, ambivalent noises that came from the woman's mouth as h_rd worked.

Exhausting the skin of the stomach, h_rd moved on to her captive's small breasts, but the woman's movements proved too unruly. H_rd turned Rana Harter over and quarried the broad expanse of her back, and dug hard into the thicker skin of her arms and legs.

Soon she had enough, the vacuum's collector almost full. She tapped its precious cargo onto the table, carefully emptying the collector by wetting her smallest finger with saliva and probing the crannies of the vacuum's mechanism. Then h_rd doped the tube of petroleum jelly with the second needle from the medical station, and squeezed it out onto the skin cells. The admixture moved and grew hot.

Removing her own clothes, h_rd rubbed the petroleum jelly over her own flesh, skipping the flexormetal soles of her feet, the exposed hypercarbon of her knee and shoulder joints, and the metal weave of microwave array on her back. She was a commando, not an intelligence operative, and she would never look human while naked. But hopefully security at the polar base would be too overextended by the horde of new draftees for full physicals. H_rd's path here to the pole had been well disguised, and the Imperials were looking for a single infiltrator on an entire planet. Presumably, her identity would be confirmed by visual comparison with Rana Harter's records, gene-typing a few strands of hair, and reading the genetic material from her human thermal plume. When activated, the nano intelligence now incorporated into the petroleum jelly would sluff Rana Harter's skin cells at a normal human rate, providing constant ambient evidence of her borrowed identity.

If the security forces here demanded a retina scan or some quaint, ancient technique such as fingerprints or dental records, the commando would have to fight her way out in a hurry.

As for the face, Alexander had searched the records of the entire Legis XV military structure for a close match (also selecting for Harter's microastronomy expertise and vulnerability to drugs) and had intervened to transfer the woman here to the pole. Of course, the compound mind could have changed any electronic record to match h_rd's appearence, but human memory was beyond its reach. There was the possibility that someone at the polar station had actually met Rana Harter.

The compound mind was being very cautious. H_rd was its only human asset on the planet, and might have to pass as the woman for several days, even weeks, while she prepared for the transmission. At least, the commando thought, she would no longer be alone. She would need to keep Rana Harter with her to restock her supply of skin cells.

H_rd emptied her captive's kitbag on the floor and sorted through the contents. Most of the woman's civilian clothes wouldn't fit her larger frame, but the baggy militia fatigues covered her adequately.

H_rd glanced at her timestamp. The hairpiece should be done by now.

On the table, the hemisphere of plastic had stilled. She

picked it up cautiously, but it had cooled to room temperature. With a quick, snapping motion, the commando turned it inside out, revealing Rana Harter's hair, now inset into the plastic.

She lifted the hairpiece onto her shaved head, where it fit snugly, incorporating the medical station's exact measurements of her skull.

Alexander caused the cabin's window to opaque and then mirror.

The Rixwoman regarded herself.

H_rd experienced a brief dislocation as Rana Harter seemed to stare back at her from the mirrored window, mimicking her movements. The wig worked perfectly; the nanos had even managed to reconstruct Rana Harter's haircut from the mass of hairs. The resemblance was eerie.

The commando heard a stir from the bed.

Her captive rose slowly, a confused look on Rana's face as she touched her own tender skin. The dreamy expression of dopamine overdose sharpened a little as she stood next to h_rd, comparing her own shaved, naked, and raw figure to her impersonator's.

She spoke the crude words of her Imperial dialect.

Not bad, h_rd's translation software supplied. *But what about your eyes?*

The Rixwoman looked in the reflection at her violet, artificial eyes, then at her captive. Rana Harter's eyes were almond.

H_rd blinked.

The woman's eyes sparkled with tears from the relentless abrading of her skin. No amount of drugs could suppress the reactions of the body to pain. The commando shuddered inside. Death, hers or another's, meant little to her measured against the scope of the Rix compound gods. But she wanted nothing of torture. She turned to the woman, lifting her fingers to point at the woman's eyes, requesting words from her software.

The woman backed away, fear defeating the dopamine to mar her beatific expression. She was talking again.

You're going to take my eyes, aren't you?

H_rd grasped Rana Harter's wrist, firmly but softly.

"No," she said. She knew that word.

The look of fear didn't leave the woman's face. H_rd suspended her previous request; asked for new sentences.

"Just eyedrop dye," the Rixwoman said. "The medical station will make it for me when we get closer."

"Oh." The woman stopped trying to pull away.

"Let's talk now. Please," h_rd said.

"Talk?" Rana Harter repeated.

A pause; new sentences delivered.

"I need to learn your language. Better than this. Let us make . . ." The word was too long, full of slurred sounds.

"Conversation?"

"Yes. I want your conversation, Rana Harter."

Executive Officer

Katherie Hobbes reached her captain's cabin door at 1.88 hours.

She took a moment outside to gather herself, wondering if she was getting old. A few years ago, a missed night of sleep had seemed routine. Now, she'd been awake a mere fourteen hours, barely more than a day, but Hobbes felt her emotions beginning to fray, her mask of calm efficiency growing more brittle by the minute. She only hoped that her intellectual capacity wasn't suffering as well. This would be a disastrous time to start making tactical errors.

It wasn't simply age, though. The last few days had been a

rollercoaster of adrenaline, fear, anguish, and relief. The whole crew had been through the wringer, and now they faced ten days at high acceleration, followed by a battle in which they were overmatched. All of Hobbes's simulations put the *Lynx*'s chances against the Rix battlecruiser at the raw edge of survivability.

Hobbes doubted for a moment her purpose here at the captain's cabin. Was it just wild emotion that had brought her? Perhaps she should wait until after the battle with the Rix to confront this question. She could simply turn around and head for the command bridge, where the senior staff would be assembling in twelve minutes to present their detailed battle plans. But however confident she and the captain might act for the crew, they both knew that the *Lynx* would probably not survive the battle. If she didn't ask now, she might never know the answer.

Hobbes watched her fingers requesting entry.

That common gesture felt suddenly alien, as it had when she'd first left home to enter the Navy.

When Katherie wanted a door to open on a Utopian world, she'd just ask it. Aircars went where they were told, handphones heard and obeyed. But the military never talked to their tools. Such anthropomorphism was too decadent for the grays—machines were machines. Here on the *Lynx*, opening a door required a gestural sequence, a tongue click, perhaps even a token of some kind; it was all secret handshakes and magic rings. The grays preserved spoken language for use among humans, as if conversing with the ship would somehow bring it to life.

In retaliation, gray machines seldom talked to their masters. Instead, they employed a bewildering conglomeration of signifiers to get their messages across. Back on her Utopian birthworld, a burning house would simply alert its occupants with the words, "Excuse me, but I'm on fire." Navy alarms, however, were composed of unpleasant sounds and flashing lights.

But Katherie had discovered that she had a gift for the codes and icons. Imperial interfaces had a curt efficiency that she enjoyed. Like a jetboard or a hang-glider, they responded instantly to subtle motions. They weren't slowed down by politesse.

And so, the captain's answer came all too quickly.

"Come," he said, his voice raw from lack of sleep.

The door opened to reveal Zai. His tunic was unclasped, its metal ringlets hanging slack, his hair glistening from a recent shower. His eyes were lined with red.

Hobbes was brought up for a moment by the sight of her captain in disarray. In their two subjective years together, she had never seen him at less than parade readiness.

"What is it, Hobbes?" he said. He ran his fingers through his hair and glanced at the tactical stylus in her hand. Captain Zai smiled. "Couldn't wait for the meeting to regale me?"

Her eyes fell shyly as she took a step into the cabin. The door closed behind her.

"I'm sorry to disturb you, Captain."

"It's time, anyway. We can't be late for this briefing. 'Work your staff hard, work yourself harder,' aye, Hobbes?"

"Yes, sir. 'And make sure they notice,'" she completed the quote.

He nodded, and began to work the clasps of his heavy woolen uniform. Hobbes watched the fingers of his gloved, artificial had move, momentarily unable to speak.

He pointed to his conference table.

"Ever actually seen sand before?"

The table was covered with a galaxy of bright, hard shapes. Hobbes leaned closer and picked one up. The tiny object was sharp in her hand, with the familiar facets of structured carbon.

"So, this is sand, sir?" Hobbes knew the battle specs on ten different types of sand, but she'd never held the stuff between her fingers.

"Yes, what poets and politicals call *diamonds*. I intend to use quite a bit of it in the battle, Hobbes. We can synthesize a hundred tons or so in the next two weeks."

She nodded. Sandcaster drones were used in any space engagement to spread confusion in the enemy's sensors, but at this battle's high relative velocity, the stuff could be lethal. At high speed, enough of the hard, sharp particles could eat away even hullalloy.

"Pretty little things, sir."

"Keep one, if you like."

Hobbes put the diamond in her pocket, closed a fist on its hard shape. There was no delaying her purpose here any longer.

"I just had a question, sir. Before the meeting."

"Certainly, Hobbes."

"To better understand your thinking, sir," she said. "You see, I'm not sure that I completely grasp your . . . motivations."

"My motivations?" he said with surprise. "I'm a soldier, Hobbes. I have orders and objectives, not motivations."

"Generally true, sir," she admitted. "And I don't mean any personal intrusion, Captain. But the current tactical situation—as we both have agreed—seems to have become intertwined with your . . . personal motivations, sir."

"What the devil are you asking, Hobbes?" Zai said, his fingers frozen on the top clasp of his uniform.

Hobbes felt her face flush with embarrassment. She wished she could disappear, or could rewind time and find herself on the other side of his door, walking toward the command bridge, having never come in.

But even mortified as she was, the emotions that had carried her into the captain's cabin pushed her to say the next words.

"Captain, you know that I'm very happy that you rejected the blade. I did all I could to convince—" She swallowed. "But now that you have, I'm just a bit confused."

Zai blinked, then the slightest smile played at his lips.

"You want to know why I didn't kill myself, eh, Hobbes?"

"I think it was the right choice, sir," she insisted quickly. It was absolutely essential that he not misunderstand her. "But as your executive officer, I need to know why. In case it has an effect on . . . our working together, sir."

"My motivation," Zai repeated, nodding his head. "Perhaps you think I've become unhinged, Executive Officer?"

"Not at all, sir. I think your choice was very sane."

"Thank you, Hobbes." Laurent Zai thought for a moment, then sealed the top clasp of his uniform and said, "Sit down."

She found herself falling into one of the deep chairs around his airscreen table. The effort of breaching the topic had exhausted her. Her legs were weak. She was glad as he sat down that he would speak now, that she could remain silent.

"Hobbes, you've known me for two years, and you know the kind of man I am. I'm Vadan and gray. As gray as they come. So I understand that you're surprised by my recent decisions."

"Happily surprised, sir," she managed.

"But you suspect there may be more to it, eh? Some secret directive from the Apparatus that explains all this?"

She shook her head. That wasn't it at all. But Zai went on.

"Well, it's simpler than that. More human."

She blinked, waiting through the interminable pause.

"After forty relative years, and almost a century of absolute time, I've found out something unexpected," he began. "Tradition isn't everything for me, Hobbes. Perhaps it was on Dhantu that I changed, that some part of the old Laurent Zai died. Or perhaps when I was rescued and rebuilt, they didn't put me back together in the same way. However it happened, I've changed. Service to the Emperor is no longer my only goal."

Zai absentmindedly attached his captain's bars to his shoulders, where they slid to their correct positions.

"Hobbes, it's quite simple, really. It seems I have fallen in love."

She found that her breath had stopped. Time had stopped.

"Sir?" she managed.

"And the thing is, Hobbes, it seems that love is more important than Empire."

"Yes, sir," was all she could say.

"But I am still your captain, as before," he said. "I shall still follow the Navy's orders, if not every tradition. No need to worry about my loyalties."

"Of course not, sir. I never doubted you, sir. This changes nothing, Captain."

It changed everything.

Hobbes allowed herself to feel for a moment, tentatively to sample the torrent of emotions that built inside her. They poured from her heart, ravenous and almost frighteningly strong, and she had to clench her teeth to keep them from her face. She nodded carefully, and allowed herself a smile.

"It's okay, Laurent. It's human."

With an effort of will, she rose. "Perhaps we should continue this conversation after the battle with the Rix is concluded." It was the only possible solution. The only way to survive was to push this down into hiding for another ten days.

Zai glanced rightward, where she knew he kept the current time in his secondary sight, and nodded in agreement.

"Right, Hobbes. Always efficient."

"Thank you, sir."

They took a step together toward the door, and then he grasped her shoulder. A warmth spread from that contact through her body. It was the first time he had touched her in two years.

She turned to him, her eyes half closing.

"She sent that message," he said softly.

She. "Sir?"

"When I went to the observation blister to kill myself," he said. "There was a message. It was from her."

"From *her?*" she repeated, her mind unable to parse the words.

"My beloved," he said, an out-of-character, beatific smile upon his face. "A single word, that made all the difference."

Katherie Hobbes felt a chill spreading through her.

" 'Don't,' the message said. And I didn't," he continued. "She saved me."

There it was again. *She*. Not *you*.

"Yes, sir."

Laurent's hand slipped from her shoulder. Now the cold in Hobbes was absolute. It stilled her raging emotions. Like a killing frost, it cut down the part of her that was confused, devastated.

Soon she would be ready to go on. She just had to keep standing here, without feeling, for these next few seconds, and everything would be back the way it was.

"Thank you, Hobbes," Captain Zai said. "I'm glad you asked. It's good to tell someone."

"Very well, sir," she answered. "The briefing, sir?"

"Of course."

They walked there together, her eyes forward so as not to see the unfamiliar expression on her captain's face.

Happiness.

Senator

"We approved the attack without objection."

Senator Nara Oxham said the words quietly, almost talking to herself.

Roger Niles frowned and said, "The *Lynx* would be just as doomed if you'd forced a vote. Losing eight to one isn't much of a moral victory."

"A *moral* victory, Niles?" Oxham asked, a faint smile softening the bitterness on her face. "I've never heard you use that term before."

"You won't hear it again. It's a contradiction in terms. You did the right thing."

Nara Oxham shook her head slowly. She'd signed a death warrant for her lover, and for another three hundred men and women, all for the political advantage of a despot. Surely this could not be the right thing.

"Senator, these won't be the last lives the War Council will vote to sacrifice," Niles said. "This is war. People die. There are real strategic arguments for sending the *Lynx* against that battlecruiser. The Empire simply has no idea what the Rix are up to. We don't know why they want to contact the Legis compound mind. It might be worth a frigate to keep the beast cut off."

"*Might* be, Niles?"

"It's in the nature of war to frustrate the enemy, even if you're not sure exactly what they're doing."

"Do you really think so?" Nara asked.

The man nodded. "The Emperor and his admirals aren't about to sacrifice a starship just to revenge a slight. The *Lynx* may be small, but she's the most advanced warship in the Spinward Reaches. Even an insult from a gray hero like Laurent Zai wouldn't warrant throwing her away."

"You should have heard them, Niles. They laughed with pleasure at making him a martyr. Called him a cripple."

Nara put her head in her hands and leaned back, letting the luxuriant visitors' couch take her form. She and Niles were in one of the docking spires above the Forum, tall spindles of crystal that sprouted from the senatorial grounds to tower over the capital. The spire rooms were used primarily to impress ambassadors and to entertain the odd powerful constituent. They were intimate despite their commanding views, the Senate's subtle answer to the Imperial glories of the Diamond Palace and the Holy Orbitals. Their slightly musty furnishings spoke of collegiality and chumminess, of retail politics and handshake deals.

Oxham and Niles had evicted the spire room's previous

occupants (Council rank had its privileges) for a hasty meeting before she returned to the Diamond Palace. The senator's palace flyer waited just outside, bobbing softly in the cold morning breeze. Nara hadn't known that the term "docking spires" was literal, but the flyer's AI had chosen the spire, recognizing that Oxham had little time for a landing.

Council would meet again in twenty minutes.

"I don't know what's worse," Oxham admitted. "The Emperor killing Zai for revenge or me voting to commit the *Lynx* for purely tactical reasons—agreeing with the overwhelming majority so that they'd listen to me when a close vote came up."

"That's sound thinking, Senator. You don't want to be branded as weak and unwilling to shed blood."

"But actually to agree with them," she continued. "To sacrifice three hundred lives on the merest *assumption* that troubling the Rix is worth the cost. That's harder to swallow than a tactical concession, Niles."

Her old counselor stared back at her. He looked diminutive on the overcushioned divan, a sharp-faced elf in the salon of some corpulent satrap. His eyes narrowed, bright blue and exceptionally sharp. There was no second sight here, ten kilometers above the concentrated synesthesia projectors of the Forum's chambers.

"You've made distasteful compromises before, Nara," he said.

"Yes, I've traded my vote before," she answered warily. It was Niles's way to debate her when she doubted herself, to bully her into understanding her own motives.

"What's the difference this time?" he asked.

She sighed, feeling like a schoolgirl repeating rote lessons. "In the past, I've bargained with the Empire's wealth. I've dealt tax relief for patent enforcement, axis protections for trading rights. Ninety percent of Senate policy is pure economics, a matter of possession. I've never traded in lives before."

Niles looked out the window, his gaze oriented on the Debted Hills, over which dawn was breaking through distant black clouds.

"Senator, did you know that the suicide rate in the Empire has been consistent since the First Rix Incursion?"

Suicide rate? Oxham thought. What was Roger talking about?

She shrugged. "The population is so large, its economic power so dispersed—that sort of consistency is just the weak law of large numbers at work. Any local spikes or troughs in suicides are subsumed within the whole."

"And what would cause those local spikes, Senator?"

"You know that, Niles. Money is the key to everything. Economic downturns lead to a higher suicide rate, murder rate, and infant mortality, even on the wealthiest worlds. Human society is a fragile weave; if the pool of resources shrinks, we're at each other's throats."

He nodded, his face growing lighter by the moment in the rising sun.

"So, when you trade tax relief and axis protections, pushing around wealth in accordance with the grand Secularist plan, what are you really trading?"

The bright sun had reached her face, and Nara Oxham closed her eyes. As often happened when she was out of synesthesia's reach, ghost images of old data danced before her eyes. She could reflexively visualize what Niles was saying. On a world of a billion people, a decrease of one percentage point in planetary product would result in well-established statistical shifts: some ten thousand additional murders, five thousand suicides, another million in the next generation who would never leave the planet. The explanations for each tragedy were terribly specific—a broken home, a business failure, ethnic conflict—but the god of statistics swallowed the individual stories, smoothing the numbers into law.

"Of course," Niles interrupted her thoughts, "the process

you're used to is rather more indirect than ordering soldiers to their deaths."

Oxham nodded. She had no will left to argue the point.

"I'd hoped you would cheer me up, Roger," she said.

He leaned forward. "You did the right thing, Nara, as I said before. Your political instincts were correct, as always. And it's possible that the council actually made the right military decision."

She shook her head. They'd condemned the *Lynx* without a clear reason.

"But here's what I was trying to say," Niles continued. "You've handled issues of this import before."

"I've traded in lives before, you mean."

His gaze swept down from the bright sky to the huge city.

"We are in the business of power, Senator. And power at this scale is a matter of life and death."

She sighed. "Do you think they'll all die, Roger?"

"The crew of the *Lynx*?" he asked.

The old advisor was looking straight at her. The sunrise had found his gray hairs, which glinted like strands of boyish red. She could tell that her anguish was revealed on her face.

"It's Laurent Zai, isn't it?"

Oxham lowered her eyes, which was sufficient answer. She'd known that Niles would find out soon enough. He knew that Oxham's lover was a soldier, and there were a limited number of occasions when a Secularist senator would come into contact with military personnel. The Emperor's parties were a matter of record, and they were monitored by an informal system of rumors, gossip sheets, and anonymous posts, all of which were filtered through celebrity newsfeeds. An intense and private conversation between a senator-elect and an elevated hero, no matter how brief, could not have gone unreported.

Any doubts that Niles might have entertained would be vanquished once he'd uncovered that decade-old conversation. It must have been obvious to him why Nara was focused on the fate of the *Lynx*.

She sighed, sadder still now. Her closest advisor knew that she had voted for the death of her lover.

He leaned closer.

"Listen Nara: it will be safer for you if they all die cleanly."

Her eyes stung now. She tried to read Niles, but she'd had to up the dose of apathy in her bloodstream to cross the city, which was bright and sharp with war lust.

"Safer?" she managed after a moment.

"If the Risen Emperor were to discover that one of his war counselors communicated privately with a commander in the field, one who then rejected a blade of error," Niles explained, "he'd have her head on a stake."

She swallowed.

"I'm protected by privilege, Niles."

"Like any legal construct, the Rubicon Pale is a fiction, Nara. Such fictions have their limits."

Oxham looked at her old friend aghast. The Pale was the basis of the Risen Empire's fundamental division of power. It was sacred.

But Niles continued. "You're playing both sides, Senator. And that's a dangerous game."

She started to respond, but the council summons sounded in her head.

"I have to go, Niles. The war calls me."

He nodded. "So it does. Just don't make yourself a casualty, Nara."

She smiled sadly.

"This is war," she said. "People die."

Militia Worker

Rana Harter was happy here on the tundra.

It had taken her a few days in the prefab to grasp and name the feeling. Before meeting the Rixwoman, happiness had only ever come to her in short, evanescent bursts: a few seconds when sunset drenched the sky in the smell of chamomile; a man's touch in the feathery moments before he became brutal; those brief flashes of trumpet and copper-on-the-tongue as Rana's brainbug took hold and the world emerged exact and clear. But the happiness she felt now was somehow sustained, awakening with her each morning, stretching across these long and listless nights she spent with Herd, constantly amazing Rana with its persistence.

Like the whorls of her fingertips in a microscope, joy turned out to be entirely unfamiliar when viewed at this new and larger scale. Rana understood now that the happy moments of her earlier life had been furtive, truncated. Like a wild tundra hare, felicity had always bolted before she could grasp it, slipping across the bleak background of her life, a mere streak forever in peripheral vision. She had been ashamed of her mind's abilities, overawed by the beautiful but brutal natural world of her cold home province, embarrassed by the pleasures she took with men. But now Rana could actually witness her happiness directly, magnified through the lens of eleven-hour Legis nights when Herd was released from duty.

Rana Harter had discovered unimaginable new textures of contentment. She could count the grains in a teaspoon of spilled sugar, listen for hours to the moaning song of the incessant polar wind as it tested the walls of their cheap rented prefab. Even Herd's intense, daily ministrations—shaving every part of her, cutting hair and nails, swabbing saliva, abrading skin—became rough pleasures. The Rixwoman's competent hands, her brittle conversation, and her strange, birdlike movements were endlessly fascinating.

Rana knew that Herd had given her a drug, and that the joy she felt had been forced upon her, leveraged by chemicals rather than events. She knew obectively that she should be terrified: suffering forcible confinement and isolation with a deadly alien. Rana even considered escape once, out of an abstract sense of duty to the militia and her home planet, and from worry that the Rixwoman would eventually dispose of her. Rana had managed to dress herself, the fabric of her old clothes sensually harsh against raw skin. Warmth had required layers and layers; Herd always took their only winter coat to work at the facility. But when Rana opened the door to the prefab, the cold poured in with the blinding glare of the white tundra. The frozen vista of the polar waste muted any desire for freedom. It only reminded Rana how bleak her life had been before. She closed the door and turned the heat up to compensate for the inrush of frigid air, then took off the chafing clothes. She could not leave.

But Rana never felt defeated here in this cabin. Somehow, her mind seemed freed by captivity. It was as if her brain-bug, no longer suppressed by shame, had finally been given the opportunity to develop to its true capacity.

Rana loved teaching the northern Legis XV dialect to Herd. While her captor was away impersonating her, Rana spent the hours diagramming the structure of basic Imperial grammar, filling the prefab's cheap airscreen with webs of conjugations surrounded by archipelagos of slang, patois, and irregulars. Her student was an unbelievably quick learner. The commando's knowledge advanced nightly, Herd's flat, neutral accent taking on the rounded vowels of the tundral provinces.

Rana demanded to be taught in return, insisting that knowledge of the Rix tongue would improve her tutoring of Herd. Rana also learned quickly, and they began to converse late into the night, Rana firing away with questions about Herd's upbringing, beliefs, and life in the Rix Cult. At first, the commando resisted these attempts at companionship, but the cold and featureless Legis nights seemed to wear away at her resolve. Soon, the conversation between hostage and captor became constant and bilingual, each speaking the other's language.

At first, Rix was easy to learn. The core grammar of the language was artificial, created by compound minds to facilitate communication between planetary intelligences and their servants. But the language was designed to evolve quickly in human use, its streamlined phonology of clicks and pops infinitely malleable, able to embrace the unwieldy tenses of relativity or the chance-matrices of the quantum.

In Rana's mind, now constantly in a light brainbug fugue, the collectivity of things Rix began to take on a definite shape/flavor/smell. The clean lines of Herd's weapons, the icy sharpness of the woman's language, the whir of her servomotors, just audible when Herd was naked, the way hypercarbon melded into skin at her knees, elbows, and shoulders—all were of a piece. This Rix-shape grew in Rana Harter's head, putting to shame the brainbugs of her earlier life, the mathematical parlor tricks to which the Empire put her ability. Here was the flavor of a whole *culture,* as deep and heady as some ancient whiskey perpetually under her nose.

Rana watched her captor as if in love, pupils dialated with the dopamine coursing through her bloodstream, brilliant revelations growing within.

After three days at the pole, Herd began to question Rana about Imperial entanglement technology. Under the current state of emergency, the entire polar facility was cut off from the Legis information web; thus the compound mind could only assist indirectly with whatever sabotage they were planning. Herd, a soldier rather than an engineer, was unable to effect the changes that the mind demanded. Rana tried to help with her limited understanding of the arrays used in microastronomy, but her answers often confused Herd; the underlying Rix concepts of quantum theory differed from the Imperial model. The two systems seemed fatally at odds. For one, the Rix standard model rendered the curves of discernible difference with a different number of dimensions than the Imperial. And their notion of discoherence escaped Rana altogether.

So she put her hours of quiet happiness to work, beginning a study of translight communications. She found the Legis library unexpectedly helpful. Almost immediately, Rana found an expert program to help her. The expert bookmarked and highlighted the primary texts, guided her through the morass of beginner's texts to build on her elementary understanding of repeater arrays. The expert seemed to understand Rana, quickly learning to mold information into the form demanded by her brainbug, pulling in the chaotic, widespread data upon which her ability feasted. Herd brought home an attachment for the cabin's airscreen, a second-sight projector that allowed Rana to go into full synesthesia. She sank into the coils of data, willing prey. Herd had never told Rana exactly what the commando's mission was here at the pole, but her study seemed to guide itself.

She found herself fascinated by the backup receivers that supported the facility, collecting the planet's conventional tranmissions and forwarding them to the translight grid. Their were many systems in place in case the hardlines were cut, but Rana was especially drawn to a colony of hardy, small, self-repairing machines that lived on the polar wastes around the facility. They were like the cheap, distributed arrays that Rana had used before in microastronomy, designed to survive arctic winters, earthquakes, and acts of terrorism.

After a few sleepless days, Rana collapsed into a sleep/fugue that lasted some untold time. When she awoke, Herd was next to her, applying a cold rag to her fevered head. The usual joy of awakening filled her, heightened now with the surety of new knowledge. It was in the lemongrass flicker of Herd's eyes, the precision of her movements as she squeezed excess water from the rag, and it animated the shape of Rana's researches in the cabin's airscreen: the flavor of her understanding reflected throughout the room.

"The expert program," Rana said in the Rix tongue. "It's the compound mind, isn't it?"

Herd nodded, and answered quietly.

"It is always with us." The sentence was one syllable in Rix.

The commando held the red wig in one hand. Rana's own hair, removed so long ago, now seemed an alien artifact to her. The Rixwoman fitted the wig onto Rana's head. It felt warm, as if fresh from an oven. It seemed to fit perfectly.

"You will be Rana Harter tomorrow," Herd said.

The thought of leaving the prefab terrified her.

"But I don't even know what you want," Rana said, slipping into Legis dialect. The Imperial language felt crude, like thick porridge in her mouth.

"Yes, you do," the Rixwoman said.

Rana shook her head. She thought hard in her native tongue: she knew *nothing*. As it had done all her life, confidence crumbled inside Rana.

"I don't understand. I'm not smart enough."

Herd smiled, and touched the cold rag to Rana's forehead. With that contact, her anxiety lifted. Separate threads began to weave themselves together: the data from her guided exploration of repeater technology, the emerging shape and flavor of Rix culture, the fast Bach and lemongrass of Herd's powerful and avian presence.

And quite suddenly, Rana Harter knew the compound mind's desire.

Herd's servomotors whirred as her hands moved across

Rana. She was applying some sort of cream to Rana's embattled skin. The touch felt delicious, a balm against the fever of realization in her head.

"Don't worry, my lucky find," the commando said. "Alexander is with you now."

Alexander. The thing actually had a name.

Rana touched her fingers to her own forehead.

"Inside me?"

"Everywhere."

Executive Officer

Katherie Hobbes let the water run into her glass in a thin, slow stream, until it had filled to the brim. The tap stopped automatically, before even a drop ran down the side; water wasn't rationed here on board the *Lynx,* but wastefulness went against the aesthetics of the Navy.

Hobbes turned from the sink in slow motion, her green eyes following each motion of her hand, carefully watching the wobble of the surface tension that held the water in the glass. She took the few steps that it took to cross the executive officer's private cabin, her movements an exaggerated pantomime. The glass felt strangely heavy, although the *Lynx*'s high acceleration was, in theory, fully corrected. Was the extra weight a stress hallucination? Perhaps Hobbes's limbs were simply tired, beaten down by the constant microshifts of easy gravity.

Or perhaps it was her disappointment. She hadn't had time to recover from Zai's revelation before the weight of high acceleration had settled painfully upon her.

Normally, the vicissitudes of artificial gravity created

only a vague disquiet in Hobbes, no worse than the motion sickness she'd experienced on the great, seagoing pleasure craft of her Utopian home. But the *Lynx* was currently accelerating at ten gees, and the slight flaws and inconsistencies of easy gravity were correspondingly magnified.

The field patterns of easy gravity were a classic metachaotic system, mined with strange attractors, stochastic overloads, and a host of other mathematical chimeras. Fluctuations of mass on one side of a solar system could affect easy gravitons on the other unpredictably, even fatally. It was not quite the case that the flutter of a butterfly's wings could cause a tornado, but the swift rotation of Legis system's seven gas giants and the massive solar flares of its sun constituted more than enough chaos to perturb Katherie Hobbes's inner ear.

Hobbes could feel the effects of high acceleration in her joints as well. Every few minutes, something as simple as taking a step would go subtly wrong, as if the floor had come up slightly too hard to meet her foot. Or an object in her hand would jump from her grasp, as if suddenly pulled by an invisible hand. The stresses were rarely strong, but the constant unpredictability of normal events had gradually worn down her reflexes, fatiguing Hobbes's faith in reality. Now she mistrusted the simplest of actions, just as she mistrusted her own emotions.

What a fool was Katherie Hobbes.

Could she have really thought that Laurent Zai was in love with her, even for a moment? When had that insane idea begun? She felt an idiot; a young idiot, suffering a classic infatuation with a distant, older authority figure. The whole episode had shaken her faith in herself, and the random jumps of gravity that plagued the *Lynx* weren't helping. She wished she could have a hot bath, and cursed the Navy for its disdain for this simple, necessary pleasure.

At least she had other things to worry about. The flexing gravity around her was real enough, and wielded outliers of lethal force. The night before, the marble chessboard in Hobbes's locker had suddenly, earsplittingly cracked, rudely interrupting her fitful sleep.

A few minor injuries had occurred on the *Lynx* in the first few days of acceleration. Ankle fractures and knee sprains were common, a young marine's arm had broken without apparent cause, and burst blood vessels were visible in the eyes of a number of her shipmates. Katherie herself had suffered an unbearable and sudden headache the day before. It had passed quickly, but the intense pain was unnerving. With the ship's doctor dead, there was little hope for anyone suffering brain damage from some wayward tendril of gravity passing through their head.

Hobbes walked carefully, and reached the black lacquer table without spilling any of the water.

Setting the glass on the table, she sat and watched the water's surface. It loomed just above the lip, quivering slightly. Was that some perturbation of the easy gravity field? Or simply the ambient vibration of the *Lynx* under high acceleration, marking the egress of photons from its churning engines?

The water shuddered once, but the surface tension held. A few drops condensed on the side of the glass and traveled slowly downward. Nothing seemed to be out of order in that tiny segment of space.

It gave Katherie a secure feeling to observe this localized example of soundness and normality.

After a minute of watching, Hobbes picked up the glass and poured it slowly onto the table.

The water seemed to turn black against the ebony lacquer. It formed into rivulets and small pools, seeking the imperceptible valleys of the table's contours. None was absorbed into the shiny blackness; the water's surface tension kept the drops large and rounded.

On a dry island in this shallow sea she placed the diamond Laurent Zai had given her, a bright spot against its blackness.

Hobbes set the half-full glass down and regarded the results.

At first, the liquid seemed to come to rest, gathered in spattery puddles, with one tiny river reaching the edge and running from table onto floor. Then, Hobbes saw something move across the blackness, a wave of force, as if the table had been kicked. A few seconds later, one of the tendrils of water flexed in agitation, twisting like a beached fish. A single, isolated droplet moved a few centimeters, as if momentarily inhabited by a live spirit, and engulfed the tiny diamond. Then the water was still again.

Hobbes waited patiently, and more flutters of motion came. Spread across the table's two dimensions, its passage on the lacquer almost frictionless, the spilled water writhed visibly with the microshifts of artificial gravity coursing through the *Lynx*. In its sinuous motion, it revealed gravitic lines of force like iron filings rendering the patterns of magnetism.

It eased Katherie's mind to watch the water move. Now that she could actually see the invisible forces that had tortured her crewmates for the last week, Hobbes felt a bit more in control. She gazed at the black table, trying to scry some understanding from the patternless figures there. But easy gravitons were chaotic, complex, unpredictable: like the ancients' concept of the gods, whimsical and obscure, pushing tiny humans around according to some incomprehensible plan. Not unlike, Katherie Hobbes reflected, the political forces that moved the *Lynx* across the black and empty canvas of space, placing them here at this nexus of a new war, condemning the captain, pardoning him, then sending them all careening toward death.

Like the drops of water before her, the crew of the *Lynx* wriggled blindly against this void. An emotion that had seemed immense to Hobbes had become suddenly infinitesimal, laughable. On the scale of the universe, the aborted love of one executive officer for her captain made no ripples at all.

Still, at this moment, Hobbes knew she hated Laurent Zai with all her heart.

When her door sounded, Katherie Hobbes started, banging her knee against the table's leg.

"Come," she said, rubbing the leg, her latest wound.

Second Gunner Thompson entered, taking slow, careful steps, like a practiced alcoholic. He smiled when he saw the water-covered table.

"Spill something? I've been doing that all week."

"Just an experiment," she said.

He shrugged, and pointed to the chair opposite her. She nodded. Thompson lowered himself carefully, mindful of the poltergeists of gravity all around them.

It occurred to Hobbes that the second gunner had never been in her private cabin before. He had always been friendly, but perhaps a bit too familiar, as if he felt that his aristocratic roots entitled him beyond his rank. And Hobbes was aware of the effect she had on some crew. Her Utopian upbringing had casually included a degree of cosmetic surgery that gray parents would never countenance. She was overwhelmingly beautiful to many of them, and to others a woman of cartoonish sexuality, like a whore in some ribald comedy. She had considered counteractive surgery to make herself more average-looking, but that seemed the ultimate affectation. Hobbes was what she was.

The man sighed when he reached the safety of the chair.

"I'm sore all over," he said.

"Who isn't?" Hobbes answered. "Just be glad you can't feel the real ten gees. *Then* you'd be sore. Dead by now, in fact."

Thompson's head rolled back slowly in exhaustion; his eyes closed.

"The worst thing is," he said, "I can't quite place where it hurts. It's like when you turn an ankle, and wind up limping for a few days. Then the *other* ankle gets sore from taking up the slack."

"Collateral injuries," she said.

"Right. But I seem to be *all* collateral injuries, like I can't remember where the original damage was. Very disquieting."

Hobbes looked down at the table. Her collision with it had spattered the water evenly across the black expanse, and now it revealed nothing but the ship's ambient vibration.

"I know what you mean," she said. "I've been trying to get a hold of it myself. To place it . . . in perspective."

Thompson opened his eyes, squinted at her. Then he shrugged.

"Ever been in high acceleration this long before, Hobbes?"

She shook her head. Few of the crew had. High gees were usually reserved for battle, a few hours at most.

"Makes you wonder what we did to deserve it," Thompson said.

Something about the man's voice made her look up from the spattered table. His eyes were narrowed.

"We lost the Empress," she answered flatly.

He nodded deliberately, as if wary of gravity even in this simple motion.

"A debt that wasn't paid," he said softly.

A slow disquiet took form in Hobbes's stomach, joining the nausea that lay there. "What are you talking about, Thompson?"

"Katherie, do you really think the Navy wants to sacrifice the *Lynx*?" he asked. His voice was as soft now, just above a whisper. "Simply to prevent one compound mind from communicating with one Rix ship?"

"So it would seem, Thompson," she said.

"But we can't keep the mind cut off forever," he said. "It's a whole *planet*, for the Emperor's sake. The Rix'll find some way to talk to it."

"Maybe. But not while the *Lynx* is here."

"However long that is," he said.

She looked down at the table, unable to think for a moment. The water looked different now. The surface tension seemed to be reasserting itself; droplets and puddles were forming again. It didn't make sense, this spontaneous organization. Was entropy giving way to order, the arrow of time in reverse?

What was Thompson talking about?

"Tell me what's on your mind, Second Gunner," Hobbes ordered.

"It's obvious, Katherie," he said, "why the *Lynx* is being sent on this mission. We're being sacrificed, to cover the debt not paid."

Hobbes closed her eyes. She only had a few seconds to respond, she knew.

Katherie Hobbes had been an above-average student at Academy, but not the best. Coming from a Utopian world, she didn't have the discipline of her gray peers. She didn't think herself truly brilliant, just savant at certain types of tactical calculations. But even in her greatest moments of self-doubt, Hobbes always prided herself on one thing: she made decisions quickly.

Katherie Hobbes made a decision now.

"Thompson, are you the only one thinking about this?"

He shook his head, so slightly that it would have been imperceptible in a low-resolution recording.

"Tell me what you're thinking, Thompson."

"We've been friends, right, Hobbes?"

She nodded.

"So you give your word that you'll be . . . discreet?"

Hobbes sighed. She'd hoped it wouldn't come to this. But her decision was made.

"The way I see it, Thompson," she said, "we're all dead anyway."

He smiled ruefully, folding his hands and shifting in his seat toward her.

"Maximum privacy," she told the room, and leaned forward to listen.

Militia Worker

As Rana Harter approached the sniffer, she felt like an impostor.

The red wig tight on her head, the coarse militia fatigues against her raw skin, the military ID bracelet—it all felt like a costume, a ruse that might be discovered at any second. In the burnished metal walls of the facility her own reflection was only distantly familiar, a holo from childhood. It was as if she were impersonating a previous self.

The sniffer created a bottleneck as the workers entered the array facility. Rana felt a moment of panic as she joined the crowd. The week she'd spent alone with Herd in the prefab seemed like months now—the lengthened memory of some summer idyll. Isolation had a purity about it, a calm order that was hard to leave behind. The jostling crowd offended her new sensibilities.

She wished that Herd were here with her, a familiar presence to guide her through the strange facility. The commando had impersonated Rana for the last week, and knew her way within these walls. But the sniffer would no doubt take umbrage at *two* Rana Harters entering together.

There was a slight updraft in the short passageway of the sniffer, slow fans assisting the human thermal plume, carrying skin cells and dust upward. With these particles the device could not only DNA-type the entering workers, but also detect the effluvia of concealed explosives or weapons, and search frayed hairs and skin cells for signs of drug or alcohol abuse. It could even sniff theft; valuable pieces of equipment in the facility were given phero patches. Whatever you were up to, the sniffer smelled you out.

Rana held her breath as she passed through. Would the device notice the difference between herself and Herd? The thought of being stopped and questioned terrified her. She might be Rana Harter down to the bone, but she felt utterly false.

She hoped her epidermis had recovered sufficiently to satisfy the machine's appetite. Herd had worked a healing balm into her skin all night, trying to restore the cells the commando had mined so pitilessly for her own use. The balm seemed to have worked, taking the pink rawness from her skin—but after the last week, any attempt to put the old Rana Harter back together seemed woefully insufficient. She felt half Rix now.

The sniffer, however, let her through without comment.

Herd had drawn a map on a piece of flash paper. Rana held the paper carefully: any friction and it would incinerate itself. She followed the map through narrow, dimly lit hallways. The tight hypercarbon spaces down here felt like the corridors of an overcrowded ship, and smelled of damp and humanity. The facility was overstaffed by half, Rana knew. Herd had said that a fresh load of newcomers had arrived two days ago, along with news of another approaching Rix warship. The signs of organizational confusion were everywhere: equipment stacked in carry-cases crowding the halls, breakrooms filled with impromptu workstations, newly assigned workers moving through the hallways carrying order chits and looking lost.

The repeater array that collected the planet's com traffic for offworld retransmission was being refitted to assist Legis's orbital defenses. The changeover from communications to intelligence gathering was taking place at breakneck speed.

When Rana met other workers in the hall, she found herself moving like Herd. Another imitation, in case any of the passersby had met the commando in her Rana Harter guise. The avian motions—sudden and tightly controlled, each joint an isolated engine—came to Rana with an unexpected ease. In a week of living with the commando, she had internalized the woman's gait, copying her avian power and unpredictability. The impersonation seemed to work, even though there was a decimeter difference in stature between herself and her captor. A few of the other workers nodded with recognition or said her name in greeting.

Rana responded to them with Herd's cryptic smile.

It would, of course, be easy to escape the Rixwoman now. She could announce herself to the facility's security forces—pulling off the wig would certainly get their attention. And she was safe from retaliation. Alexander was absent here. The links from the planetary infostructure to the entanglement facility had been physically cut by Imperial edict. The usual ghosts of second sight—timestamps, newsfeeds, and locators—were oddly absent. There was nothing Herd or Alexander could do to her.

But if she betrayed them, the happiness would go away.

Herd had already injected her with the antidote for the dopamine regulators. The nanos' influence had diminished already, the joy she had floated upon for the last week slowly winding down. Herd had insisted, and it was true, that with the gauze of happiness gone she would be more clearheaded for this job. But her undrugged mind threatened to return to its former state of indecision and fear. She could already glimpse that wavering, all-too-human Rana Harter waiting in the wings. The confident, hybrid creature she had become could crumble at any moment.

She knew she would not betray her new allies. Rana wanted to keep this reborn self. The Rixwoman and her omnipotent god had erased a lifetime of marginal existence, borderline depression, and unfulfilled potential. They had done more for Rana Harter in a week than the Empire had in twenty-seven years.

And besides, this was a mission of mercy, she now understood. Alexander must be freed.

Following the map, she found the workstation for Rana Harter, Second-Class Militia Worker. The interface was unfamiliar from her days in quantum microastronomy. As Herd had explained, she had been assigned to monitor and repair the hundreds of receivers/repeaters that funneled the world's data into the entanglement facility. Her transfer here—arranged by Alexander—had been justified by Rana's practical knowledge of distributed arrays. She'd been assigned to the GAP's remote, icy wastes all her career, and had often been required to make her own repairs.

But she would be doing more than repairs today.

Hopefully, no one would interrupt her shift. The chaos of the overcrowded station was such that a self-sufficient operator was largely left to her own devices. Rana sat, called up the workstation's help mode, and began to look things over.

By the end of her shift, Rana Harter had found everything that Alexander wanted.

The entanglement facility had been designed for exactly the type of traffic the compound mind envisioned. The facility incorporated a huge number of repeaters that gathered information from local planetary communications—phones, credit cells, taxation minders, legal governors—and pumped compressed versions of these data into the entanglement system. Despite its military provenance, the facility's primary purpose was to link the planet's civilian economy with the rest of the Risen Empire. There were even FM radio transmitters to throughput data to the other Legis planets at lightspeed; XV was the fleshpot and de facto capital of the system.

In peacetime, these transmissions came into the entanglement facility through hardlines, and in emergencies, through the repeaters. Scattered through the acres of the facility were tens of thousands of tiny civilian-band receivers, a vast colony of machines that lived on snow and sunlight. The repeater colony extended for hundreds of square kilometers, to the edge of the wire: a lethal barrier surrounding the facility. These receivers were like weeds among rare flowers, banal technology compared with the translight communications they supported, but self-repairing and hardy enough to withstand arctic winters.

Rana examined the system with growing frustration, the metallic taste of failure in her mouth. She couldn't help Alexander. Nothing could be done from her repair station to reconnect the entanglement facility to the rest of the planet. The repeater software was too distributed, too autonomous to respond to a central command. And the repeaters themselves were switched off—not ordered into sleep mode, but physically turned off *by hand*. The imperials were taking Legis's isolation very seriously.

Someone would have to go into the array field itself to make the necessary changes. Past the minefields, sniffers, and microfilament barriers of the wire. It had taken hundreds of militia workers to physically turn the repeaters off.

She sighed. There was nothing she could do herself. This was a problem for Alexander and Herd. If Rana could smuggle them the data she had collected, she wouldn't have to return to this awful place.

She searched her workstation for some way to bring the data to Herd, and settled on a memory strip borrowed from a repairbot's internal camera. A schematic of the simple repeaters fit easily into the memory strip's capacity, and she added a map of the array and the barrier wire's specs. Rana shut her station down and erased her researches; her shift was almost over.

Now she could return to the warmth and safety of the prefab, to happiness.

When the shift siren blew, Rana rose from her chair

stiffly, hands shaking. The muscles of her legs felt weak. Anxiety had built over the long shift, stealing into every tissue of her body. Rana knew that she needed the surety of Herd's drugs. Soon.

She wished now that she'd eaten something today. But she'd wanted desperately to finish her work in a single shift and never return here.

Calming herself by imagining the strip-heater glow that lit the prefab, Rana joined the other militia workers jostling their way toward the facility exit. The six work shifts of the long Legis day overlapped to prevent this sort of rush-hour crowding, but the narrow corridors of the overstaffed station were always crowded, even in peacetime. Rana found herself swept along in a human flow, and the scent of tired workers became overwhelming.

Strange, how humanity repulsed her now. The empty chatter, the profusion of colors and body types, the clumsiness of the crowd's movement around her. Without trying, Rana still walked with the avian grace of her captor; the imitation had somehow insinuated itself into her bones. She longed to shuck the wig and its pointless, decorative excess of hair. Rana closed her eyes, and saw the clean lines of Alexander's airscreen charts, the scimitar curves of Herd's weapons, the flavor of Rix. Biting her lip, she made her way through the halls.

Soon, she would be back home.

The crowd's progress slowed to a crawl as she neared the exit. Bodies pressed in closer. The overwhelming human smell made Rana's hands begin to shake. The scent seemed to leach all oxygen from the air. Meaningless conversations surrounded and battered her, a hail of empty words. She distracted herself by reading the sniffer's warning signs: *Declare Any Volatiles, Nanos, or Facility Property.*

With a start, Rana remembered that the sniffer could detect stolen equipment.

She shook her head to drive away paranoia. The memory

strip in her pocket was insignificant, the sort of cheap media that came free with disposable phones and cameras. Surely it wasn't marked with pheros. But among the signs, her nervously darting eyes now found the words: *Sign Out ALL Data Storage Devices.*

Rana swallowed, remembering the data she'd put on the strip. A map of the facility, the repeater schematics, the specs for the lethal wire. From those three files, her intent couldn't be more obvious. The sniffer was only a few meters ahead of her now. She planted her feet to resist the bodies pressing her forward.

Rana fingered the memory strip in her pocket. It was too small to hold a phero patch. But what if they'd sprayed it with pheros as a matter of course?

Security was tight here, but *that* tight?

Frantic thoughts crowded her mind. The overstaffed facility seemed utterly disorganized; such a subtle measure didn't seem likely. But she remembered an old rumor about a creeper security nano that Imperials unleashed on top secret bases. Something that propagated slowly, phero-marking each machine and human it came into contact with, so that everything could be tracked from a central station. The idea had seemed fantastic at the time, the paranoia of low-level workers.

But now it seemed just barely possible.

The crowd was pressing her impatiently from behind. One of the guards at the sniffer, a marine in Imperial black, was looking at Rana with vague interest as the other workers flowed around her. She ordered herself to move forward; there was no escaping the sniffer without calling attention to herself.

But her feet would not move. She was too afraid, too tired. It was too much to ask.

She remembered boarding the maglev on the way here, her hesitation before climbing the stairs. That old paralysis—the old Rana Harter—had returned with a vengeance.

The marine rose from his stool, eyeing her suspiciously.

Move! Rana commanded herself. But she remained put.

Then a glint of metal caught her eye. Down the sniffer hallway before her, Rana saw the flash of an officer's badge.

It was Herd, wearing her militia colonel's uniform, beckoning her forward.

At that sight, the panic that had held Rana fast was suddenly broken. She moved toward the sniffer, knowing Herd would protect her, would return her to happiness.

Rana Harter stepped into the sniffer, and was for a moment alone, separated from the press of bodies. The updraft took away the rancid smell of the crowd.

Then a siren began to scream, so loud that in Rana's synesthesia it became a towering cage of fire around her, as blinding as the sun on lidless eyes.

Executive Officer

The conspirators met in one of the zero-gee courts that surrounded sickbay. The courts were empty, of course, being unusable under high acceleration. The mere notion of playing rackets or dribblehoop in this unstable gravity made Hobbes's knee ligaments ache.

There were only five conspirators present, including herself. Hobbes had expected more, actually. Five didn't seem enough of a critical mass to warrant plotting a mutiny. There must be more, but Thompson wasn't tipping his hand yet. No doubt some of his cards were in reserve.

She knew all those present: the ringleader Second Gunner Thompson; Yen Hu, another young officer from gunnery; Third Pilot Magus, her face sour and strained; and one of the communications ensigns, Daren King. Apparently, this was no crewman's mutiny. Everyone here had stars on their uniform.

They all seemed relieved when she walked in. Perhaps as the ship's second-in-command, Hobbes somehow validated the enterprise.

But Thompson took charge for the moment. He closed the door of the rackets court, which sealed itself seamlessly, and leaned against the small window in its center to block his small handlight from spilling into the hall. The precautions were hardly necessary, Hobbes thought. Under the current cruel regime of high acceleration, the crew moved about the ship as little as possible. She doubted security was monitoring the ship's listening devices very carefully, though Ensign King or other conspirators unknown to Hobbes must be jiggering any bugs in the zero-gee court in case they were queried later.

This was to be a silent coup.

"Not really a mutiny at all," Thompson was saying.

"What would you call it, then?" Hobbes asked.

Second Pilot Magus spoke up. "I guess, properly speaking, it's a murder."

There was an intake of breath from Yen Hu. The assembled conspirators looked at him. Hobbes was sorry to see Hu in on this. He was only two years out of academy. Gunner Thompson must have worked hard to break him down.

"A mercy killing," corrected Thompson.

"Mercy on . . . ?" Magus asked.

"Us," Thompson finished. "The captain's dead, whatever happens. No point in the rest of us going down with him."

Thompson took a step back from the rest of the group, making them his audience.

"The rest of the Empire may believe that pardon, but we know that Captain Zai refused the blade of error. The Emperor knows it too."

Hobbes found herself nodding.

"This attack on the Rix battlecruiser is a pointless sacrifice of the *Lynx*," Thompson continued. "We should be standing off and coordinating with the Legis planetary defenses. Protecting civilians against bombardment, we could save millions. Instead, we're engaged in a suicide mission."

"Do you really think the Navy would change our orders at this point?" she asked.

"If the captain accepts the blade in the next day or so, they'll have time to order us back. The politicals will make up something about Zai-the-hero being the only officer who could have pulled off the attack against the battlecruiser. The *Lynx* can gracefully withdraw back into the system defenses. With Zai dead, it'd be pointless to sacrifice us."

Despite what they were plotting, it rankled Hobbes to hear the captain's name used without the honorific of rank.

"My math shows that we've got twenty-five hours to make turnaround," Second Pilot Magus said. "A few more, really. We could always get to twelve gees after turnaround."

"No thanks," Thompson said. With every gee they added, the easy gravity field would grow geometrically more unstable.

"Well, in any case," Magus said. "Any longer than thirty hours, and we'll be committed to meeting the Rix battlecruiser outside of Legis's defenses."

Hobbes wondered if Magus had taken the precaution of doing the calculations by hand. Computer use, even at trivial demand levels, was always recorded.

"And once it's done, we've got to get word back to Home that the Captain's committed suicide," said Ensign King. "Then they've got to make a decision, and get word back to us. Assuming we draw from our Home-connected entanglement store, there's no com lag."

"But how long will it take for the Navy to make a decision?" Magus asked.

The four of them looked at Hobbes. They knew she'd

worked as an admiral's staff officer before being assigned to the *Lynx*. Hobbes frowned. She'd seen complex, crucial decisions taken in minutes; she'd seen days go by before consensus was reached. And the decision to save or lose the *Lynx* was as much political as military. The question was: Did anyone expect Zai to take the blade now? Would there be a contingency plan ready to go?

But that was irrelevant to Hobbes. The important thing was to keep the conspirators from taking any precipitous actions. If they felt they were up against the clock, they would be harder to control.

"It won't matter how long it takes," she said flatly.

"Why not?" Magus asked.

Hobbes paced a moment, thinking furiously. Then it came to her.

"With Captain Zai dead, the *Lynx* is my ship. The moment I take command, I'll make the turnaround and ask for new orders," she said.

"Perfect," Thompson whispered.

"But you'll be disobeying direct orders," Yen Hu said. "Won't you?"

"If they tell us to continue the attack, there'll be time to get into some kind of position. But I don't think they will. They'll thank me for taking the decision out of their hands."

Thompson laughed. "Hobbes, you old devil. I was half certain you'd throw me to the captain for even talking to you. And now *you're* going to take all the credit for this, aren't you?" He put one hand on her shoulder, the touch intimate in the darkness.

"A subtle sort of credit," she said. "Let's just say we don't have to cover our tracks too carefully."

"What are you talking about?" Hu asked. He was completely confused now.

Magus turned to the young ensign. "ExO Hobbes doesn't care if the Apparatus suspects that mutiny occurred, as long as they can't prove it. She believes her initiative will be appreciated."

Hu looked at her with a kind of horror. He had entered into this to save the *Lynx*, not advance anyone's career. He was obviously aghast that she was thinking past the current crisis of survival. Good, she thought. Hu needed to be focused on the long term. Even if this conspiracy fell apart here and now, he'd already changed his life forever.

"So, sometime in the next twenty-five hours," Thompson said, "Laurent Zai will take the blade of error."

"The later the better," Hobbes said. "My decision to pull the *Lynx* back makes more sense if there isn't time left to get new orders from the Navy. The captain should go off his watch the day after tomorrow at 9.50, twenty-two hours from now."

"Are we all agreed then?" Thompson asked.

They were silent for a moment. Hobbes hoped that someone would say something. There must be some quiet, cutting remark, she thought, that would bring them all to their senses. At this point she could still imagine the conspiracy sputtering out. The right words could break the spell that Thompson had cast. Only, it couldn't be her to speak up. Hobbes couldn't let them suspect her real purpose in joining their conspiracy.

"There's only one thing," Hu said.

They waited.

The young ensign cleared his throat. "This makes Captain Zai look like a coward. As if he'd been pardoned, but killed himself anyway because he couldn't face the Rix."

Hobbes saw the truth of this dawn on the conspirators' faces, and wondered if Hu had found the right words.

For a few moments, no one said anything. They were all from gray families. Posthumous honor was not a thing to be trifled with. In a world ruled by the living dead, the ghosts of the past were taken very seriously.

Of course, it was Thompson who finally spoke.

"He is a coward," he said bitterly. "He couldn't face the blade. That's why we're in this mess."

Magus nodded, then King, and finally Hu, and they placed their hands palm up in the center of their little circle. An old academy team ritual, enjoined to this perverted purpose. But Hobbes joined them. Thompson placed his last, palm down.

The plan was locked.

Commando

H_rd stood still for a moment as the siren began to wail, watching the crowd's reactions at a calm remove. She noted that the siren cycled with a two-second period between 15 and 25,000 Hertz. At both its extremes, this sine wave went beyond the range of normal human hearing. It dug down low enough to shudder in the gut like a pneumatic hammer, and high enough to shatter fine glass.

The siren was evidently designed to paralyze anyone whose hearing was unprotected. Most of the crowd on h_rd's side of the sniffer covered their ears, their knees bending as if suddenly under high gravity—a few dropped straight to the ground. Poor brainbugged Rana Harter, for whom sounds were solid and visible, crumpled like a column of sand.

Only the two militia guards and the Imperial marine remained effective. H_rd waited for their slow reactions to unfold. As one, they turned their backs on the Rix commando to face Rana Harter, who lay in the sniffer corridor. They pulled weapons, activated helmet displays, took up firing poses.

Satisfied with their incompetence, h_rd sprang into action.

In a few steps, she was behind the Imperial marine, the only real threat to a Rix commando. Her monofilament knife found the seam between helmet and breastplate. The knife was so sharp (sixteen molecules diameter) and her cut so fast that she decapitated him without a drop of blood touching her. She could feel a gurgling sound vibrate the breastplate, but the marine's death rattle was drowned out by the still-protesting siren.

The two militia soldiers were side by side, stepping toward the ragdoll Rana Harter with exaggerated caution. H_rd leapt toward the space between them. She saw one stop, cocking his head to listen to a voice inside his helmet. Someone in tactical control had seen her on-camera, was trying to warn them. It was far too late for that.

She stepped between the militia soldiers and laid a firm hand on their variguns, pulling the barrels away from Rana Harter and toward each other. One obliged her by firing, knocking his partner back three meters. H_rd punched him in the face—he had forgotten to lower his visor—and pulled the weapon from his grasp. She turned it on him. The varigun was set to a concussion stun, a wide-area effect meant for crowd control. At a range of ten centimeters, it burst the man's eyeballs and pushed his jawbone back far enough that it severed his jugular. H_rd reached the sniffer before his body, limbs still flailing with old, irrelevent intentions, hit the ground.

Rana Harter was light as a bird. She draped over h_rd's shoulder like something without bones. The siren was focused here in the sniffer corridor, almost loud enough to damage even Rix hearing. Some sort of gas was drifting upward in the sniffer's draft, but h_rd hadn't breathed since the siren began sounding, and had another thirty seconds or so before she would need to.

Her burden secured, the commando began to run at speed in a zigzag course away from the facility entrance, dropping the few standing workers in her path with the appropriated varigun's concussion effect. She was a hundred yards away when the siren cut off, leaving a staggering silence. For a few moments, static filled her ears, and h_rd thought that her hearing was damaged. But with a quick glance backward she saw the dust rising behind her and realized what the sound was.

A pair of small flechette autocannon were raking the outer grounds of the facility, orienting on the sound of her thudding steps. According to Alexander's researches on the array facility, these cannon used listening devices in the ground to triangulate an intruder's position. But they were falling short, callibrated to hit someone running at normal human velocity. Even in the few meters between her footfalls and the listening devices, the tardy speed of sound made a difference. The incompetence of local militias here in the Spinward Reaches always amazed her; she was glad the few hundred Imperial soldiers had been stretched so thinly across the planet.

Suddenly, the dusty arcs of flechette fire rose up in front of her. Someone was recalibrating the autocannon in real-time, trying to compensate for the Rixwoman's inhuman speed. The gun would catch her soon enough, if only by trial and error; at the moment, she was only a single-variable problem. H_rd asked her internal software for a string of random numbers, and shifted directions to irregularize her course.

But the autocannon were spraying wildly now, their screeching reports pitched above a thousand rounds per minute. They would find her eventually. A few hits wouldn't kill her, but she didn't have time for wounds. One arm wrapped around Rana Harter, h_rd adjusted the varigun to a new setting at random with her teeth. *Damn,* the thing was badly designed—if only she had a spare second to pull her own weapon.

H_rd aimed blindly, without turning her head—her eyes were a soft spot where even a mere flechette could kill her—calculating on the fly the center of an arc of impacts before her. Her weapon recoiled with a satisfying *thump*. Three seconds later, a sharp boom rang out and one of the cannon was silenced.

She swung the varigun the other way, aiming at the center of the remaining arc of dust that swept toward her. Her finger closed on the firing stud.

The gun beeped twice, with that apologetic timbre recognizable in all simple and stupid machines. The weapon had contained only one round at that setting. The stream of flechettes raced along the ground, reaching for her, and h_rd made a rare mistake.

She timed the jump perfectly to clear the arc of fire, but didn't fully take into account the burden of Rana Harter over her shoulder. The commando's leap reached only two meters vertical, and four flechettes plunged into her.

One struck her kneecap, flattened against the exposed hypercarbon, and slid off without leaving a scratch. Another hit a buttock, the small metal arrow tearing bloodily across a broad swath of skin as it bounced off the flexible subdermal armor that protected Rix soldiers from falls. A third passed through her abdomen, nicking the impervious spine and shattering. The shrapnel perforated her stomach, which began healing itself immediately, and destroyed two of her seven kidneys—an acceptable loss.

The only real damage came from the round that struck her left arm. It lodged in the radial notch, wedged as tight as a doorstop in the hypercarbon. Her forearm's flexibility was suddenly reduced to zero. A workaround radius activated itself instantly, allowing the arm to move again, but the strength of the needle-thin workaround was less than ten percent normal. As they landed, Rana Harter fell from h_rd's suddenly weakened grasp, and tumbled across the tundral grasses like a lifeless body thrown from a train.

The commando regained her footing and turned to face the still-shrieking autocannon. With the shaking hand of her damaged arm, she twisted the varigun's controls through its settings, raking the cannon's emplacement with infralaser, magnetic sniper rounds, antipersonnel explosives, a burst of tiny depleted uranium slugs, and a stream of microfoil chaff that set the air to sparkling brightly around her.

The autocannon stuttered to a halt a few seconds before its firing arc would have found her again, either destroyed or overheated.

H_rd's eyes spotted the thermals of more militia soldiers emerging from the array facility, now a kilometer away. They were staying low, moving forward nervously. She fired more microfoil chaff in their direction to baffle any sensors that could image Rana Harter's body heat, then emptied the rest of the chaff straight into the air. She scooped up her fallen burden. The glittering microfoil drifted along with h_rd, the wind at her back, falling like metal snow as she plunged into the tundra waste.

She traveled twenty kilometers before she thought to check Rana Harter for wounds—another mistake.

A host of bruises from the fall covered the woman's skin, and h_rd's thermal vision showed increased bloodflow, the body responding to a sprained wrist. Rana's lower lip was bleeding. Her eyes were starting to flutter open; only time would tell if a head injury had been sustained. Then h_rd saw, barely visible in the winter night's starlight, the fingertip-sized, dark circle of blood staining the militia fatigues.

H_rd knelt, blinded momentarily by a wave of some strange and awful emotion. Then she gathered herself and inspected the wound more closely.

A flechette had passed straight through Rana's chest, hardly slowed by the flimsy calcium rib cage. The projectile was meant to turn to shrapnel inside the body, but had been designed for an armored target. Nothing in the woman's chest had resisted the shell enough to shatter it. It had missed her heart and spine, but had holed one lung.

The woman's breath was fast and shallow. H_rd put her ear to the wound and listened for the telltale whisper of tension pneumothorax, but no pressure was building in the chest cavity. The bleeding had stopped.

H_rd sighed with relief, and something filled her, vibrant and expansive. Not the mere satisfaction of a mission parameter fulfilled, but an animal feeling like the vigor of sex or the calming scent of her home orbital's familiar air.

The cause of this feeling, this swelling of joy: Rana Harter would live.

Senator

The war changed everything.

The council met throughout the week, setting broad guidelines for the tumultuous shifts that would shake the Eighty Worlds for the next few decades.

In the Spinward Reaches, the council altered the reproduction and education laws. The next generation would have to be numerous, and it would have to grow up quickly. The Expansionist senator on the council presented the proposal, using terms like "replacement population." Nara Oxham found the euphemism repulsive: why not simply call them war orphans?

But she voted with the unanimous Council, setting a generous birth dowry to be paid off in lands from the Imperial Conservancy. On twenty planets, virgin climax-stage forests

were parceled into bribes, remuneration for the most productive parents. By the time the hundreds of warships from
anti-spinward reached their new assignments on the Rix
frontier, the babies of this demographic bulge would be old
enough to become marines, ground troops, replacements for
the technical personnel sucked into the war effort. This over-
sized generation raised in the hinterland would stand ready
to repopulate smashed cities, to recolonize dead planets if
necessary.

The stately pace of the constant was a convenience in the
prosecution of war, Oxham realized. Across the thirty-light-
year diameter of Empire, war was slowed to a time scale in
which human seed could be sown like summer crops,
stacked and stored in preparation for leaner times. Even on
her native Vasthold, seven light-years from the Rix frontier,
Oxham was forced to accept population increases that would
cut deep into the unspoiled continents of the planet: biomes
that had taken centuries to stabilize razed overnight to make
room for a generation of cannon fodder.

The Empire girded itself for a bloodbath that might consume tens of billions.

The Expansionist senator sometimes waxed ecstatic as
she outlined these plans, her mind alight with partisan fever.
Her faction had long called for increased birthrates. The
Expansionists shared with the Secularists and Utopians a
wariness of the growing power of the dead. But their motto
was "Bury the dead with the living." They sought to redress
the balance of power through sheer numbers, an ever-
expanding population (and thus, an ever-aggressive Empire)
in which the dead would never predominate.

The Utopians took the opposite, equally unpragmatic
tack: they promised universal elevation, in which the symbiant would be bestowed upon every citizen of Empire upon
death. Thus, the dead would represent all classes, and everyone would have a stake in immortality.

To Senator Oxham and her Secularist Party, both these

strategies were patently absurd. The great living masses of the Expansionist vision were doomed to become an underclass. As an ancient philosopher had once said, "The poor are only poor because of their great number." Add the immortality of the wealthy dead to the equation, and the class divisions in the Risen Empire could only worsen. The Utopian future, in which billions were elevated every year, was equally untenable. It would choke the Eighty Worlds and bow the vital living under the weight of their ancestors. Both schemes would create population problems that could only be solved by conquest.

The Secularists had a simpler plan. They were, as Laurent had put it so long ago, simply pro-death. Universal and irrevocable, natural death leveled all members of a society. Of course, the technology of the symbiant could never be uninvented, but its effects could be ameliorated as much as possible. Elevation should be rare, its rejection celebrated. And the Secularists wanted the living to hold as much power as possible; the dead could stay in their gray enclaves and stare at their black walls, but could not use their unanimity and accumulated wealth to steer the course of Empire.

Thus three parties, a clear majority of the Senate, stood against the Emperor, but theirs was a divided opposition.

To bolster her case for increased population, the Expansionist senator showed recordings from the First Incursion. Eighty years before, the Rix had sought to break the Empire's will, to force acceptance of compound minds within all Imperial infostructures. The Incursion had opened with appalling terror attacks. Living cities were ruptured by chaotic gravity beams fired from space, buildings rended as if made of straw, crowds sucked into scrambled piles, in which human forms commingled with metal and plastic and clothing. Gray enclaves were decimated with special munitions, flechette cluster bombs that shredded victims beyond the symbiant's ability to repair. In rural areas not covered by nuclear dampening fields, clean bombs were used to destroy human and animal populations.

Oxham contemplated the images: death enough for anyone.

Perhaps that was the seductive nature of war: it gave all parties what they thought they wanted. Millions of new elevated war heroes for the Utopians, vast population increases for the Expansionists, and plenty of true death for the Secularists. And for the Emperor and Loyalty, a period of unquestioned authority.

The dead sovereign nodded when the Expansionist finally finished. Darkness was falling, and Oxham realized that she hadn't slept for two of Home's long days. The dead needed little sleep—they seemed to drift into an internal world for short, rejuvenating meditations—but the living members of the council looked exhausted.

"I am glad you have chosen to prepare for the worst, Senator."

"Thank you, Your Majesty."

"Any objections?" the sovereign asked. Nara realized that this was it. The whole package of population increases, of childhoods spent in military training, of countless virgin biomes raped, it all came down to a simple vote among a few exhausted men and women. It was all happening too fast.

She cleared her throat.

"Does it not seem to the council that this Rix Incursion is different from the first?"

"Different?" asked a dead general. "It has not yet begun in earnest."

"But the last began so suddenly, with a clear ultimatum, followed by a wave of simultaneous terror attacks on several worlds."

"Hasn't this incursion begun suddenly, too, Senator Oxham?" the Emperor asked. Nara had grown more adept in reading the man; he seemed intrigued.

"As suddenly, but with greater restraint," she began. "Only

a single planet was attacked, and no civilian targets were destroyed."

"They accomplished by blackmail what they could not by terror," the dead general answered. "A compound mind, forced upon us by hostage-taking."

Oxham nodded, concealing a look of disgust. Though losing four billion lives, the Empire had never relented in the First Incursion. But when the beloved Empress was threatened, they had let the Rix inside.

"However appalling their choice of targets," she said, "the Cult has shown tremendous focus in their attack. A single world, a single hostage, a limited result."

"But with absolute success," the Emperor said.

"An unrepeatable success, Sire," she finished.

She felt the council recognize the truth of her words. The Rix could hardly take another hostage of the Empress's stature; no one except the Emperor himself would warrant the restraint that Zai had shown.

"Do you think that they'll stop now, Senator?"

"I think, Sire, that they tried to bludgeon us into submission once, and failed. This time, they have decided on a more subtle approach."

She looked around the circle, saw the counselors' attention beginning to focus through their fatigue.

"We don't know what their ultimate plan is," she continued. "But it would be odd for them to begin the war with such a precisely delivered stroke, only to return to the crude terror tactics of the First Incursion."

The dead general narrowed his eyes. "Granted, Senator. As you said, their *subtle* victory is an unrepeatable one. But surely it is also purposeful. They have a viable mind on an Imperial world, and they are moving to communicate with it. They clearly intend to gain some strategic advantage from their occupation of Legis."

"An advantage that could lead to terrors like those of the

First Incursion," the Emperor continued the thought. "If they can tap the knowledge of their mind on Legis, they will know us better than they did a century ago."

"Would that they knew our fortitude," Raz imPar Henders said.

"An interesting expression, Senator Henders," the Emperor said. "Perhaps we should demonstrate how great a sacrifice we are willing to make."

"What sacrifice could be greater than the four billion lost in the First Incursion, Sire?" Ax Milnk asked. "The Rix should know us well enough by now."

The Emperor nodded in contemplation, and the council stayed respectfully quiet.

Finally he said, "We shall have to consider that question."

Nara Oxham saw it then in the dead sovereign's thoughts—the hulking shadow of his fear, the strength of his resolution. The Emperor's will had reached an absolute condition. He would do anything to prevent the Rix from communicating with their mind.

If the *Lynx* failed, something awful was going to happen.

Executive Officer

They met the next time in Hobbes's cabin.

She didn't want this grim rehearsal, sullying her small, private domain. But hers was the cabin on the *Lynx* most similar to Zai's; the same size and shape except that it lacked the captain's skyroom. It was close enough.

The conspirators stood in their positions uncomfortably, mock assassins playing at a game they were still afraid to make real.

"Are you sure you can get us in?" Magus asked her again.

Hobbes nodded. "I've had the captain's codes for months. He sometimes sends me to his cabin if he's forgotten something."

"What if he's changed them?"

"He hasn't," she said flatly. Hobbes wished that Magus would shut up about this. It didn't do for them to examine her claims too closely.

"Trust Hobbes," Thompson said to the third pilot. "She's always had the old man's ear."

The words struck Hobbes with palpable force, a wave of guilt, like some tendril of gravity whipping through her stomach. Gunner Thompson trusted her completely now, and there was more than trust behind his eyes. Her Utopian beauty complicating things again.

She saw the others reacting to Thompson's words, questioning his blind faith. Magus was still far warier of Hobbes than he, and Hu had apparently started to think that this had all been her idea rather than Thompson's. She would have to watch her back.

"Come in, King," Thompson ordered.

Ensign King entered the cabin, a nervous look on his face. His job during the murder would be to block the ship's recording devices; he would be at his communications station. So he was standing in for Captain Zai.

Magus and Hobbes took his arms, exchanging the timid looks of an unsure rehearsal, and pulled him forward carefully. This was during the daily half-hour break from high acceleration—the *Lynx* was under a mercifully steady single gee—but they all still moved with exaggerated care, their bodies conditioned to caution over the last five days.

Thompson crouched in the center of the cabin on the ceremonial mat, a blade of error in his hand. The blade was a gift from his father, he had explained, for his graduation from the academy. What a morbid present, Hobbes thought. She hadn't known Thompson's family was so gray. Indeed, all the conspirators were from conservative families. That was the irony of this situation; mutiny was hardly an Imperial tradition. But of course, it was the grays who were most appalled by Captain Zai's rejection of the blade.

Hobbes and Magus pushed King forward, and Thompson rose to thrust his empty fist into the ensign's stomach. He mimed the crosscut of the blade ritual, and stepped back as King crumpled convincingly to the mat.

The conspirators regarded the still body before them.

"How do we know this'll fool anyone?" Magus complained. "None of us has ever worked in forensics."

"There won't be a full investigation," Thompson said.

"A suicide with no recording? Won't my equipment failure be a little suspicious?" King said, rising from the mat.

"Not under heavy acceleration," Hobbes said. Seven days into the maneuver, systems were failing intermittently throughout the ship. The ship's circuitry was at the bleeding edge of its self-repair capacity. So was the crew's nervous system, Hobbes reckoned. Tempers had grown short. A few times over the last ten hours, she'd wondered if the conspirators would fall to fighting amongst themselves. She had hoped the mutiny would have crumbled under its own weight by now.

"Don't worry," Thompson said. "Any anomalous forensic evidence will be put down to easy gravity effects."

"Even the blood all over your uniform?" Magus said.

"I'll space the damn thing."

"But a thorough investigation—"

"—is at *Captain* Hobbes's discretion," Thompson insisted.

They all looked at her. Again, she felt the weight of the conspiracy upon her. Hobbes wondered when she had become the leader of this mutiny. Was she leading them all further into this than they would have gone if she'd simply ignored Thompson's insinuations? She forced the doubts from her mind. Second thoughts were an exercise in pointlessness. Hobbes was committed now, and had to act the part.

"This will be deemed suicide, officially," she said. "That will be the reasonable and *politically* acceptable interpretation."

They nodded, one by one, agreement a virus spreading through the room. By mentioning the political situation, she had suggested that they were following the Apparatus's implicit wishes. With every utterance, her hands were dirtier.

"So, it's settled," Thompson said. Then, to Magus and Hobbes, "You two can handle Zai?"

"No problem," Magus said. She stood almost two meters tall. Under normal conditions, she alone could easily murder a man of Zai's slight build. But Captain Zai was integrally part of the *Lynx*. The conspirators couldn't give him time to shout to the ship's AI or work a gestural command. If he had prepared himself for mutiny, defensive orders programmed into his cabin's intelligence could be invoked with a gesture, a syllable. For the plan to work, they all knew, the deed had be done in seconds, and in total surprise.

It was time to press this point.

"He might have time to shout something," Hobbes said. "You'll have to cover his mouth, Thompson."

The gunner looked at her with concern. "While I stab him? I've got to hit him square in the stomach. No one will believe a messy wound."

Magus looked worried. "Maybe Yen Hu?"

The gunner's mate swallowed nervously. He didn't want to be included in the actual violence. Under Thompson's plan, he was supposed to be lookout, to warn them if anyone was with the captain, and to let them know when they could exit the cabin without being seen.

"He needs to stay outside," Thompson said. "You do it, Hobbes. Just hit him in the mouth."

"I've got to keep a hold on his hands," Hobbes argued.

"You've seen how fast he works airscreens. He could send an alert with one finger."

"Maybe we should just knock him out," Magus suggested.

"Forget it," Hobbes said. "The Adept is bound to notice any trauma to his head. The politicals will at least take a look at him."

They were silent for a moment. Hobbes watched their unsurety rise as they cast glances at one another. However many times they had all fired weapons in anger, the physical nature of a murder by hand was dawning on them. Maybe this would be the moment the conspirators would come to their senses.

"I'll take the risk. Let's knock him out," Thompson said. Magus nodded.

Hobbes sighed inwardly. They were set on their course.

"No," she said flatly. "I'm the one who has to cover this up. I say we need another person."

Hobbes watched Thompson carefully. Her reason for continuing this far—besides the hope that the conspirators might relent, and redeem themselves to some small extent—was to flush out any unknown mutineers.

She saw Thompson start to speak, but he swallowed the words. He was definitely hiding something, still keeping someone in reserve. Perhaps he had plans for Hobbes herself after the ship fell into her hands.

The thought chilled Hobbes, steeling her will.

"I know someone," she said. "He's quick and strong."

"You can trust him?"

"I don't want anyone else—" Magus protested.

"He's with us already," Hobbes interrupted. She looked coolly into the stunned faces. "He came to me, wondering if there was anything he could do."

Thompson shook his head, on the edge of disbelief.

"You think you're the only ones who don't want to die?" she asked.

"He just came to you?" Thompson asked. "Suggesting a mutiny?"

She nodded. "I'm the executive officer."

"Who is it, Hobbes?"

"A marine private." No sense giving them a name; they'd have time to check her story.

"A grunt?" Magus cried. Daren King looked appalled. They were both from solid Navy families.

"As I said, he's fast. In hand-to-hand, he could take us all."

"Do you trust him?" Thompson asked, narrowing his eyes as he watched her reaction.

"Absolutely," she answered.

That much, at least, was true.

Commando

The recon flyer was kept aloft by both fans and electromagnetics. A sensible design: limited by Imperial technology, neither propulsion system alone was sufficient for a fast, armored vehicle. Moreover, if either system failed suddenly, the other would provide for a relatively soft landing. Only a hit that crippled both would crash the flyer.

It was h_rd's intent, however, to keep the vehicle in good working order. She would have to bring it down intact, although both of the soldiers on board would have to die.

She could see one of them clearly. Silhouetted against the aurora borealis, his head low as he peered into the glowing northern quadrant of the sky. They were bringing the craft in slowly toward their find, unsure yet whether to call for reinforcements. They were duly cautious, no doubt aware that the fugitive Rix commando had killed twenty-one of her pursuers—and shot down one other flyer—to date. But h_rd knew that they would hesitate to ask for assistance.

H_rd had been tracking this flyer for three hours, arranging a series of false targets for the crew. At the beginning of their shift, she'd set out a sack full of trapped arctic hares. As intended, the animals' combined body heat had shown up as a human-scale thermal image on Imperial equipment. The recon flyer crew called for backup. The militia surrounded the squirming sack with fifty troopers, then peppered the captive hares with stun grenades. The hares had somehow remained conscious when a grenade burst the sack, resulting in a sudden explosion of dazed and fleeing rabbits. And that was only the first embarrassment of the day for the two recon soldiers.

During the short daylight portion of their shift, the pair in the flyer had heard a rain of hard projectiles pounding their craft's armor and seen muzzle flashes. They reported themselves to be under hostile fire. A squadron of jumpjets soon arrived, but the projectiles turned out to be a freak occurrence of localized hail; the muzzle flashes that the pilot had seen were merely reflections from an exposed, mica-rich escarpment. The calculations required to bend Legis's cloud-seeding dirigibles to this purpose had strained even Alexander's computing resources. But shining up the mica with her field laser had been easy for h_rd.

In the few hours since this last embarrassment, the luckless recon flyer crew had been traveling in slow circles. Its onboard computer, like all military AIs, was independent from the planetary web and therefore immune to Alexander's control. But it still relied on data from the planet's weather satellites to perform dead-reckoning navigation. The shape of the terrain below changed constantly with snowdrifts and glacial cleaving, and the flyer's computer received frequent updates. Alexander had spoofed it with subtle manipulations of the data, gradually reducing the navigation software's democratically redundant neural net to total anarchy. By this point the troopers knew their machine was confused and lost, but however tired and threadbare their nerves were, the two were reluctant to call for help a third time.

And now they'd found another target: the glacial rift before them held a heat signature of human scale.

Rana Harter was inside, feverish from her wound and breathing raggedly. The flyer crew would soon be certain that they finally had a real target.

A small shape lowered from the flyer, h_rd's sharp ears picking up the whine of its propulsion fan. The remote drone wafted down from the safe, high altitude that the flyer maintained, and moved into the mouth of the rift.

Using her communication bioware, h_rd scanned the EM range for the drone's control frequency. She could hardly believe it: the drone was using simple, unencrypted radio. H_rd linked into its point-of-view transmission. Soon, the ghostly figure of Rana Harter appeared, at the edge of discernibility in the drone's crude night vision.

The commando jammed the connection with a squawk of radio, the sort of EM bump often caused by Legis's northern lights.

H_rd waited anxiously. Had she allowed them too clear a view of Rana? If they called for backup now, the situation might spiral out of control. Rana might be killed by the militia's clumsy, paranoid doctrine of overwhelming force.

The recon flyer hovered for a few interminable minutes, almost motionless in the calm air. No doubt the tired, harried troopers were debating what to do.

Finally, a second recon drone descended from the flyer. H_rd jammed it the moment it entered the rift.

This time, the recon flyer moved in reaction. As h_rd had hoped, it descended, trying to reestablish line-of-sight with the lost drones. The craft's forward guns targeted the rift's opening. The commando allowed a few images to pass through her electronic blockade, tempting the recon flyer farther downward. She noted that Rana had moved out of the drones' sight—good, she was still thinking clearly. Rana's concussion worried h_rd. The woman was lucid one moment, incoherent the next.

Taking the bait, the flyer lowered itself one last critical degree.

H_rd burst out of her covering of snow and thermal camouflage skin. The commando threw her snare at the rear of the Imperial machine.

The polyfilament line was anchored on both ends with depleted uranium slugs. It flew with the orbitlike sway of a bola, rotating around its center of gravity as it rose, the polyfilament invisibly thin. H_rd's aim was true, and the makeshift bola tangled in the rear fans of the flyer. The machine screamed like a diving hawk as the unbreakable fibers exceeded the fans' tolerances. H_rd's night vision spotted a few metal shapes spinning from the wounded flyer. She ducked as a whirring sound passed close by her head, and set her jamming bioware to attack every frequency the flyer might use to summon help.

The recon flyer's front reared up like a horse, the undamaged forward fans still providing thrust, and it began to slip backwards as if sliding down some invisible hill. H_rd drew her knife and ran toward the careening craft.

She heard the front fans shut down, an emergency measure to level the flyer. The electromagnetic lifters flared with an infrasonic hum, the static electricity raising small hairs on h_rd's arms. She felt lightning in the air as the recon flyer's descent began to slow, rebounding softly just before it reached the snowy ground.

H_rd had timed her approach perfectly. As the flyer reached its lowest point, she jumped.

The flexormetal soles of her bare feet landed on the flyer's armored deck without a sound. The craft tipped again as her weight skewed its balance, and the rearmost crewman—the gunner—spun in his seat-webbing to face her. He started to cry out, but a kick to the temple silenced him.

The pilot was shouting into her helmet mike, and heard nothing. H_rd decapitated her with the monofilament knife, cut her body from the webbing, and threw her overboard. H_rd had studied the controls of the other flyer that she'd shot down in preparation for this attack, and easily found the panic button that triggered the machine's autolanding sequence.

The unconscious gunner's helmet was chattering in the local dialect. Some emergency signal from the flyer had gotten through to the militia. H_rd hoped they would be slow in responding to this third alert from the flyer. Her jammer was chopping the incoming transmission into bits and pieces of static-torn sound.

She tossed the gunner from the craft, saving his sniper's rifle and crashland rations. (Despite her small size, Rana ate more than a Rix commando—the two fugitives were running out of food.) As the craft settled onto the ground, h_rd whistled for her accomplice and leapt from the flyer.

Tilting up the rear fan cases, h_rd saw that she was in luck. Only one of the fans had disintegrated, the other had shut down when the polyfilament had arrested its motion. H_rd sprayed a solvent with the polyfilament's signature onto the intact fan, and it soon spun freely under the strokes of her hand.

Rana emerged from the rift, wrapped in thermal camouflage against the bitter arctic cold. Her ragged breath was visible against the aurora's light. She labored to carry the heavy fan blade that they had salvaged from h_rd's earlier kill. The commando turned to the shattered fan before her, and lased the small rivets that held on the remaining pieces. By the time the spinner coil was free of detritus, Rana was by her side.

H_rd threaded the salvaged fan onto the naked coil. It fit, spinning in perfect alignment. However crude the Imperials were, they did make their machines with an enviable interchangeability. With her blaster, h_rd burned the fan blade fast.

The commando lifted Rana gingerly into the gunner's seat, pausing to kiss her midway. The gesture brought a smile to Rana's lips, which were cracked with dehydration despite all the snow-water she consumed.

"We'll go somewhere safe now?" Rana asked in Rix. Her voice had changed, the chest wound giving it a strangely hollow sound.

"Yes, Rana."

H_rd leapt into the recon flyer and brought the fans up to speed. She closed her eyes and listened to their purr.

"They sound true," Rana Harter said. "It'll fly."

H_rd looked back at her captive, ally, lover. The woman could hear things outside of even Rix range. She saw things too: results, extrapolations, meanings. She could predict the day's weather with a glance into the sky. When h_rd hunted hares with her bola, Rana knew in the first second which throws were hits, which would fly long. She could deduce how far glacial rifts—their hiding places these last days—extended, just from the shape of the cracks around their mouths.

H_rd hoped Rana was right about the flyer. The machines were quick, but their Imperial metals were terribly fragile in the brittle arctic cold.

The commando boosted the fan drive's power, gunned the EM, and the small craft pitched northward into the air. They flew toward the shimmer of the fading aurora, her eyes narrowing as the frigid wind of their passage built.

At last, she had acquired the means to assault the entanglement facility, and to finally escape the Imperials' fumbling search for her and Rana. They were headed to the farthest arctic now, to await the proper time to continue their lonely campaign.

To await Alexander's command.

Marine Private

Private Bassiritz did not understand his orders.

Normally, this was not much of a concern for him. In his years as a marine, he had performed crowd control, jumped into friendly fire, executed snatch-and-runs, and even carried out an assassination. Ground combat could include myriad possible tactical situations, and generally the details were complex and beyond his ken. But as long as Bassiritz knew ally from foe, he was happy.

Bassiritz had always thought of the crew of the *Lynx* as his allies, however. As the Time Thief stole more and more faces from home, his shipmates had effectively become his family. But here he was, under orders delivered *straight from the captain,* ready to do violence to some of them. This didn't make sense. It seemed as if the tribulations of the gravity ghost over the last week—the jittering of his bunk, the reeling of floors and walls, the complaints from his sense of balance—had begun to affect the very fabric of reality.

For the thousandth time, Bassiritz went through the orders in his head, visualizing the motions his body would take. It was simple enough. And he knew that he would follow orders when the time came. He could comprehend no other course of action. But he didn't like the feeling it gave him.

Bassiritz felt out of place here in Navy country. The floors and the freefall handholds were the wrong color, and everyone had given him slanty looks as he'd followed Executive

Officer Hobbes down the corridors. And now they were here, waiting in the *captain's* cabin. The room seemed fantastically large to Bassiritz, bigger than his parents' house; the skyroom alone could have held the bunk coffins of his entire squad. What did the captain *do* with all this room?

There was no way to guess. The captain wasn't here.

Executive Officer Hobbes was. She would be the only friend in this operation, Bassiritz knew. The other three officers had gone bad, mutinous.

There was a tall woman waiting beside the door across from Hobbes, with pilot's wings on her shoulders. She was sweating, twitching from nerves or intermittent bumps from the gravity ghost. Outside, a slight gunner waited on watch. He was bad too, but Hobbes had asked Bassiritz not to kill him unless it was absolutely necessary. The marine private hoped he wouldn't have to kill anyone.

The last conspirator, another gunnery officer, stood in the room's center, holding a short, wide knife. Bassiritz had never seen a blade of error before. He had hoped he never would. They were bad luck, it was reckoned back in his village. Once you possessed the tool, you'd eventually be called on to do the work, they said at home.

When Bassiritz was done with this operation, he was going to use up his payment of privilege chits and take a long, hot shower.

There were two quick raps on the door. Hobbes had explained to him that this was the signal that everything was going right. The captain was approaching alone. Bassiritz shook his head involuntarily—none of this was *right*. But he was pretending to be a conspirator, so he smiled, wringing the old rag he held in one hand.

The smile felt wrong on his face. He didn't like this one bit.

ExO Hobbes stole a look at him. She winked one lovely green eye—a sign, but one that meant nothing really. Just a reminder that he was here under orders.

"Stay cool and everything will go fine," she had said to him an hour ago. "That's what a wink will mean."

Nothing was fine, though.

The door opened. The captain entered.

The four of them leapt into action. Hobbes and the pilot grabbed Captain Zai (striking the *captain*—an Error of Blood right there) and propelled him forward. Bassiritz's quick eyes could see Hobbes slip something into Zai's hand, but he knew from long experience that the subtle motion had been too quick for normal people to see. As the captain fell toward him, Bassiritz's reflexes took over and he forgot the gross impropriety of his actions. He pushed the rag into Captain Zai's mouth with his left hand, stifling the cry that uttered from it. Bassiritz felt the captain's roar of anger vibrate his hand, but the marine was already focused on his real task here. The big gunnery officer was jumping forward, his blade of error leveled at the captain's stomach.

Bassiritz's right hand shot out. To the rest of them, trapped in their slow-motion world, it would look as if he were steadying himself. But the marine's armored hand (they all wore gloves to cover their fingerprints) grabbed the blade of error, guiding its wild trajectory straight into the center of Zai's stomach.

Those were his orders. No near misses, no wounds to the chest or groin. Right into the stomach: dead center.

ExO Hobbes hadn't told him exactly why. Bassiritz hadn't asked. But the recorded message from the captain had assured him that this was all part of the plan.

Bassiritz felt the knife go in, right on target. There was a sickly squelch, and a warm fluid spurted over his and the murderous gunner's hands.

Captain Zai made a hideous grunt, and tumbled face-first onto the ritual mat they'd spread out for him. The gunner pressed down on Zai's back, having left the blade in him.

"No footprints," the man whispered, pointing at Bassiritz's

boots. One of them had a fleck of blood on it. Blood. *What had they done here?*

Bassiritz looked at Hobbes for the next signal.

The executive officer shook her head almost imperceptibly. *Not yet.*

The room grew silent, a last shuddering sigh coming from the captain. Bassiritz gazed in horror at the blood that flowed from him and across the floor. It moved strangely, tiny rivers branching out like the living tendrils of a sea creature, shuddering with odd tremors. The gravity ghost was moving it. Bassiritz reflexively stepped back from a finger of the red liquid that reached for his boot.

The captain was not breathing. *What had they done?*

"It's over," Hobbes said.

The pilot leaned back against the wall, covered her face with her hands.

The gunner stumbled back, a nervous smile on his lips.

"All right, then," he said. He lifted a small transponder and spoke a single codeword into it. Bassiritz remembered to look at ExO Hobbes.

Hobbes winked her *left* eye. Now.

The marine's fist shot out, catching the gunner's throat. The man crumpled to the bloody floor, most likely still alive. Bassiritz turned to watch the rest.

Hobbes was already in midswing, delivering a slap to the pilot's face with a loud crack. The larger woman reeled backward, her face blank from the blinding shock of the slap. A good way to confuse someone, but only for a few seconds. Bassiritz stepped forward. But before he could strike, a second crack rang out.

The electric smell of a dazegun filled the room. Bassiritz felt the small hairs on his arms rise and tingle.

The pilot dropped to the floor.

The captain leapt up, the dazer in his bloody hand. He whirled to face the fallen gunner, but the man was motionless. Bassiritz knew from experience that he wouldn't be getting up for hours.

"Captain?" Hobbes asked.

"I'm fine, Hobbes," he answered, nodding. "Well done."

The door burst open; more marines, Bassiritz noted happily. The Navy was too complicated for him.

The small gunner who had been watching for the conspirators outside was among them, his arms pinned. His eyes swept the room, then glared with hatred at ExO Hobbes.

"Any reaction from that transponder signal?" the captain asked.

Hobbes listened, then nodded. "Two crew from gunnery left their posts, sir. Headed for my cabin, apparently."

"Don't take them yet. Let's see what they're up to," he ordered.

The captain pulled the ringlets of his tunic with a single ripping motion, and the garment parted. One last rush of blood spattered onto the floor. Bassiritz noted the armor strapped to his undershirt; it only covered his stomach.

Bassiritz smiled. The captain certainly had confidence in him. If the blade of error had missed its mark, Captain Zai would be bleeding for real.

One of the other marines checked the gunnery officer crumpled on the floor.

"Alive, sir."

Suddenly, the young mutineer in the doorway lunged forward in his captors' arms. Bassiritz slipped between him and the captain, an arm raised to strike. But the marines held the man fast.

"The blade!" the gunner cried. "Let me take the blade."

All had gone according to plan, but Bassiritz found his relief turning bitter in his mouth. These were his crewmates, condemned to death for their shameful actions. Hobbes looked away from the young man, her eyes downcast.

"In due time," the captain said quietly.

They pulled the gunner from the room weeping, an animal howl coming from the young man.

Executive Officer Hobbes spoke up again. "Another response to the transponder. A notice went up on a public board, a few moments after your 'murder,' sir. An anonymous noise complaint, for the Section F gunnery bunks."

"A coincidence?"

"There is no Section F, sir."

Captain Zai shook his head. "How many of my crew are in on this?" he wondered aloud.

"At least two more, sir. One to send, another to receive. Whoever posted it was clever, though. We can't crack the anonymity."

The captain sighed. He stepped over the unconscious gunnery officer and sat heavily on his bed. "I seem to have injured my knee, Executive Officer."

"Bad gravity for a fall, sir. I'll get medical up here."

"Think we can trust them?" the captain said.

Hobbes was silent.

Then she said, "Well, at least the marines are with us, sir."

Captain Zai looked at Bassiritz and smiled wanly.

"Good work, soldier."

"Thank you, sir," Bassiritz answered, eyes front.

"You managed to stab me dead center."

"Yes, sir. Those were my orders, sir."

The captain wiped some of the fake blood from his face.

"Well, Private, with your help I seem to have accomplished something very unlikely."

"Sir?"

The captain stood, wincing as he shifted weight from one knee to the other.

"I doubt that many men have avoided two blades of error in their lives. Much less in the same week."

Bassiritz knew it was a joke, but no one laughed, so he kept his mouth shut.

Senator

"This pit is lined with an old and simple material," the Emperor began, gesturing to the floor beneath the counselors' feet. Nara Oxham had noticed before that of all the Diamond Palace she had seen, only the council chamber was made of the pearly substance.

"From the casein, or lactoid group of plastics," he continued. "A beautiful white, almost milky in appearance. It is, in fact, made from cows' milk and rennet, an enzyme from the stomachs of goats. Hardened by formaldehyde."

Senator Oxham lifted one foot from the floor uncomfortably. She had always liked the hard-plastic feel of the council chamber, but this pillaging of animals' guts seemed a bit perverse.

"It was discovered almost a hundred years before spaceflight, when a chemist's pet cat knocked a bottle of formaldehyde into its saucer of milk."

Save us, Oxham thought, from those agents of history.

She realized that the pit they all were perched around might well be a giant saucer of milk, a meal set out for some gargantuan housecat.

"The hardening effect was noticed, and plastic—the ancestor of our smart carbon—was created," the sovereign said. "Such disasters can always be turned into opportunities. But it is good to be prepared."

Disasters?

"The time has come to consider the possibility that the *Lynx* will fail."

The Emperor nodded at the dead admiral, who waved an

image into the War Council's airscreen. Between the counselors hovered the familiar shape of the coming battle. The sweeping arcs that represented battlecruiser and frigate now almost intersected.

"The two ships are nearing contact even as we speak," the admiral said. "The elements of their drone fleets will engage shortly. Against such a powerful foe, the demise of the *Lynx* could come suddenly."

Senator Nara Oxham took a deep breath. She had marked this moment for days; she didn't need some dead woman to explain its significance. Nara had hoped that she would be able to spend these hours alone, waiting for word to come from the Legis ground stations that were intently watching the battle. But the council summons had invaded her vigil.

Now she might learn of Laurent's death in the company of these politicians and gray warriors. She steeled herself, pushing fear and hope as far down as she could, forcing a cold absence into her heart. This diamond chamber was no place to weep, or even feel.

"If the *Lynx* is destroyed, and has failed to destroy the Rix array," the admiral continued, "we should know some eight hours after the fact, assuming standard models of simultaneity. That calculation includes lightspeed delay between Legis XV and the battle, and a decision window for the local military. They'll have to be a hundred percent sure of what's happened."

"In those eight hours," the Emperor added, "the Rix ship will be forty billion kilometers closer to Legis."

"We will have to reply to Legis rather quickly," the general said. "For any decision to reach them before the Rix draw within range."

The counselors looked at each other in some puzzlement. They had been swept up in the greater war, and had lost track of the *Lynx*. The council had been determining the lot of generations—hundreds of billions of the living, dead, and unborn—and again the fate of a single ship demanded their attention.

"Then we should discuss our options, Sire," the Utopian senator said.

"Are there any?" Oxham asked.

"We believe that there are," the general said.

"I move to invoke the hundred-year rule," the Loyalist Senator Henders said.

There was a stir at these words. The rule was an old privilege of the Emperor's War Council, a means to ensure that His Majesty's counselors could speak freely, without fearing that their words would be openly repeated. With the council so far acting unanimously, there had been little reason to invoke the rule. The counselors never discussed their decision-making in public in any case. And under the rule, the consequences of an inadvertent slip would be unthinkable.

"I second," the Emperor said.

Nara felt cold fear come into the room. The sovereign had seconded, and the rule was invoked without objection.

Now nothing of this discussion could be repeated outside the chamber, not to anyone at all, not for one hundred years Imperial Absolute. The price of breaking the rule was as old as the Empire itself.

Execution by exsanguination: the common traitor's death.

Of course, Nara realized, she and the other senators on the council would be technically protected by their own senatorial privilege: freedom from arrest and Imperial censure. But breaking the rule constituted proof of treachery, and would be the end of any political power they might wield.

The discussion began with a speech from the Emperor.

"If the Rix compound mind is able to communicate with the rest of the Cult, then Legis has, in effect, been captured a second time. The mind is constituted of every piece of information on the planet: every line of code, every market datum, every technical specification. It has access to all our technological secrets."

Nara took a deep breath. They'd heard all this before. But the Emperor's next words surprised her.

"But that isn't our concern," he said. "The strength of Empire is not in our technology, but in our hearts. And that is where we must be most vigilant. The mind is more than computers and comfibers. It also contains every child's diary, every family legacy recording, the prayers of the living to their ancestors, the patient files of psychoanalysts and religious counselors. The mind has grasped the psyche of our Risen Empire; it knows us in every aspect. The Rix seek to steal our dreams."

The sovereign paused, challenging each of them with his stare.

"And we know what the Rix Cult brings: absolute disdain for human life except as a component of their precious minds. No terror was beyond them when they sought our submission in the First Incursion. Back then they didn't understand our strength, didn't realize what bound us together. Now, they have reached into our minds to discover what we most fear. They seek to pull out our secret nightmares and make a lever of them."

Nara Oxham felt the Emperor's fear clearly now. It spread slowly to the others in the room as his speech continued. She could see the source of his passion: the reasoning behind his hatred of the Rix, his horror at the mind's takeover of Legis, his willingness to sacrifice the *Lynx*. Finally, perhaps, he was telling the truth.

"If the *Lynx* fails," he said, "we have lost this war."

The words shook even Oxham. The old childhood conditioning, the imagery of fables and songs made the concept unthinkable. The Emperor of the Eighty Worlds spoke of losing a war. The sovereign wasn't allowed to entertain such an idea. He had beaten death, after all.

For a moment, the emotions in the room threatened to overwhelm her. Nara reached instinctively for her apathy bracelet, but forced herself not to resort to the drug. She needed to maintain her sensitivity. But the fear remained at the edge of her control.

"What must we do?" asked Senator Henders. Nara could see that he'd been coached for this question, as he had been to invoke the hundred-year rule. Henders already knew what the Emperor's answer would be.

"We must be prepared to kill the mind."

A chill ran down Oxham's spine.

"How, Your Majesty?" she asked.

"We must be ready to make any sacrifice."

"Sire," she pleaded. "What do you propose?"

"We must kill the mind," he said flatly. Then he turned to the dead general.

The ancient warrior raised his head and looked at them. His gray face shone a little, almost as if he were sweating.

"We switch off the nuclear dampening fields on Legis. Then we detonate four hundred clean-airburst warheads in the hundred-megaton range, at an altitude of two hundred kilometers, directly over population centers, control points, and data reserves."

"Nuclear weapons?" Nara said in disbelief. "Over our own people?"

"Very low yield on dirty radiation, optimized for electromagnetic pulse."

The admiral spoke. "Every unshielded machine on the planet will be rendered useless. Unlike a normal power grid failure, all the distributed, self-maintaining components of the infrastructure will be eliminated. Every phone, handheld device, and computer on the planet will suddenly stop working."

"Every aircar will fall from the sky," Oxham protested. "Every medical endoframe will fail."

The admiral shook his head. "Before the blast, a standard space-raid warning drill will run. Aircars will ground themselves, medics will be standing by."

Oxham willed herself silent, trying to read the council's reaction. Their minds were in chaos. The Emperor's speech about the Rix had raised old fears, but those were nothing compared to the truly ancient horror of nuclear weapons. The counselor's minds had gone wild, like those of animals trapped within a ring of predators.

"The main power stations are shielded from EM pulses," the general continued. "But they will be shut down voluntarily. Ether-power substations will be destroyed by conventional explosives. Other shielded facilities, such as hospitals and emergency shelters, should remain in good working order."

Oxham shook her head. An isolated hospital might keep functioning for a few days, but with the world around it crippled, remote consulting doctors would be cut off, emergency transport would fail, and supplies would soon run short.

Ax Milnk spoke. "The short-term casualties might be limited, but we must consider what will happen over time. It might take months to return to a functioning infrastructure, during which millions could die from lack of food and medicine. The Legis population is all in the northern hemisphere, where winter is coming."

"We have fully analyzed the situation, Counselor Milnk."

The dead general looked at the Emperor, who nodded.

"We expect there to be roughly one hundred million deaths total," the old warrior said.

A howl came into Nara's head, a whirlwind like the city when she awoke from coldsleep. The naked fear of the counselors pried open her mind, and the war lust of the surrounding capital rushed in. She could see better than ever the bright, raging face of Empire at war: the popular clamor for revenge, the hunger of profiteers, the unpredictable shuffling of power as new alliances formed.

For a moment, Nara Oxham was lost to herself. She became the Mad Senator, subsumed into the cries of the city's animal group-mind.

The cool hand of apathy reasserted herself. She looked down, almost surprised to be conscious. Then she saw her fingers at the bracelet. Old reflexes had moved her to increase the flow of the apathy drug, saving Nara from dropping to the floor mewling and insane.

She breathed deeply, wiping the sweat from her forehead and trying not to vomit.

"This will show our true strength," the Emperor was saying. "It will show that we would rather destroy ourselves than accept Rix domination. We will have surrendered them nothing. And they will never doubt our resolve again."

"A hundred million, dead by our own hand?" the Expansionist senator said. "Won't that do more damage to morale than the Rix ever could?"

"We will say the Rix did it," the general said flatly.

Oxham bowed her head. Of course, this was why they had invoked the hundred-year rule. She doubted that even a century from now anyone would learn what they had done.

"A new Rix terror to motivate the Empire," the sovereign added. "Many war aims met with a single act."

"I move we accept without objection," said Senator Henders.

Senator Oxham raised her head. She had no time to think, no time to calculate. But given only these spare seconds, making the choice turned out to be easy.

"I object," she said. "I call for a vote."

Relief. Even with her empathy dulled, she saw it on the living counselors' faces. They were glad someone had spoken against the Emperor's plan.

And they were glad it hadn't been them.

The sovereign looked at her coolly, his expression unreadable now. His gray young face seemed as remote as the night sky. But she knew that someday there would be a price for her action. Nara Oxham had crossed the Emperor.

"A vote, then," he said quietly.

"Can we have more time?" Ax Milnk asked.

The Emperor shook his head. He had calculated this to the minute, had left revelation of the plan until time was too short for discussion. His best opportunity was now, before the horror of the idea could sink in.

"There is little time," he said. "The *Lynx* might be dead in hours. The Rix battlecruiser will be within transmission range a few days later."

"Give us those days, then," Oxham asked. Her voice sounded hollow in her ears.

"The lightspeed delay between Legis and the *Lynx*, Senator," the admiral said, shaking her head. "Round trip several times, to be sure. We have only hours to decide."

"And the earlier the space-raid warning is sounded, the fewer casualties will result," the general said. "More medical personal can be standing by. Grounded aircars will have time to bring their passengers to populated areas rather than depositing them in the wild. We owe the population of Legis a quick decision."

Their arguments were illogical, Nara knew. The Apparatus could sound a raid warning in any case, and wait for a final decision. They could have prepared the planet for this over the last few days. The Emperor had simply chosen to spring this on the council, to grind their will against an artificial emergency. But she was too dizzy to make these arguments, to bring specific points against the steamroller that the Emperor had created. Her stomach roiled now, the first sign of a mild apathy overdose. Nara's blind fingers had unleashed too sharp a dose of the drug after all the days she had kept her sensitivity high. Her empathy was absolutely flat, her body barely able to function.

Council sessions had been called at odd hours for ten days. They were all exhausted; the Emperor had wanted them that way.

Senator Oxham gritted her teeth in anger. She had been outmaneuvered by the sovereign, betrayed by the weakness of her own psyche.

"A vote, then," she said. "I say no. 'No killing of worlds.' "

There was a gasp from someone. She had quoted the Compact, the old document that a few gray worlds interpreted as validating Emperor's authority. He smiled at her coldly.

"I vote yes," he said. The Emperor leaned back, supremely confident.

The War Council almost stopped him.

The Expansionist and Utopian senators voted against the action, as Oxham had known they would. And Ax Milnk showed unexpected strength, joining the opposition senators against the Emperor.

In a foregone conclusion, the two dead warriors voted with their sovereign, as did the Loyalist Henders. The measure was tied at four votes to four when the counselor from the Plague Axis spoke. He was an unknown quantity, this host of all the ancient terrors that humanity had put to rest. Living, and yet not fully alive, he was on the borderline that split the Risen Empire. He was a cursed thing.

"Let us show our strength," came the voice from the suit's filter. "Destroy the mind, at whatever cost."

The motion had passed, five to four.

Roger Niles was right, Nara Oxham thought coldly as the vote was entered into the council's records. There were no moral victories. Only real defeats.

Then a glimmer of hope entered her mind. This unfathomable genocide might not actually occur; the *Lynx* might succeed in its mission. But even this slim chance had a dark side.

If my lover fails, a world dies, Nara realized.

She shook her head.

More blood on the hands of Laurent Zai.

Lieutenant-Commander

Laurent Zai dressed quietly, thinking his lover asleep.

His arm was clever enough to come to him when he clicked his tongue for it. The limb turned itself slowly, orienting on the sound, then finger-crawled a bit too quickly for Zai's taste, for a moment a fleshy insect. Supposedly, it was smart and agile enough to reach its master even in zero-gee, but that was not a feature he had tested.

The arm had fallen close to the fire, and felt feverishly hot when he meshed its control surface with the tangle of interface threads that hung from his shoulder stump. But the warmth wasn't unpleasant. This house, the fire, Nara: these things were warm, and were good.

Zai flexed his fingers, their artificial nerves awakening with a tingle like returning bloodflow. When a chime assured him of the arm's strength, Laurent pushed himself upright with both hands, looking for his legs. They were close by.

His remaining natural legs were short stumps, and Zai could sit up easily on them. The floor was soft with some kind of plant growth; it felt like a fine animal pelt, chinchilla or mink. He made his way to the artificial legs with two quick movements, swinging forward like a gymnast on parallel bars. Over the subjective months since his torture, he had exercised his remaining arm until it was almost as strong as the prosthetic one. Vadans valued balance.

He reattached his legs. The smooth gray of their exterior melded with his pale flesh, edges sealing with a familiar tug of suction. He saw his tunic, and pulled it over his head as he flexed his toes.

Zai turned to see Nara gazing at him.

A chill in his chest pushed aside the warmth of the fire, of their lovemaking. Other than a few medics, none of his crewmates—no one—had ever seen him naked before, much less without his limbs. He tried to say something caustic, but his voice failed him and he scowled.

Nara shook her head.

"I didn't mean to embarrass you."

"It's your house," he said, pulling on his trousers.

When he looked at her again, she seemed puzzled by the words.

"Take your pleasure as you will," he explained sharply.

"Have I taken advantage of your nakedness?" she said with a small smile. Zai realized that Nara was still completely unclothed. He felt foolish now in his disheveled fatigue tunic, grasped some piece of her clothing on the floor, and flung it to her.

Nara pushed it aside and sat up, reaching for his hand. It was the artificial one, which had somehow lost its glove. She pulled the metal thing toward her breast.

Zai's anger faded abruptly. At Nara's touch, he felt safe and whole again, as he had in her arms. Sighing, he closed his eyes and imagined the hand to be real. The returns of the false nerves were very convincing. He opened a second-sight menu and increased the hand's sensitivity, basking in the warmth of Nara, the change in texture from dark skin to pink aureole, the slow ripple of her heartbeat. He felt a tremor like distant running water as blood rushed into the erectile tissue of her nipple.

He opened his eyes. She was smiling.

"I'm sorry I snapped at you, Nara."

"No, Laurent. I should have realized. But you seemed so . . . comfortable before."

"Eager, more likely."

"Oh." Was there a note of pity in her voice? A look crossed her face, and she nodded. "You don't use . . ."

He shook his head. *Surrogates,* she would have said, but on Vada they used the old words for professionals.

The playful smile again. "In that case, Laurent, you must be famished."

He could not disagree.

But Laurent Zai pushed her hands away. He'd felt so broken under her eyes. "Nara?" he pleaded.

"Yes," she answered. "You can keep your limbs. Your tunic too if you want."

He nodded, and a sound came from his chest that was like a sob. But he ignored it, hastening.

House

The missive came over the general net, looking for Laurent Zai. The lieutenant-commander's presence here at the polar estate wasn't registered with the comnets—the mistress had specifically requested privacy—but the search was energetic enough to ping every private domicile on Home. Not an emergency, just standard military persistence. The house quietly snatched a copy, investigating its security before passing it on to the mistress's guest.

The message bore the telltale marks of midlevel military cryptography. It hadn't been buried under the absolute noise of a onetime pad, or the self-similar swirls of fractal compression, so it was neither top-secret nor very large. The missive seemed to be double-ticket encryption, with a long enough key that Zai must be carrying it on his person, not in his head. The house set a host of micromaintenance bots—normally used to repair optical circuitry—to the task of discovering this object. This effort was illegal, and against Imperial AI guidelines, but the Rubicon Pale extended around the house whenever Oxham was here. The transgression was also justified by the fact that the house was sometimes called upon to encrypt the mistress's Senate business. And the best way to learn the craft of security was to attack the systems of one's peers.

Besides, the house was curious. And the mistress always encouraged it to indulge its curiosity, to gather information relentlessly. It was relatively sure she wouldn't mind this bit of harmless snooping.

The key was disappointingly easy to discover. A Vadan fetish on a strap around the lieutenant-commander's neck proved to be subtly bit-marked. The titanium cladding on its front was brushed to resist fingerpints, and upon close inspection, the tiny ridges of the burnishing were actually sawtooth waves, which reversed direction with suspicious periodicity. The house read the two directions as one and zero, fiddled with the results, and in a few seconds had cracked the missive.

It delivered the message to *Captain* Laurent Zai (the first half of the message was a promotion) as it absorbed the contents.

A new class of ship was described in the missive's second part, an experimental vessel of which Zai would be taking command in a few days. The specifications were not given in great detail—hence the shoddy encryption—but they were certainly stimulating. The warship was officially a frigate, but in the range of its weaponry and ground troops, the *Lynx* was sui generis. Its design had some of the characteristics of a patrol craft: fast and maneuverable, full of intelligence drones, capable of long-range operation with minimal logistical support. But the "frigate" also possessed extensive ground-attack and orbital insertion capacity, a smattering of heavy weapons, and excellent survivability. It had punch.

The house figuratively raised its eyebrows. This was a fine little warship. Perhaps it was intended to serve as a roving ambassador, showing the flag, equipped for crisis management and gunboat diplomacy.

As the house expected, the AI component of the warship was woefully insufficient for its range of possible operations. Imperial design tended toward underpowered artificial intelligence. (The house had recognized long ago that its own distributed processing was at odds with strict Imperial AI regulations. Some sort of damage at the beginning of its existence had allowed it to expand without the usual self-governors. The mistress had always approved, however, as long as it was discreet. There were advantages in being down here at the end of the earth, and it was pleasurable to be illegally smart.)

The house took care to note Zai's reaction, wondering what he would think of his new ship.

Captain Zai and the mistress were together on the western balcony, overlooking a few ice sculptures of aboriginal Home insect life that the house had attempted in the dead of winter, smoothed to abstraction now by the arrival of summer. Zai hadn't even accessed the entire missive yet, but he seemed upset by what he had read so far.

"Ten years out," he said. Was it pain in his voice? Or just the cold? "Ten years back."

The mistress stepped toward Zai, put a hand on his shoulder. He looked at her and laughed sourly, shaking his head.

"I'm sorry to react this way," he said. "You hardly know me, after all."

The house scanned the missive and spotted a section it had ignored. The newly promoted captain had been assigned to the Rix frontier, to a system called Legis, ten light-years away, for a tour of indeterminate length.

"I'm sorry too, Laurent," the mistress said.

Zai placed his hand on hers, blinking from his eyelashes the first flakes of a light snow. He spoke carefully.

"I know we've just met. But to lose you already—" He shook his head. "I sound foolish."

"You don't, Laurent."

"But I thought I'd be here on Home for at least a few months. I was half hoping they'd stick me on training staff."

"Would you want that, Laurent?"

"A staff position? My ancestors would wail," he answered. "But *twenty years*. And facing the damned Time Thief again. I suppose I've grown tired of his tricks."

"How long has it been, Laurent? Your career, in Absolute years?"

"Too many," he said. "Almost a hundred."

Nara shook her head. "I didn't know."

"And now another thirty, probably," he said. "Fifty, if there really is a war coming."

"A senator's term of office," the mistress observed.

The man turned, his expression changing.

"You're right, Nara. We may both lose the next fifty years. And you senators have your own Thief. You're frozen half the time, aren't you?"

"Much more than half, Laurent."

"Well," he said, meeting her eyes, "that's hopeful, I suppose."

She smiled. "Perhaps it is. But I'll still be older than you, subjectively. I am already."

"You are?"

She laughed. "Yes. Give me another decade in subjective, and you'll notice."

Zai straightened himself. "Of course I will. I'll notice everything."

"Is that a promise?"

He took both the mistress's hands.

"We have four days to make promises, Senator-Elect."

"Yes, Captain."

"Four days," he repeated, and turned back to the ice sculptures.

"Stay here with me," she asked. "Give us those days."

The house became alert. The mistress had only announced a weekend stay; never before had she extended a visit unexpectedly. Meals had been planned in excruciating detail, supplies obtained in exact amounts. Despite the vast resources of the estate—the underground gardens, the caves full of food and wine, the cargo drones ready to launch from a hundred high-end stores on the Imperial homeworld—a surge of anxiety almost resembling panic swept through the house's mind. This was all so *abrupt*.

And yet, the house wanted Zai to agree.

It waited anxiously for the man's answer.

"Yes," he said. "I'd love to."

The house took its attention from their sudden kiss. There was so much to do.

EPILOGUE

Captain

The *Lynx* exploded, expanded.

The frigate's energy-sink manifold spread out, stretching luxuriant across eighty square kilometers. The manifold was part hardware and part field effect, staggered ranks of tiny machines held in their hexagonal pattern by a lacework of easy gravity. It shimmered in the Legis sun, refracting a mad god's spectrum, unfurling like the feathers of some ghostly, translucent peacock seeking to rut. In battle, it could disperse ten thousand gigawatts per second, a giant lace fan burning hot enough to blind naked human eyes at two thousand klicks.

The satellite-turrets of the ship's four photon cannon eased away from the primary hull, extending on hypercarbon scaffolds that reminded Zai of the iron bones of ancient cantilever bridges. The *Lynx* was shielded from the cannon's collateral radiation by twenty centimeters of hullalloy. They were removed on their spindly arms four kilometers from the vessel proper; using the cannon would afflict the *Lynx*'s crew with only the most treatable of cancers. The four satellite-turrets carried sufficient reaction mass and intelligence to operate independently if released in battle. And from the safety of a few thousand kilometers distance, their fusion magazines could be ordered to crashfire, consuming themselves in a chain reaction, delivering one final, lethal needle toward the enemy. Of course, the cannon could also be crashfired from their close-in position, destroying their mother ship in a blaze of deadly glory.

That was one of the frigate's five standard methods of self-destruction.

The magnetic rail that launched the *Lynx*'s drone complement descended from her belly, and telescoped to its full nineteen-hundred-meter length. A few large scout drones, a squadron of ramscatters, and a host of sandcasters deployed themselves around the rail. The ramscatters bristled like nervous porcupines with their host of tiny flechettes, each of which carried sufficient fuel to accelerate at two thousand gees for almost a second. The sandcasters were bloated with dozens of self-propelled canisters, whose ceramic skins were cross-hatched with fragmentation patterns. At the high relative velocity of this battle, sand would be Zai's most effective weapon against the Rix receiver array.

Inside the rail bay, great magazines of other drone types were loaded in a carefully calculated order of battle. Stealth penetrators, broadcast decoys, minesweepers, remotely piloted fighter craft, close-in-defense pickets all awaited their moment in battle. Finally, a single deadman drone waited. This drone could be launched even if the frigate lost all power, accelerated by highly directional explosives inside its dedicated backup rail. The deadman was already active, continuously updating its copy of the last two hours' logfiles, which it would attempt to deliver to Imperial forces if the *Lynx* were destroyed.

When we are destroyed, Captain Laurent Zai corrected himself. His ship was not likely to survive this encounter; it was best to accept that. The Rix vessel outpowered and outgunned them. Its crew was quicker and more adept, so intimately linked into the battlecruiser's systems that the exact point of division between human and hardware was a subject more for philosophical debate than military consideration. And Rix boarding commandos were deadly: faster, hardier, more proficient in compromised gravity. And, of course, they were unafraid of death; to the Rix, lives lost in battle were no more remarkable than a few brain cells sacrificed to a glass of wine.

Zai watched his bridge crew work, preparing the newly configured *Lynx* to resume acceleration. They were in zero-gee now, waiting for the restructuring to firm up before subjecting the expanded frigate to the stresses of acceleration. It was a relief to be out of high-gee, if only for a few hours. When the engagement started in earnest, the ship would go into evasive mode, the direction and strength of acceleration varying continuously. Next to that chaos, the last two weeks of steady high acceleration would seem like a pleasure cruise.

Captain Zai wondered if there was any mutiny left in his crew. At least two of the conspirators had escaped his and Hobbes's trap. Were there more? The senior officers must realize that this battle was unwinnable. They understood what a Rix battlecruiser was capable of, and would recognize that the *Lynx*'s battle configuration had been designed to damage its opponent, not preserve itself. Zai and ExO Hobbes had optimized the ship's offensive weaponry at the expense of it defenses, orienting its entire arsenal on the task of destroying the Rix receiver array.

Now that the *Lynx* was at battle stations, even the junior officers would be able to spot the ill portents that surrounded them.

The boarding skiffs remained in their storage cells. It was unlikely that Zai's marines would be crossing the gulf to capture the Rix battlecruiser. Boarding actions were the privilege of the winning vessel. Instead, the Imperial marines were taking up positions throughout the *Lynx,* ready to defend it from capture should the Rix board the vessel after pounding it into helplessness. Normally under these conditions, Zai would have issued sidearms to the crew to help repel boarders. But after the mutiny this seemed a risky show of faith. Most ominously for any crewman who chose to notice, the singularity generator, the most dramatic of Zai's self-destruct options, was already charged to maximum. If the *Lynx* could draw close enough to the enemy battle-cruiser, the two craft would share a dramatic death.

In short, the *Lynx* was primed like an angry, blind drunk hurtling into a barfight with gritted teeth, ferally anxious to inflict damage, unconscious of any pain she might feel herself.

Perhaps that was their one advantage in this fight, Zai thought: desperation. Would the Rix try to protect the vulnerable receiver array? Their mission was obviously to communicate with the compound mind on Legis. But would the dictates of saving the array force the Rix commander to make a bad move? If so, there might be some slim hope of surviving this battle.

Zai sighed and grimly pushed this line of thought aside. Hope was not his ally, he had learned over the last ten days.

He turned his mind back to the bridge airscreen and its detailed schematic of the *Lynx*'s internal structure.

The wireframe lines shifted like an oriental puzzle box, as walls and bulkheads inside the frigate slid into battle configuration. Common rooms and mess halls disappeared to make space for expanded gunnery stations, passageways widened for easier movement of emergency repair teams. Crew bunks transformed into burn beds. The sickbay irised open, consuming the zero-gee courts and running tracks that usually surrounded it. Walls sprouted handholds in case of gravity loss, and everything that might come loose in sudden acceleration was stowed, velcroed, bolted down, or simply recycled.

Finally, the coiling, shifting, expanding, and extruding all came to a halt, and the schematic eased into a stable shape. Like a well-crafted mechanical bolt smoothly sliding into place, the vessel became battle ready.

A single claxon sounded. A few of his bridge crew half-turned toward Zai. Their faces were expectant and excited, ready to begin this fight regardless of the ship's chances. He saw it most in ExO Hobbes's expression. They'd been